PUNCH DRUNK

D J Keogh

Thomas Fewtrell
The Gentleman Jaw-breaker

Punch Drunk

David J. Keogh

Paperback Edition First Published in the United Kingdom
in 2017 by aSys Publishing

eBook Edition First Published in the United Kingdom
in 2017 by aSys Publishing

Disclaimer

This is a work of fiction. All characters and incidents are
products of the author's imagination and any resemblance to
actual people or events is coincidental or fictionalised.

ISBN: 978-1-910757-87-1

aSys Publishing
http://www.asys-publishing.co.uk

DEDICATION

Dedicated to all of you who bought my first book, The Accidental Gangster, your support helped drive my debut book into the bestseller's list and soon to be a six part TV series. I am eternally grateful to you all.

I would also like to dedicate this book and to personally thank the award-winning journalist Mike Lockley of the Birmingham Evening mail who wrote the original article which sparked the interest that led to the book becoming a bestseller, your encouraging words and continuing support is very much appreciated. Thank you.

D J Keogh

Thomas Fewtrell

PART ONE

Pistols, Punches & Honeypots.

CHAPTER 1

The rider sat motionless amongst the moon-shadowed trees, his dark, woollen cloak pulled tightly around his black neck scarf in a futile attempt to keep the frosty night from his bones. The horse stomped and snorted steamy clouds of breath which hung in the air, illuminated by the bright moonlight. He patted the animal's neck, calming the beast lest it give his presence away at the side of the dark highway where he waited for his prey. He ran his fingers over the pistols that hung either side of the saddle pommel just as he had done many times before on nights like this. An instant of self-doubt sent a tingle of cold sweat prickling along his spine, but the touch of the gleaming, brass tips on his deadly, cap-locked pistols calmed his nerves and one last time he ran through the carefully laid plans for the robbery he was about to commit. Even though he was content with his preparations, the consequences that would befall him should things go awry and the prospect of what would happen to him if they did, hung about him like a black cloud as he tried to quell the fear that threatened to overwhelm him. A fear that had manifested itself into what seemed like a thousand horseflies that danced and buzzed around his stomach, making the freezing night even more uncomfortable.

The days of the English highwayman were at their height, and the daring deeds of these heroic robbers captured the imagination of the public. To counter this, the government of the day were constantly having to invent ever more Draconian ways to punish the brigands. Indeed, at the public execution of the highwayman William Gordon in 1785, a crowd of nearly five thousand people gathered at the triangular gallows named *the Tyburn Tree*. William Gordon took the drop to rousing cheers from his adoring public and was hung until pronounced dead but the robber was then pulled down from the scaffold and resuscitated at the foot of the gallows. As soon as the prisoner was fully conscious and thought himself saved, they strung the poor fellow up again only to kill him and revive him once more. Five times Gordon hung, and five times he was brought back to the land of the living. However, if the second coming of William Gordon was seen as proof of life after death, the fourth and fifth coming proved nothing but tedious to the baying mob and on the sixth drop, Gordon remained where he was until the crows had had their fill of him.

This should have had the effect of discouraging anyone from following a similar life of crime, in this world or the next. Yet here sat Thomas Fewtrell, one week later, in a freezing hoar mist, a shadow amongst the shadows, awaiting the midnight Royal Mail coach from London to Birmingham and all the riches he was sure it contained.

Thomas shuffled in his saddle, his feet and hands were tingling with cold, and his backside was almost numb. He nestled himself into the velvet collar of his thick, bottle-green cloak and allowed his mind to wander in a vain attempt to escape the cold's grip. Thomas dwelled on all manner of things, his childhood, favourite taverns he frequented, even allowing himself dreams of the future if indeed he had one after tonight's heist. All of this helped to keep his nerves in check as he fought to stop the uncontrollable chattering of his teeth.

A shuffle of hooves on frozen leaves interrupted Thomas's

reflections. He turned to see his accomplice approaching through the dense tree line behind him. Thomas recognised the silhouette of his friend and forced a weak smile. The approaching rider returned the welcome with a more optimistic grin. His teeth gleaming white in the bright moonlight, his crafty eyes shadowed beneath the black tricorn hat that sat on his mop of dark hair, tilted fashionably as was the style of the day.

"It won't be long now Thomas." He whispered, his breath hanging in the freezing air like a ghost.

"Well, it had better not be Sykesy, my arse is starting to freeze. How long have we been sitting here anyway?"

Sykesy tilted his head and pushed the brim of his hat back on his forehead. He stared for a second at the position of the moon, before holding his hand up and spreading his thumb and forefinger, pinching the two digits together, he positioned his hand so that the waning moon was at the centre of the circle he'd made with his fingers. Thomas watched, enthralled that his companion should know how to tell the time of day by the position of the moon. After almost a full minute, Sykesy turned back to Thomas.

"Well, how long have we been here?" Thomas whispered excitedly.

"Fuck knows!" Thomas sat motionless, a bemused look on his face.

"What do you mean 'fuck knows'? What was all that about with your fingers?" He said, bringing his leather-gloved hand up, imitating the action of his friend.

"Oh that!" replied Sykesy, creating the loop between finger and thumb again. He held it up to his eye and stared at Thomas through the open circle, trying to stifle a laugh. Thomas pressed him.

"You were measuring the movement of the moon to see how long we've been here weren't you?"

"Nah, I was just thinking about that old tart I shagged at the Red Lion last night." Sykesy giggled, "Her honeypot was massive, I could barely touch the sides!" Sykesy burst into laughter, disappearing behind a cloud of steaming breath.

"*Shhh!*" Thomas grabbed the other man's bridle and pulled the horse's head toward him angrily. "Shut the fuck up Sykesy, you'll give us away!" The man tried to stifle his laughter. Thomas's panic subsided, and he joined his friend giggling.

"*Honeypot?*" Thomas whispered incredulously. "What the fuck is a honeypot?"

Sykesy stopped laughing, his eyes growing wide at his friend's naivety.

"A honeypot, *you know …* " he searched Thomas's face for a second, " …what, you're telling me you *really* don't know what a honeypot is?"

Thomas laughed briefly, before answering sarcastically.

"Well, I've never heard it said in this context before, have I? So not unless you've been shagging a beekeeper's daughter with a rather large pot of fucking honey, no, I *don't* know Sykesy."

"*Honeypot*, it's a nice way of describing a lady's … " he stopped for a second, trying to find the right word, finally settling on, " …minge, it's a nice way of saying minge, the ladies love it when you call it a honeypot, Thomas."

"I very much doubt that the women you've been saying it to are ladies, Sykesy!"

Before Sykesy could answer, the high-pitched jingle of horse bridles in the distance broke the silence. The two accomplices froze for a second, listening for sounds of any kind. Thomas looked his friend over before nodding that they should prepare themselves for the business at hand and pulling his black neckerchief up around his face he waved his friend off.

"Good luck." Sykesy did the same before turning his horse to go to his own hiding place on the far side of the road.

Captain Henry Sykes or Sykesy as he was known to his friends, was same age as Thomas. The two had met accidentally while brawling drunkenly at one of the many taverns that encircled the Birmingham Bull Ring market. Neither man could remember which tavern it had been or the fact that the fight had begun with the locals taking offence to Sykes's London accent and his battle cry '*to hell or the hangman!*' which always seemed to proceed this sort of bar room brawl. His battle cry had aggravated the

Birmingham locals to the point of violence, but all Thomas and the Captain could remember was that it had been a mighty fight and a bloody good laugh. Although an expert with a pistol when the moment demanded it, Captain Henry Sykes also considered himself a genius with both sabre and dagger, both of which always hung at his side. If fate had not led him down the road of the highwayman, he would surely have made a very capable soldier serving his majesty on some far off battlefield, had it not been for two things; his hatred of authority and his addiction to thievery and honeypots. If truth be told, he had swindled his commission of *captain* in a card game in the London suburb of Whitechapel two years before, also duping the member of the landed gentry out of over one hundred gold guineas too. The toff hadn't noticed the hidden card up the sleeve of the card-sharp, and the simple trick had fooled the old man easily. However, the old toff had friends in high places and more to the point, paid killers in low places. The word about Sykes's trickery soon spread, aided by the Lord's particularly vicious, Scottish manservant around the gambling dens of London and as a consequence, London was now a no-go area for the Cockney 'captain'. Nevertheless, Henry wore the stolen title of captain with great pride in front of his name like a shiny medal that had been won at a great battle rather than at a drunken, midnight card-table. He was small of stature compared to Thomas; but strong in mind and handsome in a dark, roguish way, and much to many a tavern master's daughter's delight, was also blessed with the ability to make a woman laugh and orgasm in equal measure, whenever the opportunity arose, which it did on a regular basis. Indeed, if tonight's heist went well, he'd be feeding once more on a honeypot like the greedy little bear he was.

The jingle of bridle grew louder as the coach drew nearer. In the blackness it was difficult to judge distances, so Thomas climbed from his horse and removing his glove lay his hand on the frozen ground. He remained in that position for nearly a minute until he felt the soil vibrating as the eight horses' hooves drew closer, stomping their metal shoes into the hard-packed, dirt road, sending shock waves through the ground. Thomas's fingers picked up the tiny vibrations and reacted, donning his glove he climbed back into the saddle. Drawing one of the heavy pistols from its holster, he pressed his spurs softly into the horse's flanks. The black mare stepped from the trees and trotted to the middle of the road. Thomas raised his pistol and pointed it at the two candlelit lamps coming towards him at full pelt. His moonlit silhouette filled the dark highway. The bottle-green cloak hung from his broad shoulders, draping across the black mare's hind quarters, his tricorn hat with its dark green, feather plume stood tall on his head, giving the impression that man and horse were one single gargantuan beast barring the road to Birmingham.

The pounding hooves and rattle of the coach thundered closer, but Thomas remained unmoved, his pistol held high. The highwayman waited for the driver or guard to see him in the dim pool of light that shone from the two large lamps either side of the carriage. Thomas's horse became jittery as the noise of the coach grew louder, he held the reins tightly, forcing his horse to look away from the approaching black shape lest it scare his mount and make her bolt. Thomas knew there was always a very real chance that the coachman or guard wouldn't see him at all and the charging horses and coach rig might crash into him at full pelt, killing him and the mare outright. However, his upbringing as a farmer's son had taught him horsemanship, and he knew that the coach companies always used stallions as their lead horses. The highwayman had chosen his mare carefully because she was in season, Thomas knew the stallion would smell his mount a long time before he ever saw her, or at least that was the idea anyway. There was always the last resort of shooting the lead horse, but that would leave the highwayman with one less weapon to discharge and open to a devastating shot from one of the blunderbuss shotguns regularly carried by the coachmen, something that had to be avoided at all costs.

"Stand!" Thomas shouted. The coach pressed on, "*Stand!*" Thomas stood in his stirrups trying to make his outline larger in the silver moonlight. Still, the coach closed on him at speed. "*Stand, damn you!*" he screamed, his eyes wide and bright beneath the shadow of his tricorn hat. Suddenly the dark highway was filled with the deafening sound of screeching metal as the coachman caught sight of the shadow ahead. He pulled hard on his reins whilst pressing his foot on the brake pedal, straining his other foot on the duckboard against the power of the eight horses, save he should be pulled under the wheels of the coach and crushed to death. The shotgun-toting coachman slid off his bench and into the footwell of the driver's platform. His huge cap-lock weapon fell from his hands and onto the dirt road as he tried desperately to stay aboard the coach as it ground to a halt, only inches from Thomas's position in the middle of the highway. The silence that followed was deafening against the night. The horses stomped, whinnied and snorted their protests at the interruption to their gallop and the smell of the fresh mare, finally settling into submission at the driver's command. Thomas summoned up his courage before calling out to the coachmen once more so that there would be no mistake as to what was about to take place. "Stand, and throw your weapons to the floor!" He let the words hang in the still air for a second before driving home his command. "I'll have your wealth, or I'll have your life. Throw down your weapons *now*!" The two burly coachmen at the front of the wagon knew that they were caught under fire and slowly raised their hands high. The man that sat high above the vehicle on the rearguard's seat still held his blunderbuss but had no clear shot at the highwayman in front of him. The heavy weapon with its flared barrel was hopelessly inaccurate. In a normal gunfight this would have been a drawback, but in a situation like this, its ability to hit anything in front of it with a pepper of heavy lead shot was the main reason the coach companies issued this type of gun to its guards. It didn't need to be aimed only pointed in the general direction of its target and fired. Unfortunately for this particular coach if it *was* fired, it would most certainly kill both driver and forward guard. The highwaymen knew this, hence Thomas's position in the road. The chubby rearguard raised the gun to his shoulder, looking for a shot at the robber's silhouette in front of him. At that moment Sykesy rode from the dark trees to the coach's rear. The rearguard froze as he heard the unmistakable click of a pistol hammer being drawn back.

"Whoa fatso, drop the fucking gun, or I'll blow your balls off!" He said, trying to sound as aggressive as he could. The chubby man didn't move. "You might be fat but you ain't deaf, drop the *fucking* gun!" There was a moment of hesitation from the guard. "Drop it you bastard!" The loud click of Sykes's second pistol hammer being drawn back brought the young guard to his senses. He laid the blunderbuss on the coach's roof. "No, throw it to the *ground* there's a good boy!" The man followed his orders, and the heavy weapon fell to the road with a dull thud. On seeing this, the highwaymen began working a routine they had practised many times before, controlling the scene with ease.

"You three, down *now!*" Thomas ordered. The driver rose and lumbered stiffly from his perch, followed by his companions. The chubby man began grumbling to the others as they did.

"We don't get paid enough for this shit." The driver said under his breath.

"Shut it skinny, it ain't your money, it's the King's and he's got plenty. If you do as we say you won't get hurt and you'll have a bloody good tale to tell your grandchildren won't ya?" Sykesy had trotted his horse around the side of the coach, Thomas who was still at its front, covered the area with a pistol in each hand and the reins wrapped around the pommel of his saddle.

"Ok, ladies ..." Thomas said sarcastically in his deepest voice, trying to sound authoritative. "Let's not fuck around. We want the strong box from the coach." He pointed the pistol barrel in his right hand at two of the guards. "You pair of plonkers, climb in there and bring it out." The men turned to each other, a look of confusion on their faces. Neither man moved. Thomas raised his voice. "Are you pair deaf or stupid? Get in there and bring the strong box out, *now!*" Once again neither man moved. Sykesy dropped from his saddle and came behind the guards, bringing his pistol up into the nearest man's face.

"Move it sunshine, before I turn your head into a fucking soup bowl." Suddenly the man seemed to shake himself into life and dropping his hands he stepped towards the coach door and placed his hand on the handle to the carriage. Sykesy turned to Thomas, a broad smile growing across his face. Thomas sniggered.

"You're a smooth talking bastard, I'll give you that Captain Sykes!" The guard turned the heavy metal latch to the coach's compartment, its dry internal mechanism squeaked as the lock opened. He pulled the door back, gingerly releasing a beam of light from within the coach's interior. The light caught the highwaymen by surprise. This was meant to be a Royal Mail carrier, not a passenger coach. The guard stood frozen in the doorway for a second. Sykesy stepped closer to the man, placing his hand on the shoulder of the guard. Just as he was about to push the man out of the way and peer into the light within, a deafening pistol shot roared from within the coach. The guard's head exploded as a pistol shot shattered the silence of the night. The man's brains showered Sykesy in blood and gore, knocking his hat from his head. The robber stood in the pool of light cast from the coach's bright interior, his dark eyes bright against the thick, red blood and brain matter that had splattered all over his face and shoulders. Thomas's horse shuffled and stomped from the noise of the shot, almost throwing him from the saddle. The gunshot left a loud ringing in the robber's ears on the silent highway, catching all in a moment of shock.

"Anyone who steps through that doorway will get the same as the last poor wretch!" An aristocratic voice came from inside the coach. The highwaymen turned to each other. Neither of them knew what the next course of action should be. In all their rehearsals for this crime, they had never covered the possibility of someone actually being *inside* the mail coach. The Royal Mail had stopped carrying passengers on this particular coach a few years before to prevent inside jobs and leaving an empty coach also meant it could carry a greater amount of post.

Sykesy gagged at the sight of the gore and the smell of fresh warm blood which suddenly filled the air around him in a bright red mist which glistened in the coach's lamplight. He tried desperately to stop himself throwing up but the realisation that he was covered in another man's brains finally sank in and he began to retch. Thomas dropped silently from his horse, pistols in hand.

Sykesy saw him and understood his intentions, still gagging he addressed the man inside.

"We only want the strong box." His demand was met by silence. "Throw out the box, and we'll be on our way."

"Come in and get it . . . *Captain!*" was the reply, the last word spoken in a drawn out, sarcastic manner. Then another voice spoke, this time a much deeper voice with a strong Irish accent boomed.

"Yeah, *Captain Sykes*, ye heard his lordship, if ye want it, come in and get it, ya wee gob-shite!" The men inside the carriage were making the most of Thomas's earlier slip of the tongue. The situation had changed dramatically for the two highwaymen, the blood and gore that covered Sykesy testament to that.

"You've already killed one of the guards, would you kill another innocent man?" Sykesy reasoned.

"I shall kill whomever I see in that doorway!" the aristocrat retorted viciously. Thomas crept around the far side of the carriage whilst Sykesy kept the men inside occupied. Reaching the far side of the coach, Thomas used his pistol barrel to slowly and silently push the black leather curtain that covered the interior of the window to one side. The leather folded back to reveal a tall, thin gentleman in his early thirties, a grey wig sat atop his elegant head, his thin neck covered by a white lace scarf. By the look of his blue brocade coat, Thomas thought he looked exactly the gentleman his accent betrayed. The other man with the booming Irish brogue was hidden from sight, due to him sitting on the other bench opposite the gentleman. Thomas slid the pistol into the window until the barrel's cold metal touched the gentleman's neck.

"Don't move an inch!" Thomas half whispered. The cold touch shocked the man and seeing he was undone, all but froze except for his eyes, which darted this way and that in an attempt to find an escape. "Drop the pistol toff, I have no intention of hurting you but I will if I must!" Thomas raised his voice to Sykesy. "Take the man's pistol, Henry!" Sykesy stepped forward onto the carriage step, his cloaked figure filling the doorway. He looked the gentleman over and was pleasantly surprised to see Thomas's pistoled hand pointing through the far window of the coach, its muzzle resting under the thin man's chin. The candlelight shone from the small lamp fixed to the far wall illuminating the gentleman in all his finery. Sykesy scanned the man's appearance for signs of riches, his eye finally came to rest on a large, gold brooch on his coat lapel. The highwayman stepped towards the seated man, his hand unconsciously rising towards the bauble, almost hypnotised by the gleaming beauty of the brooch. Just as he was about to touch the golden treasure, he was grabbed by a huge hand which belonged to the gigantic man who sat in the dark shadow cast by the lamp above his head. Before Sykesy could warn Thomas, the giant's other hand came up with lightening speed and grabbed the barrel of Thomas's gun, pulling it away from his master's throat and forcing the trigger to be pulled. The caplock snapped shut on the powder pan at the end of its barrel which sparked and set the powder alight. A split second later the muzzle of the pistol burst into a tongue of flame, sending the shot harmlessly into the coach's roof with a loud crack. The giant pulled the gun as hard as he could, forcing Thomas's head into the side of the coach and causing him to drop his other weapon. He fell unseen to the ground outside after cracking his nose into the frame of the window. Sykesy reached into his belt to draw his own pistol. However, the giant had predicted his intentions and was already throwing his first punch of the night. *Bam!* The punch came without warning, knocking Sykesy full in the face, driving the already-unconscious highwayman back through the doorway he'd just stepped through. He fell onto the packed-dirt highway like a sack of potatoes. A thin smile broke the aristocrat's features.

"Well done, O'Donahue, now get out there and finish the pair off and we can be on our way!" On hearing his master's command the giant Irishman stood as best he could in the cramped carriage.

"Yes, your Lordship!" The aristocrat followed the big man outside to where Sykesy lay at the feet of the driver and surviving guard.

"You two, tie him up, he'll be doing the Tyburn dance by the month's end." Turning to the Irishman he continued. "O'Donahue, you go and get the other rogue and bring him around here and we'll have some sport!"

"My Lord." The driver stepped forward taking his hat from his head, holding it with both hands at his chest. "My Lord," he said again, eyes lowered, "but what about him?" He nodded towards the decapitated coachman at their feet. The aristocrat gave the body a quick glance.

"There's little we can do for that poor wretch, murdered by these pair of highway robbers. We all saw it, didn't we? *Murdered* in cold blood . . . " He left the words hanging, turning towards the Royal Mail men, his white-powdered face glowing in the moonlight like a spiteful spirit. "Well?" He pressed. The men reluctantly nodded their obedience. "Don't worry gentlemen, there shall be an extra ringing of coin in your pocket after we reach our destination." The two coachmen smiled.

"Yes, your Lordship. Thank you, sir." The driver fawned. "But, but where exactly *is* your destination, sir?" The aristocrat gave the men an impatient look which made the coachmen bow even lower than they already were, finally answering with a question of his own.

"You!" He pointed his white leather gloved hand at the driver. "How far are we from Birmingham town?" The driver looked around him at the surrounding forest track, trying to find a landmark in the pitch blackness.

"It's hard to say in the darkness your Lordship, but we passed through Warwick two hours past, so I'd say we're not far from Druids Heath, sir. Maybe about another hour more to go, I'd say, four, maybe five miles from the town of Birmingham, depending on exactly *where* in the town your Lordship wants to be taken?" The elegant man took in the driver's words before answering.

"I'm . . . " He stopped himself, " . . . *we*, that is, Mr O'Donahue and myself are going to an area of Birmingham called the *Froggery*. Do you know it driver?" The driver's fawning smile dropped.

"Yes sir, but . . . but . . . " The aristocrat became more impatient.

"But what man? Spit it out, do you know it or not?" The coachman and driver turned to each other before stepping forward into the pool of light. "We do, sir." The coachman said, removing his hat. "But the *Froggery* isn't somewhere your Lordship would want to go, it's, it's full of thieves and cut throats." His companion joined the conversation.

"Yes, sir, the likes of people like him!" The driver gave the still unconscious Sykesy a kick. "No, you don't want to go down the Froggery, sir!"

"*Damn you pair of insolent ingrates!*" The gentleman screamed. "It's not for the likes of *you* to tell me where I can or cannot go." He pulled a thin-foiled blade from a jewel-encrusted scabbard that was concealed beneath his coat sleeve and pointed the blade, letting it dance between both men. "You've both been paid handsomely for our concealment in your infernal mail coach so shut your filthy mouths and take me where I want to go. Unless of course, you would both prefer to end up like this bag of rags you called a friend." He raised his booted foot and placed it on the dead man's chest. The speech had put the driver and his companion both in their place, and they nodded obediently. "Good, now we understand each other!" He tapped his foot on the dead guard's chest and ordered. "Now take this poor bastard and place his body on the luggage rack, if I'm not off my mark, someone will pay a pretty penny in Birmingham for your friend here." He gave a short chuckle. "Don't worry, you can keep whatever his body raises, I am a firm man, but never let it be said that I am not a fair one!" The irony of his words was lost on all there. The moment was broken by the entrance of Thomas Fewtrell. O'Donahue had picked up the semi-conscious highwayman up and literally thrown him to the ground at his lordship's feet. Thomas fell with a sickening thud on the hard-packed dirt. His face covered in blood where his nose had been cracked by the carriage's window frame.

"Here's the other one, me lord." The Irishman laughed.

"Ah, we have another guest for our little party." Nodding to the coachmen, "Pick him up!" The men stepped forward simultaneously, bending and picking up the groaning robber from the floor under his arms. The aristocrat stepped forward and flipped the tricorn hat from Thomas's head, before pulling the black scarf to reveal the robber's face.

"Well, well, we have a handsome Highwayman at our mercy, eh O'Donahue?" The gentleman scanned Thomas's features, his long, dark-blond hair hung over his brow, the aristocrat brushed the hair back to reveal Thomas's bright blue eyes. He removed a silk handkerchief from his laced sleeve and wiped the dried blood from the younger man's nose. "My, my, you are a handsome young man, such a shame to ruin such a noble face as yours." Thomas opened his eyes slightly, wincing with the pain from his nose. He glanced at his unconscious companion.

"Is he dead?" The aristocrat grinned.

"No, but he soon will be, just like you. I've a good mind to bring you both back to London to dance on the Tyburn tree." He stopped mid-sentence. "But I dare say Birmingham has as good a gallows as anywhere else, so you can both hang here for all I care!" He raised his finger and ran it over Thomas's cheek. "But that's in the future my sweet highwayman, for now, we must make the most of what fate has handed us whilst we still have time." Thomas grimaced at the man's touch.

"Fate?" The aristocrat laughed.

"Yes, fate, you see this fine beast of a man is James O'Donahue, a man of rare talent as you and your unfortunate friend have just found out. O'Donahue here is a pugilist." The gentleman let the word sink in. "Do you even know what a pugilist is?"

Thomas rolled his eyes, finally understanding why Syksey and himself had suffered so much.

"He's a fighter." Thomas said reluctantly.

"No!" The gentleman said in surprise. "Not a fighter, anyone can fight young man, O'Donahue here is a boxer, an expert in the gentleman's sport of pugilism, do you understand?" Thomas shrugged his shoulders nonchalantly, trying not to show any signs of fear. The aristocrat continued. "Well, just in case there's any confusion between fighting and boxing, O'Donahue here is more than happy to give you a display of his boxing prowess." Thomas forced a smile.

"Oh there's no need for that, tell your Irish friend he should save his strength for when he gets back to Ireland. I've heard there's plenty of sheep that need shagging over there and by the look of his ugly mug, I'd say he needs all the help he can get, cos those sheep can be fussy buggers." The gentleman snorted at the joke.

"Did you hear that O'Donahue? The scoundrel has wit, maybe you should show him what *you're* good at and we'll see if he's still laughing when he has no fucking teeth left in his head!" The man's smile dropped. "Hold him tight!" He ordered the coachmen. They nodded, grabbing Thomas's arms tightly. "No, damn you, not like that, hold him by the wrists. O'Donahue needs space to work!" The men slid their hands down to Thomas's wrists, each holding tightly. Thomas stood crucified between the two, waiting for O'Donahue to finish removing his jacket, allowing the enormous Irishman the freedom of movement needed for the beating about to commence.

O'Donahue struggled with the tight jacket sleeve for a few seconds before ripping the garment from himself with impatience. The huge, thick-set man looked ridiculous in his tight breeches, waistcoat and shirt, a ruffle of lace at his chin contrasted with his brutal face, scarred from previous boxing bouts. He came in close to Thomas.

"Alright so let's see how tough ye are without those pistols in your hands." O'Donahue stepped back, rolling his sleeves up to the elbow. Thomas mustered up his courage and said laughing,

"Jesus man, who dressed you in that bloody suit?" The Irishman stopped in his tracks. "Was it him?" He nodded towards the aristocrat, who had taken up a perch on the footstep of the carriage. On hearing Thomas's comment the Irishman looked down at himself, becoming embarrassed by his bright-green, silk breeches and waistcoat that matched the suit jacket he had torn off so violently. "What colour is that by the way?" Thomas continued. "It's a cross between puke green and piss yellow." The gentleman laughed loudly, the guards joining in with stifled sniggers. O'Donahue flushed self-consciously. "And what are those embroideries?" Thomas gestured with his head towards the dark green detailing on the waistcoat. "Oh, shamrocks, I see, just in case people didn't notice you were Irish, you've got bloody shamrocks all over your fucking suit, stone the crows." Thomas laughed loudly, joined by the other men. The giant man snorted, his eyes wild and brow furrowed. O'Donahue began to massage his knuckles which creaked and cracked as he pulled his fingers back and forth.

"Oh you're a funny man, so ye are, well you ain't gonna be so funny after the feckin hiding O'Donahue's gonna give ye tonight, ye little gob-shite!" Thomas, gulped, trying to conceal his fear, but he knew he had the man on the hook so continued with his jibes.

"I don't know what I'm more upset about, being hung on the gallows for tonight's shenanigans or being beaten up by a six foot six leprechaun!" The aristocrat burst into laughter, joined once again by the driver and coach guard. Thomas's face broke into a huge grin, the smile just for show. Thomas braced himself for the first punch, a feeling of dread creating a void in his stomach. On hearing the laughter the big man went into a rage, snarling. O'Donahue came forward with a flying, haymaker punch. For Thomas, the whole thing happened in slow motion. The Irishman bringing his arm back and counterweighting it with the other arm, making his movements predictable and slow. As the huge fist came through the air towards Thomas, the highwayman drove his heels into the dirt and pulled his head backwards away from the fist. As he did so, Thomas pulled both arms together with all his might, dragging the driver and guard both into the space where a split second before Thomas's face had been. The surprised coachmens' heads cracked together painfully, where only a millisecond later they were joined by O'Donahue's giant fist. There was a sickening thud as the Irishman's clenched fist landed squarely on the guard's jawbone, shattering it completely with a loud *crack*. The fist had so much momentum behind it that it carried on through the guard and full into the driver's face which was at a different angle to his companion's and so took the full power of the blow squarely in his face which exploded in a fountain of blackened teeth and crimson blood. Thomas's move caught everyone by surprise, most of all, Thomas himself, who hadn't been sure if his plan was going to work at all. The jibes had wound the Irishman up so much, that he'd thrown a wild, angry punch with all the power he could muster. The coachmen had been too busy laughing at Thomas's comments to take any notice of O'Donahue's actions, both now paying for it with a scattering of teeth and blood. The two men dropped to the floor, the driver out cold, the other man, screaming with pain at his dislocated and shattered jawbone. Thomas shook himself free of their grip and stepped towards the big man, his fists held up in front of his face.

"Ok, leprechaun, let's see what you've got!" On seeing this the aristocrat suddenly became animated, clapping his hands together in a short burst of excitement. O'Donahue, his eyes wide with surprise, looked at the two injured men at his feet. He seemed unable to comprehend what had just happened. The rage gripped him once more. The giant stepped forward with the same hay-maker he'd floored the unfortunate coachmen with, Thomas saw it coming and ducked beneath the swing easily. The Irishman's fist flew over his head with a swoosh of air, but Thomas was already in, underneath the swing, with his own punch to the big man's ribs. *Bam, bam,* two punches in the same rib, *crack,* then he was back out from under O'Donahue's huge arm, already searching for the next opening. The giant buckled at the broken rib but came on in a snarling rage, trying to grab at the younger man. Thomas ducked beneath the man's grasping right arm, coming out behind the Irishman. *Bam, bam,* another couple of punches to the ribs, *crack,* another lower rib snapped by the lightning blows. The big man spun with a painful howl, his arm extended, trying to catch Thomas with a blind blow to the head but the highwayman was already crouched, the powerful throw once again missing his head by inches. Thomas brought his right fist upwards as hard and as fast as he could, his two legs springing from the ground, his full weight behind the punch, as if his open hand was a hammer. Then right at the last second, just before the open hand landed on the Irishman's thick-set face, Thomas twisted his wrist, clenched his fist and brought his knuckles to land with a loud thud on O'Donahue's cheek, smashing the man's cheekbone, which collapsed inside the Irishman's mouth. The giant took the blow without falling. He stood in a punch-drunk stupor, staring at the highwayman in front of him, his lower mandible protruding at a weird angle, his rotted teeth still attached to the bone. O'Donahue stepped forwards then backwards, unable to comprehend what had happened. Thomas watched the man's stumbling, with a growing sympathy.

The aristocrat had stopped clapping and had risen to his feet. He watched his prizefighter stumble around in the pool of dim moonlight, like a drunken buffoon in his pea-green, shamrock livery. Thomas turned to look at the gentleman and saw that the man was occupied with the injured Irishman's oncoming demise.

Thomas stepped behind O'Donahue and bent to pick up the still unconscious Sykesy. He struggled with the weight of his friend, finally lifting him onto the saddle of his horse, throwing him over the horse's flank unceremoniously. A loud thud behind him made Thomas spin just in time to see the Irishman come to rest in a cloud of dust at his master's feet. The aristocrat stood, tall and thin, immaculately elegant, his narrow white-powdered, chiselled features glowing in the freezing moonlight, staring down at the semi-conscious Irishman like a hovering angel of death. Thomas broke away from the scene to fetch his mare from the far side of the coach. He scanned the area for his fallen pistols and finding them easily in the bright moonlight, he dropped them into the saddle holsters and with a strange calmness he climbed into the saddle. As he trotted his horse to Sykesy's side he heard the click of a hammer being drawn and saw the figure of the aristocrat aiming one of the blunderbuss rifles at him but before he could react, the trigger was pulled. The weapon boomed in an explosion of flame and metal into the darkness. Thomas winced at the sudden, stinging he felt in his thigh, his mare's neck burst into a peppering of bloodspots, instantly rearing onto her hind legs, ready to bolt. Thomas struggled to bring her under control and glancing at the gentleman by the coach who had thrown down the single shot weapon and was already bending to pick up the other discarded blunderbuss. The mare rose onto her rear, sending the highwayman forward, grasping for her mane for balance, grabbing the reins, Thomas desperately tried to force the mare to obey his commands but the horse had other ideas. *Click,* the second weapon's hammer drew back, Thomas braced himself for what must be a deadly, point-blank shot.

"Run, Thomas, run!" Sykesy screamed. His friend, who had regained consciousness, lay across his saddle, kicking his horse's flanks, bringing his horse between the aristocrat and Thomas. "Run,

God damn you, *run!*" He screamed desperately. Thomas struggled to hold his own horse, which was stomping and snorting its protest in clouds of steam in the cold air. *Boom*, the second weapon fired, Thomas saw the dark silhouette of his comrade and horse fall to the ground with a mixture of noise and pain from both man and beast. Thomas's horse could not be controlled any longer. The deafening sound of the second shot made any attempt to calm the beast useless and so, she bolted, the highwayman clinging to her mane for all he was worth. The animal sprinted into the darkness towards Birmingham town like a black Pegasus running from the fires of hell. With some difficulty and pain, Thomas managed to turn in the saddle as he left the scene of the robbery. In the dim pool of soft, yellow lamplight, Thomas had just enough time to see the elegant aristocrat standing over Sykesy's crumpled body, a fresh pistol in hand. The gentleman was staring into the darkness as the shadow of the highwayman grew smaller, his horse's hooves throwing up tiny dust devils spinning in the blue light of the moon.

The Rookery

CHAPTER 2

The card table sat in the centre of the wide, wooden-framed mezzanine balcony that ran the length of the cavernous room. The bright-green, felt material covering the table top contrasted against its grimy surroundings. Strange, golden hieroglyphic symbols crisscrossed the green surface, giving the gaming table an almost mystical appearance, making *this* table different from the other ten or so gaming tables scattered around the busy, smokey room. The Egyptian table, as it was called, was reserved for only the richest of punters at the Rookery gambling house. However, it didn't matter how rich one was, one was only allowed to play *this* table if they belonged to the most prestigious of Birmingham's many secret societies or had been invited to play there by the club's godfather Mr William Blackfoot.

Bridget O'Hara leant across the rickety, old bannister rail that ran the length of the mezzanine level, her back to the room below. Her dark hair gathered in an untidy mop around her mocha-coloured skin, a pile of dark gypsy-like ringlets fell in curly tousles over her shoulders, as she drew lazily on the thin clay pipe that hung from the corner of her mouth, sending a thin plume of smoke into the already eye-wateringly smokey air. Her sharp, green eyes scanned the group of finely dressed gentlemen that had gathered around the table, in various states of excitement and drunkenness. She was tired, partly from the amount of gin she had consumed and partly from the fact that she had been trying to work these punters since sundown, without one of them taking a bite of her cherry. If things continued as they were, she would have to resort to her former trade as a pickpocket, a job she'd always had a talent for and the idea made her ponder why she had turned to whoring at all. She puffed out a cloud of smoke into the soft glow of the yellow candlelight that struggled to illuminate the huge room. The inadequate candles guttered on their massive wrought-iron candelabras which hung on chains from the high roof. The night was dragging. She hadn't been able to entice any of the young dandies that visited the gambling house into the room she'd rented for the purpose of prostitution, at the back of the Rookery's main hall. Although the tubby Quaker who frequented the place, ostensibly trying to save souls, *had* been giving her the eye, whether it was a sinful eye or not she couldn't tell. Anyway, the Quakers she'd come across were usually penniless, unapproachable and liked to look down their long judgmental noses at the prostitutes of Birmingham or maybe that was just the chip on her shoulder, she couldn't tell these days. Many of the girls who had worked the Froggery area of Birmingham, were, due mainly to the ever-increasing pimping prices, forced away from the Rookery, and onto the dark streets around the Froggery. However, after the bodies of three well-known bawds had been discovered mutilated, she was beginning to have second thoughts about her new career. In a time when violence against whores was all part of the job, Bridget O'Hara made sure that she was always within earshot of one of the hard men she gave a free one to in exchange for the protection they granted. The Rookery itself had seen better days, it had once been a grand ornate building, a place of worship for the Jewish community, who had lived in this part of the town fifty or so years before. However, times and fortunes had changed. The Jewish pedlars had done well for themselves and when the area now called the Froggery, had fallen from grace, the Jews had simply moved on, making way for the next community to take over the area, namely, the poor, of which there were thousands. Their numbers were made up of folk streaming into the town looking for work; Irish, Scottish, black and Chinese could all be found rubbing shoulders with the local Brummies looking for an honest living. Of course, when there was no honest work, the life of thieving or prostitution was the only option, unless you wanted to drown yourself in gin and drink away your miserable life. An option which, by the standards of the day, seemed very attractive to many people, rich or poor.

Bridget spun away from the gamblers, who had all but ignored her darkly, attractive, flirtatious smiles. She leant over the wooden railing and observed the throngs of peasantry that went about their business in the room below, the busy scene partially obscured beneath a thick cloud of tobacco smoke hanging in the air like a blanket of brown, sweet-smelling fog.

The balcony was reserved for men with plenty of coin; lords, gentry, dandies and the like, however, the ground floor was open to all and sundry, and tonight the lower level was thriving. Bridget's idea to rent one of the whoring rooms had cost her more than she could afford. She had been coerced into the decision by talk of tonight's boxing bout which had been banded around the town for weeks, creating a fervour of betting and wagers, which in turn had the effect of pulling a huge crowd to the Rookery to see the fight. However, much to Bridget's annoyance, everyone was waiting until *after* the boxing bout before spending their cash on a taste of her expensive cherry. She watched the cockfight taking place in the wooden-railed, circular ring ten feet directly below her. The large, brightly-coloured birds crowed and squawked at each other as they fought frenziedly with the long, razor-sharp metal spurs that had been attached to their legs with thin, leather throngs, by their greedy owners. Men gathered around the ring screaming their delight as the animals tore each other to pieces. The scattering of straw lining the floor of the ring was already covered in blood from previous cockfights of which this was the last before events moved on to the next gambling attraction. Most events generally ran in the same order starting with cockfights, dogfights, then something unusual, maybe a bear or wild boar fighting a dog or pack of dogs which always sounded much more exciting than it actually was. This was followed by the most dangerous of all beasts, mankind, usually just amateur scrapping, uncontrollable, untrained fighting with fists and feet or occasionally a knife fight between two enemies, sometimes till first blood *or*, much to the delight of everyone who frequented the Rookery, to the death. Tonight was a bout between two experts of the new gentleman's sport of Pugilism. Bridget had no interest in such pursuits, and so with growing boredom, she searched the heads of the punters for a potential shagger, only to find ragbag losers and hard on their heel prostitutes in the chaotic drunkenness amongst the two hundred or so peasants in the pit below. She sipped on her glass of gin in between pulling on the smouldering tobacco of her clay pipe. She allowed herself to reflect on her climb out of poverty from her penniless upbringing as the daughter of a black servant girl and a drunken, red-haired Irish father. She had learned to use her buxom assets to her best ability in the only way she knew. The realisation that Bridget O'Hara could literally *fuck* her way out of the desperate poverty, suffered by herself and all around her, had been a most liberating moment. When finally, she had found to finance her way to cross the ocean to some new world where with coin in her purse, she would be able to begin her life again by opening her horizons instead of her legs. Where and when she hadn't considered as yet, but she knew that she must escape the streets of Birmingham.

Bridget's thoughts were interrupted by a commotion near the huge warehouse door at the front of the building. A crowd had begun to gather around the smaller entrance hatch that sat to one side of the door. She watched a large, brutal-looking man duck inside the small frame followed by an equally mean-looking fellow who proceeded to push back the crowd which had formed a small circle around the entrance. In anticipation of whoever was about to step through the hatch, many of the crowd were craning their necks to see over the shoulders of the people at the front of the circle. Suddenly from out of the blackness of the entrance stepped another large man. Only this man was *smartly* dressed in a long, grey greatcoat which almost reached to his ankles. Its massive collar of brown, curly, beaver fur stood tall behind his neck in the latest Regency style, all of this weighed down with one hundred silver buttons which ran the length of the coat from collar to toe. Underneath the heavy garment, a bright red waistcoat contrasted against his white, linen shirt and neck scarf. The outfit was topped off with what Bridget thought was the tallest hat she had ever seen. A grey, tapered, top hat which sat on the man's head precariously, its large plume of bright red feathers protruding from the hatband reaching almost two feet above the man's head, giving him the impression of being eight feet tall. From underneath the small brim of the hat, a face, just as brutal as his minders, stared around him, peering from beneath a pair of black, hairy eyebrows at the excited faces of the chaotic crowd. Red blusher ran in smudged lines along his jowls, in an attempt to create the impression of cheekbones on the flabby, white skin. Another smudge of eyeliner shadowed his eyelids, making his dark, animalistic eyes sparkle with a mixture of triumph and distrust in the yellow candlelight.

"Black Foot!" Bridget muttered under her breath at the sight of the host of tonight's little soiree. William Black, or *Black Foot* as everyone around the town called the Rookery's owner, was Birmingham's self-proclaimed *King of Thieves*. An ex-redcoat soldier in his mid fifties, he was a little older than most of the people he made his living from and *what* a living it was. Gambling, protection rackets on almost every ale house and inn within the town limits, prostitution, and even the occasional dirty deed for the town's high and mighty. All of which brought in enough money to keep Black Foot and his beautiful daughter Eleanor in a high life that most of his clientele could only dream of. When he wasn't extorting money from the good people of Birmingham, Black Foot liked to boast about his military prowess of old; the men he'd killed with musket shot or hand to hand, all of which was a figment of his imagination. He bragged loudly to the ignorant and naive of battles and spoke of how he had walked into showers of lead gunshot at the head of his regiment or of desperate midnight attacks on imaginary forts at the head of a forlorn hope. The stories were told with such a dramatic conviction that the listener not only believed Black Foot had been at these fantasy battles, but also that he still carried the deadly prowess he had possessed in that far off time of war. The hidden truth was far less dramatic. William Black *had* served in the Redcoat army under the Duke of Cumberland and had even seen action against the Jacobite army of Bonny Prince Charlie at the battle of Culloden Moor in 1746, but far from being a heroic Achilles at the head of his army, William had been a twelve-year-old drummer boy in the ranks of the British forces. That's not to say he didn't join in with the plunder, murder and rape of any unfortunates that the redcoats happened upon following the massacre of the Jacobites on that bloody day. As a matter of fact, William Black gained his nickname following the battle when he came across a dying clansman, a chieftain from the market town above the Loch of Invergordon, who, on realising that his time on this earth was up, decided to take the little plundering drummer boy with him. He lashed out with his long, basket-hilt Claymore, ripping the tendons in William's ankle, almost crippling the lad. Indeed this was the *only* thing Black Foot had in common with the Ancient Greek hero, Achilles, and his famous ankle. William's life was saved by a watching officer who took pity on the boy and took his own sword to the chieftain. Unfortunately for William, the Highlander's blade had been a filthy one and the wound festered before gangrene set in, turning the foot black. A gentleman surgeon upon finding the lad, saved both life and leg. However, William's right foot refused to return to its former colour, remaining a mixture of black and dark blue. and so, the wound that had so quickly ended William's army career inadvertently gave him the nickname that would later become synonymous with violence and fear amongst the peasantry of Birmingham, William Black Foot.

Bridget O'Hara watched the commotion at the front entrance spread through the throng of folk below in a wave of excitement. The cockfight all but forgotten as the Brummies, one by one, became aware of the entrance of their very own royal family. After allowing the sycophantic crowd to gaze upon him for a full minute, Black Foot stepped to one side, allowing his daughter to cross the threshold from the real to the surreal that existed inside the Rookery. Bridget leaned further over the bannister rail to try and get a better look. An elegant stockinged leg appeared through the small gateway. She watched as Black Foot's daughter stepped fully into the room, her gown crushed by the door's narrowness. A small gasp could be heard clearly throughout the warehouse as this vision of beauty in eggshell-blue walked into the middle of the clearing and through the crowd. Bridget, like almost everyone else inside the building, couldn't take her eyes from the girl, whose perfection of un-pockmarked skin, blonde hair, white teeth and cleanliness, was most rare to behold in these days of open sewers and the ever-present smell of human excrement. A light-blue hat sat atop a mop of blonde hair which had been piled delicately upon her head. The broad brim of the hat partially hiding the lady's perfect features from almost everyone in the room. Only the lower part of her face could be seen, her bright, cherry-red lips glistened in the dim light, promising a sexuality that was out of bounds for all but the chosen. Her lips contrasted against her pale, powdered face its only blemish a tiny, hand-drawn, heart-shaped mole, just above and to the side of her mouth. Eleanor Black took up a stance, one foot in front of the other, her fragile weight upon the thin glass cane she held in her white, silk-gloved hand and she slowly raised her head until the brim of the hat revealed her face fully. Another gasp went through the room as if the crowd had just realised there was an angel in their midst. Bridget joined them, clapping her hands excitedly at the sight of such perfection. Then, as if the mere presence of Eleanor were not enough, the lady broke into a broad smile, which seemed to illuminate the room itself. Her smile was more infectious than the plague and almost everyone who gazed upon the girl broke into broad but not so beautiful grins of their own. Bridget smiled too. She didn't know why, maybe it was because beauty such as this was a rare commodity in the streets of the town, or maybe Bridget saw something in the lady that reminded her of the secret fantasies that came to her at night. There was no mistaking the sexual tingling in her loins whenever she'd seen Eleanor, whether it was a sexual attraction or one of materialistic envy was uncertain. There was even talk amongst the whores about Eleanor's secret interest in the girls that worked the Rookery. Bridget had never seen it though and so concluded that this was probably just gossip between envious prostitutes of which there were plenty. She watched from the balcony as Eleanor twisted her head elegantly from one side to the other, smiling that disarming smile amongst the roughest crew the town had to offer. Then, with the slightest twist of her long, pale neck, Eleanor was staring right at Bridget, a direct stare, one Bridget thought could see right into her heart, which fluttered with flattery at the girl's attention. The prostitute froze, as if caught in a trance, hypnotised by the gaze of a wild yet beautiful predator, wanting to, yet unable to break away. The tingling in her loins grew and Bridget wondered if it carried on whether she would orgasm there and then as the stare became more and more intense. The lady's bright-blue eyes bore into her and for the first time Bridget saw that although Eleanor had that disarming smile still painted across her face, her eyes were not smiling, they were cold circles of intent, simmering with hidden sexual desires and all of it aimed towards her. Bridget O'Hara's knees began to tremble as the intensity of the stare grew and flashing visions of lust danced within her mind's eye and her heart pumped excitedly in her breast, anticipating what might await her later that night.

The Bear

CHAPTER 3

Black Foot turned to the large minder at his shoulder who leant forward and placed his ear next to his master's face. Black Foot muttered something inaudible over the din of the crowd. The minder turned and stretched up to pull on the wrought-iron bolts that held the huge gates shut, separating the room from the street outside. As he did, Black Foot began to bang his blackthorn cane on the floor, its silver cap making tiny sparks on the cobbles beneath it. The loud ringing brought the people to a forced hush. He watched with an expressionless face as the crowd around him grew quiet around him. When he saw that the room's attention was focussed on him, he spoke.

"You filthy animals!" He screamed. "Vile, filthy scum of the Froggery, every single one of you!" The crowd stood, enthralled by the outburst. "Villains!" He began walking around his daughter, who stood motionless in the centre of the circle of people, with that beautiful smile on her face, pointing with his Blackthorn cane at various characters in the crowd. "Thieves!" Each time he pointed his cane at someone a cheer of approval rose from the excited crowd. "Whores, pimps, sluts, vagabonds, cut pockets, horse thieves and ... the most beautiful of all the *scum* of Birmingham ... " He left a pause for dramatic effect, knowing that he had his audience in the palm of his hand, finally bringing his cane to point in the direction of a table of homosexuals dressed in women's makeup, clothing and finery, " ... n*one other than our very own mollies!*" A deafening roar of laughter and cheering went up, joined by a shower of tricorn hats and caps being thrown into the air. The group of homosexuals joined in the laughter, one of them even climbed onto the ale-ladened table and lifted his great ringed-skirt and exposed his genitals to the crowd, which brought even more drunken cheering and wolf whistles. Black Foot let the cheering quieten before continuing.

"Tonight, my lords, ladies *and* gentlemen," He bowed mockingly to the group of well-dressed dandies peering over the railing on the mezzanine next to Bridget.

"I have brought you something very special, my friends. Something to entertain you and tickle those purse strings in a boxing bout to beat all bouts, some of you will leave here rich men, when the wagers are placed, others ... " he raised his index finger, waving it enticingly " ... not so rich!" He laughed at his own comments before changing his tone. "I ask myself, why William Black Foot, why do you treat these people as if they were your own children ... " He ran his fingers across the cheek of his daughter's soft skin. She turned her face toward her father, her broad smile replaced by a mischievous smirk. " ... and I say ... " Black Foot continued, in answer to his own question, " ... if God almighty has forgotten these poor unfortunates, then never let it be said that William Black Foot has not. I tell you Satan himself, could not provide you with such a show of brutality as I will tonight and so, you horrible rabble of humanity ... " he gestured the minders to pull the huge wooden doors apart,

" ... I give you, *the Bear!*" As he said the words the massive doors behind him opened with a squealing creek as the rusty hinges ground together, to reveal a giant of a man, standing in the broadening gap. His hairy, wide chest pumping in and out as the man flexed his pectoral muscles. His thick, hairy arms hung at angles as he tensed his arm muscles to show his physique in all its masculinity. The man opened his deep-set eyes as wide as he could as he tried to take on the features of a wild animal and he roared his anger and fury at the crowd inside. On hearing the animalistic noise, the crowd stepped backwards as one, trying to get as far away from the beast in the doorway as they could. The Bear stepped across the threshold, bare-chested, his only protection from the freezing night was his doe skin breeches and the thick coating of hair upon his back, no shoes or stockings on his huge feet as he walked upon the cold cobbles. The Rookery was silent as the gargantuan man took his place next to Eleanor. She raised her hand, and the giant took it delicately. The crowd stood in silence, wide-eyed, hypnotised by the beauty and beast before them. The two stepped forward, into the crowd, which parted with their every step until they reached a table that sat on a risen platform next to the gaming pit. The lady sat, the man bent and kissed her hand delicately before turning to the crowd and slowly bowing. The audience burst into applause and whistles filled the hall. A small, smiling urchin of a man stepped forward and gave the giant a tankard of ale which he drained in seconds, throwing the cup into the gaming ring at the long-forgotten, half-dead cockerels. Slowly the audience resumed their conversations and gambling. After a short time Black Foot joined them at the table and climbing onto the bench, he scanned the heads of the crowd as if searching for someone.

"Where is this Irish challenger, James O'Donahue?" He asked himself, raising his hand to his brow as if he were ship's captain searching the sea, a look of confusion growing on his face. He beckoned a tall, balding man to his side. "Where is he?" The man shrugged in reply.

"I ain't sure, Mr Black Foot sir, he was meant to be here around midnight, but it's well past that now." Black Foot shivered with anger, the man stepped back expecting an explosion of insults at any moment, but Black Foot, seeing he was still under scrutiny from some of the crowd, especially the higher-class men on the balcony managed to bring his emotions under control and smiling falsely, he said through gritted teeth.

"I don't need to remind you that I have a very large wager on tonight's fight, you suggested we put the fight on and I agreed, and now . . . " He checked himself, lest he talk too loudly, " . . . and now, I'm gonna be left out of pocket and looking like a prize prick if this bout doesn't go ahead. So unless you want to be propping up a gravestone in Hockley fucking cemetery, I'd get your skinny arse moving and find out where my fucking challenger is!" The man shuddered at his boss's words.

"Yes, Mr Black Foot sir, I'll, I'll ... " The thin man seemed to be lost as to what he should do about the late arrival of O'Donahue and his master Lord Percy Whip. Black Foot, seeing this confusion, broke in.

"Get some fucking riders out looking for them, you useless ponce. Lord Percy's letter said they should be arriving on the midnight Royal Mail coach, which comes along the old Warwick Road. He'll be in a big, red, fucking coach with Royal Mail painted on the side, it can't be that hard to find, can it?" The thin man almost bent in two as he backed away.

"No, sir I'll get some riders out right away, sir." He backed into the throng and vanished amongst the drinkers gathered around the gaming pit. Black Foot sat at the table opposite Eleanor.

"Fucking ingrates, all of em!" Eleanor reached across the table and placed her hand on his.

"I'm sure there's a reasonable explanation as to why they aren't here father." He raised his head and looked at his daughter. His brutish face lit up as he gazed upon her beauty and he held her stare as if it were the first time he'd ever seen the girl. The anger fell from him, replaced by a resigned smile.

"Yes, I'm sure you're right my dear, but if this fight doesn't go ahead ... " Eleanor patted the back of her father's hand.

"I'm sure it'll be all right in the end father, your riders will find the man. Come now let's drink, after all, we didn't get all dressed up for nothing now did we?" Black Foot nodded and smiled, turning to the gaming pit his attention was grabbed by the two large, black dogs being led into the wooden circle. Eleanor craned her head and looked directly above her straight into the eyes of Bridget O'Hara. The two women held each other's gaze for a few seconds. Realising her father's attention lay on the dogfight about to take place, Eleanor rose from the table and crossed to the stairs leading up to the mezzanine and climbed them. Bridget was waiting for her at the top of the small rickety staircase. Eleanor stepped in closely to the young, mixed-race prostitute. "Do you have a room?" Bridget's surprise at the unexpected question was obvious, but nevertheless, she answered matter of factually.

"A room . . . yes, in the back of the building my lady!" Bridget fawned. Eleanor's seductive smile dropped from her face, she came close to Bridget, touching the dark-skinned girl with her white-powdered cheek and whispered in her ear.

"Well, my beautiful little whore, I think I'll have to take you to your back room and punish you, for you've *just* made your first mistake." Bridget shook her head.

"Mistake my lady?" She questioned. Eleanor raised her arm slyly and grabbing Bridget around the waist, she pulled the girl into her roughly.

"Yes, *mistake,* my little mulatto whore. You called me a *lady!*" Bridget's eyes widened in a mixture of surprise and embarrassment. In the guttering candlelight of the smokey room, the half-Irish, half-black girl could see just how much Eleanor's face had changed in the few seconds it had taken to say those words. From the innocent girl who had made such a grand entrance into the dominant woman filled with sexual desires that stood in front of her now. Eleanor giggled mischievously.

"You're about to find out, just how *un*ladylike I am!"

Dog Fight

CHAPTER 4

Lord Percy Whip waited for over an hour for one of the unconscious men to come around in a spluttering of blood and teeth. His lordship wasn't used to having to wait for anything, well, that wasn't entirely true, he'd been waiting for his doddering dear father to shuffle off his mortal coil for the last few years.

"The old fucker just won't die!" He would rant to any one of his fellow dandies, drunk enough to put up with the annoying aristocrat's irrelevant ramblings. Until only two months before, Old Lord Percy senior had mysteriously suffered an agonising, black-lipped death that had more than just a resemblance to arsenic poisoning. The old man's death left young Lord Percy Whip free to gamble, drink, and whore himself stupid, pursuits he had taken to with an almost biblical conviction, even before the old man's body was cold.

He looked down at the injured man at his feet and for a second even considered offering the wretch a swing of brandy from his silver hip flask. However, the thought of wasting such a rare French liquor on the underclass was beyond any level of empathy he could muster. Besides, it was their incompetence that had delayed him, and now he was too near his destination to turn back to London. He must now face the infamous William Black Foot without a fighter to compete in the heavy wager he had arranged with the scoundrel. He cursed himself for taking the wager at all but needs must, he could not see himself in the debtor's jail with all the other poor gentlemen who had fallen for a card trick or tart's tit. He sat on the step of the coach and took a swig from the small flask, the brandy's warmth filled him immediately, perking him up in the increasingly freezing night.

"Get up you dolt!" He screamed at the coach guard. "Get up and get that damned fool up too, broken or not, I'll not miss this appointment!" He stood and crossed the space between the coach and the prostrate coachmen and kicked the man nearest him. "Up, up, damn your insolent bones!" He turned to the fallen Irish man next to the coach's wheel. "And you, Irishman!" His voice rising higher. "Get up off the dust and pull yourself together!" O'Dona-hue didn't move. Lord Percy took the man's stillness as a personal affront and crossing back to the coach he undid his britches and took out his penis. "Come on you oaf, up, up, *up* !" He shouted the last word with such anger and volume it woke the sleeping giant in the road just as a shower of his Lordship's piss splashed onto the Irishman's face. O'Donahue blinked against the yellow shower, as it cascaded into his eyes and mouth. The sight made Lord Percy laugh loudly. "That's it you Irish bastard, I knew a bit of brandy piss would awaken you. Now stand sir, and we'll be on our way!"

The coach guard and driver took another fifteen minutes to raise themselves from the dirt. O'Donahue took considerably longer but eventually, after loading the dead guard onto the rear rack and the still unconscious and bleeding, bound highwayman into the carriage's rearmost bench, the broken Irishman climbed into the carriage, and the Royal Mail coach went on its way, if somewhat slower than it had before. The driver taking care to miss the pot-holes and track-lines that sent jolting shock waves through the coach's primitive suspension, directly to the broken jawbones of the agonised men aboard the vehicle, as it trundled its way towards the high town of Birmingham.

Just outside the town centre, the coach was met by the group of four cloaked horsemen sent on Black Foot's orders. As the Royal Mail men could barely talk due to their injuries and O'Donahue had passed out again, Lord Percy took control of the situation. He ordered the men to take him to the Birmingham town watchmen in order to report the crime. However, the horsemen informed him that Black Foot was waiting for him at the Rookery. The aristocrat was also persuaded by the muffled protests of the driver and guard, who said that the attempted robbery should be kept a secret from their superior, as the gentleman shouldn't have been aboard the coach anyway and they would lose their jobs if it were ever found out. The aristocrat eventually agreed with the men and instead ordered the horsemen to lead the way through the dark, moonlit streets of the Froggery to the Rookery doors.

Black Foot was drunk by the time Lord Percy Whip arrived. Lord Percy was ignored at first as the gang leader refused to turn his attention away from the vicious dogfight taking place within the gaming pit. Lord Percy presented himself properly with a short bow and a bemused smile.

"William Black Foot?" He enquired, his question had to be shouted over the din of a hundred or so gamblers that were baying for blood, watching four, large alpha-dogs in the ring tear each other apart. Black Foot glanced over his shoulder, looking the man up and down, before turning back to the ring. The Aristocrat lifted his cane and tapped Black Foot's shoulder. "I say, are you Black Foot or not?" he asked arrogantly. The man didn't move.

"It's William Black foot to the likes of you!" He screamed above the cacophony without turning to the man. Almost instantly, the din around the dogfight began to hush. The dog-handlers looked towards Black Foot, who drew a line across his throat, indicating that the dogs be separated. The two dog-handlers nodded to each other, before pulling hard on the set of four chains connected to each dog. They reluctantly dragged the snarling hounds away from each other, who continued to snap their slavering jaws at their enemies with wide-eyed, malevolent and uncontrollable rage. As the room fell silent the only sound that could be heard were the dogs snarling their hatred. All eyes turned to the scene around Black Foot's table. The crowd were intrigued why the fight had been stopped. The sudden quiet discomforted the aristocrat, but he tried to hide his growing unease behind a display of breeding.

"The likes of me? I am a gentleman sir, a Lord of the realm and you sir will address me as your Lordship!" He poked Black Foot's shoulder again with his thin cane. The crowd became even quieter as they waited to see how the gang leader would react to such a provocative order. Black Foot turned to the voice, his face changing in an instant. The rage fell from him as he bowed humbly to the thin, elegant man.

"Oh yes, your Lordship, please pardon my ignorance, your grace!" He said, a sarcastic smile growing across his face, turning to the watching crowd he continued. "Come on you common bastards, bow to his *Lordship!*" One by one, the audience began to bow, stifled sniggers breaking the silence. The sarcasm was lost on the aristocrat.

"Good, we all have our place in society and you Black Foot should know yours!"

The gang-leader bristled but caught himself before he reacted.

"Oh yes your Lordship," he fawned. "Please allow me to apologise on behalf of myself and these poor wretches." He swept his hand around the room before continuing. "Now if it pleases your highness, we would like to see your man O'Donahue." Lord Percy raised his eyebrows with impatience.

"There will be no fight tonight Black Foot, my man O'Donahue is injured." William Black Foot stood again, the audience followed his example. The smile dropped from his face.

"No fight you say?" Lord Percy felt a growing feeling of dread in his stomach.

"That's what I said Black Foot. Are you *deaf* man?" Black Foot turned to the crowd.

"No fight?" The group of Brummies began to murmur their disapproval. "But I've promised these ingrates a fight, what shall I tell them?" Lord Percy tried his best to hide the growing prickle of unease.

"What you tell these people is of no concern to me Black Foot, I am telling *you*, that my man is injured due to a facade with two highwaymen on the old Warwick Road. My man floored one of them, he's still unconscious out there in the carriage, but

O'Donahue was..." he stopped, searching for the right way to explain the destruction of his indestructible fighter to the gang-leader."...He was caught by surprise by the other robber who broke his jaw and now cannot fight."

"Your man, the best pugilist in London, was beaten by a...a highwayman?" Black Foot said in disbelief. The aristocrat pulled a handkerchief from his sleeve, bringing the silk material under his nose before noticing it still had the highwayman's blood on it. On seeing the blood, he threw it to the floor instead. "I don't have to explain myself to the likes of you, I said he's hurt so he can't fight. There, sir, you have my answer, he can't fight, and that is that."

"That is that?" The gang leader repeated. "Well, *your Lordship*." He said, barely hiding a snarl. "This is this!" Black Foot clicked his fingers. Suddenly the Bear appeared from the crowd, pushing his way through the still-silent throng. He stood next to the aristocrat. "*Lord Percy Whip*..." Black Foot snarled, "...m*eet the Bear*!" The gentleman turned with horror to see the huge man next to him, his knees buckling at the sight of the monster. Black Foot began to laugh at the discomfort of the aristocrat.

"Perhaps you'd like to explain to the Bear why he can't fight anyone tonight?" The gang-leader turned to the crowd, shouting, "Did you hear that, Lord Percy said that there won't be a fight tonight." The audience burst into loud booing, some of the men cursing the tall, elegant man before them. Lord Percy's eyes darted around him at the filthy, disfigured faces, and the realisation that he should have taken the coach-guard's advice and not come to the Rookery at all dawned on him.

"Look here Black Foot, I have explained myself, and now I'm leaving, what you do with these ragged beggars is your business, not mine." Black Foot exploded his face flushing as red as the blusher on his cheeks. He stepped into the man's face.

"You ain't going fucking anywhere sunshine, and I've told you, my name is *William* Black Foot." Without turning his face away from the now terrified aristocrat, Black Foot slapped the chest of the giant who stood next to him. "Throw this cunt to the dogs!" Without hesitation the Bear lifted the aristocrat by the collar of his fine silk coat, the man's feet rose from the cobbles beneath him kicking his protest into the air around him. The man's panicked kicking brought a round of laughter from the watching crowd, dropping his cane to the floor, the Bear held him in front of Black Foot for a second.

"But . . . I'm a lord or the realm . . . You can't do this to me. I'll have each, and every one of you scoundrels flogged for this. Do you hear me? You'll all hang for this!" Black Foot gestured with his head towards the gambling pit.

"Feed the dogs, Bear!" The big man grabbed one of Lord Percy's legs and propped the man high above his head. Before Lord Percy could protest any further, he threw the unfortunate aristocrat unceremoniously into the straw and bloodstained fighting pit. Percy landed with a sickening thud. The crowd fell silent again as they waited to see what the dogs would do. The silence was broken by the soft jingle of chain, as all four dogs were released from their metal tethers. None of the dogs ran forward as the crowd expected, all were cautious, creeping forward on their crouched legs ready to spring at any moment. Fighting another dog was one thing but the beasts knew instinctively that this animal of lace, silk and powder, whatever it was, would have to be taken as a pack. And so, all the dogs, who only a few minutes before, had been willing to tear each other to pieces, now formed a pack to bring down the elegant creature that was trying to rise to his feet from the from the floor of the pit.

Lord Percy gathering himself together clambered to his knees, breathless from the fall, he stuttered pleas to the men who held the dogs on their thick chains.

"Call them off Black Foot! Please, I implore you. My man is *injured!*" He begged desperately. "I have gold, lots of coin and you can have it all if you call them off, please . . . please!" The dog-handlers glanced at each other at the mention of gold. Lord Percy saw their reaction and pressed the point further. "I have gold and silver, more than you'll ever earn from these brutes, you can have it . . . " Black Foot interrupted.

"Don't bother trying to bribe em, your lordship, they'll get their fair share of gold once the dogs have had their fill of you. You say your man was injured?" Lord Percy nodded, producing a purse from his pocket.

"Yes, yes, a highwayman broke his jaw. O'Donahue beat one of them, but the other robber must have been a trained fighter because he beat my man easily. I have never seen a punch as hard as the one he laid on O'Donahue!" Lord Percy held the purse higher giving the small, leather sack a little shake, jingling the gold coins inside. "I have the gold about me, sir, the dogs will get at it, surely you don't want that?" Black Foot burst into laughter.

"How very considerate of you, your lordship but you needn't worry, we'll collect the gold coins when the dogs have a shit tomorrow morning, won't we boys?" He slapped his thigh with laughter, the dog-handlers laughed too, joined by almost everyone else watching the exchange. "After all, didn't you say that everyone should know their place in this world. Well, as of tomorrow morning, your place in this world is gonna be in a big pile of dog shit in the corner of the yard! "

Percy began to whimper towards the creeping dogs, trying to reason with animals, whose only reason for existence was to kill or be killed. Unfortunately for him, his reasoning fell on deaf ears as one of the dogs mistook his open, pleading hands as a sign of weakness, falling upon him wild-eyed. The other dogs followed the lead, their mouths a mixture of saliva, fresh, red blood and bone piercing pain. The scene exploded into a frenzy of screams and snarls, shrouded in a blood-red mist as the hounds did their deadly work. A low gasp rose from the crowd who all stood frozen, unable to turn away from the bizarre sight. Black Foot wasn't watching. Instead he looked around the faces of the Rookery and smiled to himself. The guttering candles illuminated the gleeful bloodlust in the eyes of all that watched, enthralled by the macabre performance that played out for their entertainment.

"A highwayman brought down Lord Percy's man." He said to himself and just who was this accidental pugilist that had beaten London's best on the highway? A whimpering scream caught his attention, and he turned in time to see the now bloody mess that was Lord Percy be taken by the throat by one of the dogs. He turned back to his nearest minder and pulled his arm.

"His Lordship said that one of the highwaymen was in the carriage, go get him, bring him in to me! He'll tell us exactly who this highwayman scrapper is." A loud intake of breath brought his attention back to the bloodbath inside the pit. The crowd's mood had changed from bloodlust and excitement to pity for the poor, limbless devil who sat on his stumps. His tongueless mouth flopped open and closed. Lord Percy was still very much alive, unable to die and his eyes pleaded with the voyeurs of his final agonised moments in this world to find it within their cruel hearts to put him out of his misery.

Not a man moved. Black Foot scanned the stone faces and climbing onto the bench table in front of him he called out over the whimpering of the aristocrat in the pit.

"Anyone who can bring me the man that beat Lord Percy's fighter will receive a purse full of Lord Percy's gold, enough to make you rich!" His voice rang out through the warehouse, bouncing around the tall, red-brick walls, reaching every corner of the Rookery. The throng of people temporarily lost interest in the gaming pit and turned towards the powerful voice. A silence came over the crowd as every rogue, rascal and whore listened as one and far behind the crowd at the rear of the room, the tubby Quaker listened too, rubbing his hands together, unable to control the surge of excitement that quivered through his body. He tried to control the emotion, lest those around him saw his elation. He stopped ringing his hands and mopped his brow with the sleeve of his black jacket, wiping away the tiny beads of sweat breaking from beneath his tall hat and rolling down his face. Whether his glee came from William Black Foot's words as he orated from the table or from the sight of Bridget O'Hara standing on the balcony directly above him, her arm draped through the beautiful lady Eleanor's, it was hard to say.

"Do you *hear* me?" Black Foot continued, raising his voice to a military bark.

"Be you a rich man or pauper, a gambler or . . . " he raised his face looking directly at the people leaning over the mezzanine balcony where Bridget O'Hara and Eleanor stared down at him, " . . . or whore, know this. If you bring me the other Highwayman, I will share this poor bastard's gold with you. Enough to get yourself and your loved ones out of this shit-hole of a town and make something of yourself . . . " he looked around him at the turned up filthy, desperate faces before him adding, " . . . or by the look of most of you, allow you to finish the job of drinking yourselves to death!" He said laughing. "It makes no difference to me. I have one highwayman, bring me the other, and you shall be *rich*!"

A Heavy Hangover

CHAPTER 5

Thomas Fewtrell was awoken by the spattering sleet upon the tiny window of his casement room at the top of the town-centre lodgings at the Market Tavern. He was warm beneath his thick, green cloak. He exhaled a long cloud of steam into the freezing air in the room and glanced over to the small fireplace. The black hole in the wall was filled with cold ash and half-burned logs. A thin line of smoke drew up the chimney like a spirit leaving the body of a dead friend which, only a few hour ago, had burned brightly, filled with life and warmth but was now dead and gone, leaving only a smouldering pile of nothingness. The wisp of smoke only served to remind Thomas of his fellow highwayman and drinking partner, Henry Sykes. The drink hung on Thomas like a lead hat, making it hard to lift his head from his pillow. When he did, he wished he hadn't. This pain was intense, but as he swung his legs out of his bed, he soon found out the tiny peppering of gunshot holes left in his thigh were quite another level of pain. He examined the wounds for any signs of shot in his leg. The whole thigh had turned black with bruising. He was sure he'd managed to retrieve all of the lead from the tiny holes that had punctured his skin from the blunderbuss shot. His only worry was that a small piece of material from his breeches had entered one of the wounds and might fester and turn gangrenous which would probably kill him. He had performed the operation when he'd been drunk and so wasn't certain about the extraction of the cloth, but he *had* soaked the wounds in gin and set fire to it. He wasn't sure why he'd done that, he had seen his grandfather do the same thing after a farming accident, and the image had always remained with him. Whenever there was blood, there was always gin or brandy followed by flame, to burn off any infection. Thomas lay back on his bed and stared at the ceiling. This was not how he'd pictured events playing out.

A highwayman's life wasn't what Thomas Fewtrell had planned for himself when he'd left the tiny hamlet of Easthope, Shropshire three years previously. The family had fallen on hard times. Only one generation had passed since the Fewtrells had fallen from landed gentry in the early 1740s, to subsistence farming barely forty years later. The Fewtrells had held onto their land and large manor house through the six hundred years of warfare and anarchy that followed the days of the Norman conquest, only to have it all snatched away in a moment of weakness during a crooked card game against their old rivals and fellow landowners, the Lutwhiche brothers. *They* were now the new Lords of the manor, strutting around like arrogant peacocks, rubbing the salts of success into the Fewtrell's wounds whenever the opportunity presented itself.

The family's farm hadn't been profitable enough to cater for Thomas and *all* his siblings, so their father Samuel had made the decision that the two elder brothers would have to leave Easthope and seek out whatever fortune fate had in store for them without his help. So one spring morning Thomas and his twin-like brother Edward marched into the distance with a small jingle of coin in their breeches. They climbed the dusty track to the crest of the hill that had been their horizon for almost all of their young lives and left the sleepy vale for the foreseeable future. Life amongst the country folk of Shropshire had done nothing to prepare Thomas and his look-a-like sibling for the corruption, filth and depravity that awaited them in the high town of Birmingham.

Those far off memories of life on the farm were always more pleasant than they had been in reality. The years had softened the memories of the beatings he'd suffered at the hands of his father's various relatives, dubious alehouse friends and Lutwhiche brothers.

Unable to accept the loss of the family's fortune, his father Samuel had turned into a spiteful, violent man who took great pride in the family's reputation for fighting. Samuel rarely smiled but when he did it was more of a toothless grimace than an actual expression of happiness. The evidence of his violent side could be seen quite plainly by the lack of teeth in his head, proof if ever there was, of how the family's bad reputation had been acquired. However bad that reputation was, everyone in the area knew that Samuel Fewtrell was the only man capable of keeping the lid on the Lutwhiche brother's pot of violence which promised to spill over at any time and when it did would scald all who were not strong enough to withstand their gangsterism. The ever-present promise of a good thumping gave young Thomas an almost sixth sense to spot trouble before it arose. On the occasion that it *did* arise, he had become nimble enough to duck and weave between the punches and kicks that came his way, avoiding any would-be attackers, wearing out his opponents without them ever landing a blow or Thomas even throwing a punch. That is until, at the age of fourteen, during a particularly vicious bout between Thomas, his father and *three* of his older relatives, he decided, at long last, to punch back. Eventually flooring all three attackers and breaking his own father's nose who, until that point had been considered by all in the sleepy hamlet, the toughest fellow around.

Life in the countryside had been tough, that was a fact, but if the innocence of those long gone days amongst the country folk of Shropshire seemed hard, life in the booming town of Birmingham made his childhood seem idyllic and golden. It was as if the Brummies were just waiting for the country bumpkins to arrive. The jingle of coin in the breeches of the brothers acted like a magnet to the pockmarked whores and pimps of the town who soon silenced the jingling by emptying their pockets, leaving both siblings with no choice but to graft alongside other poor wretches who had made the big mistake of trusting a pretty face.

After a week of exhausting whoring and drinking which had become Thomas's favourite pastimes, he had a rare moment of clarity. He realised that he and his brother were only a day or so away from becoming one of the many destitute beggars that littered the outskirts of the town; and sobered up enough to find work loading and unloading animal carcasses from the merchant wagons at the epicentre of the beehive that was Birmingham town, namely, the Bull Ring market. Edward Fewtrell on the other hand didn't find work. Instead he found God and joined the growing number of Quakers that could be found patrolling the inns and taverns in search of souls to save in this Brummie Babylon. Edward was the spitting image of his older brother, tall, muscle-bound with a dirty, blonde mop of straw-like hair. So similar in fact, that the siblings were often mistaken for each other wherever they showed their faces. The only thing it seemed that *was* different was the colour of their souls.

****

In 1780 the Bull Ring was a chaotic pandemonium of humanity and beasts. On any given day, traders and buyers bartered with the well-to-do. In the background, an unseen army of cut-pockets, rogues, vagabonds and horse-thieves worked nonstop to relieve these *toffs* of their coin, purses, horses and shiny things like a flock of raggedy, flea-infested magpies. Thomas, being of able body and bright mind endured the punishment of honest work for twelve long months before deciding to join their ranks. Spending other people's hard-earned cash was a great deal more enjoyable than earning his own pittance of a wage carrying pig carcasses around the town. Besides, his wages had barely covered his favourite pursuit of whores, ale and gambling, which, it must be said he indulged in six nights a week in an almost hedonistic frenzy. The only thing the hard labour *had* given him was muscles, not just any muscles though, Thomas's arm and leg muscles were long and lean. His shoulders and neck were thick and solid, his waist slim but his chest broad, his stomach ripped with clearly defined abdominals, all held together by a spider's web of sinew. In the heat of the summer months, Thomas walked shirtless amongst the malnourished peasantry of the Bull Ring like a golden-haired Apollo.

Like many a young man, he liked to think of himself as a worldly fellow, talking eloquently in his deep voice to the other punters of the various, packed taverns around the town centre's marketplace. A protective disguise to hide the fact that although he spoke with the self-assurance of a man who'd seen all the world had to offer, in fact, the only experience he could draw on was his farmyard childhood and the long road from Shropshire to the high town of Birmingham; a trek of some fifty or so miles as the crow flies, hardly *the Odyssey*. Nevertheless, he was honest, as far as his word was his bond, loyal to his friends and fierce in a bar-room brawl.

Thomas limped to the fireside and clumsily knelt beside the hearth, he blew at the ashes looking for any life within the dull pile. As he blew, a soft orange glow grew deep within the embers, the very sight of which warmed the kneeling man. Thomas grabbed a handful of kindling and pushed the twigs delicately into the embers, blowing softly at the pile until he could see a solid draw of smoke when finally the twigs caught fire. He dropped some heavier logs into the tiny fire-basket. The kindling cracked and spat tiny sparks as the flames caught true and the fire came back to life. Thomas grabbed his cloak and pulled it around himself again. He squatted painfully beside the little grate listening to the sleet landing loudly on the casement window betraying what the day outside held in store for him. He searched the room for a drink, tipping various bottles of different shapes and sizes but all were empty. His leg throbbed, but he tried to put it to the back of his mind. He crossed to the old oak door that separated his room from the steep staircase that ran down to the bar area below. He peered into the darkness of the bar and wondered what time it was and how long he'd slept. He couldn't remember getting back the previous night, however, as with all of Thomas Fewtrell's drinking bouts what he couldn't remember now, would all come back to haunt him at some point the following day. He called down the stairwell.

"Mrs Bakewell!" He heard the tread of feet on creaking floor-board below him as the landlady came to the bottom of the crooked staircase. The face of a woman in her late forties but who looked much older, popped around the corner of the bannister rail.

"Mr Fewtrell?" Thomas smiled at his landlady who returned his smile with a black toothed one of her own.

"Ah, Mrs Bakewell, I need some food and some warm ale, I shall be down shortly." The woman cackled.

"I'd say you'd be wanting a hearty breakfast with all that moaning and groaning you were doing last night, Mr Fewtrell, sir." Thomas stared down at the woman, somewhat bemused.

"Moaning and groaning you say?" The landlady cackled again.

"I expect the young lady you've got up there will need feeding as well." Thomas' brows furrowed. He turned back to the small room and scanned it in case he'd somehow missed seeing this young lady his landlady was speaking about.

"I have no lady here Mrs Bakewell, you must be mistaken."

"I know what I heard Mr Fewtrell, you was moaning and groaning like a good-un, so you were, you must've got your money's worth out of her." Thomas tenderly touched his bruised leg with his fingertips.

"Ah, I see." Realising the noise he made when treating his wounds must have carried further than he'd hoped. "No, Mrs Bakewell, I can assure you I'm on my own, any moaning and groaning was all my own work." The woman's smile turned to a grimace as she peered up at him.

"Well, that's come as a surprise Mr Fewtrell, a handsome young man like you, moaning and groaning all on his own and these beautiful young whores down here throwing themselves at ya. I had you down as plenty of things sir, but a *wanker* wasn't one of em!" Her head disappeared again as she walked away in disgust. "Your breakfast will be on the table in the bar." Thomas called after her.

"No, it's not what you think, I was ... " A door slammed somewhere beneath him, indicating the woman had left the room. Thomas stood in his doorway for a second. What could he tell her anyway? That he'd been shot whilst robbing a Royal Mail coach? There would surely be a reward for the highwaymen's capture and a woman like Mrs Bakewell wouldn't think twice about collecting it. No, better to let her think of him as a wanker than a thief. Anyway, he was sure that the posters telling of last night's robbery would be all over the town by now, so he'd best let sleeping dogs lie.

As promised, breakfast was waiting for him by a table next to the huge fireplace in the dark, wood-panelled bar. The ale was weak but warm and sugary, Thomas gulped its goodness down, the misty liquid's sweetness reviving him somewhat. The meat was what had been left over from last night's ham, but he was glad of it, and at least the bread was fresh. The warmth from the fire made his leg hurt and with each throb of pain images of last night's debacle on the highway returned. Who was the gentleman and his Irish giant? What had happened to Henry's body? Everyone knew that Sykesy and Thomas were best friends so it wouldn't be too much for the imagination for the city watchmen to put the two together in this bungled robbery. Thomas's mind raced over the possibilities of retrieving the body but realised that it was already too late, as the gentleman in the wig would have already reported the attempted robbery by now.

The jingle of coins on the table brought Mrs Bakewell scampering through to the bar. She smiled before scraping her hand across the table, collecting food scraps and Thomas's coins into her filthy apron.

"Thank you for the food. I'll be back after dark, I have some business about the town." The landlady gave him a quick look of disapproval.

"Well, let's hope it's a little more healthy for you than what you were getting up to last night ... that'll make you as blind as a church mouse!" Thomas blushed as he gathered his pistol belt that hung over the back of his chair and gave a small laugh as he buckled the heavy, leather belt around the outside of his waistcoat.

"It wasn't what you think Mrs Bakewell." He said half-heartedly, picking his pistol from the table and sliding it into the loop on his belt.

"What I think?" She said horrified. "I am a Christian sir, I don't think of things like *that*."

"A Christian?" Thomas said with more surprise than he'd

intended. The images of the landlady's drunken debauchery he'd witnessed on many a night before ran through his mind.

"Yes, sir, a Christian and what of it?" The small woman snarled, challenging him. Thomas raised his brows.

"As I said Mrs Bakewell, I must be about my business, good day to you." Thomas smiled weakly and tossed a small coin onto the dark, oak table. He could feel the woman's disapproving stare burning into the back of his head as he headed towards the exit. He peered through the small, leaded window in the door and saw that the sleet had turned to heavy flakes of snow which had already begun to settle on the cobbled street. Pulling the collar of his cloak around his ears he yanked the heavy door to the street open but just as he did a beautiful, mixed-race girl almost fell into the doorway and into his arms. He caught the girl and raised her to her feet. She looked up at him in shock.

"Oh, forgive me sir. I slipped upon the snow, thank you, sir." She said, trying to curtsy in the tiny doorway, her eyes lowered in subservience. Thomas could see that the woman had been crying. Her bright-green eyes sparkled against her mocha skin, but as he looked closer, he noticed speckles of tiny, red blotches that stood out against the whites of her eyes, where the blood vessels inside her eyes had burst. Thomas was taken aback for a few seconds before pulling himself out of the bedazzlement of her beauty. His eye followed where the tear trails had run down her face and onto her freckled cheeks. It was then that he noticed the redness around her throat, it was as if someone had tried to throttle her. She had made an attempt to hide the marks beneath a tatty, silk scarf. Thomas raised his finger and dragged the material down to reveal the girl's delicate neckline. The red marks were far worse than he'd thought at first. The thickest of them had already turned from red into a dark-blue bruise. Thomas frowned at the sight of the choke-marks. The girl looked up at him, her eyes a mixture of sorrow and defiance.

"What brute did this to you?" Thomas enquired in half-whispered words. The girl could plainly see the empathy in the man's face, and he looked trustworthy enough, handsome too, in a rugged sort of way. She had seen him around the tavern before, usually drunk and gambling with his cockney side-kick but she wasn't in any mood to make small talk with a relative stranger. She stepped back as far as the cramped space would allow and pushed his hand away from her scarf. As she did, her shawl fell from her shoulders onto the wet puddle of melting snow on the floor. Thomas bent and picked it up. As he passed the woollen shawl back to the girl, a small roll of parchment fell from within its folds. Thomas's reactions were fast, catching it before it reached the floor. The girl made a snatch for the parchment, but Thomas was too fast for her. She took her shawl with a reluctant smile and held her hand out for the roll of parchment. Thomas noticed that the girl suddenly seemed nervous.

"I, I need that ... " she stuttered, " ... I have to give it to Mrs Bakewell to put up in the tavern." Thomas smiled,

"Of course." He held the roll out in the palm of his hand but as he did the parchment unravelled. Thomas could see it was a small poster, freshly printed, its ink still shiny on the cheap, beige parchment. Thomas read the large, ornate print.

His smile dropped from his face, his rosy complexion replaced with a white palour. He'd been right about last night's events being all around town. The poster pronounced the hanging of his friend Henry Sykes for the crime of highway robbery.

The girl saw the expression on Thomas' face turn from shock to bewilderment.

"How could this be ... " he thought, he'd seen Sykesy fall from the shot with his own eyes, " ... how can they hang a dead man? There hasn't even been a trial." The image of the aristocrat standing over his friend's slumped body filled his mind and a fleeting moment of remorse washed over him that he'd been unable to go to Sykesy's rescue. "Where did you get this?" Thomas said sternly. The girl's defiance disappeared when she saw the sudden worry on the man's face. Thomas screwed the poster up in his large hands. "Where did you ... ?"

"Bridget O'Hara, is that you my girl?" Mrs Bakewell called through from the bar area. Thomas and the girl turned together, startled by the brash voice of the landlady. "What are you doing girl?

Come in and warm yourself by the hearth, you must be frozen!" Then turning her attention to Thomas, Mrs Bakewell said. "I thought you were about your business sir, now come, let the lady pass, sir!" Thomas turned back to Bridget O'Hara.

"This man is my . . . " the girl cut Thomas short,

" . . . your friend. I know." Thomas, already shocked by the information on the poster, was taken aback by the fact the girl knew of his friendship with the man mentioned on the pamphlet. Seeing Thomas's reaction, she continued. "It's no secret sir, that you and Captain Sykes are good friends." Thomas came closer, aware that Mrs Bakewell could hear the exchange. He whispered.

"Tell me what you know of this!" Bridget turned towards the landlady and smiled, then turning back to the man opposite her and in as low a tone as her injured throat would allow,

"I am tired and injured sir and as you can plainly see . . . " They both turned towards Mrs Bakewell who was making no secret of trying to eavesdrop; craning her neck towards them as if the action would increase her ability to hear the softly spoken words, " . . . there are large ears and even larger mouths about us sir, come to me later, I will be here for the rest of the day. When I have eaten and rested, you can ask your questions freely." Thomas frowned.

"But the poster says they are going to hang my friend, a man who I saw shot down on the highway last night with my own eyes. Tell me, how can they hang a dead man? Is it a trap?" Bridget became impatient but tried her hardest to hide it.

"I can assure you sir, your friend *is* very much alive. William Black Foot has him on display like a wild animal in a cage at the Rookery. I have just come from there."

"William Black Foot?" The man shook his head. "Why isn't he being held in the jail by the parish watchmen?"

"Black Foot owns the watchmen, Black Foot owns everyone, including myself, if he knew I was sharing this with you he'd . . . " She caught herself and returned to the subject. "Anyway there's nothing in it for Black Foot if the watchmen hold him, he's charging a shilling to all and sundry to view the poor fellow in his cage at the Rookery." Thomas slumped back against the wood-panelling behind him, a mixture of relief and anger washing over him, so his friend was alive. He sighed deeply. There was hope for Sykesy after all. Bridget saw his expression.

"He's not due to hang for another week or so." She whispered. "Black Foot wants to make as much money as he can out of the wretch before offing him on the scaffold they're building in the square just outside the warehouse. He wants to sell tickets to the hanging, you can say what you want about old Black Foot, but he certainly knows how to make a few bob when the occasion presents itself. Anyway, I am tired, so come to me later, I will tell you all I know." As she turned to leave, Thomas grabbed her arm.

"My purse!" Bridget turned to him with a feigned look of hurt and innocence.

"I beg your pardon, sir?" Thomas frowned.

"My purse, you took it from my pocket when you stumbled into me, hand it back please!" She shrugged and raised her eyebrows in a form of apology and reaching inside the deep pocket of her dress she produced Thomas's small, suede purse. Bridget bounced the bag in her hand, weighing it. The bag was light, and the sound of two or three coins jingling together betrayed the lack of money within.

"Looks like it wasn't worth having anyway!" The girl's sorrowful demeanour had all but vanished now, she smiled. "I must be losing my touch." With that, she tossed the purse into Thomas's open hand, turned and walked away. Thomas watched her as she approached Mrs Bakewell. The older woman threw her arms around her and began to fuss about the markings on the girl's neck. Bridget turned her head and mouthed the words 'sorry' to Thomas before allowing herself to be ushered into the bar and into a seat next to the roaring fire. Thomas Fewtrell felt the weight of guilt lift from his shoulders only to be replaced by one of apprehension about securing Sykesy's release. If Henry Sykes was alive then there was hope for his emancipation. Thomas swore an oath to himself that he would free his friend from Black Foot's cage even if he had to fight the devil himself. However, the highwayman may never have sworn such an oath and might have just walked away and learned to live with his guilt, if he'd have known just how close to the truth that would turn out to be.

Bread & Dripping

CHAPTER 6

E dward Fewtrell had gone to ground since joining the Quakers. His new friends in the religion had fed and clothed him, and now he had a direction in life that led to heaven itself. Whatever he was going to do, be it kneeling, praying, listening to the never-ending sermons or wearing the ridiculously tall, black hat and clothing that identified him as a Quaker, he *wasn't* about to rock the boat. His days were spent contemplating God's existence and more importantly trying to find that God in *everyone*, however, lost they were. Edward felt as if he were at the spearhead of something new. In reality, it had been over one hundred years since the founder of his new found religion, George Fox, had seen the gleam of God's light shining from every human being on Earth. Since then the Quakers had already left their mark on society by campaigning for the abolition of slavery fifty years before Edward had even been born. In some circles though the Society of Friends, as it liked to call itself was thought of as a dangerous and almost revolutionary movement. Anyway, anything was better than the depravity Edward had seen around the Bull Ring, a biblical like debauchery that his older brother Thomas seemed to absolutely revel in. The fact that the good or should we say the *bad* people of Birmingham kept mistaking him for his older brother would put Edward into a very unchristian-like mood whenever it happened.

No, Edward secretly thought that Thomas and his ilk could

not be saved, no matter what the elders said, they were all lost to Satan, and there was nothing he or anyone else could do about it, he was certain of that. So it was with some trepidation that Edward answered the loud knocking on the front door of the Quaker meeting house and reluctantly allowed his brother Thomas into the warmth of the scullery on that snowy day.

Thomas stepped across the threshold removing his snow-laden tricorn hat and banged its brim against the top of his tall, knee-high riding boots. The snow fell onto the slate floor where it instantly turned to a puddle in the heat of the room. Thomas looked about him at the sparsely decorated but clean room. Its tall, shoulder-high chimney breast glowed and a bright, crackling fire in the deep hearth heated the room whilst the bread ovens either side of the hearth made the room smell delicious, welcoming and homely. A tall woman entered the room, her head covered with a blue scarf, her long blonde pigtails poking out of either side of its folds. Thomas bowed as best he could with his injured leg which had now become stiff as the swelling around the wound had taken hold. The woman did not acknowledge him and retreated back into the hallway, a look of horror on her face. Edward seemed lost for words.

"You've landed on your feet here little brother." Edward seemed bemused by Thomas's words.

"My feet?" Thomas pointed towards the woman in the hallway.

"Pretty girl, she yours?" The words seemed to take his brother by surprise and he stood open-mouthed. Thomas turned to the fireplace. "Fresh food, a warm house and good-looking girls. I bet you think you've died and gone to heaven little brother."

Edward lost his patience.

"Why are you here Thomas? What do you want? Is it money?" Now it was Thomas's turn to be shocked. The two stood facing each other for a few seconds before the facade of decency was dropped.

"Well, so much for the grace of God, these bastards have certainly got their claws into you!" Thomas shook the remaining snow from the shoulders of his green cloak. It fell on the top of the bread oven and sizzled there for a few seconds. "Have you forgotten me after such a short time Edward? Or is it I'm all right Jack and fuck everyone else!"

"How dare you come here and say such things!" He glared at Thomas, losing his temper. "I am saved Thomas, saved by these good people who took me in from the gutter you left me in and brought me to the light of God." Thomas bristled.

"Well, just in case you didn't notice little brother. I was lying right next to you in that gutter and it was *you* who left me there not that I would have followed these ... " he searched for the right word, " ... *weirdos!*"

"Please leave!" Edward shouted. "You're not welcome here Thomas!"

"What is all this shouting about brother Fewtrell?" A small, round man with a rosy complexion and a serious look stood in the doorway. Thomas looked over the man, trying to stifle a snigger. The man glared at the arguing brothers before wobbling into the scullery.

"*Brother* Fewtrell?" Thomas laughed. "He might be a bleeding brother to you mate, but he's more or less disowned me since he met you lot of God-botherers?" A short silence followed, and the three men stared at each other as the older man assessed the situation. Edward broke the silence.

"Brother Tumbold, this is my older brother Thomas. Thomas this is Brother ... "

" ... Tumbold, yeah I get it." Thomas finished his sentence. The older man seemed disturbed by Edward's lack of empathy towards his blood brother and clapping his hands called the women, who were waiting in the adjoining corridor, into the room.

"Come, come, we must show our guest the hospitality of God's house, you must be hungry, sir. Please take a seat by the fire and warm your bones." Thomas smiled sarcastically at Edward as he sat at the table next to the fire.

"Thank you Brother Tumbold, I don't mind if I do!" Edward rolled his eyes, drawing in a deep breath of irritation.

"What do you want Thomas?" Edward said impatiently. Brother Tumbold shot Edward a look of horror.

"Brother Edward this is not how we treat our guests. How are we to guide this man to God if we treat him with suspicion and distrust?" Two women came into the room and began to fuss around the fireside ovens. "Sisters, bring Thomas here some of your bread and take some dripping lard from the pan. I'm sure he would enjoy that?" Thomas nodded, returning his younger brother's growing irritation with a smirk.

"That would be lovely, Brother Tumbold." The round man smiled at his visitor's acceptance of food. "I don't suppose you have any warm cider to wash it down with do you?" The smile fell from Brother Tumbold's face, replaced by that same look of horror and the women froze at the mention of the alcohol.

"Warm cider, oh, no, no, no, we don't allow the devil's drink in God's meeting house!" The round man spluttered. Thomas shrugged.

"Ok, how about a glass of port or some gin? You know, just to take the cold off me chest?"

"Oh, sweet Jesus no!" The round man shook his head and raised one of the palms of his hands. "Please Jesus, help us to save this poor soul." Thomas looked around the room at the four Quakers who all had the same subservient expression on their faces, all except for Edward who had suddenly become flushed with anger.

"What do you want Thomas? Is it money for your ale and whores?" Brother Tumbold turned towards Edward again, who, on seeing the elder's expression shook his head at the man's naivety. "He's after money Brother Tumbold, I really don't think he's come to cleanse his soul, there isn't enough holy water in heaven to do that, he's here for hard cash, that is all!" Thomas interrupted.

"No, you're wrong, but I do need your help." Thomas interrupted, and Edward rolled his eyes again.

"Here it comes!" Brother Tumbold took over.

"Oh ye of little faith brother Edward!" Turning back to Thomas the elder enquired. "What help do you need my son? Is it a conflict between good and evil?" Thomas tried to hide his smile.

"You could say it is sir, yes, good and evil." One of the women brought a large slice of fresh bread smothered in a thick layer of goose fat to him. Thomas, thanked her and snatching the bread which was still warm from the oven, he took a large bite. Thomas closed his eyes, enjoying the deliciousness of the thick dripping. "Mmm, if this is the bread of the Lord then I'll have another slice!" Edward's temper flared.

"These good people are not used to the likes of you brother. Do not take advantage of them by blaspheming. Eat your bread and leave!" Thomas dropped the bread back onto the plate.

"Look, I ain't here for your money, but I do need your help. I want you to come with me and petition someone for the release of my friend." Edward folded his arms, shaking his head.

"Your friend is being held, where and for what?" Brother Tumbold enquired, suddenly interested.

"Yes, my *best* friend, a good Christian like you lot." He lied, "Henry Sykes, he needs help. Isn't that what you lot do, help people?" Brother Tumbold nodded.

"Indeed sir, indeed we do help those unfortunate souls that have lost . . . " Edward had heard enough.

"What did this good Christian do? Kill someone, cheat at the cards, beat a whore? I know the type you hang around with Thomas, I used to be one of them." Thomas looked between his untrusting brother and the naive Tumbold. Turning to the older man, he pressed his argument.

"No, he killed no one. It is all a simple case of mistaken identity. My friend was in the wrong place at the wrong time, and now he is to be hanged." Brother Tumbold turned to Edward, a look of shock on his face.

"Mistaken identity Brother Edward!" Edward Fewtrell laughed.

"He's lying brother Tumbold, don't believe him!" The elder turned back to Thomas and examined his face. Thomas returned his look, mustering as much innocence as his features would allow which in truth, wasn't a great deal. He lowered his face, raising his eyes as if he were a scolded puppy. The elder stared at him for a second before turning on Edward.

"How can you say he's lying, he looks as innocent as the driven snow to me?" Edward laughed again.

"Oh, he's lying all right." Edward sighed. Brother Tumbold raised his voice.

"But how can you be sure brother Fewtrell?" Edward pointed at Thomas.

"It's always easy to tell when Thomas is lying . . . his lips move." Edward's words had the opposite effect than he'd hoped for. Tumbold came beside Thomas's side and placed his hand on his shoulder. The women joined the elder, standing either side of Thomas as he sat by the fireside.

"Your blood brother needs your help Edward, you may not realise it but God works . . . "

" . . . in mysterious ways!" Thomas finished the older man's sentence. He sat there looking pleased with himself as if he'd just quoted the whole bible. He felt Tumbold's hand grip his shoulder as the words were spoken and knew he'd won them over. Thomas looked up at his younger brother suddenly becoming serious.

"*Please* Edward, I need your help. My friend *will* die if I cannot get him freed and it will be all my fault!" Edward Fewtrell recognised the sincerity and sorrow in Thomas's voice. Thomas needed his help, and he saw now, how hard it had been for his older brother to come to him and ask for it. How could he refuse?

"Ok, Thomas we'll help." He said reluctantly. Brother Tumbold took over, crossing the room to Edward's side and embraced the young man.

"God has given you the gift of forgiveness brother Fewtrell." Turning back to Thomas he continued. "Tell us how we can be of service to you and your unfortunate friend." Thomas sighed his relief.

"Thank you Mr Tumbold, I won't forget this." He let his head drop, relief overcoming him. His leg had begun to throb again and with the pain of his wounds came the regret of last night's bundled robbery. Thomas suddenly realised how serious the situation was. His hangover had clouded the desperateness of Sykesy's position and just how precarious the idea of his friend's rescue was. Thomas stood and crossed to his brother, ignoring the others in the room. "I am going to find out exactly what the situation is later tonight. I have someone who is on the inside of the Rookery." Edward perked up.

"The Rookery!" Thomas saw the alarm on the faces of the

Quakers. Brother Tumbold who had begun ringing his hands and shaking his head at the mention of the drinking den began to step from one foot to the other muttering prayers under his breath. Thomas thought he saw a slim smile growing on the man's lips but when Tumbold saw Thomas looking at him, it vanished replaced by a look of deep worry.

"Oh holy Jesus, protect us from Satan and all his evils!" The man muttered to himself.

"Yes, do you know it?" Edward nodded, his face suddenly pale.

"Yes, well, we know *of* it." Edward said, his face suddenly ashen. "It is a den of iniquity and sin Thomas, a real Sodom and Gomorrah owned by the devil incarnate, William Black Foot." The room fell silent. The Fewtrell brothers stared at each other. "He isn't a man that you tangle with, Black Foot is best avoided at all costs." Edward's voice had dropped to a whisper. "Why is your friend being held at Black Foot's Rookery and not in the jail with the town watchmen?" Thomas shook his head.

"As I said Edward, I'll find out more tonight when I talk to the girl I know who works there."

"A whore?" Brother Tumbold exclaimed, unable to contain himself anymore. Thomas turned towards him.

"Yes, a prostitute," he replied impatiently, "Bridget O'Hara, she said she would help me free my friend." The tubby Quaker began tumbling his hands one over the other.

"Bridget O'Hara . . . a mulatto *Catholic* whore, the worst kind of the devil's sirens!" Thomas frowned, wondering how the man knew the woman was mixed-race, shrugging off the question, he turned back to Edward and continued.

"I shall call again tonight Edward, we shall go there together, and then you and Mr Tumbold can petition this Black Foot fellow." Thomas gave a thin smile of gratitude before continuing. "But for now Edward, this is what I need!"

The Cage

CHAPTER 7

"No, you've had enough!" The burly, bald man had lost his patience with the Cockney inside the makeshift cage who, by the amount he was smoking, drinking and eating was acting as if he were a guest of honour at the Rookery. As a matter of fact, Sykesy was having a whale of a time. If it hadn't been for the two black eyes, the broken nose that had caused them and of course the prospect of being hung till dead in the next few days, the highwayman would have moved into the cage for good. There was also the prospect of one of the many whores giving him a free fuck when he was ready to play the sympathy card, which he would when he had finished his one man party.

"Come on me old pal, give me another ale!" Sykesy rattled his manacles.

"I ain't got long, have I? So I've gotta get a lifetime of drinking and eating in over the next few days. If I'm going out, it'll be with a fucking good hangover!" The big man tutted more to show his position as jailer than any disapproval he felt. In truth, the jailer felt like getting inside the cage with the outlaw himself who he'd grown to like over the last twenty-four hours. The things he'd seen around the Rookery lately made the interior of the cage the safest place to be. The bodies of the murdered whores were still top of the list in the nonstop gossip around the Froggery even after aristocrat's death last night. The burly minder had never seen anything like that, and he'd seen plenty of horrible stuff over the time he'd worked for Black Foot. He had been involved in most of it, but the way those dogs had ripped that elegant man to pieces was enough to turn anyone's stomach, well, anyone except William Black Foot.

"All right, fair enough pal." He said trying his best to give the captured man a sympathetic smile. "I'll get you some port, that's pretty much all we've got left. The ale won't arrive until after midday, but you'd best have a good sup now, your cash-paying public will be arriving soon." Sykesy shook his head, knowing what he meant, Sykesy had done enough sightseeing himself over the years. He'd especially enjoyed the freak shows he'd seen at the travelling carnivals, although he'd never imagined that one day *he'd* be the main attraction. He pointed towards his sabre and dagger which hung from the back of the jailer's chair in their black leather sheaths on his sword-belt.

"Well, just make sure they don't go looking for any mementos to take home!"

The big minder shrugged.

"Nah . . . I'll wait until you dead before I sell em Mr Sykes sir!" The jailer's words were of little comfort to the highwayman, and he watched as the fat jailer crossed to a tall counter which acted as a bar in the warehouse. As the jailer poured Sykes's drink, he glanced over towards the huge mastiff dogs who were tethered in the corner of the large room. They were all asleep stuffed to the brim with aristocrat. He glanced at one of the many piles of dog shit that littered that part of the room and unconsciously shivered.

The queues of sightseers had begun to arrive around midday. The cash-paying public always had time to see freaks, cruelty and torture or hopefully all three in one sitting. After all, it was good for the soul, or so they were given to believe by the pompous sermons pouring from the pulpits of almost every church in the kingdom on every Sabbath.

Even though he would never have believed it and even if he could have even grasped the concept if he did believe it, over night Henry Sykes had become a very rare commodity. He was a man about to leave this world and stand before God's all seeing eyes for his final judgement, but if Henry was worried about his impending demise, he didn't show it. He lay across a small wooden bench, his hat pulled down over his blackened eyes, trying to sleep off the creeping hangover.

"Satan must be rubbing his hands together at the prospect of such a one as you Mr Highwayman." An elegantly dressed, plump woman giggled, her arm draped through the arm of her skinny fiancee who was trying to stifle a snigger.

"Fuck off you ugly, fat tart!" Sykesy said without any emotion. The big minder burst into laughter as did many of the people in the queue behind them. The girl's smile fell from her face as is she had been slapped, and her fiancee suddenly became animated.

"I say, you rogue, apologise to my fiancee right now!" Henry pushed his hat back onto his forehead and stared at the two gentlefolk. He squinted at the midday light that flooded through the vaulted, roof-windows above him as the pain of his hangover from that mornings over-indulgence dug in. He stared at the two and decided to kill a bit of time with them.

"What you're gonna marry that?" he said to the gentleman, pointing at the tubby girl beside him. He stood and crossed to the bars of his cage and stared through the gaps in the wrought iron. "You're a good-looking, young man." He smiled. "Why the hell are you gonna tie yourself down to that cannonball?"

"H . . . how *dare* you, sir!" The young man blustered, Sykesy started to enjoy himself.

"Come on, don't be coy, you've been thinking the same thing yourself, ain't ya?" Sykesy sniggered. "She'll eat you out of house and home son." The girl burst into tears.

"Rodney, are you going to let him get away wth that? Do something!" Henry laughed.

"Rodney!" He imitated the girl's high-pitched voice. "Yeah, Rodney ain't ya gonna *do* something?" The young gentleman banged the cage with his cane.

"Do not cry my dear Madeleine, I've a good mind to get inside that cage and teach him a bloody good lesson, you, you filthy villain!" Sykesy knew he had the two on his hook now and so started to enjoy himself.

"Oh Madeline, that's right, I recognise you now, you're the tart who used to visit us down at the guard's barracks last year, do you remember this?" Henry pulled the gusset of his breeches until his cock was free and lay flaccid in his open hand.

The woman screamed, before swooning into her lover's arms. Sykesy laughed.

"Ha, that's what she did last time she saw it." The fiancee held the woman in his arms. "Don't worry mate," Sykesy continued, "she ain't really fainted, she's seen it all before, ain't ya Madeline? Oh yeah, she's been cocked more times than King George's hunting rifle." The now, bright-purple fiancee began to drag the half-conscious girlfriend away.

"You utter scoundrel sir, I have a good mind to . . . "

"TIME UP!" The big minder stepped forward and grabbed the gentleman by his collar. "Come on, there's others in the queue you know." The fiancee turned on the minder.

"Did you hear what that robber said about my dear Madeline?" Without missing a heartbeat, the big man replied.

"Oh Madeline, now I recognise her, she was down here two weeks ago, giving us all a taste of her honeypot for free. If I was you sunshine, I'd give her the heave-ho before you catch the clap, she's probably riddled with it."

"I . . . I . . . " The man stuttered. The minder stopped him

"I . . . I would fuck off rather sharpish if I were you." He leaned into the man and breathed his stinking breath into the young gentleman's face who on smelling it, suddenly came to his senses as if given a dose of smelling salts. The well-dressed pair scuttled away under a shroud of shame with far less elegance than they had arrived.

"NEXT!" Without hesitation, a thickset man in the dark clothing and a tall hat stepped into the space before the cage.

"That'll be me, sir!" The man tugged on the brim of his hat, pulling it even further over his face than it already was. He bowed his head in subservience to the jailer, his collar pulled high around his ears hiding what little of his face could be seen from under the hat. Henry gave the man the once over, raising his gaze from the man's silver-buckled shoes, his black stockinged legs, a waist-length cloak and to finish the outfit the tall, small-brimmed hat.

"Oh that's all I need." Sykesy said. "A bleeding Quaker!" Bored of the sightseers already, he slumped back onto the wooden bench and had pulled his hat back over his eyes.

"I say, is that a London accent by any chance?" The Quaker enquired.

"Yeah, what's it to ya?" Sykesy said without looking. "Don't God like Cockneys or something? Maybe you could put in a good word for me?" The Quaker gave the minder a quick glance and seeing that he was sitting back at his table, he came closer to the cage.

"Yes, maybe I will!" He said loudly before whispering. "Wake up you cockney tosser, I ain't all dressed up like a prize prat to come here and talk to myself have I?" Sykesy flicked the brim of his hat back in recognition of his friend's voice.

"Well, you took your bleeding time!" he said laughing and rising from his bench. Thomas flinched at his friend's outburst. The jailer stared at him with a look of distrust and Thomas held his index finger to his head and crossed himself.

"Oh mighty Lord, save this poor wretch from his life of sin!" Thomas said loudly. The jailer went back to making himself comfortable on his chair, leaning back and closing his eyes, trying to nap. Thomas placed his finger to his lips with one hand whilst pointing to the minder with his other. Sykesy rolled his eyes whispering,

"Sorry mate." The two men both turned their heads towards the jailer who, much to their relief was now resting his head against the back of the gaming pit, snoozing.

"You ok?" Thomas asked quietly. Henry held his hands in front of him displaying his manacles.

"No, I'm pretty fucking far from ok, Thomas!" Sykesy whispered through gritted teeth. "What happened last night? One minute we were robbing the coach, the next thing I woke up here with a broken fucking nose!" Thomas glanced behind him at the long line of sightseers.

"We ain't got much time Sykesy, I'll tell you all about it when I get you out of here."

"Oh yeah and how you gonna do that? And anyway, what's with all the Quaker get up?" Henry said trying to stop himself laughing. "You look a proper fucking molly!"

Thomas smirked irritably.

"Well, I wasn't gonna walk in here wearing me hat and mask, was I? These are my brother Edward's clothes." Thomas could see the bemused look on his friend's face. "I'm gonna get the Quakers to petition for your release." He said, a thin smile on his face, trying to hide the vagueness of his plan and hoping it would be infectious enough for Sykesy to pick up on, it wasn't.

"You're gonna get the Quakers to come and ask them to let me go?" Thomas nodded, not knowing what else to say. "Are you fucking mad Thomas? These bastards are gonna hang me and charge the good people of Birmingham a pretty penny to come watch me dangle. They ain't gonna just hand me over to a bunch of God-botherers with the promise of saving their souls at some point in the future!" Sykesy swept his hand around the cage towards the snoozing minder. "From what I can tell, this lot ain't got any fucking souls!" Thomas's eyebrows furrowed.

"Shh!" he said, angrily grabbing the cage. "Shut the fuck up Henry, I'll get you out of here, just keep your hair on and don't do anything stupid." He saw his words were having the right effect on his friend and continued. "I'll be back later tonight with the Quakers, don't worry, I got someone on the inside, and I've got a plan!" If he didn't have a plan *now,* he was sure he could come up with one by the time he returned tonight. "Just sit tight mate, don't do anything to wind these fuckers up!" He gestured to the crowd behind him who were starting to grow impatient in the queue, a growing murmur growing amongst their ranks, making the jailer stir from his slumber.

"Ok, Mr Quaker, time up, now fuck off and save some other fucker's soul!" The big minder slurred. Some of the crowd behind Thomas gave a little cheer. Thomas nodded and touched the brim of his hat.

"Would you be interested in selling your sabre, Mr. Highway-man?" Thomas's question took Sykesy by surprise but comprehending his intentions, nodded his head.

"Yeah why not? I ain't gonna need it where I'm going, am I?" The jailer smirked at the prospect of money being exchanged. Thomas pulled his purse out of his jacket and shook it, it gave a pleasing jingle.

"There you are, sir. I think you'll find enough to cover the weapon and belt!" Sykesy took the purse and nodded to the jailer.

"Go on mate, give it to him, I'll share this with ya!" The minder shrugged and taking the heavy sword-belt from the chair dropped it into Thomas's open hand saying angrily,

"Come on, you bible-thumping bastard, you've got the poor man's sword as a souvenir . . . now fuck off . . . there's others in the queue!" Thomas turned and nodded towards the jailer.

"Bless you my child!" He said raising his hand with the sword-belt in it, marking a cross in the air with his fingers. Henry burst into laughter. Thomas slunk off into the midst of the crowd until he finally disappeared through the main door to the Rookery.

The next people arrived at the cage's bars.

"I say, can I buy his hat?" Henry rolled his eyes and returned to his bench trying his best to sleep whilst the paying public gawped at him through the bars of the cage.

Baiting the Trap

CHAPTER 8

Black Foot raised his glass of port to Eleanor as she entered the dining room of their large house on the outskirts of town in the wooded countryside area of Bearwood.

"Come in my dear, come in." Black Foot beckoned as he leant against the huge fireplace puffing on a long, clay pipe. "Drink my dear?" Eleanor nodded.

"Yes, please father." She plonked herself down into the green, leather chair next to the fireside, any ladylike composure forgotten in her father's company. "That was quite a night last night father!" Black Foot chuckled.

"Yes, my dear, it certainly was, especially for that posh bastard from London." The girl raised her eyebrows as the memory of the bloody stump of a man came to mind.

"I'd say he got a little more than he bargained for." Black Foot turned from pouring her drink to look at his daughter. He took in the girl's youth, his daughter was only nineteen years old and that scared him. Such beauty on young shoulders was bound to be a recipe for disaster. However, he quelled his nerves with the fact that she not only had the innocence and beauty of a young lady but also the cunning of a fifty-year-old court whore, easily a match for any would-be suitors on the make.

"You are a strange thing Eleanor, most ladies would find such a topic disgusting!".

"It is you that made me the way I am father." Black Foot turned his attention back to the drinks and without turning he said.

"If I have made you the way you are my dear, then I think I have done my job well." He turned with a small glass of port and crossed to his daughter beside the fire. "You are beautiful, intelligent *and* independent, you are more than I ever dreamed you would be." Eleanor took the glass and held it towards her father who clinked his against hers. The fine glass rang a high-pitched note that floated around the room. The two listened to the sound until its vibration dissipated behind the crackle of the fire. Black Foot's face became serious. "The world is a serious place my dear, full of . . . " he searched for the right words, " . . . *cunts,* who would take all you have and leave you with nothing. You must ready for them, you must be the biggest thief of all. Take everything and *give* nothing. It is my job to prepare you for the time when I'm dead and gone, and you'll have to fend for yourself me dear." He took a sip of the strong, sweet port, savouring the liquid on his tongue for a second before continuing. "You realise you're at the right age to marry my darling?" Eleanor rolled her eyes.

"I'm having much too much fun for that father. Anyway, I simply haven't met the man that could tame me!" Black Foot burst into laughter.

"My god, I pity the man that tries to do that my girl!" Eleanor looked at her father with a sly smile. She could see he was mulling the idea of his daughter's impending marriage around his mind, as he always did when he *jokingly* brought up the subject. The girl decided to change the subject.

"The man last night . . . " Black Foot nodded.

"Lord Percy?"

"Yes, Lord Percy, won't anyone miss him?" She enquired.

"Yes, I'm sure they will!" The girl smiled thinly as she mulled over her father's answer.

"He was from London?" Black Foot became serious.

"Yes, London, from a *gentlemen's* club." He suddenly broke into a mock aristocratic pose. "The *Hellfire* club, don't-cha-know." He pulled a handkerchief from his sleeve and waved it about him before bowing to his daughter. Eleanor giggled at her father's impression of the dead man.

"The Hellfire club, sounds very exciting father." Black Foot's ceased his antics.

"Bah! . . . Lords, dandies and rakes, a shower of wankers the lot of em, that's all they are me dear. I mean if you've got to *join* a fucking club to act like an arsehole, then what type of arsehole are you?"

"True father, but as I said, surely they'll miss Lord Percy?"

"They might miss him but they won't fucking find him will they? Not unless they fancy poking around in the dog shit at the Rookery." The man laughed. The girl perked up.

"Why so father?" Black Foot smirked to himself.

"What the dogs don't eat, the pigs finish off."

"Pigs?" The girl shook her head at the image.

"Pigs, Eleanor, that's why we keep the sty behind the Rookery, they eat anything, we pour the slops from the night before into the sty every morning. They get rid of the animals that are killed in the pit on the gaming nights, and the food slops go in there too, that helps keep the rats down in the building." Eleanor seemed puzzled.

"But you said the dogs ate Lord Percy?" Black Foot nodded.

"Yes, yes, the dogs will ravage a man . . . but they won't eat him, well at least not all of him. No, my dear, you need pigs for that, they'll go through anything, eat a grown man in no time at all. Of course you have to crack the man's skull as the pigs can't get the mouths open wide enough to break it, but they'll eat the flesh bones *and* clothes, save the buttons . . . which could choke them, you can't be cruel my dear. What was left of Lord Percy went straight into the pigsty!" The girl was still bemused. Black Foot saw her confusion. "It's nothing for you to worry your pretty head about my girl."

"Do they eat gold father?" Black Foot turned on his daughter, his smile turning into a troubled grimace.

"Gold . . . mmm, yes the gold, I see where you're going with this Eleanor." The girl continued.

"The dogs and pigs have had their fill father but the gold remains, and surely the *Hellfire* club won't forget that. Someone will definitely come sniffing around after it." Black Foot returned to his jovial self.

"Nonsense, they wouldn't dare come onto my turf, if they did they'd be sent back to London with their over-privileged tails between their legs very fast, I can tell you that for nothing." Eleanor watched her father. She could see through his false smile of assurance but wasn't fooled for a second. She recognised the concern in his eyes, and she knew he wasn't telling her everything about the situation with the Londoners and the Hellfire club. However, Eleanor knew that pressing her father for more information would just make him clam up completely, so she gently changed the subject towards the man in the cage.

"Well, I hope you're correct father. Although I wouldn't underestimate them if I were you. After all, you don't become an over-privileged lord, dandy or rake by letting someone like you steal their gold and get away with it, do you?" Black Foot tried to smile his way out of the corner he found himself in. He looked for a change of subject but Eleanor beat him to it. "Anyway why didn't you do the same to the highwayman?" Black Foot turned on the girl, eyes wide, almost indignant at the very suggestion.

"We *can't* kill the highwaymen yet!" Eleanor placed her glass down on the small mahogany table by her chair.

"Why not? His death would be just as good sport as the aristocrat's!" Black Foot looked at the girl, a look of disappointment on his face.

"We can't kill him because we need him my dear."

"Need him, what for? Surely his death would bring in some good business at the Rookery?" Black Foot smiled.

"Yes, you're right my love, and he *will* hang, I assure you but not before we get him to tell us who his accomplish was."

Eleanor seemed even more confused.

"Why would we want to find out that, isn't that the business of the town watchmen?" Her father laughed sarcastically,

"The watchmen? That's a bloody joke. Those buffoons couldn't find their horses underneath their own arseholes. No, my dear, we need to find out who the other robber was because he was the man that broke the jaw of one of the best boxers in England."

"Oh, boxing!" The girl's bright eyes sparkled at the mention of the new sport. She felt a familiar tingle in her loins whenever she thought of the violence she had witnessed during the pugilistic bouts at the Rookery. "You think he might be a boxer too?" Black Foot shrugged.

"He could be yes, but we won't know that until we can find him."

"What if the highwayman won't talk?" Eleanor asked. Her father raised his eyebrows.

"Oh he won't talk, I can assure you of that my dear. Not that we won't try and get it out of him if it comes to that. I've known men like him my whole life. I fought alongside them in the army, hard as nails, cunning as foxes. He'll tell us everything except what we want to know." Eleanor sighed, expecting her father to go into one of the old army stories she'd heard a thousand times but surprisingly Black Foot remained on subject. "The Cockney in the cage is just the bait for our trap and if my judgment is right, the man that cracked the jaw of one of the toughest men in England will try and spring his fellow highwayman from the Rookery in the next day or so." Eleanor gave her father a serious look.

"And if he succeeds father?" Black Foot laughed again.

"Well, there it is my girl, we must be ready for him!"

"And *are* we ready for him?"

"We are my dear, we most certainly are!" He said triumphantly. "This highwayman boxer will walk into our trap like a drunken sailor after the smell of quim." Eleanor giggled at her father's crudeness, barely able to hide her excitement, enjoying the exchange.

"And when he does?"

"And when he does, the jaws of our trap will spring shut, and our mysterious boxer will show us his pugilist prowess." The man held his hands up in front of him like a boxer.

"What about if he isn't a boxer?" Black Foot dropped his arms and returned to the fireside. H picked up his glass of port and slugged it back. Shrugging he replied,

"Well, that's simple me dear. He'll have two choices, either he'll be a boxer, or he'll be pig food me dear . . . oink oink!"

The Hell Fire

CHAPTER 9

A deep blanket of freezing, grey fog rolled along the Thames during the first rays of the weak, winter sunrise, spilling over the river's banks and nestling into the low-lying areas around the city of London. It lay unmovable and thick, creeping into every crack and cranny of the houses of rich and poor alike. The usually busy streets were deserted this morning. Market traders and merchants found trading impossible on days like this and the fog had brought the city to a virtual standstill. If trading during one of London's many whiteouts was hard, there was also the danger of being robbed by one of the city's footpads on the way to market. And for many, running risk of losing their goods for the trivial amount of cash they would make on a day like today, just wasn't worth it. Anyway, a day in a local alehouse was much more appealing, at least until the winter sun broke the fog's spell and gave the city's inhabitants some sort of respite from the mist. Hopefully, by the time that happened, many of the merchants and traders would already be too drunk to function. Even the affluent areas such as Highgate and Balham were lost in the dense mist, as the yellow glow of the city's oil-lamps did nothing to cut through the thick veil.

The stillness of the morning was broken by a loud clatter of hooves on cobbles and jingling bridal brass as a coach slowly emerged from the fog as it negotiated its way through the streets of

Highgate, towards the humble but well-presented house of Daniel Mendoza. The coach's lone passenger winced at every jolt in the road as his dislocated jawbone sent lightning bolts of pain deep into his brain.

James O'Donahue could just about make out the wrought-iron railings that ran the length of his friend and fellow professional pugilist's house as the coach drew near. The large Irishman closed his tired eyes and sighed with relief after the nightmare twelve-hour journey back from Birmingham. The last few hours of travelling had taken it out of him, made all the worse by his lower mandible's dislocation.

The carriage pulled to a halt directly in front of Mendoza's home with a noisy protest from its four horses. O'Donahue could see a glow of light from within the building and knew his friend would be there. Grabbing his small canvas bag of fighting breeches and bandages for his hands, he wearily stepped from the carriage and stood in the deserted street. He was glad to be out of the confined space inside the coach. He stretched his arms and yawned, forgetting momentarily about his agonising jaw and broken rib. His actions brought a yelp of pain as he stood shrouded in the morning fog for a second, listening to the distant sounds of the city coming to life.

"*Ahem!*" The voice of the waiting driver caught him by surprise. O'Donahue, forgetting momentarily he wasn't on his own, turned to the driver with an embarrassed look on his face. He dug in his pocket for a coin, finally finding one and flipping the guinea towards the exhausted driver, who sat atop the coach, all but a dark silhouette in the morning twilight. The driver on seeing he'd been over paid, bit the coin with his rotted teeth. The small, silver coin bent slightly, surprising the driver by its authenticity, he nodded down towards the Irishman.

"Thank you sir, thank you!" Without replying, O'Donahue turned and walked up the short entrance path towards the large front door of the property. He stood at the door and swept his hand across his head, trying to tame the unruly mop of red hair that spilt in a tangle over his ears. Raising his hand, he found the large brass door-knocker. The ornament was the shape of a man's fist, indicating the profession of the owner of the property, the sight of which brought a painful chuckle from the Irishman.

Bang, bang, the metal fist slammed against the dark-green door-panel, harder than he wanted it to. He raised the hinged knocker again and intended to slam the door once more, only this time a little more delicately, however, as he brought the hinge back, the dim glow of a candle filled the small, stained-glass window above the door. Placing the brass fist back against the door softly, O'Donahue stepped back to watch the approaching candlelight from within the hallway. The loud clunk of a bolt being drawn back broke the silence of the street. O'Donahue stepped towards the door clutching his canvas bag to his chest, as he did so the door cracked open and a thin line of candlelight filled the doorframe. Without warning O'Donahue came face to face with the muzzle of a pistol, O'Donahue froze.

"Who is there?" Came a man's voice, a touch of a Portuguese accent making his voice sound exotic to the Irishman's ears. O'Donahue went to answer but the searing pain in his jaw stopped him, he gave a muffled reply. The door swung wider until a small, dark-haired man in a nightgown peered around the doorframe. The two men stared at each other for a few seconds before the smaller man recognised the man on his doorstep.

"Oh my God, James, what are you doing here at this hour? Are you all right?" O'Donahue nodded, pointing to his injured chin. The Irishman rolled his eyes as if trying to explain his injury to the Portuguese man who suddenly seemed to wake up. "Come in O'Donahue, my friend. My God, what has happened to you?" The man called over his shoulder to no one in particular. "Wake, wake, we have a friend in need upon our step, he needs food and drink!" Turning back to the Irishman, he gestured for him to enter. "Come in man, come in!"

The waiting coachman watched the big Irishmen step into the pool of light streaming from the doorway. The little scene enthralled his curiosity as well as his greed, after all, a ruffian like O'Donahue calling at a house, all be it a humble one, in one of the most affluent areas of London at this unearthly hour of the day was something that someone somewhere might be willing to pay handsomely for. The driver sat motionless, trying to hide within the fog's veil as best he could. His questions would be left unanswered as the small dark-haired man in the doorway peered into the gloom of the morning from the large door and on seeing the watching coachman guessed his intentions and called out,

"Have you been paid?" The driver, realising he'd been spotted in the mist and suddenly feeling very conspicuous, answered as cheerfully as he could.

"Yes, sir, handsomely!" Mendoza nodded.

"Good, so now you can fuck off, can't you?" With that, the door slammed shut with an echoing bang leaving the driver to clatter away into the grey shroud.

Inside the hallway, Daniel Mendoza ushered his guest into a small room at the foot of the elaborate, elm staircase. The room was the cheerfully bright colour of pastel yellow which lifted the spirits of James O'Donahue somewhat, and the Irishman wondered if indeed that was the intention of whoever had decorated the room. Daniel gestured for the big man to sit in a large, leather armchair near the fireside. The big man sat stiffly, his broken ribs scraping together as he did so and he let a muffled yelp jump from his lips unconsciously. Daniel leant over him and examined his jaw, running his fingers softly across the jawline and joint position to see if it was broken or dislocated. He nodded his approval.

"You're a lucky man, it's all in one piece, but it's dislocated and lodged against something I can't see or feel. I can fix it for you, but it'll take a little messing around. What about your ribs?" O'Donahue shook his head, indicating that the broken ribs although painful were nothing in comparison to the injured jaw. The men were joined by a young, dark woman, whom Mendoza instructed to fetch some gin from the scullery. The woman nodded, disappeared for a minute and upon her return, Mendoza poured a large glass of the clear liquid and offered it to the Irishman.

"You'll need to drink plenty, James. I'd like to say this wasn't going to hurt, but we both know I'd be lying!" He turned back to his wife. "This is no sight for a lady, my dear, you had best go and prepare some food for our guest, we'll try and be as quiet as we can!" The slim woman nodded a subservient smile and withdrew to the kitchen. Daniel turned back to O'Donahue, he glanced at the empty glass, pouring another for the Irishman he sighed. "Ok my big friend, are you ready?" O'Donahue nodded, closing his eyes as he did. "I shall count to three, and then I shall put your jaw back into its rightful place." Mendoza let the words sink in before continuing. "Right I'll count to three . . . " O'Donahue braced himself, " . . . one . . . "

BAM! A thousand stars exploded in the Irishman's head like a cheap fireworks display. The tiny stars bounced this way and that until finally turning into a spiralling psychedelic pattern, changing constantly through a spectrum of colours. As the line of stars drew nearer to each other, so the pain grew until O'Donahue's jaw cracked back into place under the power and weight of Mendoza's punch, the jaw's tendons pulling the bone back into the position it had been in before Thomas Fewtrell's punch had dislocated it. O'Donahue's eyes opened. He caught a quick glimpse of the small man in front of him who had thrown the punch. Mendoza had removed his shirt, and the Irishman could see the rippled muscles on the stocky man's body. Just as the Irish prizefighter lost consciousness, he finally understood why Daniel Mendoza was one of the most respected boxers and trainers in what was Britain's fledgeling sport of pugilism.

Daniel Mendoza, the son of a half-Portuguese merchant, was small, solid, stocky and cunningly intelligent. He found he had a natural ability for fighting at a young age and soon took to the gaming pits around London as a prizefighter where he quickly built a reputation as a man to be taken seriously. Unlike many of the bare-knuckle scrappers of the day, Mendoza approached fighting from a more scientific standpoint. No matter how violent a man's reputation, Daniel Mendoza knew it was fitness and health that won the fight. Good food, hard training, discipline and the most importantly, no drinking on fight day. Fights and fighters were his game, study the opposition; learn his weaknesses, his attack and defence techniques. In the late 1700s, he had virtually invented a new way to fight bare-knuckle. Due to his small size, he was at best a middle-weight fighter although this never held him back from battling and beating many a man twice his size. As a matter of fact, many who fought him viewed his sleight stature as a weakness when in fact it was his biggest strength. He fought small and tight, getting in close, getting inside the haymaker throws of the much bigger men he battled. Mendoza concentrated his punching on specific areas, the nose, jaw, eyes and ribs. He trained for hours every day perfecting techniques to lay a man low with punches strong enough to crack a rib or an eye socket with one blow, and he was fast, very fast. In under the defence, *bam* and out again before the bigger man even knew what had hit him. He also knew how to take a punch, absorbing the normally devastating blows by shifting his weight back and forth, thus taking the slamming power from an attack out of the equation. Yes, there was a reason James O'Donahue had travelled through the night, braving the thick London fog in the early hours of that freezing morning to Daniel Mendoza's front door.

O'Donahue woke from his nightmare with a start, thinking he was still caught in the dream, his fists shot up to protect himself from the devil he'd been fighting in his gin-induced sleep. He took a few seconds to accustom himself to his surroundings. The pastel-yellow walls of Mendoza's study seemed brighter than they had in the misty twilight of the dawn, they now reflected the glow of the winter sun which streamed in through the large window. The fire in the small hearth crackled away under its small but intricately carved mantle warming the draughty room and comforting him. The Irishman felt his jaw, the pain was still there, just less intense but now at least he could move his mouth. He stretched his jaw open as far as he could ignoring the pain more interested in the movement. He opened his mouth and poked a dirty finger inside to see if his teeth wobbled beneath the injured and now bruised skin. The few back teeth he had left didn't move which pleased him, and he slumped back into the armchair sighing with relief. Last night's drama was over and he was glad of that. However, the realisation that he would have to explain to the members of the betting consortium from the *Hellfire club* what had taken place and why he had returned empty-handed and without his Lordship was dawning on him.

Mendoza had warned him not to get involved with the likes of the *Hellfire club.*

Advice O'Donahue had happily ignored at the time but now sadly regretted. Lord Percy had been chosen as an escort and chaperone to represent the club at last night's fight in Birmingham. He had on him an undisclosed amount of gold to bet on the outcome of O'Donahue's fight against a Brummie fighter known as *the Bear.* But here he was, back in London with no answers, no Lord Percy and more importantly, no gold pieces. The Irishman who had lived what could only be described as a colourful life was scared of nothing, but the bizarre things he'd witnessed at the *Hellfire* club had often brought him out in a cold sweat. He knew that to fall foul of the powerful aristocrats within the club didn't just mean death, it meant a long, drawn-out, torturous, humiliating death. Even worse, one's ending would be staged for the entertainment of the uber-rich members of the Hellfire at one of their secret meetings. O'Donahue had seen it first hand when he'd attended as a celebrity fighter as a guest of one of the blue bloods. The sight of a young girl being mutilated by a bear was enough to turn the toughest stomach, and it had taken the Irishman all of his resolve to stand there and watch the macabre, blood-soaked struggle.

London was rife with such organisations; the Gormogons, the Calve's Head club, the Golden Dawn were just some of the names of clubs in London society at that time. The *Hellfire club* was different. Its members included the rich and famous and on occasion even royalty. Their secret meetings were held purely for the love of sexual debauchery and violence. Usually, the unfortunate victims had been kidnapped from one of the outlying villages of the city of London where a never-ending supply of poor could be picked up for a piece of silver. They were chosen for many reasons, beauty, ugliness or deformity. Whatever the reason for their abduction, the end result was always the same, sadomasochism, sodomy, rape, torture, bestiality and sometimes on a special occasion, death, which would then lead to a wager on who would commit the sin of necrophilia. Oh yes, the *Hellfire* club made Sodom and Gomorrah look like a Sunday afternoon's canter through Hyde Park and why James O'Donahue felt a prickle of cold sweat creeping up his spine as he sat beside the fire in Daniel Mendoza's yellow study.

O'Donahue turned to see his friend enter the room, a small wooden tray in his hands.

"Ah, you are back from the dead!" Mendoza laughed.

"I didn't think death could be so painful Daniel." He moved to rise and take the tray, but the Portuguese man shook his head, gesturing that he should sit again.

"No, James, you are still weak, eat first and then tell me what happened to you." He placed the tray across the O'Donahue's lap before taking a small parchment, quill and a tiny glass jar of ink from the mantel. He plonked himself on a low footstool beside the fireplace and sat watching the big man eat, his quill in hand and the parchment over his knee ready to take notes on the previous evening's bout.

O'Donahue on seeing the quill sighed.

"I'm afraid you'll have no need for that my friend." Mendoza stared at the man as he took a large bite from a chicken leg.

"Oh and why so?" He leaned forward and dipped the sharpened end of the long, white feather into the ink at his feet. "I always take notes from the bouts if I can, you know that James? How else are we meant to learn and improve our skills if not from each other?" O'Donahue was struggling with the bird's leg due to the soreness of his injury and finally placed it back on the plate. He took a gulp of wine from the small glass on the tray, draining the glass.

"But there was no bout!"

"No bout?" Mendoza asked, his dark eyebrows drawing together with a growing expression of puzzlement. "No bout? What do you mean, no bout?" The Irishman had started on some bread and dripping which was going down much easier than the chicken, and he wouldn't be disturbed from the food. Daniel continued. "But if there was no bout, tell me what happened to your jaw?" O'Donahue held his index finger up, he began chewing faster, finally swallowing the mouthful.

"Sure, I said there was no bout. I didn't say there wasn't a fight!" Mendoza shook his head.

"You're not making sense James." O'Donahue apologised.

"I'm sorry my friend allow me to explain as I eat. I'm bloody starving!" Daniel nodded.

"Yes, of course, we don't stand on ceremony in this house, please, do go on."

****

The winter sun slowly travelled along its low arc until it fell towards the horizon in a glorious display of orange and red, finally vanishing into the growing fog bank that had once again begun to roll back along the River Thames and into the heart of London. As the day drew to a close, the two men talked for hours about the events of the previous night. The Irishman told Mendoza about the highway robbery in all its detail, how he'd punched the smaller highwayman and knocked him out cold and how Lord Percy had travelled onto the venue to explain the Hellfire club's fighter's absence. However as the story was told, O'Donahue became far more reticent about how he'd received his injuries dodging Mendoza's questions far better than he had dodged the punches. Daniel Mendoza finally became impatient with the dithering storyline and interrupted him.

"Come on man, tell me about the attacker! Did he use a weapon or catch you off-guard?" Mendoza realised he'd raised his voice and had lost his normally controlled temper. He took a deep breath and gathered himself. "I've seen you take punches from some of the hardest men in London James, *none* of whom have even scratched you. Yet this morning you show up at my door with your jaw nearly hanging out of your mouth so put your pride to one side and tell me who and how this happened!" O'Donahue sighed, realising that he'd been called out by his mentor and friend.

"I'm sorry Daniel, I guess I'm coming to terms with the idea that this man had something that I haven't."

"That prickle you feel in your heart is pride, James. You have been bettered, which would be bad enough if it were a *fellow pugilist* but a highwayman on the road *that* is a hard thing to come to terms with." The Portuguese man let his words sink in before pressing for the information he was really after. "But however much this brigand has hurt your pride, I must know more about him in order to establish whether it was just a lucky punch or not." O'Donahue shook his head in disbelief.

"Oh be God it was no lucky punch Daniel. Sure if I didn't know better, I would have sworn the man I was fighting was spring-heeled Jack!" Mendoza laughed at the reference to the folklore bogeyman.

"Let's just stick to the facts James. The man that hit you was no imaginary sprite, he was flesh and blood and we must establish if he was a trained boxer or not." O'Donahue rolled his eyes.

"I tell you, this man moved like a ghost. He was so very fast, I couldn't get a punch on him at all and believe me I tried. The fecker was in low under my arms and punching my ribs before I knew what was happening." The Irishman flinched unconsciously at the mention of his broken rib. "He ducked and weaved this way and that almost as if he knew what I was going to do before I knew it myself. I tell you Daniel, he *was* spring-heeled Jack!" Mendoza smiled at his friend, realising that the Irishmen couldn't come to terms with the fact he'd been beaten by a mere man and not a folklore devil.

"Well, if I were you I wouldn't be seen around London for a while and I wouldn't mention any of this to those animals at the Hellfire. If they do find you, tell them you were attacked by highwaymen and leave it at that." O'Donahue's face became pale at the mention of the club's name.

"But what about Lord Percy and the gold wager?" Mendoza frowned.

"Gold wager?" The Irishman nodded.

"There was a big purse on last night's fight. The club members will think I've stolen it!"

"Nonsense my friend, they'll think Lord Percy has stolen it. From what I've heard he was up to his ears in debt and about to pay a visit to the debtor's jail at Fleet. As a matter of fact, I'm surprised the club chose the man to accompany you in the first place, he's a bloody liability. You say he carried onto Birmingham after the attack?" O'Donahue shook his head.

"I only know what the coachman who brought me here told me, I was unconscious from the punch for most of the way here after all." Daniel laughed.

"Well, that's a first James. Tell me the name of the venue and did the coachmen say anything?" Daniel Mendoza rose from his stool by the fire and placed the quill and unmarked parchment on the mantle, deep in thought. O'Donahue perked up.

"The gaming house was called the Rookery. It's owned by a gentleman called William Black Foot, he's new to the pugilist world, plenty of cash though by the size of the wager he'd put on his man they call the *Bear*." O'Donahue waited for his friend to acknowledge his words but the Portuguese man seemed lost in his thoughts. The Irishman continued. "The driver said that Lord Percy had flagged him down as he was returning along the road from Birmingham to London. They loaded me into the coach and he told the driver to take me to his address in Balham but as I regained consciousness I told the driver to bring me here instead. I knew you could put my jaw back into place. The coachman said that Lord Percy had travelled onto Birmingham to hang the other Highwayman who they had tied up in the Royal Mail coach." Mendoza turned.

"So they have the man's accomplice?" O'Donahue nodded.

"Yes, they are going to hang him."

"Well, that's good news and bad news." The Irishman was puzzled.

"Good news and bad, why so?" Mendoza crossed the room to the door, opened it and stepped into the doorway.

"Good news because they have the accomplice which means we can find out who his boxer friend is, if indeed he is a boxer!" The Irishman's face scrunched up into a bemused grimace.

"And sure why should we want to know that?" Mendoza smiled.

"We want to know that because this man has shown that he can better the best James. He must have a natural talent for pugilism, if he has, I intend to bring him into the brotherhood of boxers and train him or learn from him." O'Donahue was impressed by Mendoza's sharpness of mind.

"And the bad news?" He enquired.

"The bad news is that they are going to hang the accomplice and if that happens, then we will never know the true identity of this highwayman pugilist." O'Donahue rose from his chair.

"So where are you going now?"

"*We*, James O'Donahue, *we*!" He pointed at the big man. "*We* are going to Birmingham to find this scrapper!"

The smell of a woman

CHAPTER 10

The Tavern was packed to capacity that evening as Thomas stepped in from the snow-covered street. The thick cloud of tobacco smoke hit him immediately as he stepped into the small doorway and stung his eyes as scanned the room for Bridget O'Hara. He shook the snow from his shoulders and stepped into the bar. Thomas looked at the drinkers around the room, but the pretty, mixed-race girl was nowhere to be seen. A rowdy sing-song was well under way amongst a group of market traders around one of the fireside tables who all gave Thomas the once over as he crossed to the bar. He nodded at them, touching his hat, glad that he had called at his brother's house and retrieved his own clothing, exchanging them for the borrowed Quaker's garb. Thomas felt himself again and crossing to the counter he leant across and took the key to his casement from its hook. A quart bottle of port sat on the shelf next to it, and Thomas grabbed the small bottle and a pewter goblet before retracing his steps back towards the front door. Finding an empty table, he collapsed into the creaky chair and poured the thick, red liquid into the dirty, metal cup. The image of his friend in the cage wouldn't leave him, and the long walk back from the Rookery had given him plenty of time to mull over his friend's fate. The girl had promised to help him, yet she was nowhere to be seen. He drained the goblet and poured himself another. The singers by the fireside were growing in volume making it hard for

Thomas to think clearly. He went through different scenarios of Syksey's breakout in his mind, but however elaborate his escape plans were, they always ended up with the same conclusion, blood and guts, Thomas's blood and guts.

"There's only one thing for it then, blood, guts and glory!" He raised his cup to himself and drained it again. The port had an instant effect on his empty stomach, making his head swoon. A merry smile broke his stern yet handsome face as the liquor found its mark. "I shall ride through the gates of that shit-hole and shoot any fucker that gets in my way!" He said aloud to no one in particular. Thomas poured another drink and slugged the sweet port to the back of his throat. "That's the only way you're coming out of that cage, my old pal!" Slamming the cup down, he picked up the bottle and slugged the remainder of the quart down. He tried to rise from the table, but his injured leg felt like jelly beneath him. He stumbled backwards before catching himself against a post. The crowd of singers had fallen silent and were all turned towards the drunken man as he struggled to stay upright.

"Sing!" Thomas ordered. "Come on you fuckers sing your bloody songs!" A silence fell over the tavern making Thomas feel suddenly self-conscious. He righted himself and picking his hat from the table, he bowed low in a mocking gesture of grandness.

"I beg your pardon ladies and gentlemen!" He said sarcastically, laughing at his own sudden drunkenness. "I shall retire to my casement!" He said trying to summon as much dignity as he could. "For I seem to be a little drunk . . . hic!" He bowed once more, flaying his tricorn hat around him grandly but as he stood up his head came into contact with one of the low beams that lined the ceiling of the bar. The collision was a hard one, whacking the back of his head as he came to his full height. The watching crowd burst into laughter at the man's discomfort whose aura had instantly fallen from the mocking grandness of a gentleman to an utter buffoon in the blink of an eye. He screamed obscenities at his shoes at the top of his lungs and held the back of his injured head. The crowd howled with laughter as he stumbled around the room knocking into tables and fellow drinkers.

Suddenly two cold hands caught him by the shoulders.

"Thomas!" He looked up into the face of Bridget O'Hara, her shoulders covered with fresh snow from the street. She rolled her eyes as the man returned her concern for him with a look of drunken arousal. "Come on, let's get you to your room, never mind this lot, you need to sleep this off before we go to the Rookery tonight."

"Ah my exotic beauty!" He said smiling. Then he lowered his voice leaning into Bridget's ear. "I bet you've got a lovely ... " Thomas searched for Sykes's description from the night before finally blurting, "honey..p..pot!" The girl shook her head in mock disbelief.

"From what I've heard from Mrs Bakewell, I don't think you'd know what to do with my *honeypot* even if I handed it to you on a plate!" The girl raised her voice. "Apparently you're a bit of a *wanker*!" The crowd cheered at the girl's response. The gleeful crowd's laughter brought Thomas back to his senses.

"I'm sorry miss, I don't normally talk to girls like that!" The girl nodded.

"I know, I know, come on let's get you upstairs, we've got plans to make and places to be!"

With that Bridget gathered Thomas's cloak over her shoulder and placing her head under the big man's arm helped Thomas up the rickety stairs to his casement where he dropped lifelessly onto his small bed, asleep before he'd even hit the mattress.

****

Thomas awoke to the sound of a loud crackling fire in the tiny hearth. The port had done its job on his empty stomach, soaking through the bread and dripping he'd enjoyed at his brother's that morning with ease sending him into a drunken stupor. He lay there hung over on the small bed and tried to remember how he had gotten there. The only thing that came to him was the face of the dark-skinned girl, the shadow of her face and small breasts in the glow of his room's fire. The room was dark except for the flickering firelight. He felt around the bed, his hands searching for the girl in the darkness but she wasn't there. Thomas's mind ran over the sexual images that had begun to roll through his mind with increasing speed. Turning his head he could suddenly smell the woman on his pillow. The scent sending more images of sexual exploits from earlier in the day. Was he recalling a real moment with Bridget? Or were the dreams all part of his desire to have the girl? Shaking the beautiful girl's image from his mind he rolled to the side of his bed and threw his leg over the edge. His thigh stung sorely and he gave a short gasp as he moved into a sitting position on the bedside. The bruising had gotten worse and he examined the injured thigh for a short while before realising that he was only in his shirt. He wondered how he'd managed to undress himself in his drunken state. Reaching beneath the bed he pulled out the china chamberpot, looked inside it and was relieved to see that Mrs Bakewell had emptied it. He recalled her making a big deal out of the fact that she emptied the chamberpots in all the rooms, charging extra for the service. Thomas knew that she was selling the piss to one of the leather tanneries in the Irish quarter of Digbeth who used it to cure their skins as did almost all of the taverns in town. Thomas reached under his shirt and fumbled in the folds of the long gown for his manhood. The folds were thick and tangled, he reached further underneath, fumbling even more around his crotch, finally finding his penis which was almost erect because of the passionate images of the girl.

"You'll go blind doing that all the time Thomas!" The girl's voice made him jump.

"*Fuck*!" He turned to see the girl's pretty face peeking over the back of the tall armchair next to the fire. "You scared me, I thought I was alone." The girl giggled.

"So I can see!" She nodded towards his groin. He looked down at himself, his semi-erect penis in his hand.

"No, it's not like that, I was just *having* a piss!" He said angrily. The girl, on hearing his raised voice replied in a similar tone.

"Yeah, and I was just *taking* the piss!" The woman had changed her clothes and had made herself up for her night's work. Thomas was taken aback by her beauty. Her wild black hair hung around her face in tight ringlets and her smokey-green eyes, glowed against her dusky skin. His eyes followed the line of her faded silk gown from its once elaborately embroidered but now frayed neckline, down to her breasts which had been forced together by the wires of the dress. The line of the gown had been altered so that the gown's material only just hid her nipples. Thomas had to force himself to look away from the woman so seductive was her allure. Bridget turned and knelt on the chair, peering over its tall back at Thomas. She began to giggle as the man tried to dress himself, struggling with the doe-skin breeches and his bruised leg.

"What happened to your leg Thomas?" The man spun his head towards the girl before losing balance altogether and falling backwards onto the chamberpot, spilling its yellow contents all over himself.

"Fuck it!" He snorted, sitting in the pool of his own urine. The puddle began to soak through the floorboards, leaving a yellow stain on his long cotton shirt. "For fuck's sake, this is my best shirt and now it's sticking of piss." The girl jumped from the seat.

"Wait here, I've got something in my room you can wear." The girl sprang across the room and vanished through the door. Thomas tried to rise from the floor but his leg was stinging again as the urine seeped into his wounds. He struggled from the floor until he stood fully, the wet shirt clinging to his body. He pulled the garment from himself and threw it at the fireside where it landed on the small fire-surround, a cloud of foul-smelling steam rising as it instantly began to sizzle on the hot tiles. Thomas could hear the girl's footsteps stomping on the wooden floorboards somewhere in the recesses of the tavern and before he could find anything to cover his nakedness the girl was back in the casement. She stopped just inside the doorway, the look of initial shock on her face was almost instantly replaced with one of mischief. Thomas saw the girl's eyes run over his body and did nothing to hide himself, being still irritated by ruining his shirt, he was in no mood for games. Bridget bit her bottom lip, as she let her eyes wander over the ripped, lean body of the man in front of her.

"You said you had something I could change into?" He pointed at the bundle of material in the girl's hands. She looked down at the bundle and remembered why she had gone to her room.

"Oh . . . yes, I'm sorry, I was distracted." She nodded towards Thomas's nakedness, giving a small sexy giggle as she threw the bundle at Thomas. "The clothes belonged to my pimp, you can have them!" Thomas caught the clothes.

"Your pimp you say, well won't he need them?" The girl became serious and turned away towards the fire trying to hide her expression of sadness.

"No, he's dead!"

"Dead?" Thomas held the garments up in front of him.

"Yes, dead, typhus, he shit himself to death!" Thomas dropped the clothing and wiped his hands on himself.

"Typhus!" The girl nodded and looked at the pile of clothes Thomas had dropped on the bed.

"Don't worry, they've been cleaned. I was going to sell em, but you can have them if ya like, they cost him a lot of money!" Thomas pulled the breeches out of the bundle and laid them out on the bed. They were made from a light-brown leather yet were as supple as silk, drawn low at the waist and buttoning up at the crotch, their legs reaching just below the knee. He nodded with approval. He reached for the jacket which was made from the same leather, reaching to the thigh, the jacket's front was lined with a long line of dull, grey buttons which covered the cuffs of the sleeves. As he held the jacket up a white shirt fell from the coat's folds onto the bed. A smile grew across Thomas's face. A fine suit of clothes he thought to himself. He bent and picked up the suit's matching hat and holding the leather tricorn in his large hands, he examined the bottle-green, feather brocade which stood four inches tall from the hatband.

"I shall pay you for these of course!" The girl giggled.

"Well, excuse me if I'm stating the bloody obvious Thomas but you ain't got a pot to piss in!" She pointed at the broken chamberpot, then gave another giggle. "I'll tell ya what, you can pay me in kind Thomas." She looked at him, a serious look growing on her face as she began to mull over a new idea in her mind.

"In kind?" Thomas raised his eyebrows and smiled.

"Not like that, you saucy bugger!" Thomas's face fell like a disappointed child, suddenly feeling exposed he hid his manhood behind the hat.

"Oh, I thought you meant you wanted me to sha . . . "

"Yeah, I know what you thought!" She giggled again. "If you want that, then you gotta pay for it Thomas."

"But didn't we just . . . last night?" Thomas stopped himself when he saw the girl's confused face. She broke the embarrassing moment.

"I mean, you can look after me, you know, protect me."

"You mean pimp you?" Thomas exclaimed. The girl shrugged.

"Yeah, I suppose that's what I mean."

"I ain't a pimp girl, I'm a . . . " he left the sentence unfinished,

" . . . a highway robber and how's that working out for ya then?" Thomas frowned, holding his finger to his lips.

"Shhh girl, you wanna get me hanged!" He looked around the room. "Walls have ears you know Bridget!" The girl burst into laughter.

"Are you bleeding joking? Everyone in the tavern knows everything about everyone. There ain't no secrets here you know, anyway, what's wrong with being a pimp?"

Thomas shook his head.

"I make me own way in this world Bridget. I don't intend to cream my cash from your open-legged shenanigans!" She laughed.

"Oh I see, you're a proper man are ya? Taking other people's cash at gun point is ok but a bit of rough and tumble and you're all offended, do me a favour, Thomas." The pair stood on either side of the bed, the oppressive silence only broken by the hubbub from the busy bar below. "Look I only need someone to look after me. I nearly got throttled last night, look!" She pulled her hair aside to reveal the black bruising around her throat. Thomas crossed the room and ran his finger delicately along her neck.

"Who did this?" She shook her head.

"I don't know, I was drunk and whoever it was, came from behind." Thomas's finger ran along her jawline to her chin. She turned her head towards him, looking into his eyes. He drew his breath at her smokey beauty, her eyes glowing like flickering emeralds as they reflected the light of the fire. She smiled softly, and he could see that her confidence was a front for hidden in those green eyes was a twinkle of fear, suppressed far beneath the surface but there nonetheless. "Please," She said, almost whispering, "I'm scared that I'll end up like one of them poor bitches they keep finding in the streets of the Froggery. They found another last night, that's five now." Thomas nodded.

"Okay, I'll look after you, but if you're scared, why don't you just stop?" She sighed.

"I can't, I got a plan, and plans need coin."

"You got a plan?" Thomas tried to stop himself smiling. "What's this plan of yours? To open your own whorehouse?" She pulled away from him.

"I'm not opening myself to you for you to mock me!" Thomas's smile dropped.

"I'm sorry Bridget, I didn't mean to ... "

"Oh yes you did, you're just like all the others, that's why I'm going to get out of here so I can start again, away from this shit-hole."

"What Birmingham, what's wrong with Birmingham?" The girl's voice raised.

"Birmingham, it ain't just Birmingham, is it? It's fucking England. Look at me, Thomas. A nigger, that's what they call me, a bloody, half-breed nigger. That's all anyone sees. The toffs think they can do what they want to people like me and do you know what? They fucking can cos the law don't give a shit about some mulatto whore. I ain't worth my weight in shit here, but in the new world I could be free!" She pulled a small fold of paper from the folds of her gown. "Look!"

She passed the tatty old sheet of paper over to the man. He took it and unfolded it.

An etched black picture of a mountain range around a lake with a ship moored in it took up most of the page. *Come to the new world of America* ran across the top of the sheet. The flyer went on to say that America needed men and women and for those that were willing to brave the three-week journey across the Atlantic ocean the newly designated American government promised *free* land west of Massachusetts. Bridget leaned across the paper and pointed at the words.

"Free land Thomas, *free* !" Thomas handed the paper back, raising his eyebrows.

"Well, they have slaves there just like they do here Bridget . . . do you think the Americans will think of any differently of you than they do here, it's probably worse there." The girl's eyes narrowed.

"I ain't no one's bleeding slave!" Thomas levelled his hands, trying to calm her rousing temper. "My old ma was . . . " Bridget stopped talking abruptly, she drew in a deep breath. Thomas could see now just how alone and vulnerable she was in this cruel world. She had asked *him* of all people for help, and suddenly he wanted to wrap his arms around her. "My ma was a slave girl out of the Bristol slave markets, sold, bought and paid for by an innkeeper by the name of Liam O'Hara. He was married, but made a point of *enjoying* his investment in flesh as often as he could, so after two years of rape and servitude, my ma." Bridget made a quick sign of the cross on her forehead before continuing. "God rest her soul. My ma became pregnant with me. Of course Liam O'Hara's wife wasn't all too happy about the pregnancy so he signed my mother over to a workhouse at Bristol Docks where I was born." The sparkle of anger still lingered in her eyes as she talked and Thomas could see that, however low the girl had fallen from grace, if indeed she'd ever had any grace to fall from, Bridget O'Hara was a proud, powerful and determined woman. "It was a blessing in disguise really the workhouse, if I hadn't been born there and at the innkeeper's instead, I would have been born into slavery but I weren't, I was born free, and I'm gonna die free, so you see Thomas." Bridget's voice rose in the tiny casement. Thomas couldn't work out if it were anger or pride that had caused the change in volume but the slightly built dark-haired beauty in front of him seemed to fill the room with her presence as she said the words, hands clenched into fists, eyes reflecting the orange glow of the fire like some African spirit. "I ain't no *slave*!" He looked at her for a second not knowing what to say, finally blurting.

"I ain't saying you are a slave, no one could think that Bridget, anyone can see, you're your own woman and God help the man who says otherwise. All I'm saying is . . . " he sighed, " . . . America might not be all it's painted up to be. I mean, haven't you heard the saying, the grass is always greener on the far side of the hill?" She folded the flyer back into its tatty wrap and shoved it back inside her gown.

"Yeah, I've heard that one before, and it might very well be true, but it'll be *my* hill Thomas, *my* hill . . . If I could find somewhere to hide away from this horrible world, I think I'd be happy!" Another silence fell between them. Thomas placed his hands on her shoulders. Outside the tiny roof window, the bell of St Martin's church struck eleven times. The sound brought them both back to the moment, and both stood in silence as the bells counted down the hour.

"Look, let's just take one day at a time. Here's the deal, I need to get my mate out of that cage tonight, you said you'd help me, so let's concentrate on that, and when Henry Sykes is free, we'll talk about protection for you and getting you to America if indeed that's where you want to go. Until then let's keep our minds on tonight's events." She nodded, pleased that he was taking her idea of the New World seriously. He continued, "My brother Edward's coming here to meet us at midnight."

"Right then, before we go to the Rookery you need some food inside you. I'll go downstairs and get Mrs Bakewell to put something together for us. You get dressed in your new suit, we'll eat and then free your highwayman friend from his cage."

The Order of the Second Circle

CHAPTER 11

S ir Francis Dashwood stood with his back to the scene of bestiality taking place on the altar of the abandoned old chapel. The church had been left to ruin after the English civil war, one hundred years before. The brutal battle on the Rye near the hamlet of High Wycombe was only three generations ago, and the stories of the slaughter of Royalist Cavalier forces passed down to them by their mothers and fathers were still fresh in the mind of the old folk that lived in the area. It was said that on a night when the moon casts no shadow, the ghosts of those poor soldiers who took sanctuary in the small chapel all those years ago could still be heard screaming their death songs as the roundheads surrounding the tiny church, burned the Cavaliers to death inside. The screams of agony floating across the fields and pastures around Rye on a dark winter's night were enough to keep any prying eyes away from the debauchery taking place inside the stone walls of God's house.

Sir Francis was bored. In his late seventies, he'd seen all the vulgarity, torture, and vileness that could possibly be conjured up by London's blue-blood elite. Nothing surprised him anymore. He'd tried or watched others try, pretty much everything that Satan and his spawn had to offer. He stood with his back to the scene of the young serving maid stolen from the filthy streets of London's east side being held down by four masked men being forced to have sex with a monstrous dog.

"My God," he rolled his eyes at the man next to him, "how many times do we have to put up with Lord Harrington's obsession with dogs and wenches?" Lord Dashwood's Scottish manservant laughed. "Och, I don't know me Lord, I think it's got a certain . . . je ne sais quoi." The French sounded clumsy when spoken with a strong Scottish brogue.

"Bollocks man!" Lord Dashwood said angrily and turning, he walked away from the scene, eagerly followed by Flint. "Even the fucking dog's bored, look man!" They turned to watch the debacle at the end of the aisle. "Even the floundering beast can't get a bloody hard on, what hope have we?" Lord Francis' manservant chuckled.

"Ai . . . well it has na stopped Lord Harrington enjoying himself, me Lord!" He pointed at a red-faced man in his late fifties who was sat on one of the old, rotted pews that ran along the front of the church around the old stone altar, watching the show. The grey-wigged man had his breeches around his ankles and was masturbating furiously, his eyes rolling into his head beneath the black eye-mask that all the members of the club wore on such occasions as this, totally unaware of the hundred or so other masked men and serving wenches around him. "Och, he seems to find tonight's entertainment terribly erotic, your lordship!"

"Nonsense Flint, that fucker would wank himself stupid over a squirrel eating nuts!"

Lord Dashwood turned back to the crowded church's dimly lit front entrance.

"Astounding isn't it me lord?" Flint addressed his master in the familiar. "Considering Lord Harrington is married to one of the loveliest roses in all of London, that he's here wanking himself blind over a wee tart and a smelly mutt." Lord Francis stopped walking and turned to Flint.

"Ah, well there you have it Flint, don't you see?" Flint raised his eyes.

"See what me Lord?" Dashwood slapped his servant's broad shoulders.

"That's what the *Order of the Second Circle* is all about, Flint." The servant's eyebrows furrowed.

"You mean the *Hellfire* me lord?"

"Yes, yes, Hellfire, well that's what some call us but to be sure, there seems to be Hellfire clubs sprouting up all over the bloody place at the moment. I've heard they even have them in the bogs of Ireland." Flint nodded.

"Oh, ai me lord."

"Bloody bogtrotters." Flint saw his master's mood change.

"I don't think those wee clubs are as good as ours!" Dashwood slumped heavily into the large armchair that had been pulled out for him by one of the young, black serving boys.

"Well, they wouldn't be, would they Flint? This club is the original, 1722, Flint *1722*. We are the first and only Hellfire and that's the way it's going to stay, man." Flint reached across the table for the large bottle of port. "Debauched and anonymous to each other and all!" He said laughing. "Although in truth, I know every man in here tonight whether they wear their masks or not. *Sit,* Flint, *sit!*" The servant sat on the small bench opposite his master and poured the dark, red liquid into two pewter goblets. He handed one to his master and took the other himself.

James Stuart Flint was the son of a Scottish chieftain from the mountains to the east of the small market village of Invergordon. A life wandering the Highlands guarding the cows of a distant Edinburgh-based Laird was to be the ten-year-old boy's destiny. However in the late summer of 1745 during a visit to the Inverness market to trade, fate played its hand in the form of Bonny Prince Charlie and his quest to wrestle the crown from the ruling Hanoverian head, King George II. The young prince intended to place it on the rightful monarch's head, namely his father, James Stuart or as he was called in England, *the Old Pretender*. The boy's father, being staunchly patriotic towards Scotland and the Stuart household, declared himself and his son in favour of the Jacobite cause. Although in truth, the old Chieftain was driven less by his love of the Scottish blood in his veins more by the Scottish Whisky that could be found running through them. Being a chieftain, he and his son were permitted entrance to the Jacobite war council where Flint's father was called upon to serve the Prince as his bodyguard in the battle to come. He was presented with a ceremonial dirk by the Bonnie Prince himself, an honour that brought the rough high-lander to tears. Taking the weapon, he later passed the dagger onto his son for safekeeping. He prepared himself for battle by drinking his fill of the rough, Highland *Uisce Beatha* until the time came for the tartan army to march south under the shadow of the blue and white flag of St Andrew and a dreadful hangover. The father left his ten-year-old son to fend for himself for over ten months. On his return, he joined his fellow clansmen as they charged into the hailstorm of grapeshot, bullets and death on that infamously barbaric day on the snow-covered heather of Culloden Moor. The boy, on seeing the day was lost and driven by hunger as much as panic, followed his fellow refugees from the battlefield towards any escape route possible. In Flint's case, the open sea where he found passage on one of the Jacobite ships taking the fleeing men to France and to safety. That is, if they could avoid the Royal Navy. The boy told all aboard the packed brigantine, exactly how the battle had played out and if they didn't already realise it, all aboard now knew for *certain* that *the cause* was now a lost one. During this voyage, the young man came into contact with a member of the ruling class, namely a forty-year-old Jacobite blue-blood, by the name of Lord Francis Dashwood who as it happened, was a paying passenger on the brigantine returning to Scotland to bring fresh food and powder to the half-starved Highlanders. Flint, despite being only eleven years old was about to be hung from the yard arm for his part in the killing of a junior rates officer aboard the brigantine, over a derogatory comment about the Bonnie Prince. The boy had used the vicious dagger given to him by his father. On seeing the weapon, the captain confiscated it. The wound inflicted on the young officer was a fatal one, too deep to treat or heal by itself due to the narrow width and length of the dirk's blade and so, after the unfortunate officer's burial at sea, the convicted lad was dragged on deck by the officer's friends. A long streak of blood ran down the right cheek of the boy. A testament that the young murderer hadn't had it all his own way in the argument; for just before the dead officer had been gutted by Flint, he had delivered a blow of his own; with a small sail knife to Flint's young face, leaving a long, red stripe running down the right side of his face, temple to chin. Even by the standards of the day, the scar was an impressive one, especially on a child.

His Lordship had stood on the poop-deck looking over the condemned boy who stared back at him with a defiant stare. The Captain had asked Flint if he would name his fellow murderers for no one believed a child of Flint's age could deliver such a deadly wound but the boy wouldn't have betrayed his comrades even if he'd had any. Even as the noose was hung around his neck, Flint had the presence of mind to see a man for what he was and had winked mischievously at Lord Dashwood. Whether it was this gesture or the fact that the young Highlander in his great kilted plaid was the epitome of one of Dashwood's homosexual fantasies that made him act as he did we will never know. But as Flint stood in the stiffening breeze, the hangman's noose around his neck; his emaciated body tiny in the huge piece of tartan material, his scarred, yet handsome face, staring back at Dashwood with a bold disobedience, Lord Francis Dashwood was compelled to save the boy and so stepped forward and tapped the captain's shoulder, asking for reprieve for the child. The captain or course remonstrated about his Lordship's decision, but Dashwood would hear none of it and after paying the captain handsomely, he took the lad on as his personal servant. Flint, on hearing his Lordship's command, turned and smiled at the officer's around him as they untied his hands and removed the noose from his neck. When he was free of the rough bonds, he marched across the poop-deck and took his place behind the right shoulder of Lord Dashwood and there he had remained ever since until ultimately the Lord and the murderous young Jacobite had become inseparable.

"Some men are too *manly* to be trapped by a hearth, home and woman, some of us need to . . . " he searched for the right words as he sipped at the port, " . . . shake off the weight of the establishment and just fucking enjoy ourselves. *That's* what the Hellfire is all about Flint, one face for society and one face for debauchery, it's as simple as that. Although . . . " the Lord raised his hands to a pendant around his neck and began to play with it, twisting the picture-pendant around his fingers unconsciously, " . . . I *do* crave something real, Flint!"

"My lord?"

"Some *real* danger . . . rebellion Flint, *rebellion*!" He said the words as if he were saying something sacred, something blasphemous, relishing the word as it rolled across his tongue, all the while fiddling with the silver pendant that hung on a long chain around his neck. "The King across the sea Flint, remember?" Flint took a sip of his port, he knew exactly what his master was getting at. After all, they had fantasised about it on many a drunken evening.

"To the King across the sea!" Flint raised his glass and smiled.

"Ai, the King!" Flint pointed at the locket around the old man's neck.

"My Lord, may I have a wee peek at it again?" Dashwood stopped fiddling with the small pendant. He pulled the locket up in front of him and flicked the silver latch on the tiny ornament. The silver locket flipped open to reveal a tiny, hand-painted picture and a young blonde man with large, dark eyes. The young man was wearing an indigo bonnet with a large, white cockade to the front, an illegal sign of Jacobite allegiance and to the left of the tiny picture was a small lock of human hair.

"May I touch it?" Dashwood laughed.

"How many times over the years have you ran your fingers over the hair of the true King, every time you see Prince Charlie's lock of hair, it's as if it's the very first time boy!" Flint laughed, more from the fact that his master still called him *boy*, even though he was nearly fifty years old, than any embarrassment about his obsession with the lock of hair. The locket brought back good memories for Flint, and he reflected on his good fortune meeting the old man all those years before. His life had been a barrel full of quim, arse and alcohol ever since. The buggery he had suffered at the old man's hands as a child had been a small price to pay and as the years rolled by he had passed the mantle onto other young boys, even indulging in the acts himself. However, the best thing about serving the old Lord was that in order to repay his Lordship for saving his life, all

Flint had to do was to beat the shit out of anyone Lord Francis Dashwood thought needed a seeing to. Flint was only too happy to oblige and as a matter of fact, beating the bejesus out of men, women and the occasional street urchin had become one of Flint's favourite pastimes. Indeed the idea of actually being paid in silver, women, boys and booze to do it was like a dream come true. Of course, this was on top of the fact that Flint also actually liked his master. Dashwood snapped the locket shut.

"Those days are gone boy, never to return, the mighty Highlanders have been scattered to the winds by those bastards in the house of Hanover, sold into the slave markets of the Caribbean and America, never to return!" The Lord lowered his voice, "The new rebels are to be found amongst the colonials in the new world, and if there is anyone that could overthrow the crown of England, it is surely them." Flint nodded agreement. The two sat listening to the dog barking its frustration at the other end of the room. "Tell me Flint, Lord Percy, where is he? More importantly, where is my gold?" Flint leant forwards in order to speak into his master's ear over the din. The growing female screams and barking had risen gradually, until now the bestiality show on the alter, threatened to deafen the whole group inside the old church.

"Och . . . I was gony tell ye . . . Lord Percy is dead."

"Dead?"

"Yes, my Lord, those Brummie savages fed him to their dogs." Lord Dashwood frowned.

"Dogs?"

"Ai dogs, big bastard dogs, they ate him!" Lord Francis stared at the servant with some disbelief.

"Why Flint, why?" The servant nudged up the bench a little closer to the elderly man.

"He turned up at the Rookery without our boxer O'Donahue and Mr Black Foot decided to make an example of him." Lord Dashwood shook his head in confusion.

"Turned up without O'Donahue, what the fuck did he do that for?" The old man took a gulp of port, "So where's the Irishman now?" He spluttered the claret liquid, which dribbled down the sides of his face as his anger grew. Flint smiled.

"According to our man in Birmingham, Lord Percy was robbed by two highwaymen on his way to the fight. O'Donahue knocked one out but . . . " Flint raised his eyebrows. "And you'll find this wee detail very interesting me lud . . . the big Irishman was knocked out cold by the second highwayman, broke his jaw apparently." Lord Francis stared at him, unable to comprehend the words, finally repeating.

"Broke his jaw, what do you mean he broke his jaw? O'Donahue was in the top three pugilists in England, how could some highway robber break his fucking jaw? The bloody thing was made out of granite for God's sake!" Flint nodded.

"Ai . . . very true my Lord, I've seen that big Irish bastard take a punch that would kill an ox and still would ne go down, it does ne make any sense!" Lord Dashwood snarled.

"Well, it had better start making sense Flint, I want my fucking gold back or we're done for, I don't fancy spending my remaining days in the debtors' jail!" Flint saw his master's mood blacken and unconsciously felt the need to reassure Lord Dashwood that he could deal with the situation. However, there was more bad news to come.

"It gets stranger me lud." Dashwood scowled.

"*Stranger*, how the fuck could it get stranger? They fed poor Lord Percy to a fucking dog, Flint, a dog!"

"The Highway man me lord, the one O'Donahue knocked out . . . " Dashwood drained his goblet and handed it to Flint. The servant poured another cupful and placed it back in front of the indignant Lord.

"Yes, yes, go on, man."

"The Highway man was none other than Captain Henry Sykes, my lord."

"Henry Sykes?"

"Ai, *the* Captain Henry Sykes the same one that scammed your lordship out of a hundred gold guineas and a commission in your Royal regiment two years ago." The old man perked up at the sound of the highwayman's name.

"Yes, yes, I know him now Flint, cheeky bastard as I recall. You have him?" Flint shook his head.

"Nay not yet but I'm putting things in place to find out what happened to your gold and to get Captain Henry-fucking-Sykes back into our hands for a wee bit of . . . "

Dashwood cut him short.

"Punishment and revenge Flint, punishment and revenge!" The servant nodded.

"I was thinking, maybe we could use Lord Harrington's dogs for a bit of entertainment other than fucking wee tarts me Lord!" Dashwood burst into laughter.

"Yes, Flint, that's the style man. We'll feed the bastard to *our* dogs, let's see how they like it!" William Flint smiled.

"I was hoping you'd say that, I've already got a crew bought and paid for me lord."

Lord Dashwood scowled.

"You mean *I've* got a crew bought and paid for Flint, I commend your organisational skills but be careful with my cash Flint. I've already wasted enough gold on this debacle without my manservant blowing my ill-gotten gains on a mob of horrible bastards!" Dashwood turned on Flint with an inquisitive eye. "I trust they *are* horrible bastards Flint?" The manservant broke into a handsome, yet brutal grin. The lord's heart fluttered at Flint's roguish smile.

"Och ai me Lord, I dug em out meself, nasty horrible cunts to a man." Flint saw his master's eye wander over the gap in his open shirt, Flint recognised the glimmer in the old man's eye and pulled the garment collar apart slightly exposing his bronzed skin beneath. "I'll be leaving for Birmingham in the wee hours." Lord Dashwood nodded, barely hearing his servant's words over the howling dog at the far end of the church, his attention captured by the sight of Flint's pectorals, the first tinglings of arousal creeping into the old man's loins. Flint smiled . "Would ye like me to . . . ?" Dashwood cut him short.

"I hope you're going to deal with this Black Foot character. I want my fucking gold back Flint." Lord Dashwood's eyes flickered with excitement in the dim light as Flint's hand slid from his chest to his groin. The lord's eye followed his hand as it disappeared beneath the table, where it came to rest on the buttons of the

Lord's breeches. The dog began to whelp in the background as Lord Harrington kicked the beast, becoming impatient with the dog's refusal to shag. Without breaking his stare, Dashwood continued,

"And Henry Sykes, Flint, don't forget our little captain, I want to see him bleed Flint, bleed!" The old man stopped talking as the manservant released the buttons on his crotch and dug inside the doe-skin breeches, finally releasing his master's semi-erect manhood. The lord's eyes became two thin lines of intense desire as he stared deeply into Flint's. Holding his penis with one hand, Flint reached with his other across the table and pulled Lord Dashwood's hand towards him. Guiding the old man's hand to his groin, the old man grabbed the servant's erect manhood and began to pull and push it vigorously, "The man that broke O'Donahue's jaw. I want to know who he is, find him and bring him to me! If he can beat the Irishman, he can beat others . . . that's worth gold Flint, gold!"

"And if he will nay fight me Lord?"

"It's not a question of *if* he'll fight Flint but *who* he'll fight and how we can profit from it!"

Dashwood's eyes became two, thin, cunning lines, their watery pupils glistening beneath the lids. The talk of rebellion had stirred a feeling deep inside of him, a feeling he hadn't felt since the days of the 1745 rebellion and it made him feel young again. As if he were still aboard the brigantine on his way to help the Scots all those years ago and somewhere inside that feeling there was a thought, a thought of a new rebellion, only this one would come from the new world and it would start with a single punch that would shake the house of Hanover to the ground. A punch that would come, not from an English champion but a rebel, an American rebel.

The trap is sprung

CHAPTER 12

The clatter and chatter of three hundred or so men, women, mollies and rakes rang around the tall, brick walls of the Rookery in a cacophony of sound, punctuated every now and then by the howling of a crazed dog or scream of an affronted whore.

At the feet of the oblivious revellers, a carpet of long, grey, greasy rats, scampered this way and that, enjoying the festivities almost as much as the humans as they fed on the abandoned slops of chicken, bacon and bread. A flock of grime-covered pigeons watched from their shit-covered perches on the rafters of the old building, as the mass of life below danced around each other in the never ending opera of the poor and wicked. Even above the stink of humans, animals, tobacco smoke, food and shit, the excitement in the room was almost palpable as the colourful beehive of humanity awaited the arrival of their beggar king, William Black Foot.

Henry Sykes's cage had been dragged to the centre of the room and stood beside the gaming pit covered in slops of food thrown at it by the baying mob. Sykesy sat on the bench, head in his hands, his hat pulled low over his eyes, trying to protect himself from the barrage of food and spit thrown and spat at him by the cruel throng. The last twenty-four hours had been stressful, to say the least, and if the tension inside the cage was bad enough, it was nothing in comparison to the tension that had built up inside

Henry's head, which the unfortunate highwayman thought would explode at any moment under the constant harassment from his jailers. The bombardment had turned his fear of the gallows into one not so dreadful, and he found himself almost looking forward to the noose around his neck.

A loud cheer from the crowd brought Henry out of his nightmare and back to the moment. The barrage of slops stopped momentarily, giving the caged man enough time to raise the brim of his saliva-covered, tricorn hat. He could see the crowd had turned towards the huge doorway as their master Black Foot and his beautiful nymph-like daughter made their entrance into the chaos. Sykesy watched as the gang-leader parted the crowd with his very presence, like some sort of gangster Moses parting a sea of peasants. Henry couldn't actually see the gang-leader from his position, all he could see was the heads of the throng stepping aside as the beggar king came near and then suddenly, he was there, in front of the bars of Sykes's cage. Henry automatically stood up and bowed his head. Black Foot nodded and tapped the cage with his cane.

"Ah, the highwayman!" He said, trying to adopt an aristocratic air, but only managing to make his thick, Brummie accent sound ridiculous. Henry pulled his hat from his head, his eyes lowered subserviently. Sykesy hated people like William Black Foot. The robber had a natural dislike for anyone who thought they were born better and therefore had the right to look down their nose at those less fortunate. There was a time and a place for such feelings though, and however much it turned his stomach to bow to such a man, Henry's instincts for survival had subconsciously taken over, and so he bowed his head lower as the gang-leader spoke again.

"Captain Henry Sykes at your service sir!" Black Foot laughed at the man's attempt at elegance.

"Captain?" The word seemed to surprise Black Foot momentarily. "I didn't realise you were a military man sir, I dare say we have much in common, what a shame we shall not have the time to share our battle stories." Sykesy smiled weakly, hiding his lack of battlefield stories as best he could. "However, you are our guest of honour tonight my dear Captain!" He turned to the crowd triumphantly and scanning the eager expressions on the men around the Rookery, he could see that the crowd were a new bunch, only recognising a few familiar faces in the mob. Turning, he looked above him at the men peering over the bannisters on the mezzanine level. He didn't see anyone he knew there either. The usual dandies on the raised floor above him were intermingled with another crowd, a rough-looking bunch, many of whom were wearing black neck-scarves around their shirt-collars instead of the customary white ones as worn by almost everyone at that time. The black-scarfed men stood in groups of four or five along the railings. "Who are this lot above us? I ain't seen any of em before?" Black Foot asked his burly minders who then glanced at the men above him.

"I don't know Mr Black Foot, sir. They just started to show up in small groups, we didn't notice them until they were almost filling the place." Black Foot scowled.

"Filling the place?" The minder nodded.

"Yes, sir, they're all wearing black neck-scarves sir!" The gang-leader looked around himself once more, only this time, he could see the small groups of men in the black scarves, scattered throughout the warehouse. His senses prickled at the sight of the ruffians.

"How did you not notice this lot getting in? Who are they anyway, have you asked?" The big man shook his head.

"I dunno who they are Mr Black Foot sir, as I said, they came in small groups and there must be thirty or forty of em." Black Foot's eyes darted around him, trying to make sense of the situation, realising he was being watched by the groups of black-scarfed men, he smiled, before whispering to his minder.

"Well, just keep and eye on em, they might be here to free this bastard!" He nodded slightly towards the highwayman, as he did, Henry caught his first glimpse of Eleanor standing behind her father. The sight of the young woman in the blood-red gown stopped his heart momentarily, literally making him step backwards with shock. Whether it was the filthy surroundings of the Rookery or perhaps the deformed ugliness of the crowds that crowded around the woman, the effect was the same. The contrast between the girl's perfection and the filth around her seemed to make her glow in the candlelight like some sort of supernatural vision in red. Captain Henry Sykes fell for the charms of Eleanor Black Foot, and like every other man in the warehouse, he felt as if his feelings would somehow be reciprocated if he could just get the chance to speak to her. Henry stood up.

"My lady!" He said, sweeping his saliva-covered tricorn from his head once more, he bowed lowly to the girl. Eleanor giggled at Sykesy as if he were a monkey that had learned a new trick. Black Foot turned to his audience.

"This Highwayman is to be given anything he wants tonight. He is a man in a special place, somewhere we shall all find ourselves someday, somewhere between the veils of life and death, for tomorrow he will *hang*!" He shouted the last word triumphantly. A loud cheer surged from the Rookery's regulars at the very mention of a hanging. The gang-leader watched the faces of the black scarves for any indication as to their intent but found none. He turned back to the caged man and said under his breath.

"You will hang Captain, that is unless your associate turns up and frees you, which is looking highly unlikely at the moment sunshine, so it is!" Black Foot held his hand up as if holding an imaginary rope around his neck, he yanked on the spirit rope whilst at the same time crossing his eyes and letting his tongue flop from his mouth with a loud comical groan. Sykesy didn't hear the man. He hadn't taken his eyes from Eleanor's face, who it must be said, was enjoying the handsome captain's gaze and was returning his stare with a playful look of her own. Black Foot stopped talking when he saw this. He turned to Eleanor.

"For God's sake girl!" He said sarcastically. "Leave the poor bastard some dignity!" He turned back to Sykesy.

"A bit of advice for you Captain, I wouldn't get any ideas about my daughter. I've got a feeling that unless we see a miracle tonight, you're not long for this world!" He rapped the cage with one of his large, gold rings and gave Sykesy a smirk. "Bring him some ale and food!" Nodding his approval to the caged man, he walked away towards his table with a self-assured grin, dragging Eleanor away from the star-crossed highwayman.

****

Thomas, Edward and Bridget approached the Rookery with some trepidation. The dark streets of the Froggery area of Birmingham were dodgy, to say the least. Limbless beggars, desperate cut-pockets and down on their luck prostitutes were just some of the residents of the old, run-down, Jewish quarter. The trio picked their way through the horse-shit and cobbled-stone streets towards the Rookery. The sound of laughter and music could be heard from a few streets away, echoing in and out of the alleyways and lanes. Thomas had a sinking feeling in his stomach.

"I thought Brother Tumbold would be coming Edward?" Edward shook his head.

"Yeah, me too but he's just vanished, no one's seen him since this morning."

"Tumbold, who's he?" Bridget enquired.

"*Brother* Tumbold to the likes of us Bridget . . . !" Thomas laughed.

"Brother Tumbold?" The girl said, bemused.

"Yes, Brother Tumbold, he's my sponsor, he's the one that saved my soul!" Edward said, an innocent smile growing across his face.

"Saved your soul!" Thomas laughed. "I doubt it, brother. I've heard about these priests, the only soul he's interested in Edward is your arsehole!" Thomas burst into laughter at his own joke, Edward shuffled ahead, his smile gone, already bored with his brother's banter.

"Brother Tumbold isn't a priest, he's a . . . " Bridget cut him short.

" . . . a Quaker, yes, we understand Edward, don't let your oaf of a brother wind you up!" She slapped Thomas's arm, trying to hide a smile. Thomas returned the slap, with a crafty wink and a smile of his own, all three trying to hide the feeling of dread that was slowly creeping into the pits of their stomachs as they approached their destination. "Anyway, we're here," Bridget said in a low tone, just stopping short of a crossroads ahead of them. The trio stood in the shadow of an abandoned building on the corner of the dimly lit street. The only light came from the bright winter's moon which had broken through the snow-clouds, shining its pristine, blue light down upon the grime of the Froggery. Thomas peered around the corner of the street into the shadowy gloom that hung around the Rookery like a black cloak. He could see the carriages coming and going dropping their upper-class punters outside the huge, doors of the venue. They had been painted in a bright shade of red which stood out dramatically against the contrasting filth of their surroundings, and even in the moonlight, the doors seemed to make a statement about the depravity that lay within. Thomas could make out a shape painted in black on the door's long timbers. After a few seconds he was able to see that it was a painting of a bird, a rook, its wings spread across the huge doors with its head turned to the side. From its beak in a darker shade of red were blood-drops falling down the door's length to the ground.

"That looks welcoming!" He exclaimed, Bridget laughed. She turned to Edward, who had an ashen-grey hue.

"Are you all right Edward?" He nodded reluctantly.

"You look like you're about to be sick!" Thomas patted his younger brother. "Come on, it ain't gonna be that bad." Thomas's huge hands gripped his brother's shoulders and gave him a friendly shake, trying to shake him from his fear-induced trance.

"I mean, what's the worst that can happen?" Thomas said cheerfully, Bridget and Edward turned to the big man.

"What's the worst that can happen? Did you actually just say that?" Edward asked incredulously.

"William Black Foot!" Bridget said, matter of factly. "It don't get much worse than him." She turned to the men. "Come on, it's your funeral!"

****

The gloriously chaotic atmosphere inside the venue washed over Thomas the moment he stepped over the threshold of the Rookery. He cursed himself for not having visited the place before. The filthy dilapidation he'd witnessed during his daytime visit to his caged friend had been replaced with one of joyful, hedonistic exuberance. A celebration of depravity that was right up Thomas's street, if only he was there under different circumstances. The trio shuffled as best they could through the crowd towards Henry's cage at the edge of the gaming pit. Thomas didn't know if it was his rising paranoia but he could feel the gaze of a hundred eyes upon him as he pushed through the milling crowd. On seeing his friend Sykesy he stood unsteadily and crossed to the cage's bars.

"Thomas!" Sykesy shouted, a broad smile on his face. "You're here mate, I thought you'd done a bunk!" Thomas was horrified by his friend's outburst.

"Shh . . . for God's sake, otherwise we'll both end up in that bleeding cage!" He pulled the brim of his hat lower and glanced around him to see if his presence had been noticed.

"Ah, don't worry about this lot Thomas!" Henry flayed his arm around grandly at the crowd around the cage who were chatting, drinking and smoking their long, clay pipes and cigars. "They don't give a fuck, they're all too pissed to care about anything. Look, they keep giving me coins, they think it'll bring em luck giving a condemned man a silver coin." He held a handful of coins out towards Thomas. "I'm fucking loaded Thomas!" The big man rolled his eyes.

"Yes, I can see that Sykesy, perhaps you can spend it on the way to the gallows tomorrow?" Henry laughed and pocketed the coins.

"That's *exactly* what I intend to do Thomas, Mr. Black Foot has arranged for me to visit his tailor tomorrow morning and have a new suit of clothes for my appearance at the tree. Very kind of him, don't you think mate?" Thomas sighed impatiently.

"How very considerate of him Henry!" Thomas's patience finally snapped. "You're bleeding pissed aren't you? I told you *not* to get drunk!" Thomas's words didn't register with the caged man who had just noticed Thomas's new suit and companions.

"Well, la-de-fucking da, look at you, I see you've already got yourself some new togs; brown leather from top to toe, very nice, tough but elegant, very nice, although it has to be said, you resemble a fucking lizard!" Thomas, suddenly felt conspicuous in his new outfit. Sykesy had already moved on to his friend's companions. "Hello darling!" He said to Bridget who was peeking from behind Thomas at him. She nodded and smiled uncertainly.

"Come and give a dead man a kiss, it'll bring ya good luck!" Sykesy laughed. Bridget tugged Thomas's arm.

"He's blind drunk Thomas, he's gonna be no help whatsoever." Thomas nodded.

"Yeah, I know that much. I'm in half a mind to turn around and leave the twat where he is!" Bridget's brow furrowed.

"You can't do that, we gotta at least *try* and free him!" Thomas laughed.

"*I was joking!*" He said turning to Edward. "Come here, brother!" Edward stepped towards the cage. Thomas introduced his younger brother to his friend inside the cage. "Henry, this is Edward. He's the Quaker I told you about. He'll talk on our behalf with this Black Foot fellow and bargain your freedom."

"A *Quaker?*" Sykesy sniggered. "They already have a Quaker Thomas." He gestured with his thumb towards the milling crowd behind him. Thomas and Edward began to search the faces but couldn't make out anyone in particular. Sykesy turned and pointed towards the risen table on the other side of the gaming pit. "Over there, the chubby bastard at Black Foot's table!" The three turned towards the direction of Sykes's pointing finger.

"Shit!" Bridget turned back immediately. "They're watching *us*." Edward looked confused for a second before breaking into a smile of recognition.

"*Brother Tumbold!*" He shouted over the din, waving at the tubby Quaker who returned his smile with a glaring grimace. Edward watched as the Quaker leant across the table towards a large, dark-haired, bizarre-looking man who was wearing too much makeup. He sat in a huge, ornate wooden chair, his legged draped over one of its arms. The Quaker whispered into the man's ear and as he did, Black Foot turned his gaze to the trio by the cage. Edward smiled and waved again.

"It's ok Thomas, it seems Brother Tumbold has already sorted things out for us. He's talking to someone that looks very important." Bridget grabbed Edward's arm and pulled it to his side.

"Shut the fuck up Edward! You're confusing *important* with dangerous, that's Black Foot!"

"Brother Tumbold is here to help us Bridget, you must have faith!" Edward said shaking the woman's arm off. Thomas watched with a growing feeling of dread as Black Foot rose from the chair and leaning forward swept the decanters and food to one side of the table forcing the expensive-looking cut glass decanter over the edge of the table where it fell, in an explosion of port and glass onto the stone floor. The noise of the smashing glass caught the attention of Black Foot's inner circle of associates, a nasty-looking bunch of scruffy minders and over-dressed whores who all turned to see what the disturbance was. The tubby Quaker left the table and began to push his way through the crowd towards the cage followed by two of the burly minders who swept the tightly packed punters aside with their thick-set arms. The dark-haired man rose from his ornate throne and stepped onto the table, and as he did, a hush began to spread through the throngs of people. Bridget came in close to Thomas.

"I recognise that Quaker. He's always down here, ogling the girls and young lads. He's a right creepy old sod!" Edward overheard the girl's words and became angry.

"Brother Tumbold is a true Christian, he would never *ogle* anyone!" Bridget turned on him with an angry look of her own.

"I know what I've seen Edward. Your brother Tumbold is about as much a Christian as I am!" Just as Bridget finished her sentence, Brother Tumbold and the four minders broke through the crowd and into the small space around the cage. Bridget O'Hara stepped into Thomas's shadow, hanging her head subserviently as the tubby man approached. Edward scowled at the girl before crossing to his Quaker associate, a friendly smile breaking across his face as he did so.

"Brother Tumbold, I am so pleased to see . . ." a huge arm belonging to one of the minders reached across his chest and stopped him in his tracks. The old Quaker stood for a second, his cunning little eyes scanning the group, finally settling on Bridget. The tubby Quaker's bright blue eyes were now just dark, untrusting slits in his swollen rosy-cheeked face. He stared at the girl's breasts for a few seconds entranced by the mocha-coloured orbs encased in the lowered bosom line of her red gown. The hush became absolute silence that spread through the room into every corner of the building as if the punters of the Rookery had been waiting for this moment all night. Thomas's eyes darted this way and that beneath the brim of his leather tricorn hat trying to work out exactly what was going on as the now familiar feeling of dread, he'd felt so often over the last couple of days, began to create a void in his stomach once more. The ugly, pockmarked, toothless faces of the mob stared back at him in silence. Even the billowing tobacco smoke that hung a foot or two over the heads of the resentful faces seemed to become absolutely still as the crowd waited with bated breath to see what would happen next.

"*Well?*" Black Foot shouted from his table. "Which one is it?" Tumbold shook himself out of his breast-induced stupor and placed his hand on Thomas's shoulder.

"This one Mr Black Foot, sir!" Bridget half turned towards Edward.

"You've led us into a fucking trap!" Thomas brushed the Quaker's hand from his shoulder.

"Bridget, my brother may be a fool but he ain't no traitor. If this *is* a trap then it's not of his making." Then turning to Tumbold he said. "If you lay your grubby little hands on me one more time, I'll tear your arm off and stick it so far up your arse you'll be able to pick the food out of your teeth from the inside!" The silence was broken by Sykes's manacles rattling against the bars of his cage.

"Is that the Quaker you said was gonna free me Thomas?" Sykesy said incredulously. Thomas, now under no illusions as to which side Brother Tumbold was on, rolled his eyes and sighed his reply.

"Yep, that's him!" Henry sniggered sarcastically.

"Stroll on!" he said pointing at the chubby man. "This is the God-botherer you was telling me about today, the one who was meant to be me Christian saviour, gonna barter for me life with Black Foot?" He slurred angrily. "Well, fuck me, I'm as good as bleeding dead!" He shuffled back to his bench and slumped down inside his cage, head in hands, trying to come to terms with the sudden realisation that his oncoming demise was all too real. Black Foot became impatient.

"Bring him over here and let's get a good gander at this scrapper!" Thomas was suddenly grabbed from behind by two of the large minders. He made a brief struggle but when the men were joined by two more ugly brutes, he realised there was no point trying to resist. The jaws of the trap had been sprung and Thomas Fewtrell was well and truly caught in its teeth. The mob, who it seemed had been holding their collective breaths, suddenly burst into a loud cheer.

"Brother Tumbold!" Edward shouted. "How could you betray us like this?" The Quaker laughed and grabbed Bridget's arm.

"God helps those that help themselves Edward, you'd do well to remember that." Edward stepped between the man and the girl bringing his face into the other man's.

"Judas!" He snarled.

"Judas . . . ha, do me a favour boy, Judas sold himself cheap, thirty pieces of silver!" He sniggered. "I'll be getting a purse full of gold for this." He pushed the shocked young Quaker out of his way and pulled the girl towards him. "And this little tart will be included in my price!" Stepping away from the man, Tumbold dragged Bridget through the crowd towards Black Foot's table following the path through the mob created by the minders and their captive. Reaching the table, Thomas was thrown to the floor, cutting his hands on the shattered glass around table as he landed. Black Foot stared down from the table at the young man on his knees. One of the minders pulled the hat from the kneeling man's head before grabbing a clump of hair on the back of Thomas's head and pulling it back, forcing him to look up at the gang-leader. The two men stared at each other for a few seconds, weighing each other up. Black Foot stood tall on the table above him and Thomas thought that, even though the man was in his mid fifties, and even taking into account that he had tried to gentrify himself with blusher, powder and a small beauty spot on his chin, he still looked like a tough old bastard and must have been a handful of trouble in his younger days.

The gang-leader pointed down from his elevated view towards Thomas but addressed Tumbold.

"This is him?" The Quaker, who had now joined the small group around the table, Bridget still clenched tightly in his right hand nodded.

"Yes, Mr. Black Foot sir, this is the fellow." Tumbold raised his voice so all could hear. "This is the second highwayman!" The regulars amongst the crowd cheered at his words. The small groups of men wearing black neck-scarves began to gather together within the mass forming larger groups of ten or more, scattered around the old warehouse. Tumbold continued. "This is the man that beat London's best!" Another cheer rang around the building. Tumbold looked around him at the smiling faces as the crowd swayed with excitement, arms reaching from the throng, patting his shoulders and back. As the cheers began to quieten, Tumbold turned towards Black Foot.

"You say this is the man that beat James O'Donahue?" Tumbold nodded.

"All I know is this is the man that came to my house asking for help to free his friend, the man in the cage. So if this is the second highwayman, then it stands to reason, sir . . . " Tumbold raised his free arm and staring at the roof of the Rookery as if talking to God himself, shouted triumphantly, " . . . that *this* must be the man that beat the Londoner, James O'Donahue?" He brought his arm down in a dramatic sweep and pointed to the back of Thomas's head.

Black Foot jumped from the table landing in the shattered glass in his heavy knee-length boots. He crossed to Thomas bent down to him and pushing the large minder's hands away, helped Thomas to his feet.

"Let him up, let him up!" He scowled at the minders, who all stepped away from him, fearful expressions on their faces as if he were a wild dog. "Give him some space, you wretches, back I say, *back*!" The mob began to shuffle backwards crowding together even tighter than they already were. "I need to see him!" Thomas stood a head taller than his captor. Black Foot stood directly in front of him, his eyes running over the man's chest, slowly raising his head until he looked directly into Thomas's face. He leant in close to Thomas and whispered. "Did you beat the Londoner?" Thomas blinked away the salty beads that had now begun to roll from his brow. He knew there was no point denying anything so he answered as truthfully as he could.

"Truly, I don't know what the fuck you're talking about?" Black Foot became animated.

"Don't fuck around boy, the man on the highway, was it you that broke his jaw?" Thomas shrugged.

"I hit someone, a big bloke he was, but he weren't no Londoner, he was Irish or at least that's what it sounded like to me." Black Foot's eyes lit up at his words.

"And was it you who broke the jaws of the driver and guard?" Thomas shook his head.

"No, that was the Irishman, he did that, although, the punch that did the damage *was* aimed at me." Black Foot's voice changed to a more questioning tone.

"So was it just a lucky punch or could you do it again?" The larger man looked down at the gang-leader and shrugged.

"I don't know, if it were the same situation, I may be able to do it again." Black Foot smiled.

"Ah, I see, so it *was* a lucky punch!" Thomas shook his head.

"I didn't say that, I said . . . " Black Foot cut him off.

"What say you daughter was it a lucky punch my dear? Shall we let him try his lucky punch against *the Bear* or maybe just hang him *and* his companion for highway robbery?" Eleanor had risen from the table and joined her father in the circle of people. She thought the question over for a second, all the while, staring at Thomas's shadowed face intensely.

"I say we free the man in the cage and make this fellow fight the bear." The girl's answer caught her father by surprise.

"Free the highwayman, you say and why would we do that?" Eleanor smiled.

"This one . . . " she pointed at Sykesy who had risen from his bench and was watching the proceedings with a growing mixture of hope for himself and concern for his friend, " . . . is an honest thief, he is a highwayman and was caught robbing the King's Royal Mail coach and when I look around this room I can see many amongst us that would deserve death far more than this honest thief father, especially one that robs the King's highway!" She began to search the faces of the crowd who all began to lower their heads lest they should be recognised by the girl for some crime or other. Black Foot nodded, "Besides father, you made a deal." She crossed to her father and ran her elegant finger along her father's powdered chin, smirking at him lovingly. "You did say that if the highwayman's accomplice showed up tonight, you would free him, did you not father?"

"I don't recall making any such deal but I do recall promising our friends here a hanging." Many of the watching crowd began to nod eagerly. He turned to Edward. "What about him? Shall we hang a Quaker instead?"

"Why don't we concentrate on the boxing father *that's* what our friends want to see, is it not?" She spun around and shouted her words. The crowd erupted, cheering whilst the Gentry on the higher, mezzanine level broke into more refined applause craning over the bannister rail to watch the scene from above. The black-scarfed men scattered around the room, just watched, hidden within the throng.

Black Foot nodded, and he slapped Thomas's back.

"Will you fight sir?" Thomas stared blankly at the gang-leader's powdered face, shrugged and raised his eyebrows in a non-committal way. Black Foot's face dropped to a scowl.

"Maybe I should rephrase my question?" He crossed to one of his minders and pulled a long pistol from the man's belt. Levelling the flintlock at Thomas's head he pulled the hammer back with a loud click. "You *will* fight sir!" The room fell silent. Eleanor suddenly stepped towards her father and raised one hand to the pistol's long barrel and with her other hand, she cradled Thomas's sharp jaw. Pushing the barrel downwards, she stood on her tiptoes and whispered into the young man's ear. Black Foot let the gun drop, a bemused expression growing on his face. The girl grabbed Thomas's thick arm for balance bringing herself even closer to his ear. She stood teetering next to him, her beautiful face next to his, talking in a low tone. He bent to hear her words, and as he did, her perfume washed over him in a wave of wild flowers and desire, the delicate scent contrasted against the stink of the Rookery, its intensity almost making him swoon. Thomas turned to face the girl. Their faces only inches apart, their lips almost touching. She reached up and pushed the hair back from his brow, and for the first time she could see his handsome features, his face suddenly free of the hair's shadow. The sight of the man seemed to take the breath from the girl who froze for a second. Thomas stared into the girl's bright eyes, and in those few seconds, the world seemed to grow still for the pair. Every other person in the Rookery seemed to melt into a blurred, distant backdrop of filth and grime, as Thomas and Eleanor stood alone amid the mass of watching men and women, both of them helplessly trapped in each other's gaze. Black Foot stood in a stupefied astonishment, blinking his eyes as if trying to shake the image. The gang-leader's face began to take on a purple glow as the anger within him grew. He raised the pistol to the back of Thomas's head, his eyes glaring with rage.

"Take your eyes off my fucking daugh . . . !"

"*Mr William Black Foot*!" A man's voice rang out over the scene. "Mr Black Foot!"

He turned to see a short, dark man with a long, black ponytail approach him, accompanied by a huge, red-haired man, both were well dressed. The man's voice had a hint of an accent, Black Foot couldn't work out if it were Spanish or Portuguese. His rage suddenly suspended, he dropped the gun again as he studied the two uncertainly, his eyes darting between the two men in an animalistic, distrustful way. "My name is Daniel Mendoza." The small man continued, bowing slightly, removing his tall hat as he did, sweeping it before him as if addressing a king. Standing straight again, he turned to his huge companion. "And this is my associate, James O'Donahue, the famous London pugilist." Black Foot perked up at the mention of the Irishman's name. O'Donahue bowed with a little less elegance than his friend. Black Foot shook his head.

"James O'Donahue, you say?" both men nodded.

"Yes, the very same!" Mendoza smiled. Black Foot's face returned to its usual magnanimous expression.

"Well, you're a bit fucking late ain't ya? You were meant to be here *last* night!"

Mendoza bowed again.

"Yes, Mr Black Foot, but the unfortunate delay couldn't have been foreseen." Black Foot's expression became darker. A hubbub of mumbling spread throughout the watching crowd. The men in the black scarves began to stir, grouping together secretly in larger numbers.

"Unfortunate for who, Mr . . . ?"

" . . . Mendoza sir, at your service!" The Portuguese bowed slightly again, all the time never losing his controlled smile as he spoke.

"Mr *Mendoza* unfortunate for me, I had money on the bout and O'Donahue's absence meant I couldn't collect my winnings, *sir* . . . " The gang-leader began to smile manically, " . . . and it was even more unfortunate for that silly, fuck-wit Lord Percy you sent on behalf of the Hellfire club. I had to feed that cunt to my dogs." Eleanor spoke up.

"Maybe they've come for Lord Percy's gold father?" Black Foot reached for his daughter's hand, she didn't move. Black Foot glared at her surprised by his daughter's reluctance to leave Thomas's side.

"Yes, maybe they have." Turning to Mendoza, he enquired. "Well, have you come for . . . ?" Mendoza shook his head.

"No, we are not after gold, we are here for something far more important than that." Black Foot's brow furrowed.

"More important than gold?" he shook his head in puzzlement. "And what be God, is more important than gold?" Mendoza ignored the question, turning to O'Donahue he gestured towards Thomas.

"Is this the man James?" The big Irishman shrugged, his flame-red mop of hair hung around his brutal face as he examined the man. "It's hard to say Daniel, his face was covered, but he *is* the right build." O'Donahue leant forward and squeezed Thomas's thick bicep. "Yeah, I'd say this man has the power in his arm to be a fighter." Black Foot snarled.

"Don't ignore me, *sir*!" He stepped forward. Mendoza stepped into meet him, all the time the line of minders separating the two groups.

"I shall speak plainly to you, Mr Black Foot. Gold is important to you, is it not?" Mendoza asked, his eyebrows raised in question. Black Foot nodded.

"Gold? Of course it's important to me, it's important to every man in here!"

"Are you aware of the old story of the goose that lays the golden eggs Mr Black Foot?" The gang-leader began to lose his patience.

"Golden fucking goose, do I look like the type of person that reads nursery rhymes? If you don't start making sense soon, you'll be joining Lord Percy in that pile of dog shit in the corner!" Another murmur rose from the crowd. The men in scarves began to huddle closer together. Black Foot was too immersed in the conversation with the Portuguese man to notice.

Mendoza smiled and continued, unfazed by Black Foot's anger.

"It is the story of a goose that lays golden eggs . . . "

" . . . I know what the fucking story is, what the fuck has it got to do with *him?*" He levelled his finger towards Thomas. Mendoza knew he'd pushed the man as far as he could take him.

"If you shoot this man . . . " the dark-haired man stared straight at Eleanor and Thomas, but addressed her father, " . . . then sir, you are shooting the golden goose!" Black Foot stared blankly at him. "This man bettered my friend James O'Donahue by dislocating his jaw." The Irishman bristled at the words, turning to stare at the highwayman who seemed to be lost for words in the middle of the circle. "I am a pugilist myself Mr Black Foot, and I know what I am talking about sir, I trained this man to fight myself, and I have seen him battle against bigger men than this, this . . . " he seemed stuck for a description, Black Foot finished his sentence,

" . . . *usurper!*" Mendoza could see that Black Foot was upset and his words were aimed more towards his daughter's attraction to the young highwayman, than anything to do with the subject at hand. Mendoza smiled.

"Ah young love, even the devil cannot control love." The gang-leader's indignant stare turned on the dark man in front of him.

"Young love?" He said, almost incapable of understanding what the Portuguese was saying.

"Young love, someday I hope to be a father myself sir, so understand how hard it must be to let go of ..."

"I'm letting go of nothing sir. My daughter may enjoy flirtations sir but I see the lad for what he is, a robber on the make hoping to steal my daughter away from me. Something he's going to find very difficult to do with no head on his fucking shoulders!"

"So you mean to shoot him?" Mendoza enquired.

"Shoot him, no sir, I intend to watch the Bear rip his fucking head off in the gaming pit, that is what I intend to do!" Mendoza turned to O'Donahue and patted his friend's shoulder.

"Well, Mr Black Foot, this highwayman landed a punch on my friend's jaw so hard it dislocated it completely, something no one else has been able to do in over twenty fights."

"It was a lucky punch, nothing more!" Black Foot sighed.

"Not according to my friend, it was a well-timed and well-aimed punch." Eleanor butted in.

"Let him go free, I like him father!" Black Foot ignored her.

"You say he can fight?" Mendoza nodded.

"Yes, sir, based on what James has told me, I think he can." Black Foot looked over the young man.

"Maybe he *can* fight, but *will* he fight?" Edward patted his brother's shoulder.

"Of course he'll bloody fight, won't you Thomas?" Mendoza crossed to the younger man. "Will you fight Thomas?" Thomas gave Eleanor a quick glance. The girl stared up at him, her pale skin glowing in the yellow candlelight.

"Will you fight Thomas?" She said softly, Thomas tore himself away from Eleanor's beauty with a deep sigh.

"Do I get a bloody choice in this?" Black Foot laughed, raising his voice to the crowd.

"Oh, you've got a choice all right." He raised the gun back towards Thomas's head. "You can fight or I can blow your fucking head off. It's up to you sonny!"

"Oh, well now you've put it like that." Thomas laughed. "Of

course I'll fight, but you'll have to release Sykesy first!" Black Foot pushed past the minders.

"You ain't in any position to make demands sunshine." Thomas nodded towards Henry.

"That may be the case Mr Black Foot but I ain't gonna fight anyone until Henry Sykes is set free. As your daughter said, you made a deal with him that if I showed up here tonight, you would release him, well, here I am. Anyway, we didn't rob you did we? So there ain't no reason he should hang, is there?" Black Foot stared at the young man and Thomas could see that the gang-leader was mulling the idea of pardoning Sykesy over. He decided to press the point.

"If you let him go, I'll fight any bastard you want!" Although Black Foot couldn't remember making any such deal with Sykesy. He glanced at his daughter who smiled back at him and nodded towards the man in the cage.

"Free the robber and let's see the lad fight!" Someone shouted from the crowd.

"Let him fight!" Another screamed from the mezzanine above. Black Foot could feel the mood in the room change as the volume of the punters' protests grew. He stared around the room and could see that he was no longer in control of the room. The power in the Rookery had shifted to the mob. Recognising the danger in fighting against the shifting tide, Black Foot turned, climbed back onto his throne and held his hands in front of him, quelling the rising tempers of the throng.

"Ok, ok, my friends, calm yourselves." He could see more and more of the black-scarved men scattered around the room but caught in the moment he turned and pointed to the caged man. "You shall make the choice for me!" Sweeping his hand around the room, he said, "Do we release the highwayman?" The crowd erupted into a cacophony of approval. Black Foot levelled his hands again and turning to one of the minders he threw a long, wrought-iron key towards him before shouting dramatically, "Release the highwayman!" Another cheer went up around the crowd as the minder crossed to the cage and pushed the key into the large lock on the base of the cage's door. He pulled the bars, which opened with a loud creak and Sykesy stepped through the doorway holding his manacled hands out in front of him. The jailor slid the two rods holding the shackles together out of its socket. The cuffs fell to the floor with a metallic clank. The sound brought another cheer from the crowd and a bemused smile from the freed prisoner who began rubbing his wrists, attempting to rid the numbness from his hands. Henry turned to Thomas and gave him a wink trying to hide his relief at being released.

"I hope you can fight mate cos this lot want blood!" Black Foot heard the man's comments.

"Ai and its blood they'll have an all!" Pointing to Thomas, he shouted, "You'd best prepare yourself boy." Then turning back to the watching mob he screamed. "Charge your glasses gentlemen and place your bets. The boxing is about to begin!" Mendoza placed his hand on Thomas's arm.

"Follow me!" He started to walk around the willow wall of the gaming pit, Thomas followed him but stopped when he heard the sound of his name being called.

"Thomas!" Bridget shouted trying to pull herself away from Brother Tumbold who was still gripping her arm tightly.

"What about my reward Mr. Black Foot sir? Lord Percy's gold purse!" Tumbold said struggling to keep his hold of the girl. Black Foot turned on the Quaker.

"Well, as you can see Mr Tumbold, the circumstances have changed somewhat. Any gold will be placed on the fight!" He looked the girl up and down. "Anyway, it looks like you've already found your reward, you can have the nigger Tumbold, she'll have to do!" Bridget glared at Black Foot.

"I ain't no one's nigger!" She screamed, finally releasing herself from the Quaker. Black Foot shrugged his disinterest in the girl's opinion on the matter. Tumbold tried to grab her again. "Especially not your's, you weird old bastard!" She turned on him with the fury of a wild cat, running her long fingernails down his face, gouging three long cuts into his puffy, white skin. The group around her started to laugh at the Quaker's discomfort. The gang-leader sniggered.

"I hope you like em lively Tumbold cos this one will cut your balls off given half a chance, a proper bush bitch if ever I saw one!"

"The *girl's* with me Black Foot!" Thomas shouted, turning on Brother Tumbold, who was about to strike the girl with the back of his hand. Thomas grabbed the man's hand mid-air and held it in a vice-like grip. Thomas stared into the Quaker's face and squeezed his wrist. Slowly Tumbold's expression of furious anger turned to one of surprise before a grimace of pain and humiliation crept across his features. Thomas came in close to his ear and whispered. "You're already in my bad books Quaker, but if you touch the girl again, you die, get it?" The tubby man looked up into Thomas's bright, blue eyes and nodded subserviently.

"Whoa, whoa, if there's any beating happening, it'll be in that pit, Fewtrell!" Black Foot shouted. Thomas let go of the Quaker and turned to the gang-leader who was still standing on his chair.

"I've said I'll fight, but the girl's with me. Anyone touches her I'll . . ." Black Foot cut him short,

" . . . You'll fucking what sunshine? You'll do nothing, that's what you'll do. I'm the boss here and don't you forget it. I say who lives or dies and who does what. Now, you'd best forget the nigger cos your head's still in my noose and if you wanna walk out of here alive, you had better be as good at fighting as these gentlemen believe you are. Now shut your trap and get in that fucking ring and fight, damn you!" Thomas felt a hand gently rest on his arm, turning he was surprised to see Eleanor.

"Is she your woman?" She said earnestly, Thomas turned to Bridget, then back to Eleanor.

"She's a good friend, that's all." He turned back to Bridget who stared back at the couple with a confused expression. Thomas opened his mouth to talk but was stopped by Mendoza who had returned to his side.

"Come, Thomas, we haven't got much time!" Thomas pulled his arm away but the smaller man reached for it again, this time pulling him towards an opening in the waist-high willow fence that surrounded the gaming pit. "I am not your enemy Thomas. O'Donahue and myself are here to help you, we are on the same side, we will act as your seconds, and if you are to beat that bastard I only hope you can truly fight!" Thomas turned towards the direction of Mendoza's gaze. In the shadows beneath the hangover of the mezzanine, hidden in from the guttering candlelight sat a massive silhouette of a man. The figure was sitting on a wooden crate eating what looked like a whole pig's hind leg and even though he was sitting, he was still taller than Thomas was standing. The sight of him sent a cold shiver down Thomas's spine as he realised exactly what he would be fighting and the likelihood that he was probably going to be killed. Suddenly a shot to the head seemed like a better option than being beaten to death by this animal. Thomas crossed to his corner in what seemed to him like slow motion, his feet suddenly heavy as if he were walking through the wet, muddy fields he had known as a child on his father's farm. He blinked, trying to see the shadowy form under the balcony, however, the *thing's* form seemed to be fuzzy around the edges and Thomas thought that his eyes were fooling him in the flickering light. Thomas could have sworn that the brute was covered in a dark layer of fur and resembled a beast more than a human.

"Sit, sit!" Mendoza commanded softly. "Remove your shirt!" Thomas followed the man's order as if hypnotised by the shadow opposite him. "Boots and socks too if you please!" The words shook the young man from his trance.

"Boots and socks? I ain't fighting without boots on, what if I need to kick him?" Mendoza laughed.

"There won't be any kicking Thomas, this is a boxing bout. That monster you are so afraid of may look like a monkey but he has an evil reputation as a pugilist and although I'm sure he is a *hard* man, I doubt he is a *clever* one." Thomas gave the Portuguese an incredulous stare.

"He ain't here to take a fucking law degree is he? He don't have to be clever, he's just got to be fucking scary and let me tell ya, he's doing a good bleeding job of it too!" O'Donahue leaned in towards Thomas.

"Listen to Daniel, he is probably one of the best boxers in England at the moment. If you want to get out of here alive, you must listen to him and believe in yourself Thomas. I've seen what you can do with that right fist of yours and let me tell you, it is just as scary as that animal sitting opposite you!" O'Donahue rubbed his bruised jaw, raising his eyebrows to indicate the spot where, only the night before Thomas had landed his devastating blow.

"Mmm, I'm sorry about that mate, it was nothing personal. I'm sure you're an amazing boxer, I just ... " Mendoza slapped Thomas's broad shoulder.

"You two can suck each other's dicks later!" He nodded for O'Donahue to step back.

"Go get Thomas some ale James, he'll need something to revive him during the bout." Squatting down in front of the young man, Mendoza began to talk earnestly. "Listen to my words and act upon them Thomas!" Mendoza bent in low to Thomas's ear, having to speak loudly over the increasing din around the gaming pit.

"You must finish this fast what I have gathered from the other punters here tonight, this Bear has no technique, just strength. Get in quickly and take him down as fast as you can. At the moment he and everyone else in here underestimates you, so you have the upper hand of surprise but that won't last long. As soon as the Bear knows how hard you can hit, he'll turn dirty and try and bring you down any way he can." The Portuguese began to go over the boxing techniques he'd invented and used in the many bouts he'd fought. Thomas listened intently, his eyes wandering over the chaotic scene around him. Hands were flying this way and that, coins were jingling and paper bills being waved by crazed gamblers, flapping in the air as the gamblers fervently laid their bets on one fighter or the other as the gaming pit suddenly exploded into a pandemonium of greed and voyeurism. He saw the differing groups of regulars who obviously knew each other throwing their coins into the hats of local bookies who were screaming the odds for and against Thomas. Then there were the other men, the ones in the black neckerchiefs. They didn't seem to know anyone apart from their fellow companions who also wore the black garments around their necks. Having never been to the Rookery before, Thomas had no idea who these men were. He noticed that they were abstaining from the free-flowing gin, wine, whores and had disconnected themselves from the fervour, to Thomas it seemed that these men were casing the room. They were being organised by a tall, lean-looking man with a long scar down the right side of his face who was busy walking amongst the black scarves getting them into position around the room. As Thomas stared at the men's strange movements, his eye came to rest on the pale-skinned girl next to Black Foot. Her beautiful face had suddenly become lined with concern as she gazed wide-eyed at him. On the other side of Black Foot's chair, Bridget stared with the same expression. The Quaker stood behind Bridget, the red claw-marks she had given him clearly visible in the dim light. The tubby man had her arm again and was holding it for all he was worth as if she were an untrained dog. Black Foot stood on his chair next to them with his hand on Bridget's shoulder as if to steady himself on his throne. Bridget O'Hara stared back at Thomas, and he could see the desperation hidden in her bright-green eyes. Mendoza was still talking, but his words faded as Thomas's eyes darted between the two women; Bridget with her exotic, dusky features surrounded by her thick mop of dark ringlets that flowed to her shoulders and down her breast line contrasting with the pure English rose that was Eleanor, her white skin and finery glowing in the yellow candlelight. Thomas could see the different yet equal beauty in both women, and it suddenly dawned on him that tonight, he would be fighting for his future as well as his life.

First Blood

CHAPTER 13

enrietta Stokes screamed at the top of her infected lungs as the agonising pain of childbirth ripped through her decimated body in her final death throws. The never-ending work at the Wolverhampton lime pits had taken their toll on her. Breathing in the corrosive dust and a lack of decent food had slowly eaten away at the twenty-four-year-old until she was barely a walking ghost. Even taking malnutrition into account she could have survived childbirth had it not been for the gargantuan size of her unborn child. The older women in the pit works who were always on hand to help with such situations and who had delivered a plethora of little wretches had never seen anything like it. Firstly the child refused to show itself even with the magic of old wive's tricks the thing refused to be moved, eventually staying in the womb for ten months. All who witnessed the skeletal mother-to-be in her final stages of pregnancy swore that she had swallowed a full barrel of ale, her sparrow legs unable to take the weight of the keg inside her. A local clergyman who had some knowledge of medicine had been summoned in a desperate bid by the older women to shift the child but on realising the complexity of her situation refused to get involved and chose instead to retire to a local alehouse to try and unsee what had been seen. However, the image of the bag of bones with a beer barrel inside her had left a large enough impression on him to cause him to write in his journal that *"the thing is eating away at its host at an alarming rate and soon, if there is a merciful God almighty, she must surely die!*' Even by the standards of the day in a time of hardship where pain and death were part of everyday life, the death of Henrietta Stokes stands out as a particularly painful one. The poor woman went into labour around midnight on the 23rd. December 1760, the agony lasted for four long days until the mother's heart started to give out in exhaustion. The force of the child finally dislocated the woman's pelvis allowing the beer-barrel sized thing inside her to rip itself from the confines of the womb and squeeze itself into the world. Which, I'm sure you'll agree is not the most auspicious beginning to a life. Barry *the barrel* Stokes had well and truly arrived, at birth he weighed in at 23lb. 12 oz. but soon left his baby fat behind him and by the time he was 13 years old he was five feet ten inches tall and must have weighed as much as his father whoever that was. Yet still the boy continued to grow at an alarming rate. Although Barry's over-sized muscles came in very handy whenever there was work to be done. The owner of the lime pits just couldn't keep up with the boy's eating habits, and so at the age of sixteen, they passed the man/boy onto a local debt-collector who made the most of his apprentice's size fourteen feet, to kick in doors, whores and heads or anyone unfortunate enough to be left wanting for a bit of cash when Barry came a-calling. By the ripe old age of twenty-seven years, the lad was covered in a thick coat of black hair which sat on his shoulders and back like a black sheepskin waistcoat. The lad came in at six feet ten and weighed an astonishing twenty-three stone. Barry the Bear as he was now known around the high town of Birmingham was one of the most feared enforcers to be found anywhere in England. It wasn't long before the *Bear's* reputation came to the attention of Birmingham's most ruthless gang-leader Billy Black Foot and so with a little encouragement from the gang-leader in the form of an offer of one way swim to the bottom of Earlswood Lake, the debt-collector relinquished his hold over the lad, and Barry *the Bear* Stokes came to work full-time for William Black Foot. Black Foot put the Bear to work straight away. The lad spent his waking days either beating or eating. So when the new sport of Pugilism became popular in Britain, Black Foot had an epiphany and soon the lad was fighting throughout Warwickshire for prize money. Two years and fifteen bouts later *the Bear* was the undefeated and undisputed pugilist champion of the Midlands, and for two years the bookie's song sung in the inns and taverns throughout the Midlands was the Bear was the boy to bet on, and that was just the way Black Foot liked it. In truth, most boxers gave up the ghost at first sight of the monster and were more than happy to get a few punches to the head before going down without too much of a fuss. Anyone that pushed the beast past his usual three, ten-minute rounds found that he soon tired which, in a normal situation should have been a good thing. However, if the Bear didn't have the power to punch he *still* had the power and weight to grapple, bite, twist and pull his opponents to pieces, which he did on many occasions leaving dislocated and shattered arms, legs and spines wherever he fought.

And so the Bear sat on the old wooden crate in the Rookery's shadows eating his ham and watched the young, blonde bare-chested lad opposite being coerced into the willow-walled gaming pit with little interest. The growing excitement around the Rookery was of no concern to him except that when he was fighting, he wasn't eating and he liked eating. Shifting his weight forward he creaked forwards and stood to his full height dropping the ham down onto the crate with some reluctance. He gave the long piece of meat a sorrowful sigh before turning with an animalistic snarl towards the pit. The snarl brought the chaotic squabbling to a stop for a second or two, all heads turning towards the shadowy monster under the balcony, before exploding into howls of excitement. Barry the Bear's gut rumbled uncomfortably, and he let out a foul-smelling fart. He sniffed at its pungent stink enjoying the crassness whilst looking at his opponent across the pit, opponent was the wrong term he thought to himself, victim was more in keeping with what was about to happen. Another loud fart brought his attention back to his grumbling stomach and he turned one last time to the look at his beloved ham. He'd need to get this fight over and done with fast as he could before the rats plucked up the courage to follow their noses and eat his feast.

The first punch came as some surprise to the Bear, it was a low punch to the bottom rib that made the monster shift sideways an inch or two but lost its force on the mass of muscle and fat around the Bear's torso. Thomas felt the rib crack and ducked quickly under the arm of the giant as he returned a haymaker punch that would have taken his head off if it had landed. The sound of the bone breaking gave the smaller man some encouragement. If he could keep out of the way of the monster's huge fists, Thomas thought he could wear the man down over the next two or three rounds. The Bear had other ideas and stepping backwards he gathered himself together, shaking off the pain from his broken rib. He lurched towards the lad, trying to grab him around the neck. Thomas saw his intentions and bowed his head towards the big man giving the Bear something to aim for. The giant saw his bare neck and unable to resist such an easy target tried to wrap his thick arm around it but just as the Bear reached for him, Thomas dropped the whole top half of his body to the left and let the giant over reach himself. As the monster lurched over head Thomas sprung upwards with lightening speed and slammed his clenched fist into the side of the Bear's face with such force that the man's ear exploded, showering the punters gathered around the pit with a splatter of crimson blood. The dull thump sounded throughout the hall, its power forcing the huge man to stumble backwards with an instant dizziness, catching him off guard as the Bear's anvil was destroyed. Supporting his weight on one of the willow hurdles he steadied himself and looked with some disbelief at the comparatively small blonde man in front of him. The screaming wild-eyed gamblers surrounding the fight were suddenly silent as their champion faltered for the first time in his career. Black Foot snarled at the bloodletting in the pit. He gestured to the dog-handler on the far side of the hall who nodded back, understanding the meaning of his master's gesture. He gathered the long dog's chains around his fists and began to pull both of the huge mastiffs through the crowd towards the edge of the pit.

On seeing his opponent damaged, Thomas stepped forward to

try and finish off the beast, however Daniel Mendoza had other ideas and shouted.

"*No*, leave him, gather your energy and wait for him to come to you!" O'Donahue beckoned Thomas towards him where he raised a large tankard of ale. The young man snatched the pewter cup and drained it, slurping the sugary ale greedily. The ale slipped down his throat easily, Thomas was suddenly aware of his own exhaustion and was glad of the reviving liquid. He gave a barely noticeable nod towards O'Donahue and crossed back to the centre of the pit, his bloodied fists held up in front of his sweating face, wiping away the beads of pig's grease that had been rubbed all over the top part of his body and face by the Portuguese. Blinking away the foul smelling gunk he wondered why the man had insisted he use the grease, smearing it on Thomas from a small disc-shaped box.

Tumbold had no interest in the proceedings inside the pit. Still angry about being snubbed by Black Foot and the broken promise of Lord Percy's bag of gold he decided to enjoy the prize the gang-leader had bestowed on him. Still gripping Bridget's arm tightly, he began to pull the girl towards the back of the hall towards one of the coupling rooms. The girl screamed a stream of obstinacies at him but her protests were lost in the noise of the manic crowd around the pit watching the fight. Tumbold slapped her around the face with the back of his hand, the blow drawing blood from the girl's lip. Forcing her in front of him he pushed his way through the packed gamblers. The Quaker turned towards the gaming pit and glanced at Thomas. Seeing the young man was fully occupied with the Bear and certain he wasn't being watched he turned back to the girl and grabbed a handful of her dark ringlets. He pushed her violently before him and the pair vanished within the throng. On the far side of the pit, Edward Fewtrell turned his eye from his brother's battle with the monster for a second, his eye drawn to the movement of his former master just in time to see the tubby Quaker's form swallowed by the crowd. He turned back to the fight just as the Bear began to regain his balance after Thomas's fierce blow to his ear.

The bear rose unsteadily, a flood of dark red liquid foaming from the side of his head. The wound or pain didn't register though and he turned on Thomas snarling with a new level of ferocity. Edward turned away from the pit, searching the area around Billy Black Foot's table for the dark-haired whore. On seeing she too had vanished, he turned from the pit without a moment's hesitation deciding he would prefer to confront the Quaker con man about his double-crossing, rather than watch his brother being beaten to a pulp.

Thomas was secretly pleased with his opening effort. The Bear *was* huge, that was plain for all to see and there was no doubt that the man's appearance took the fight out of anyone that stood toe to toe with him. However, Daniel Mendoza was right, the Bear's bulky strength *was* slow and lumbering. The behemoth beast was not an intelligent fighter, barely a boxer at all but then again, he didn't need to be, all he needed was to land one punch, that's all it would take to destroy anyone who was brave enough or stupid enough to fight him.

The Bear pushed himself from the willow hurdle with a grunt, stomping across the straw-layered floor. Thomas backed away keeping space between himself and the beast. He looked towards Mendoza for some sort of instruction but all the Portuguese did was raise his fists in a classic boxing stance. Thomas copied the action bringing his clenched fists up in front of his face, his left fist to the fore, his right held back in readiness. The Bear saw Thomas's stance and copied him. The men began to circle each other slowly, each trying to find a gap in the other's defence. The dance went on for nearly a minute until Black Foot began to scream at the Rookery's champion.

"What the fuck are you waiting for, you lumbering ass? Get in there and kill the bastard!" The man's voice seemed to cut through the noise of the crowd as if he were a sergeant major on a battlefield shouting over the noise of the cannon's roar. "*Kill him!*" Eleanor slapped her father's arm.

"Father!" The gang-leader looked down on his daughter.

"Quiet girl, I'll deal with your little show of disloyalty later but for now, shut your bloody mouth!" Eleanor stared up at her father speechlessly. He had never talked to her like that before, and she was shocked by the aggression of his outburst.

"Rip him to *pieces* Bear!" Back Foot's attention had turned back to the fight. The mob on hearing the gang-leader began to join in with the call for blood. The dance had gone on for long enough, and now they wanted blood, guts, glory and death.

Black Foot's screams had an instant effect on the Bear who came forward with such speed and ferocity that it caught Thomas by surprise. The noisy crowd roared as the action started again. The Bear brought his huge left hand forward trying to grab at Thomas, however the grab was a ruse and in an instant a counter-weight punch followed the grab. The Bear brought his left arm back and his right fist forward with tremendous speed aiming it at Thomas's face. Thomas instinctively twisted his neck away from the fist and to the right just as the massive haymaker swung towards him. The punch caught a glancing blow on the smaller man's jaw and almost knocked him off his feet. The Bear's fist slid across the grease-covered skin, unable to make proper contact with the bone beneath. The crowd erupted at the sight of the Bear's first landed blow. Thomas stumbled backwards into the willow hurdle where he was pushed back into the centre of the pit by several of the men behind him. He stumbled forward unable to catch up with his own momentum, tripping on the thick straw. The Bear was ready and waiting for him. As Thomas fell onto his knees at his feet the Bear brought his fist down in a hammer blow aimed at the back of the man's head but the strike was badly aimed and landed in the middle of Thomas's shoulder blades instead pounding him deeper into the thick layer of stinking straw. Thomas lay motionless for a second, face down, unable to breathe. He could hear the crowd begin to chant the Bear's name.

"Bear, Bear, Bear!" The chant was accompanied by spectators banging their pewter tankards on tables creating a cacophony of chaos in the high-walled warehouse. Suddenly Thomas felt himself being lifted upwards, two huge hands were gripping his torso and raising him from the dirty straw. He could feel the Bear fumbling, struggling to get a grip on his skin, his giant hands slipping because of the thick layer of pig's grease. The Bear unable to find leverage dropped Thomas unceremoniously to the ground where the young man fell on his chest. The slam took the air from him, and Thomas's solar plexus spasmed allowing air neither in or out of his lungs. He lay there in the filthy straw at the feet of the champion awaiting the killer blow from the beast standing over him. However, the Bear was lost in the moment of adoration from his adoring fans. He smiled a black-toothed grimace around the pit, eyes wide and wild with excitement. Turning to his master he nodded, Black Foot was standing on his throne screaming, Eleanor beside him, a look of horror on her face as she watched what would surely be the last moments of this handsome young man.

"Bravo, bravo!" Black Foot applauded the Bear as if he were at an opera. The Bear raised his arms and snarled his Bear snarl. The crowd who were already screaming their approval seemed to double their volume at the Bear's mighty roar. Only Mendoza, his Irish companion and the black scarves weren't cheering. The Portuguese was leaning over the willow hurdle screaming at Thomas to get back on to his feet. Thomas lay motionless, his breath caught somewhere between his throat and his lungs, unable to flow in or out. He finally stirred and turned towards the voice that was calling his name so fervently.

"Get up, damn you!" Mendoza's words seemed muffled as if coming from far away. "Get up now! If you don't, you're a dead man!" He spun his head slowly towards Black Foot's table and caught sight of Eleanor, their eyes met for a second. She stepped towards the willow wall, her bright, blue eyes sparkling.

"Come Thomas rise, rise, please I beg you!" Slowly the girl's words became clearer. As they did, the muscle spasm in his chest began to relax allowing a trickle of air that had been trapped in his lungs out in a low, uncontrollable groan. Suddenly Thomas could breathe again. The sensation of oxygen filling his lungs brought him a new level of energy.

"Get up for God's sake and fight Thomas!" O'Donahue had joined Mendoza at the sight of the young man's recovery. "Fight man, fight!" He screamed over the din, his thick, Irish brogue standing out above the Brummie accents around him. Thomas blinked away the semi-consciousness that had threatened to smother him and began to crawl through the Bear's open legs. On seeing the man's movements the noise from the crowd changed from triumphant cheers to astonishment at the sight of the defeated boxer regaining his feet. The Bear didn't notice the change in the crowd's mood. If he had he might have been able to stop Thomas from getting to his feet. He might even have been able to stop the young man from turning to face his hairy, defenceless back and been able to draw his right arm up in preparation for a punch. If his slow mind had not been so engrossed in the idea of getting back to his beloved leg of ham he might also have had the opportunity to defend against the devastatingly powerful blow to his kidneys that ruptured the organ instantly causing his already dodgy bowels to let go of their contents into his breeches. The huge man was now crumpled to his knees. He fell clutching his side with a loud belch as the wind was forced out of his lungs by the almighty punch from the highwayman. The Bear's head was now at the same level as Thomas's and the smaller man wasted no time in following his first punch with another, this time to the Bear's head, knocking the scruffy mop of hair sideways, almost toppling him. Thomas followed with a left to the other side of the his head, the Bear's ear exploding again, this time showering both boxers with a fountain of deep, red blood. *Bam, bam*, two more, right and again left, *bam*. The sound of the thud of knuckles on soft skin filled the gaming pit. Even with this level of pounding the Bear swayed but still wouldn't go down and Thomas could see him trying to get to his feet even as his punches landed with bloody ferocity. The big man was trying to turn to face his opponent, trying to bring his arms up to defend himself. However the Bear's raised forearms had little effect in blocking Thomas's blows as the attack was coming from behind. To Thomas, the sight of the Bear trying to stand brought a fresh impetus to the beating. He knew that the monster was still deadly dangerous and if he was allowed to regain himself he might not be as lucky as he had been dodging that last haymaker. The realisation dawned on him that this man mountain would happily kill him with one decent punch if given half a chance and he must put him down *now*. The pain in Thomas's jaw from the Bear's glancing blow sent a tingle of fear through him like an electric shock racing up his spine, through his shoulders and down his arms, until the electric charge finally reached his blooded fists giving his already tired limbs an energy he had never felt before in his life. Suddenly he was unstoppable, a Titan, a God of pain and destruction punishing this freak of nature with his lighting-bolt energy which he channelled mercilessly into his vicious punches. *Bam, bam,* right, right, *bam,* left, *bam,* right. A blur of punches hit the side of the Bear's head each like a sledgehammer, pummelling his skull until the bone could take no more, his left eye-socket breaking with a clearly audible crack. The large eyeball popped from its socket shooting out twelve inches in front of his face like a cork from a bottle, finally caught in flight by the grizzly, bloody threads that disappeared into the dark hole from whence it came inside the monster's head. The sight of the exploding eye brought a hush over the vast room as the mob suddenly became silent at the sight of the Bear's unexpected destruction by this young man. With the eyeball still attached, the disorientation from the Bear's split vision had an instant effect on the gargantuan pugilist. A panic gripped him and his slow mind tried to work out what was happening and why he wasn't able to see the horrified faces that gawped at him from the gaming pit's edge. A confusion washed over him rendering him useless. To the men around the pit he was no longer a giant, he was more like a helpless freak to be pitied as he knelt, bleeding in the centre of the Rookery. He rocked back and forth on his knees, eventually turning towards Black Foot's table which had fallen as silent as the rest of the room. He tried to focus on the face of his boss with his good eye. The expression on William Black Foot's face had changed from one of manic jubilation to a disappointed, low-browed scowl. The defeated boxer noticed the beautiful girl beside him shaking her head sorrowfully, her golden hair swaying as if in slow motion. He pondered over her perfection for a second wondering if her tear-filled eyes were crying for him before noticing the man who had been in the cage begin to clap his hands enthusiastically. He could see that the freed highwayman was watching something going on behind him outside the field of vision of his good eye. The big man turned his head back towards the centre of the pit. The room spun crazily as the Bear's hanging eye swung around his breast. The good eye could see a young, blonde man standing in front of him, his fists raised and poised, ready to strike. The Bear knew what was coming and he resigned himself to it, he was too battered to defend himself in his punch-drunk state. But as the blonde man stepped forward for the coup de grace the giant noticed something behind the boxer. Something that looked familiar, an out of focus shape that filled him with a warm, happy feeling. He could see his leg of ham and he longed for it. The fact that most of his stomach's contents were now in his foul-smelling breeches did nothing to quell his desire to devour the joint of meat and he gazed at it pathetically with his lone eye. Yet even through his damaged vision he could see there was something different about the ham. In the dim light he could have sworn the thing was moving and with one last great effort to focus his good eye, the Bear saw that the joint of meat was alive with a pack of black rats, feasting and fouling all over the rotted joint before him.

A movement nearer to him brought his mind back to the pit's willow walls. It was a quick movement, an incredibly fast image only glimpsed for a millisecond by the giant's brain before Thomas Fewtrell's fist slammed into the monster's bent nose and mouth which exploded in a volcano of blood and teeth. The blow was so hard and fast that it took the Bear as if it were a shot from a pistol, driving his already semi-conscious head backwards until the huge man toppled onto his back, his head smashing against the blood-stained straw which covered the stone cobbles underneath. The Bear's skull cracked loudly as it struck the cobbles. The man began to shake violently, his nerve endings creating a dance of death as his brain slowly died. The room fell totally silent for a second as Thomas stood astride the man's gibbering body exhausted. He drew in the foul air of the Rookery as if he were drinking pure spring water and watched the growing pool of blood seeping through the straw and onto the black, cobbled floor beneath. He looked down at its gory beauty, frozen for a moment in the absurdity of it all watching the last death-throws of the beast he had defeated. The electric charges in his fists had gone now, his sense of indestructibility replaced by a growing feeling of shame and emptiness as he stared down at the dying man.

****

Tumbold fumbled in his breeches with his left hand. The buttons were tricky in the dim light but he dared not let go of the hellcat he held by a clump of hair in his right hand. The whore had become almost uncontrollable as he had dragged her into the small, musky room at the rear of the Rookery. He had thrown her onto the rickety wooden bed with its filthy, semen-stained straw mattress and the girl had sprung at him instantly, attacking him viciously with her talon-like fingernails. Tumbold had nearly succumbed to the attack but a swift punch to Bridget's nose had shocked her sufficiently to give the tubby Quaker time to grab her by the hair on the back of her head in a vice-like grip. Now he spun her around and pushed her down with his sixteen stone bodyweight and held her face down across the bed. The girl was trapped beneath his bulk and he took advantage of the position to enjoy his victim. Bridget lay crushed beneath, panting in short gasping breaths unable to pull air into her lungs, squashed into the hard-packed mattress. She felt his tongue running along the back of her slim neck rising along her hairline until it found her right ear where it licked and searched inside the ear. She could hear his squelching saliva as it dribbled around her lobe. The man's stinking breath a mixture of tobacco and halitosis filled her nostrils, as he began to talk softly to her.

"You're mine now, my little black bitch." His words brought a fresh struggle from Bridget who desperately tried to push herself from the bed with her free hand. She soon realised that she was going nowhere and resigned herself to the fact the fat little Quaker was going to rape her if she didn't think of a way to distract him. He began to talk in a low, breathless tone again, almost whispering into her ear. "I'm going to fill your sinful vessel with the semen of

Christ!" he panted as he dug inside his trousers, trying to find his penis. Bridget burst into laughter.

"The semen of Christ!" She forced a sarcastic laugh. "Do me a favour, Brother *Tumbold,* this ain't anything to do with Christ, this is to do with you, you're just a dirty, little pervert that can't even find his cock in his own breeches. Your little maggot must be tiny!" Bridget felt the man stop moving as he took on her cruel words. She decided to press him further. "Go on then, fill my vessel with the spunk of God!" She snapped again, turning her head as far as she could to look into the man's eyes "But excuse me if I don't get too passionate, won't ya? I probably won't even notice it happening with your cock being so bloody small!" She could see a look of confusion growing on his face. "Or have you already started?" She rolled her eyes as if he were a naughty child. The man froze for a second before exploding into a shower of punches to the back of her head.

"Devil's bitch, whore . . . filthy . . . " Tumbold seemed to be struggling for obscenities. Bridget pushed her face into the mattress to protect herself from the punches. The man seemed to gather himself. He leant back over the girl, the exertion of his outburst creating beads of sweat that rolled down his brow into his wild, pale-blue eyes.

"You'll see whore, you will feel the pain of Christ just as the others did, just like *all* the other whores!" The Quaker's words were said coldly in a matter of fact manner. "They were all the same. Just like you they spoke the same sinful words but they all succumbed to the pain of Christ's wrath and you will too!" Tumbold pulled the girl's red gown up around her waist. Bridget froze as she tried to understand what the Quaker was saying to her. Who were the other girls he was talking about? Bridget opened her mouth to speak but the feeling of the man's penis entering her vagina took her breath and any idea of resistance away. She turned her head sideways and focussed on a small, damp patch of peeling, green paint on the doorway and decided to concentrate all her thoughts on it. The man rose and dropped in a sexual fervour that lasted around a minute before finally collapsing, an exhausted pile of flesh onto her back. Bridget's eye didn't move from the small mark on the door. She tried to stifle a sob knowing that if she started to cry she may never stop. She gathered herself together as best she could, turning her agony to anger.

"Are you finished you pathetic, old fart?" Her voice trembled slightly as she spoke, betraying the fear and emotional pain she felt inside.

"Oh no, I'm not finished with you yet, *whore*. Now I must introduce you to Christ himself!" Without warning, he sprung to his knees and grabbed Bridget around the neck with both hands. Bridget was astonished by his sudden strength. His fingers wrapped around her slim neck and gripping it tightly he began to squeeze. She could feel the blood pressure building in her head as he tried to complete the throttling he'd started the night before, only this time because of the boxing match outside he would not be disturbed. His eyes were wild, blue disks of madness as he wrung the girl's neck. Bridget grabbed his hands and tried to peel the thick fingers from her throat, but she could find no purchase, and slowly she began to lose consciousness. Her dark eyes rolled into her head leaving only the whites to reflect the light of the cold moon that streamed in through the large window. The Quaker began to mumble, talking in tongues to some invisible, supernatural spirit. Bridget could just make out some of the words between the nonsensical babbling before she passed out.

"You are . . . joining . . . all of the other . . . whores . . . I have sent . . . to serve Christ's will . . . in the halls . . . of heaven, no longer are you . . . the Devil's bitch . . . you are the whore of Christ!"

****

Thomas suddenly felt a tremendous blow to his kidneys. The unexpected punch caught the young man by surprise, twisting his exhausted body out of shape. He spun around to see Black Foot snarling at him inside the pit. The man stood motionless and watched as Thomas tried to regain his composure after the excruciatingly painful punch to his side.

"You've cost me a lot of money, boy!" Almost whispering the

words as if to say such a thing was blasphemous. "I bet my gold on the Bear to win, and now he's broken, dead, you've killed my man." Thomas steadied himself against the hurdle behind him and pointed at the dead man at his feet.

"It was kill or be killed, you know that Black Foot!" Thomas gasped, trying to talk over the pain in his kidney. Black Foot exploded. The two huge dogs at the pit's edge began to snarl viciously, the sight of such a large lump of dead meat on the gaming pit's centre driving them mad with hunger. The dog-handler struggled to hold on to their chains and to keep the beasts under control as Black Foot walked across to the dead man and grabbed at his bloodied hair, tearing a large, black clump away. He held the blood-dripping scalp up to Thomas.

"Kill or be killed? I don't give a fuck about that. I don't care about this piece of shit!" He threw the piece of scalp at the young man and pointed to the man's body with his blood-covered hand. "I don't give a fuck about life or death. I do, however, give a fuck about my gold." The crowd who were now stood in near silence watching the proceedings began to stir.

"He won fair and square, Billy!" A voice called from within the throng.

"Yeah, beat him proper!" Another joined the first. Black Foot held up his red hands.

"Fair and square . . . I don't think so lads. Tell me how many of you lost money tonight? Come on now, raise your hands!" Almost all the gamblers around the pit raised their hands or nodded their loss. Black Foot continued. "And how many of you have gained by tonight's bout?" He stared directly at Daniel Mendoza and the Irish man next to him. The Portuguese shrugged slightly nodding that he had indeed prospered by the Bear's defeat.

"It was a fair fight Black Foot. A man is free to bet in whichever way he wishes." O'Donahue spoke up.

"I knew the lad had the power to defeat your man."

"My friend is right, the fight was lost the moment your *Bear* stepped into the pit. Thomas is unskilled yes, he needs training in the sport properly, but you have seen for yourself, there is no doubt he has a natural talent for the sport. He has the potential to be a great boxer!" Black Foot glared at the dark man who had dared to answer him back so eloquently.

"No, no, no, this was a set up from the start! I see behind your scheme even if none of these scum do." This time the crowd bristled at the gang-leader's derogatory words. Black Foot pointed at Thomas who had begun to recover from the blow. "No, sunshine, I know your game. That was the plan all along, to steal my gold!"

"*Your gold* . . . och, that's a laugh!" A Scottish voice retorted, Black Foot turned to the crowd raising his hands once more to stop the rising murmur around the room. Apart from the snarling of the hungry dogs the room fell silent. The mastiff's eyes followed the sight of the gang-leader's bloody hand as he gestured about himself.

"That was nay *your* gold Black Foot!" The voice shouted again. "It belonged to the Hellfire club, Lord Francis Dashwood to be precise." The room turned their heads towards the voice. A lean, mean-looking man in his mid-forties with a long scar down his right cheek and a black neck-scarf was leaning on the handrail along the top of the mezzanine level staring down at the gang-leader.

"Ye stole the gold from Lord Percy Whip, did ye not?" The man's sudden questioning caught the gang-leader off-guard. He stood in the pit for a second staring up at the man before asking.

"And who the fuck are you to question me about Lord Percy's gold?" Flint smiled menacingly.

"I told ye, it ain't Lord Percy's gold, and it's ne your gold either, it belongs to the Hellfire club, and Lord Dashwood wants it back!" Black Foot noticed the black scarves gather around their leader on the edge of the balcony. His eyes darted around the room, and he suddenly realised that there were far more of the black-scarfed men that he'd first noticed. Gathering his wits about him, Black Foot retorted.

"The Hellfire club, you London boys are a long way from home, ain't ya? Well, let me tell ya you bastards will be lucky to leave Birmingham with your lives, never mind your fucking gold. If it's a fight you want, you've got it!" The gang-leader turned his gaze from the Scotsman and back towards Thomas, his white-powdered face with its small, heart-shaped beauty spot looking more devilish with each passing second. "But not before I put a piece of lead through this bastard's head!" he pulled the long flintlock from his belt and raised it. Thomas saw his actions and could only hold his open hands up in a useless defence against the on-coming pistol shot. As Black Foot's bloody hand raised the gun and clicked the hammer back the massive massifs jumped as one. Dragging the unfortunate dog-handler with them, they fell on Black Foot's blood-soaked right hand and lower arm with a ferocity that took the gang-leader and everyone else in the building by surprise. The lead dog's razor-sharp teeth taking Black Foot's right hand off at the wrist in one sharp snap of his jaws. The two dogs fell into a snarling mass of black hair and muscle onto the pit's floor. Both animals fought viciously over the human morsel, tearing the limb apart one finger at a time. Black Foot stood in shock, his eyes darting between the bizarre sight of his own pistol-griping hand being torn apart by the dogs and his bloodied stump. Flint, on seeing the gang-leader's shock burst into laughter joined almost simultaneously by the Londoners who had accompanied him to Birmingham. On hearing the mocking laughter, the dandies on the upper level began as one to throw punches at the black scarves and what began as a scuffle soon turned into a full-on brawl.

The sight of Billy Black Foot holding the stump of his arm up was all it took to ignite the tinder box within the warehouse. The regulars began to turn on their fellow punters as well as the black scarves, and within seconds the room was pandemonium, with small scuffles and fights breaking out throughout the Rookery's two levels. Eleanor jumped from her seat at the top table and pushed her way through the crowd. Climbing over the hurdle she threw herself at her father and grabbing the stump on his right arm, she pulled a white, silk handkerchief from her bosom and began to wrap it around her father's injured arm.

"Father, father!" As she did one of the dogs who by now had become crazed by the smell of blood in the midst of the feeding frenzy turned on her. It leapt across the body of the Bear snapping its blood and saliva-drooling jaws around the flesh on the right cheek of her face. Eleanor screamed in pain as she fell under the weight of the dog. Her father was too lost in the trance of his amputation to react to his daughter's screams as the beast began to savage her face. Thomas sprung from the willow hurdle and flung himself on the beast. He grabbed the tight, leather collar around the animal's neck and lifted the dog from the ground as if it were one of the pig carcasses he'd carried as a market worker as he did, the beast let go of the girl and she fell to the straw, holding her blood-soaked face. Thomas lifted the huge, snarling animal above his head and slammed it as hard as he could on top of the other dog. It landed with a crack of bones, yelping. The dog-handler stood motionless on the other ends of the chains gazing at the two injured animals.

Thomas grabbed Eleanor by her shoulders and pulled her to him and guiding the shocked girl towards Mendoza and O'Donahue he saw the fight growing out of control around him.

"Time to leave I think gentlemen!" The words were music to their ears. "Get my clothes and let's get out of here!" Just as he spoke, a commotion on the mezzanine level caught Thomas's attention. A scuffle had broken out between some well-dressed dandies and some of the black scarves and a group of lower-class brawlers. They had taken it upon themselves to ascend the rickety stairs to the *toffs* level in order to relieve the gentlemen of their cash whilst the opportunity and cover of the increasing violence surrounded them. The dandies were having none of it and were putting up a decent fight against the ruffians *and* the black scarves with swords, sticks and daggers. The group swayed this way and that as the battle became more serious, smashing glass, screams and shouts filled the high room. Suddenly a pistol shot rang out followed closely by a blood-curdling scream from the balcony. The swaying crowd began to be pushed back against the bannister rail that overlooked the pit. *Crack,* the sound of splintering wood brought almost everyone on the ground level to a standstill, all eyes turning towards the balcony from where the sound had emanated. As if in slow motion the rail gave way as the ruffians fighting with their backs to the drop no longer had the stability of the handrail which disintegrated into kindling against the pressure of the mob. The twenty or so men seemed to teeter on the edge of the precipice for a few seconds grabbing desperately at the air around them before finally falling, en masse onto Black Foot below. Thomas's mind slowed the horror down and he instinctively screamed a warning to the gang-leader but it was too late, the men seemed to freeze mid air, suspended by invisible strings for a millisecond, before crashing with a dull thump of flesh and groans into a heap of humans in the middle of the pit. Mendoza stepped forward to help the crushed man beneath the pile of writhing men but as he did another man fell on top of the heap, then another. Mendoza slapped Thomas's arm.

"This way, quickly before it's too late!" Mendoza led the way crossing the pit. He checked above himself to make sure he wouldn't become another victim of the falling men. Mendoza, O'Donahue, Thomas and Eleanor picked their way around the mass of men squirming on the pit's floor until they had reached the other side of the fenced-off area. On hearing the sound of another shot coming from above, Thomas turned and saw a scruffy man flaying an old oil lantern around himself using the heavy lamp as a weapon. The base of the metal lamp smashed into a well-dressed dandy's face, breaking his nose and knocking him to the floor of the mezzanine. As he fell, Flint pulled a small, metal pistol from his coat and fired a shot at the lamp-wielding assailant at point-blank range, the lead shot passed through the bottom of the lamp, hitting the attacker square in the face and killing him instantly. The man fell backwards from the balcony and landed lifelessly atop of the pile of men below. Thomas watched in horror as the lamp oil spilt from the bullet-hole in the base of the lamp, flowing freely all over the mass of men. The fumes of the foul-smelling whale oil filled the pit before finding their way towards the guttering wick of the lamp. *Whoosh,* the whale oil fumes ignited in a ball of flame engulfing the pile of humans in the pit. He watched the ball of fire as it rose to the rafters of the Rookery, forty feet above where it forced the tightly-packed flock of pigeons from their perches in a squawking panic. Every-one around the pit froze. Thomas stepped back wrapping his arm tighter around the injured girl as the scorching flames caught hold of the oil-soaked people. Suddenly the semi-conscious and dazed victims of the fall were now screaming masses of flame-engulfed humans. The agonised victims began to extract themselves from the pile, clawing against the straw-covered floor to free themselves from the crush. The blood-soaked straw began to smoke sending a putrid cloud rolling around the pit, before the floor itself began to burn creating an inferno within the willow hurdles.

"Thomas, time to leave!" Thomas, Eleanor and the Irishman didn't move, all three enthralled by the macabre sight of the human torches inside the pit as the victims beat at their fire-covered bodies with flaming hands in a sickening dance of death within the inferno. Thomas saw the flames lick against the old timber of the mezzanine for a second before the platform itself caught fire trapping the fighting men above.

"Thomas . . . *Thomas*!" The three boxers and the girl turned towards the call, searching for the voice but the acrid, choking smoke had become so thick that it was difficult to see anything on the other side of the pit from where the voice was coming. "Thomas!" The voice rang out again and this time Thomas recognised his friend's voice.

"Sykesy, where are you?"

"Let's get the fuck out of here, the whole place is going up!" Sykes's voice sounded desperate above the crackling flames. Mendoza agreed.

"We must leave now before the mob panic and we are all trapped!" Thomas and O'Donahue glanced quickly at each other before turning towards the front of the warehouse. O'Donahue pushed Thomas's leather coat, shirt and hat into his free arm before following his Portuguese friend.

"But my father?" Eleanor screamed at the pile of frenzied, burning men. Thomas stared at the fire's victims. Black Foot was nowhere to be seen within the inferno that was now the gaming pit.

"It's too late for him girl and if we don't get out of here, our fate will be the same as theirs!"

Incredibly the tightly packed crowd were still battling each other unaware of the urgency and the speed at which the flames were taking hold of the building. The group pushed their way through the pack towards Sykesy.

"Come on!" He yelled, trying to hide the panic in his voice. "This place is gonna be hotter than hell in five minutes!" Thomas stopped in his tracks.

"Where's Edward and Bridget?" Sykesy looked around himself.

"He was here a few minutes ago come to that where's that fat Quaker?" Thomas scowled.

"*Fuck* the fat Quaker!" Mendoza grabbed his shirt and pulled.

"Wherever your brother and the negro girl is, it will make no difference if we all burn to death looking for them. We have to get out *now* before the panic; before it's too late!" As he said the words a deafening crash of timber filled the room as the mezzanine level collapsed on top of the people beneath. All turned to see the bizarre sight of men still fighting as they burned.

Flint, stabbing and slashing, extracted himself from the brawl and made his way to the safety of the far end of the mezzanine. He stood on the far end of the balcony watching Thomas and his new friends make their escape. He took in the tall figure of Thomas Fewtrell watching him lead the blood-soaked, sobbing girl through the panicking crowd. Flint made a point of committing the young boxer's features to memory before climbing over the railing, dropping to the floor and making his way towards the rear of the building where men and women were escaping in large numbers through the rear windows of the whoring rooms at the back of the building.

****

Those that had escaped the fire watched the Rookery burn to the ground from the far side of the street. They were joined by other inhabitants of the Froggery who had crawled from the squalor of their tenements to witness the final moments of the infamous gambling house. All stood in silence listening to the screams coming from within the hell behind the giant, wooden doors with the huge black rook; its blood-dripping beak painted on the crimson timbers, bubbling from the heat within. Cries of fear, pain and panic rose into the smokey air as the poor wretches were roasted to death inside. The smell of burning hair and barbecued flesh floated around the filthy, cobbled streets with a deliciously putrid stink that made many of the paupers within the Froggery drool at the smell of cooking meat.

They watched the hypnotising flames as they danced over one hundred feet into the snow-laden sky. Each had differing emotions about the night's events. Mendoza wrestled with the image of the pile of burning men unable to shake the macabre sight from his mind and turning to his Irish comrade he could see the shock on the big man's brutal face. The orange fire-glow reflected the emotion in his watery, blue eyes as he stood mesmerised by the inferno across the street. Sykesy sat on his haunches, staring at the cobbles unable to bring himself to watch. His hands held over his ears, trying to block out the hellish sound of two hundred or so people roasting alive. Thomas, on the other hand, was clutching the girl, searching the scorched stragglers that crawled from the small hatch in the huge doors. Each escapee desperately fighting the other fleeing people who were now plugging the exit with their bodies. Thomas stepped forward to help several times but was driven back by the searing heat, again and again. He could only watch in horror as he scanned each of the agonised faces for that of his brother Edward and Bridget. The swirling smoke and blackened faces made it impossible to recognise anyone and he resigned himself to watch helplessly until the roof finally fell in on the people below, ending the terrible screams from within. As the huge roof timbers fell onto those inside they pulled the four walls of the Rookery down with them, crashing in a dull boom, the falling masonry extinguishing the flames in an explosion of orange sparks that shot up into the sky in every direction like thousands of tiny meteorites.

Thomas felt Eleanor's sudden weight, and he knew the girl could take no more. He examined the wound on her face and could see that the blood loss made the gash look far worse than it actually was. But the shock from the dog attack and the sight of her father's death were too much for the young woman, and she fainted in his arms. Holding her shoulders, he let her slowly down onto her knees and rested her head on his broad chest. She semi-conscious, he trying to blank out the hollow feeling growing in his stomach. He watched the meteorite shower above his head as the tiny sparks fizzed to their deaths in the grey sky until a tap on his shoulder brought him out of his melancholy.

"Thomas!" A girl's voice quivered with emotion and he spun to see Bridget standing beside him. Thomas stared at her for a second trying to work out if he was imagining the dusky beauty of Bridget O'Hara as she stood above him in the glowing light of the fire. She looked down at Thomas and Eleanor numb from what she had endured that night and reaching down to him she grabbed his large hand in hers. All three watched silently as the flames engulfed the giant doors which cracked loudly before lurching forward and falling in on themselves. The falling doors crashed to the floor in an explosion of flame and sparks exposing the true horror inside what now resembled a red-hot bread oven. Incredibly there were still people alive, trapped inside now just orange silhouettes dancing in pain-driven madness amongst burning timbers and the glowing, orange brickwork.

Thomas broke his gaze to see his brother watching him from across the street. The sight of him drove the hollow feeling of dread that had promised to engulf him away. Edward told how he had managed to save himself and Bridget via a rear window. The windows overlooking the Rookery's pig-styes in the rear of the building had been an escape route for anyone who knew of their existence which it turned out, many regulars did. He described how the lucky few men and women climbed from the windows dropping into the shit-covered yard below. The men listened to the description of the awful scenes with a mixture of awe and horror. Edward went into vivid detail about how burning men and women had escaped with him and Bridget as if the depth of his description would somehow exorcise him of the terrible things he'd seen that night. The one detail he *did* omit however was Bridget's throttling and rape at the hands of Brother Tumbold and how the rapist had met his demise. He knew that the inferno would destroy what was left of the tubby Quaker's smashed skull.

PUNCH DRUNK

Part 2

Fewtrell v Jackson 1788

Part Two

The King in a cold room

CHAPTER 14

"*Dashwood!*" The name echoed through the huge room bouncing around the parquet floor to the tall walls. Massive paintings of long dead, severe-looking men stared down from guilt-framed portraits as Lord Francis Dashwood entered the presence of the King gingerly. "Dashwood, come, man, come. Don't dither in the doorway, you're letting a draught in. I'm trying to keep the bloody room warm, but I fear I'm losing the battle!" Lord Dashwood stepped inside the threshold of the room and bowed subserviently. As he turned to close the door, he was surprised by a smartly dressed page standing just inside the tall doors. The page bowed his head slightly.

"One shouldn't turn his back on his highness me Lord!" He said sombrely as he took the handle of the great door and closed it silently.

"Come over here Dashwood by the fire!" Dashwood spun on his heel, heeding the page's words and hoping that the King hadn't noticed his indiscretion. He scanned the room quickly and crossed the room to the large empty space between the doors and the two tall chairs next to a large, marble, hearth and roaring fire. The room was completely empty apart from the chairs and a small desk in the far corner where a grey-haired man in the same livery sat in silence scribbling with a quill onto various parchments. Dashwood's tall heels clicked on the hardwood flooring, and the distance between the door and the fire seemed much further away than it had first appeared. As he approached the tall chairs a man's head peeked around the edge of the closest one. "Ah there you are, come and warm yourself, man, it's fucking freezing this morning!" Dashwood bowed again.

"Very true, your highness." The King shifted in his seat and pointing at the other chair he ordered his guest to take a seat.

"Sit man, sit, I'm not going to crane my bloody neck every time I want to say something. *Sit*!" The elderly Lord took the chair opposite and sat as delicately as he could. He saw a large pile of smashed chairs and ornate picture frames next to the fire. The King noticed Dashwood glance towards the pile. "Fucking freezing Dashwood and nothing burns better than a bit of old oak." As if to drive his words home the King leaned forward and grabbed a broken chair leg. "I'm told this chair came from the oldest part of the palace. It belonged to a fucking *Plantagenet* for God's sake. To think a *Plantagenet* sat his arse on this piece of wood, history, Dashwood, history. This old, black oak burns wonderfully though, lovely smell to it too. Can you smell it Dashwood?" The elderly man nodded and smiled even though his nostrils could only pick up the overwhelming sickly smell of French perfume which attempted and failed to disguise the King's musky body odour.

"A wonderful smell your highness!" He replied, trying to hide any signs of repugnance.

"Sport, Dashwood, sport!" The old lord smiled again bemused by the King's odd statement.

"Sport your highness?" The King leaned forward and reached for a large glass of port beneath his chair. Lord Dashwood noticed for the first time that even though the winter sun had only risen an hour before the monarch was already drunk.

"Sport Dashwood!" Lord Dashwood's brow furrowed.

"You mean hunting your highness?" The King lost his temper.

"No, not fucking hunting Dashwood, it's too bloody cold man. I'm mean sport *inside*, something my chums and I can enjoy from the comfort of a chair and a fucking big fire." The elderly Lord nodded and looked the King over without meeting his puffy eyes. The monarch was in his fifties although he looked much older. The ever-present alcohol and sugary food had taken its toll and he seemed to be swollen from his ankles to his neck. The skin on his face and neck was scattered with small, red pockmarks and for all of his finery and breeding he looked much like one of the low-life drunkards that could be found in any tavern in any town in the Kingdom; but of course he wasn't, he was King George III of England, Scotland, Wales and Ireland. Dashwood bowed his head again.

"Maybe a cockfight your highness?"

"*Bah cockfight!*" He took a long slurp of port from his glass and stared at the old lord from above his glass. "Fucking gypsy's and peasant's sport Dashwood, I want something different. That's why I've called you here, you're in the know man, *Hellfire* and all that!" Lord Dashwood blinked with surprise.

"Hellfire your highness?" The King lost his temper again.

"Don't play coy with me man, your little secret society isn't as secret as you'd like to think, Dashwood. I have my spies everywhere, I know what you're about sir. Bestiality, whoring, molly raping and all that, I know all Dashwood. There's no point denying it!"

The old Lord smiled weakly realising he'd been checked-mated by a court spy or two.

"Would your highness like to attend one of our meetings?" The King glared at the man opposite.

"Would I . . . would I? If I want to attend one of your fucking meetings, I'll just turn up man, I don't need your bloody permission Dashwood!"

"Of course you don't your highness." The King sat back in his chair impatiently.

"Of course, of fucking course!" A silence fell between the two. The King sipping his port and Lord Dashwood not knowing how to answer. King George sighed.

155

"I'm bored Dashwood, bored. I'm looking for some distraction from this, this fucking awful life I have found myself in!" He slurped at the red liquid again. "I thought you might have some . . . " Dashwood cut him short.

"*Pugilism!*" The King glared at the old man, unaccustomed to being interrupted, he intended to remonstrate with the old Lord. Dashwood realised his mistake but pressed on. "Pugilism your highness, it is the new sport, a gentleman's sport!" The bloated King opened his mouth to shout but stopped himself.

"Pugilism?" Shaking his head. "What the hell are you talking about man?" Dashwood sat back into his chair knowing that he had struck gold with the King's curiosity.

"Pugilism is the newest sport in London yet the oldest sport in the world your highness!" The King's face grimaced into a look of confusion.

"What the fuck are you talking about? Oldest sport, newest sport, you're not making any sense man! Are you talking about fighting Dashwood?" The old man had to stop himself from snapping his reply.

"Yes, your highness!"

"Fighting Dashwood, what's so sporting about fighting man? I can go into any tavern in the town and watch a couple of rascals scrap each other, where's the sport in that?" Lord Dashwood smiled as pleasantly as he could attempting to hide the rising impatience he felt towards the pock-marked alcoholic and after taking a long controlled breath he explained as if talking to a child,

"This isn't normal fighting, your majesty." The King tried to give Dashwood an impatient look of his own but only managed to look more confused than he already was.

"Oh, how so? Come, man, explain!"

"Pugilism is the *art* of fighting with one's fists your highness. A bout of numbered rounds between two equally measured and matched gentlemen in a controlled environment until one of the fellows succumbs to the other's punches. When performed properly by two trained *boxers* as we call them me Lord it can be a most exhilarating experience . . . Especially when one has wagered gold on the outcome of the bout." The King sat up and taking another swing of port he stared at Dashwood for a second before asking.

"And what type of gentlemen are these ... *boxers*?" The old Lord's mood softened knowing that the King's question was really his approval.

"Your highness, that is the greatest thing about the art of pugilism, these men come from all walks of life, rich or poor, it makes no difference once inside the fighting ring. All are equal and must abide by the rules of the art. The only thing that counts is the man's physical fitness, his prowess with the fists and his abidance to the rules of the sport and this your majesty, more than hawking, horses, hunting or cards is why boxing is the *true* sport of the modern gentleman!" The King sat back into the large chair. He turned his gaze from the old man and back to his crackling fire. Dashwood, stared at the man opposite imagining he could hear the cogs turning inside the King's mind.

"Where does one go to see one of these ... " he searched for the right word,

" ... boxing matches your majesty?" King George nodded.

"Yes, yes boxing match, that's what I was going to say, where Dashwood?" Dashwood pulled himself forward to the front of his seat and leaning forward he began talking in a low tone.

"Well, that's the thing, your majesty. Due to parliament's ban on duelling and the fact that boxing falls into the category of duelling, those parliamentary ... " Dashwood couldn't help but show his contempt towards the House of Commons. "Those Honourable Gentlemen ... " he said sarcastically, " ... have taken it upon themselves to stop all boxing bouts from taking place in any of the city's parks, halls and state houses. This has had the effect of virtually driving this purest of sports out into the countryside or some of the, shall we say, less-enlightened parts of London me Lord. Places frequented by the underworld, cut pockets, whores and ne'r do wells, not really places fit to accommodate someone such as yourself." The mention of the underworld made the King perk up.

"Nonsense man, the peasantry love me, I am their King, after all, Dashwood." Knowing the King had taken his bait the old Lord let his face drop to a concerned frown.

"But your majesty, there may be rebels there!"

"Rebels? Well, you would know more about that than *I,* sir. I remember the word around the court about your Jacobite sympathies in my father's time as regent!" Dashwood tried to look hurt.

"I can assure you sir that . . . " The King ignored him already moving on with the conversation.

"Anyway, which rebels are we talking about? Take your pick Dashwood, Irish, Americans even the Scots want another go at it! As I'm sure you know the fuckers are everywhere according to my bodyguards and if I listened to those bastards I'd never leave my palace. Anyway, you may have forgotten that as a young man I served my father in the army. I know how to rough it as much as the next man. If these boxing matches are to be held in roughest parts of my kingdom then have no fear, I shall attend." Dashwood furrowed his brow.

"Incognito, of course, your highness?" The King slapped his hands together, surprising everyone in the room.

"Of course, incognito man, do you take me for a fool Dashwood? My chums and I shall blend in with the ruffians. We shall disguise ourselves and walk amongst them. By God, Dashwood, this is exactly the type of adventure I was talking about." Dashwood tried to stop himself smirking. Thanks to him, gambling wagers around the fights would treble now that the King of England was involved, but more importantly the monarch would be vulnerable amongst the mob *especially* if he were dressed as one of the rabble. The fact that the King had so happily walked into Dashwood's well-laid snare was comical enough, but the very idea of this pompous, bloated buffoon trying to pass himself off as a peasant made the old Lord want to burst into fits of laughter.

The two discussed the art of pugilism for another hour. Dashwood telling him about the various boxers he was training like modern day gladiators at his farm on the outskirts of the city. The monarch listened intently draining his port glass three times before finally rising from his chair. He crossed the room to the grey man at the desk in the corner saying loudly, as if Lord Dashwood was no longer in the room,

"Tell him to leave now we want to sleep!" Then returning to his chair, he refused to look the old Lord in the face. Instead, he stared into the fire as if he no longer existed. The page rose from his chair behind the parchment-littered table and crossed slowly to the bemused Lord Dashwood.

"The King is sleeping me lud!" Dashwood looked between the page and the King and nodded, standing he bowed as far as his stiff back would allow.

"Thank you, your highness!" The King turned on him, his eyes glaring in the flickering firelight. Dashwood didn't recognise the man before him now, his features had changed in an instant, his mood from one of mischievous playfulness to one of total contempt towards him in the blink of an eye.

A twitching tick in the King's left eye developed and in seconds became more apparent until the blinking eye threatened to take over the King's whole face and shoulders. Dashwood had heard the rumours of the monarch's madness, and now he was witnessing it with his own eyes.

"D ... D ... Dashwood are you still here? Can't you see I'm sleeping man ... f ... f ... fuck off!"

"My Lord!" Dashwood bowed again and backed away a few steps before turning and crossing the room towards the large ornate doors and the way he'd entered.

"Go on f ... f ... *fuck off!*" The king shouted from his chair. Dashwood stepped through the doors into the long cold corridor that led into the depths of the palace. "Don't forget to tell me about the b ... b ... boxing, Dashwood." The King called after him, almost apologetically but the old Lord didn't answer. The blue-liveried page closed the door silently behind him and only then did Lord Dashwood allow himself to grin for he knew that no matter how erratic the King's behaviour became, no matter how much the puffy, red-faced bastard gibbered and croaked in his madness, Dashwood had just procured the King's approval of the new sport and now the noble art of British boxing would never be the same again. Now there was a chance for him to profit directly from the never-ending pot of gold that was the royal coffers. The King's attendance at these boxing bouts would also create an opportunity for him to humiliate, injure and perhaps even destroy the house of Hanover forever. Dashwood's Jacobite bile began to rise as he allowed himself to fantasise about another Jacobite uprising and the chance of an assassination which could spark a new insurgency. By the time the Lord had reached his carriage, the flames of Dashwood's new rebellion had already been ignited.

Carrot and Stick

CHAPTER 15

Mendoza's gym was a small affair to the rear of his modest house in Highgate, London. He had turned the unused coach house into an area given over purely to the training of boxers and the art of pugilism. The flaking, egg-shell blue walls within the gym were covered with drawings and diagrams of men in various fighting poses, their muscles, sinews and limbs all labelled and named. Small, red targets dotted the forms, all indicating various pressure points and weak areas around the human body. Life-sized paintings hung on long, canvas rolls which hung from nails driven into the damp plasterwork. For all Mendoza's efforts the gym still had an overriding smell of equine left over, no doubt, by the horses that had been evicted only six months before when Thomas had come to the capital to train under Mendoza's tutelage in the noble art of boxing.

The day after the fire had been a long one for the watchmen of Birmingham. Retrieving what was left of the corpses of the unfortunates from inside the shell of the burnt out Rookery was not a job taken lightly and would leave the watchmen with mental scars that would haunt their dreams for many years to come.

Two hundred and forty bodies were collected and arranged in a long line along the cobbled street outside. However, the overall number was probably far higher than that as the various body parts that made up another fifty or so people were so badly damaged that it was hard to tell exactly how many casualties there were. The job was made all the harder by the appearance of several feral dogs which quickly formed a loose pack around two massive black mastiffs who seemed to have developed a taste for human flesh. The dogs hounded the watchmen as they worked becoming braver as the day went on, in order to prey on the roasted meat of the cadavers. In fact, the dogs became so aggressive that a cordon of watchmen and concerned citizens had to form their own pack to keep the dogs at bay, beating the animals with anything at hand.

The crowd within the Rookery on the night of the fire was far larger than anyone could have predicted. Not everyone mourned the loss of Billy Black Foot's Rookery though. The local councillors and the Birmingham Quakers were just two of the many organisations who were, that very morning rubbing their collective hands together at the idea of so many of the city's underworld being handed up to God's judgement in one fell swoop.

Thomas had carried Eleanor, shocked and injured back to her father's large house in Bearwood followed at a distance by Sykesy, Edward and Bridget. Daniel Mendoza and O'Donahue had arranged to meet the group back at Thomas's casement at the tavern near the Bull Ring later that day. Thomas examined the girl's injury on the side of her face as he held her, his eye ran over her pale beauty which would be scarred permanently by the dog's vicious attack. Although it was difficult to see exactly how deep the dog bite was due to the dried blood around the wound. Whether the girl was in shock or not Thomas couldn't tell, God knows *he* was struggling with the memories of what had taken place and by the look of his friends, they felt the same, especially Bridget who seemed a shadow of her former self. Eleanor was different, she talked nonstop as he carried her in his arms. Thinking she may be in shock, he just agreed with everything she said. However as they walked the four miles back to what was now, *Eleanor's* property, Thomas noticed the girl's wits were returning. Her whimpering had turned to talk of retribution for the fight *and* the fire against the black scarves, especially the Scotsman with the black hair and long scar who had questioned her father about Lord Percy's gold.

She wanted to know who this man was and she was determined to take revenge on him no matter what. Eleanor believed that although the man was Scottish, he had obviously been the leader of the Cockney group. He would pay for what he had done if indeed he hadn't already burned to death in the inferno. Sykesy, Edward and Bridget followed behind and although they could only grasp the odd word or two about revenge and reprisal this gave the trio a hint about the couple's secret conversation and plan making.

Thomas listened intently to the girl's ever-expanding plans of recrimination until they reached the old rambling house in its walled gardens. Thomas was impressed as he carried the girl up the steps to the large pillared front door where they were met by a serving couple, who on seeing the girl's bloodied face burst into a myriad of insults aimed towards Thomas and his friends.

Eleanor climbed from his arms and stood unsteadily in the doorway and brushing off her servants' fussing she turned to look at Thomas sternly.

"Remember what I said Thomas Fewtrell. This isn't over by a long shot, someone's going to pay for the death of my father!" The mention of Black Foot seemed to bring back the horror of the previous night, and Eleanor's eyes began to fill with tears. Not wanting the others to see her emotions she turned and pushed her way past the serving couple disappearing into the shadowy hallway. Thomas stood in silence watching the beautiful injured girl as she walked away. The manservant stepped into Thomas's field of vision.

"You heard the lady, *piss off*, the lot of ya!" and that was the last anyone had seen of the beautiful lady Eleanor in the six months since the fall of the Rookery.

****

"*Low!*" Mendoza screamed impatiently. "Come in *low* Thomas, *beneath* his guard, don't give him a chance to use those long arms against you!" Thomas heard the words but was concentrating on not being flattened by one of his sparring partner's wide throws. He followed the Portuguese's command tucked his forearms in tightly around his face and stepped in close towards the man he

163

was fighting. A glancing blow from the other man's fists skipped off the top of his head but didn't make any real contact and suddenly Thomas found himself inside his opponent's attack. The man could no longer hit him as Thomas was too close, his head almost under the chin of his sparring partner pressing into his sweating bare chest. When the man stepped backwards to create a gap between the two, Thomas simply stepped with him and closed the space again following his feet. Thomas realised that this was how Mendoza had beaten so many men over the last few years most of whom were nearly twice the size of the small, pony-tailed prizefighter. Mendoza knew all the right people met through hard work and punches rather than through family ties or aristocratic contacts. After years and years of prize-fighting his way through London and surrounding suburbs, he was now the most respected name in boxing with a plethora of young would-be pugilists happy to pay for his tutelage. However, Mendoza was very reluctant to take on just anyone. Money wasn't a factor, only talent attracted him, and Thomas had talent in abundance. The training session inside the ring wound down until the sparring partner couldn't take any more punishment from Mendoza's star pupil.

"Enough, enough!" Mendoza clapped his hands loudly bringing the session to a halt. Thomas's sparring partner shuffled back to his corner and drained of energy, almost collapsed onto the bench. Thomas crossed to Mendoza still full of energy. The Portuguese smiled and turned to O'Donahue raising his eyebrows. "Well, James, what do you think?" The Irishman hadn't been to Mendoza's gym since returning to London from Birmingham after the night of the fire. He leant over Thomas's bench, smiling and held his hand out. Thomas smiled and took the Irishman's hand shaking it vigorously.

"My God Thomas, you've come along, what have you been doing to him, Daniel?" Mendoza laughed.

"I have been turning him from a scrapper into a real boxer like yourself James." The Irishman sighed.

"I ain't even in the same league as this lad now Daniel!" O'Donahue shook his head, amazed at the difference in the young man.

" Sure tell me, Thomas, how do ye find life in London as a boxer better than a highwayman I'd say?" Thomas laughed.

"Well, the hours aren't so accommodating, but I've heard the money is better!" O'Donahue looked between Thomas and Mendoza.

"Haven't you earned any prizes yet?" Thomas nodded towards the Portuguese.

"No, not yet, I've been living on Daniel's charity. He won't let me fight yet." O'Donahue turned to Mendoza, a confused expression on his face.

"Won't let him fight?" Mendoza shook his head, his long, black ponytail swinging behind him.

"He's not ready James, he's ... " The Irishman cut in.

"Have you lost your senses, Daniel? The lad's more than ready from what I've just witnessed he could beat anyone thrown at him!" Mendoza shook his head.

"No, he's not ready James, don't give him any ideas. He's not ready it's as simple as that!" Mendoza threw Thomas a long piece of linen. "Go and wash yourself down Thomas, cool off." Thomas caught the rag.

"James is right Daniel, I *am* ready, look!" He gestured towards the five exhausted boxers sitting on the long wooden bench on the opposite side of the ring. "I've just been twenty rounds with these lads, and I could still go another twenty. I'm ready Daniel. Besides, I can't live off your charity for the rest of my life. You said I would come to London and be a prizefighter, but if I don't fight I can't win prizes, can I?" Mendoza scowled.

"No, you're not ready Thomas. You think you are and I'm sure you could beat many a man, but if you want to be a truly great boxer, then you need to learn all I know and invent new tactics. We have only just scratched the surface of pugilism, and we are still in the shadows of fighting technics, we need to come into the light, step into the future, come at your opponent in a totally new way. Then and *only* then will we be ready to reveal your talents to the world." Thomas drew a deep breath, a technique he had learned from Mendoza to control his anger and breathing.

"But if we wait too long I'll be an old man Daniel!" The Portuguese laughed.

"Nonsense Thomas, you're thinking too small. You are still a highwayman at heart still going for a quick profit instead of long term glory." The Irishman butted in again.

"But long term glory doesn't pay the rent, Daniel."

"He has no rent to pay James, he has everything he needs." Mendoza snapped.

"Except his independence!" Mendoza became impatient with his old friend.

"Why are you here James? I haven't seen you since that night in Birmingham. I've heard you've been busy scrapping in every tavern in the town, making enemies . . . "

" . . . and *money* Daniel, lots of money!" The Irishman retorted, Mendoza raised his eyebrows.

"Hasn't anyone told you that there's more to life than money my friend!" O'Donahue laughed.

"Yes, you have Daniel, many times and no matter how many times say it, sure it still doesn't pay my rent!" Mendoza began picking up the linen cloth used to dry off the sweat of the men in the ring.

"So why are you here James?" O'Donahue stepped closer to his old friend and placed his huge hand on the Portuguese's, stopping him from collecting the towels.

"There's a fight Daniel." Mendoza stopped and turned to the big man. "Sure it'd be perfect for Thomas." Thomas swung his legs over the bench to face the men. O'Donahue nodded towards Thomas, before turning back to Mendoza. "Be God it'll be a hell of a fight Daniel." Mendoza stared at the Irishman angrily.

"Who for James? You, the boy or the Hellfire Club? Tell me how much do you owe them these days?" O'Donahue stepped back, shaking his head. "Oh, come on man. I know all about your debts to the Hellfire, they've been behind your prizefights for months now. You take the punches, they take the cash only leaving enough for you to drink yourself stupid after every bout. It's no great secret James, the world of pugilism is a small one, my friend." O'Donahue removed his tall conical black hat, his long red curls fell around his ears. He grabbed the Portuguese by the forearm tightly. Mendoza stopped what he was doing and looked sternly at the Irishman's hand. O'Donahue snatched it back.

"Ok, yes I have debts, by God sure who doesn't? But this fight would clear all of our debts."

"I don't have any James!" Mendoza replied in a flat, matter of fact tone. "I keep my house in order." The Irishman sighed.

"Well, we can't all be as organised as you, Daniel. Look sure it's a great fight too, an American fellow, Joseph Buck out of Massachusetts, he's arriving in a day or so. He's a champion from the new world, bigger than Thomas so I'm told, but it'll be a perfect fight to show off your new man. Holy, mother of God, it'll pull in a great revenue Daniel." Mendoza shook his head.

"From what I've heard of Joseph Buck he's not even in the same class as Thomas. He's a dirty fighter with no appreciation for the rules of the sport. If we are to create a real gentleman's sport, there have to be rules."

"I can fight him, Daniel, I don't give a shit how dirty he is." Thomas interjected.

"*NO!*" Mendoza snapped before drawing breath, controlling himself. "My answer is final. You shall not fight until I say you're ready to do so. Do I make myself clear?"

Thomas slumped down onto the bench with a humph, throwing his linen towel on the floor. Mendoza ignored him. "Thank you for coming to see us, James, I'm afraid I have things to do so, please let yourself out when you have finished your conversation with Thomas." Mendoza bent and picked up the discarded towel. "Your dinner will be on the table Thomas." Thomas looked up from under his brow feeling like a spoilt child.

"Thank you, Daniel. I do appreciate your hard work." The Portuguese nodded and left the Irishman and Thomas to talk. O'Donahue watched his friend leave the room. The Irishman donned his hat and bowed slightly.

"Well, sure it was great to see you again Thomas!" O'Donahue almost shouted the words. Thomas looked at him as if he were mad.

"James I'm right in front of you." O'Donahue leant in towards Thomas.

"Shh, we don't have much time." He gave a cautionary glance towards the anti chamber where Mendoza was instructing a young man on using a scrubbing board.

"If you want to fight meet me at the Butcher's Elbow on Marley Street tonight. We can talk freely there." He straightened up again and gave Thomas a wink.

"But . . . I?" Thomas stuttered.

"Shh, the Portuguese hears all!" He nodded and touched his hat. "If you're there you're there sure if not, well I'll know you don't want to fight Joe Buck. Don't forget!" He whispered. "The Butcher's Elbow on Marley Street! Good day to you Thomas!" O'Donahue bowed slightly, turned and crossed the room. "Good day to you Daniel!" He called towards the anti chamber. However, Mendoza had already left the small room and so didn't respond to the Irishman's farewell.

Thomas watched him leave through a small hatchway in the large coach-house door. The Irishman bent and stepped into the street. The door slammed behind him loudly, leaving Thomas sitting on the bench, stewing over the choice between deceiving his friend and patron and his growing impatience to test himself and to find out if the last six month's hard boxing training would actually pay off.

Mendoza's volunteers fussed around the gym cleaning the off-white padded canvas mats which covered the cobbled floor of the old stable. They already looked upon Thomas as some sort of celebrity even though he hadn't actually had a real fight. He watched the group of eight young men eagerly work as one, and it wasn't lost on him that any one of them would have sold his own mother in the market square just to be given the chance that Thomas had been given. For to be taught by the great Mendoza as his fellow pugilists now referred to the Portuguese was seen by many of the young men involved in the sport as the greatest patronage one could have.

The last six months had flown by in a blur of hard physical and mental training always working towards a point in the distant future and now it seemed to Thomas, that moment had finally arrived even though Daniel couldn't see it. The months of carrot and stick training had paid off and now Thomas could barely recognise himself. He was at the peak of his physical fitness, his body rippling with muscles, not an ounce of fat on him. Yet through all the never-ending training, running, sparring and studying the human body, Thomas couldn't shake the image of Eleanor walking away from him into the shadowy hall of her dead father's house. He ran the moment over in his mind again and again. Only in this *daydream* instead of walking away from the mansion with his friends never to see the girl again, he pushed the manservant aside and walked into those shadows alongside the girl and lived happily ever after, Lord of the manor, husband to a beautiful young wife. Sadly reality had turned out *far* from happily ever after.

Thomas had returned to Eleanor's house every day after the fire for a week but was told in no uncertain terms that he wasn't welcome there. According to Bridget, who had called at the house three weeks after Thomas's last visit, Eleanor had allowed *her* into the house where she'd been met in the huge hall. Eleanor had swept elegantly down the wide staircase, her refinery intact. On her face she wore a white plaster mask, the type worn at many of the Venetian-masked balls enjoyed by the wealthy and fashionable throughout Europe. The jewel-encrusted mask only covered her bright blue eyes and the scarred left side of her face which gave the young woman an exotically mysterious aura which in itself seemed attractive to the mixed-race prostitute. Added to the finery of Eleanor's long gown and beautifully styled hair, Bridget thought the young woman seemed somehow *more* attractive than she had done before the attack. When Bridget had visited Thomas in London weeks later she explained to him how the girl seemed to have turned into a woman. Thomas listened intently to every detail about Eleanor Black Foot as if she was *his* woman. She told him about Eleanor's plans to move to the city so that she could to socialise with the aristocrats in the capital where even a low born woman such as Eleanor could mix with the lorded gentry of England so long as she had the cash to do so and Eleanor had plenty of cash. However, if his official estate was worth a small fortune, it was nothing in comparison to the stolen treasure trove the gang-leader had hoarded in the cellars of his Bearwood mansion. Plundered loot and trophies from swindled aristocrats accumulated in late-night, drunken card games had been put in trunks and piled one upon the other until they reached the ceiling of the dark cellar. Eleanor had been shown the treasure by her father's obedient serving couple the day after William Black Foot's funeral and although surprised by her father's secrecy, took all of five minutes to begin making plans of reprisal for her father's death. For the sake of appearances she was careful to take the obligatory time to mourn, and although there was no body to mourn over, a funeral *had* taken place on the grounds of the manor house. She had finally resigned herself to the fact that her father had been burned to ashes in the Rookery and that all she would ever have to remember her gangster father were memories.

Eleanor Black Foot was now, without doubt, one of the wealthiest young women in Middle England, at least that's what all the servants who were out and about buying goods for their masters around the Birmingham Bull Ring were told by Eleanor's gossiping servants. In turn, the recipients of this gossip, would return to *their* masters' houses with wild, exaggerated tales of Eleanor's disfigurement and so gossip spread until the masked woman was spoken about as if she were a heavenly dragon sitting atop a golden hoard. The talk seeped through the walls from one room to another reaching the masters' dining rooms. Here, once again, the higher classes chattered between the sounds of bone china and cut glass; and the gossip spread further until word of the beautiful, masked Eleanor with her vast fortune, and plans to avenge her father's death spread through the small world of dining rooms and gaming tables at every summer ball attended by Britain's aristocracy. Indeed, by the time Eleanor had arrived in London and taken up her rooms in the small, upper-class community of Knightsbridge she was literally the talk of the town. Not to mention the quarry of every young dandy and fop who thought himself a city fox and Eleanor a country chicken to be fucked, plucked and eaten.

Mandrake

CHAPTER 16

The old, creaking ship rolled sickeningly as it took on the turning tide at the mouth of the River Thames. The waters that separated the English channel and the river itself were always choppy as the eddying tide danced with the channel's currents creating a maelstrom of small but violently unpredictable waves. The ship's bows had cut through larger surf on its three-week crossing from the newly independent land of America. However due to a rare and easterly wind the small waves crashing around the river mouth had a ferocity far beyond their size, and were being held higher than normal by the brisk offshore winds which was making the ship's entry into the water corridor to London a perilous operation for any ship's captain who wasn't used to the currents, shallows and dangerous sandbanks.

The American sat below decks in the relative darkness of his cabin, his legs hanging over the side of his bunk, his hands clasped around his rumbling stomach belching continuously, as he had done almost every minute of the three-week journey from the city of Boston. The rolling of the old ship was bad enough on his stomach but taken on top of the putrid smell of human waste, fish guts and the stinking stagnant water in the ship's ballast which splashed and sloshed beneath his cabin floor he had struggled to keep an ounce of food down the whole trip.

Joe Buck was a twenty-five-year-old Massachusetts farm labourer who, as his mother said proudly on his departure 'had done good'. His sudden rise to fame amongst the fellow barn brawlers and drinking-den associates of Boston town had turned him from an ignorant shit-shoveler into an arrogant fist-thrower. The whole of Boston, including Joe Buck himself, thought he was unstoppable as a fighter, as did the Hellfire club. In fact, Lord Dashwood who had been told about the man by his various slave-trading connections in Bristol had come up with the idea of an American-British fight off, a way of illustrating to King George that the loss of North America to the British crown was of little concern, because man for man the British were a finer and fiercer race of people. He would demonstrate this to the King by showing that a British pugilist could outbox an American any day of any week. Of course, that's how Dashwood would explain it to the King and his chums. In reality, the Hellfire had collectively paid the one hundred and twenty-five pounds for Joe Buck's crossing on the old ship *Grey Goose* in order to bankroll the club from the King's wagers on the bouts. For those outside of the King's circle, the word was that Joe Buck was the best and anyone that thought otherwise had better put their money where their mouth was.

A loud knock on Joe's cabin door made him jump out of his seasick stupor.

"Mr Buck, are you all right in there, sir?" A rough, rasping voice called through the rotten timber door to the cabin. Joe tried to talk, but another loud, uncontrollable retch fell from his open mouth. "Mr Buck, are you...?"

"Yes, yes, I'm ok, just leave me alone, God damn it!" The man outside just stared at the old door not knowing what to do, finally asking,

"It's just that you haven't been out of your cabin for several days Mr Buck. The captain is concerned, sir!" Nothing but silence came from the cabin, the only sound was the ship creaking its sea-battered timbers together. The sailor knocked again. "Mr Buck, sir, the captain asked if you'd like to join him on deck as we approach London sir? He thought you might enjoy it, sir."

BURP! The sailor went to knock again, but as he raised his hand, the door flew open. Joe Buck stood unsteadily in the doorway, ashen-faced and nothing like the athletic, young hero that had strutted the decks as the ship left America.

"Tell the captain I shall be on deck presently. At the moment, as you can see I am . . ."

"If you don't mind me suggesting sir. You'll be far better off with the sea wind in your face sir. The fresh air has a way of driving out the seasickness. Come on now sir, I'll help you." Buck made a minimal gesture as if to say he didn't want to go on deck but by the time he'd gathered his wits about him, the sailor had grabbed his thick forearm and was almost dragging him along the dark passageway and guiding him up the steep stairwell into a brisk but refreshingly summer breeze. Much to Joe Buck's surprise, it was almost dawn. Above him shone a bright, crescent moon lying lazily in a wisp of silver cloud in a sky still bright with starlight. Far off to the East, a thin orange line of light was already appearing on the horizon, stretching across the landscape bringing the first signs of a new day.

The Grey Goose slowly worked her way up the River Thames until after an hour of fairly smooth yet speedy sailing the first lights of the great city of London were sighted in the distance. All hands joined Joe and the captain on deck to witness the first sighting of what was considered to be the most wondrously corrupt city on Earth.

The raspy-voiced sailor had been right, Joe did feel better, and by the time the old ship pulled into its mooring he felt himself again. He mulled over whether he'd made the right choice coming to Britain in the first place however the sight of the welcoming committee, two very colourful gentlemen in the latest gaudy fashions and a grand carriage to greet him soon replaced this feeling with one more of curiosity.

"Mr Buck?" enquired one of the gentlemen, a small-faced, long-nosed man, that to Joe seemed to have more in common with a weasel than a human. The man swept his hat from his bald head and bowed. Joe nodded. "Welcome to London sir, my name is . . ."

"Where can I get something to eat?" Joe cut the weasel's grand welcome speech short. The small man turned to his companion, and all three looked at each other, not knowing what to say. "I've been trapped on that God-damned sieve of a ship you booked my passage on for the past three weeks, and all I've eaten is stale bread, brine soaked goat's meat, most of which I must tell you, is on my cabin floor. Now I was told that I would be treated like a prince if I came across the sea to fight. I see now that I am expected to box half-starved and ill-treated which I'm sure was your plan all along. I tell you, sir, I have a good mind to turn around and walk back up that gang plank and return home to America where we know how to treat our guests with some dignity." The weasel's smile turned to an expression of horror.

"Oh no, sir, return to America?" The Weasel's English accent seemed strange to the American, a lighting fast diatribe that he could hardly understand. "Don't do that sir, if it's food ya want, then you'll have the best London has to offer!" Joe threw his bag at the man's feet.

"Good, I could eat a horse!" The weasel laughed and reaching down he grabbed Joe's bag and threw it at one of the other, larger gentlemen.

"If it's an horse you want, it's a facking horse you'll get Mr Buck!" Stepping towards the carriage, the weasel pulled the door open. "This way if you please Mr Buck sir. There's someone very important that wants to meet ya!"

"Food first!" Joe said without moving. The weasel nodded with a false smile, all the time wondering where he was going to find a tavern in London that served horse flesh. The British were not big partakers of cheval but Lord Dashwood *had* ordered him to treat the American to whatever he wanted, no matter what.

"Whores, mollies, cards or gin, whatever the man wants, get it for him!" That's what Lord Dashwood's manservant Flint had shouted as the men left to collect the American.

"But horse meat, bleeding hell?" The weasel thought to himself as he climbed in behind the boxer. "God only knows what these colonials were used to eating amongst the savages of America!"

The meeting at Lord Dashwood's London townhouse didn't begin as the happy affair his Lordship was hoping it would be. This was due partly to the late arrival of the American at the huge house in Mayfair, and partly due to his incessant, non-stop belching and farting, caused no doubt by his over indulgence on the horse meat acquired at one of the only purveyors of cheval in the city. A meeting house of wayward French fishermen in the toughest taverns in London's roughest areas around the East End docks. The meat was clandestinely disguised in a beef broth, hidden in a brown slop of grease and soggy vegetables and served in the wooden bowl in a crowded bar full of fish-stinking Frenchmen and a fog of tobacco smoke. All of which battered the senses with old factory smells, sounds and sights and was certainly enough to null a human's senses into submission. However, none of this changed the fact it was putridly old meat and no matter how well the cook had worked his magic, the gristle stubbornly held onto its unmistakably rough texture and taste of horseflesh. This left the weasel thinking he'd done the American a great favour finding a meal of horse in a country of horse lovers and the American wondering how the English had become such an international power if indeed this gristly bowl of slop was the type of fayre they were happy to eat. Nevertheless, Joe Buck was hungry, *and* he had weight to recover before his first fight which he'd just been informed was in a few days time. And so belches and the occasional rancid explosion of flatulence were just going to have to be endured by all in the Joe Buck boxing camp, as his first fight in old England was something that he couldn't afford to lose. They were joined by Lord Dashwood's manservant Flint, who on being brought up to speed on the conversation made it very clear that his job was to make sure that wasn't going to happen come hell or high water. Joe Buck had instantly taken a dislike to Flint when he'd been introduced. There was something about the Scotsman who'd done so well for himself under the tutelage of his master Lord Dashwood that he didn't trust.

"So Mr Buck, are ye in good health, ready for the fight?" Flint asked seeing his Lordship's demeanour attempting to hide his attraction to the young boxer. The American noticed the old man's inappropriate gaze but chose to ignore it, thinking himself paranoid.

"No sir I am *not* in good health. The crossing on that coffin ship you put me on nearly killed me. But yeah, I'm ready for the fight, that is, I will be if..." he turned to the weasel who sat on a small table on the other side of the room, "...this weasel-faced bastard doesn't poison me first!" The American belched loudly as if to prove the point. The weasel just smiled, bowing his head slightly to stare at his silver-buckled shoes. Lord Dashwood scowled at the small bald man.

"Don't worry Mr Buck, from now on you can eat here. My house is at you disposal whilst you're staying in London." Turning to Flint, the Lord spoke more sternly than he normally would. "Make sure Mr Buck gets everything he wants. Do you under stand Flint?" His manservant nodded obediently.

"Oh ai, of course, your Lordship!"

Turning back to Dashwood, Joe questioned.

"Does anyone know who it is I will actually be fighting?" Dashwood suddenly became more animated.

"Yes, we have the perfect opponent for you Mr Buck, someone who's been in training for the past six months with London's most respected pugilist preparing himself for his debut fight."

"Debut fight?" Joe's eyebrows furled in a sudden look of confusion. "What do you mean *debut* fight? I was under the impression I was fighting London's best not some local scrapper!" Flint cut in.

"Oh, he ain't no scrapper Mr Buck!" Joe scowled at him.

"Well, is he any good?" Dashwood chuckled to himself. The American turned towards the old man.

"Is there some joke I'm not privy to gentlemen? Because as I'm sure you're aware I've travelled a long way to fight your best and..."

"Mr Buck, please let me interrupt you." The American stopped talking. The old man smiled again. "There is no joke, well, not one at your expense anyhow. You see Mr Flint here has seen this man fight and well... Perhaps he'd best describe him to you." Flint seemed to be caught off guard by his master, and there was a short silence until Joe lost his patience.

"Well, is he any *good*?" Flint's smile dropped from his face.

"Thomas Fewtrell good? Och no, he is ne good, the man's a fucking liability, that's what he is, from your reputation in the new world, I'm sure you're a grand boxer Mr Buck but in all honesty, ye have ne got a bloody chance in hell son." The silence returned to the room, Joe Buck stared at Flint for a few seconds. He could feel the stares of the other men in the room bearing down on him, and he wondered if he'd been brought to England as some sort of sacrificial lamb. He tried to decipher Flint's words as if he'd somehow misheard the man.

"What did you say?" Flint rose from his bench and crossed the room to pour himself a small glass of port and then returned to the bench where he'd been sitting. The American followed his every move.

"I said, Thomas Fewtrell is a better boxer than ye!" Joe snarled.

"But you haven't even seen me fight, damn you!" Flint raised the glass then slugged the port back in one mouthful. He closed his eyes for a few seconds savouring the alcohol on his tongue.

"I donny need to see ye fight man, I've seen *him* fight, and he's the best I've *ever* seen and over the last two years thanks to his Lordship, I've seen em all. I saw Fewtrell kill a man twice his size six months ago in Birmingham. He was fast, accurate and more importantly, imaginative with his punches which I must say were the most powerful I've ever seen. I'd have put him up against anyone back then, but now . . . !"

"Now?" Joe Buck pressed him.

"Well, now he's been training with Daniel Mendoza . . . " Flint held the empty glass up in front of him examining the rainbow prism of light filtering through its cut glass, " . . . like I said, he's a fucking liability!" Joe stood amazed, turning to Dashwood he questioned.

"Well, why the fuck did you bring me all this way to fight a man I can't beat?" Flint stood up and crossed back towards the port decanter.

"Oh, I did-ne say you canny beat him, I said, between the two of ye, he's the better boxer, given half the chance he'll destroy ye."

The weasel sniggered, Joe Buck glared at the man, his nose flared in a mixture of astonishment, anger and confusion.

"I'll have you know sir, I am the finest God damn boxer in Massachusetts, I would beat . . . " The weasel stopped sniggering.

"Yeah, but you ain't in Massachusetts are ya? You're in old Blighty mate, and if Flint says he'll beat ya then he'll bleeding beat ya, end of, mush!" Dashwood rose from his chair and crossed to the American placing his hand on his shoulder he patted it softly.

"It's all part of a ruse, Mr Buck."

"Ruse?" Joe Buck turned to the old man.

"That's correct, a ruse sir." The two men stared at each other for a second and Dashwood realised his words were only making things more confusing for the young man. "Don't worry me lad, you'll win the fight as I said, Flint will take care of it, this Thomas Fewtrell won't stand a chance once Flint here has slipped him one of his . . . " the Lord turned to his servant, " . . . what is it you fellows call these potions?"

"A manny me Lord!" Dashwood turned back to the boxer.

"There, Flint will dose Fewtrell up with a . . . *manny!*"

"Manny?" Buck said, matter of factly as if by repeating the word it would clarify what on earth these men were talking about.

"A Mandrake, Mr. Buck, it's a wee drink, something that looks and tastes nice but ain't nice once it's inside ye. It makes ye . . . " Flint pointed his index finger at his head and twirled it around, whilst crossing his eyes, " . . . makes ye mad, so it does."

"Go mad?" Buck asked, still bewildered, Lord Dashwood cut in.

"What my man is trying to say is that Mandrake is a psychoactive, hallucinogenic, plant root, shaped oddly enough like a man hence the name. The extract of which is very potent and can be hidden in a glass of . . . " the old man shook his head, " . . . port or brandy . . . even gin." He looked back towards his servant for confirmation that he'd got the latter drink correct. Flint nodded.

"It can be used in gin sir, ai."

"Colourless and odourless you see, Mr Buck. It is said that the ancient Roman women used it as a love potion giving it to their husbands in an attempt to prolong the act of love making." Joe Buck gave a sarcastic laugh.

"So what am I here for gentlemen, to fight him or fuck him?"

"No, no, hopefully, you won't have to do either Mr Buck for if given in the right amount, the mandrake root will render the man useless in fighting . . . fucking or . . . anything else you should wish to do to him for that matter. To all and sundry, Thomas Fewtrell will appear to be drunk!" Flint butted in,

"He'll never know what hit him!" The weasel sniggered again.

"That'll be you, Mr Buck, you'll be what hits him!" Joe Buck smiled,

"So the fight's rigged, why didn't you say so to begin with?" Lord Dashwood chuckled. He patted the American's shoulder again.

"You see gentlemen, our American cousins have a way of putting things, no beating around the bush. This boxing match is about far more than beating your opponent." Buck looked the old man over, a fresh look of distrust on his face.

"If the fight's fixed that's just fine by me, I don't mind telling you gentlemen, I'm here for fame and money and I ain't too fussed how I go about acquiring them. My dear mother back in America would like it if I returned home with my good looks intact." Dashwood smiled. He looked the young man in front of him up and down, his crafty old eyes darting around the man's ripped body as it strained against the constraints of his dress coat and shirt beneath, finally settling on his groin. Joe Buck watched with some bemusement as the old man's eyes ate his form. Glancing at Flint, then at the weasel, he noticed they too were watching him, and once again the American wondered what he'd got himself involved in.

"Money and fame, is that truly all you want Mr Buck?" Dashwood finally said. "I was led to believe that our colonial cousins were rife for rebellion?" The American's eyebrows furrowed once more.

"If you mean do we want to be free of tyranny then yes, that's one of the reasons I came here, I'll make no secret of it!" Dashwood smiled.

"Good, then neither shall we." Buck shook his head. Dashwood spoke triumphantly now. "You are here not only to fight, you are an American rebel sir, a figurehead for America." Joe Buck stared from man to man, searching for an answer to the riddle of Dashwood's statement.

"Why would you guys want an American figurehead to beat a British boxer?" Dashwood deflected the question.

"Your good mother will find her son not only as handsome as he was when he left home but considerably wealthier to boot and more's the point, you will return to your homeland as a hero of your revolution and I can assure you that your name shall forever be remembered in the annals of British history!" Buck, although a little confused could only assume the Lord was referring to his boxing ability. He was impressed by the Lord's words and thoughts of returning home a rich hero swam in his imagination. The old Lord bowed slightly to the young man, and Buck returned his bow. "Flint, pour some port for everyone. Let's drink a toast to fame, money and revolution!" Flint flashed the weasel a dark stare. The weasel seemed to shake himself out of a daydream and crossed to the drink's table and began to pour the port into the four small glasses.

"If you don't mind me asking, how do you plan to administer the . . . *manny*?" The American said the words awkwardly. Flint rose and joined the weasel at the table.

"Och, that's the easy bit, Mr Buck, we've got a wee fella on the inside, James O'Donahue. He's into his Lordship for a wee fortune, gambling debts, whores, cards and the like, so in his infinite wisdom, his Lordship saw an opportunity to kill two birds with one stone. Firstly, O'Donahue might be a stupid, ugly Irish bastard, but even he realises that this bit of treachery could clear his debts to Lord Dashwood once and for all. He knows only too well that if he doesn't clear them, he'll end up in the debtors' jail or at the bottom of the Thames. *More* importantly, he's a rebel like you and I and wants independence from England which puts him firmly on our side of the fence politically!" Flint smirked. "His Lordship's Hellfire club can destroy Fewtrell and Mendoza's reputations in one fell swing of the axe!" The weasel spoke up again.

"More like a swing of Mr Buck's fist, wouldn't ya say your Lordship?" Dashwood chuckled again.

"Well said, well said and quite correct too." He said giving a small clap to his weasel-faced minder as if he were a pet monkey. Turning back to the American, he explained. "You see Mr. Buck, the word around London is that even though Thomas Fewtrell has never fought professionally he is, nevertheless, so I'm told by my spies in Mendoza's camp, an exceptional fighter and to add to the general public's anticipation about the fight the word is that Daniel Mendoza is also an exceptional tutor. All of which makes him the number one fighter to put a wager on and as my man Flint put it so elegantly, a *fucking* liability. So you see Mr Buck, the city and more's to the point, the King of England himself thinks Fewtrell is unstoppable." Joe Buck perked up at the mention of royalty.

"The King of England, you mean King George, I get mixed up with all these Kings you have over here?" Dashwood laughed.

"Quite!" He said sarcastically. "Yes, unfortunately, I mean King George, well, not unless the Kingdom has a new King I haven't heard of yet? Have we got a new King Flint?" He smiled at the other man, who also began to chuckle sycophantically, copying his Lordship.

"No, your Lordship sir, still King George, the same drunken bastard as ever he was."

"Thank goodness, Flint. I thought that fop of a son of his had stolen the crown from his bloated head for a minute!" The old man spun back towards the American. "His highness *will* be there, incognito of course," he said recalling his conversation with the drunken monarch, "and he will as everyone else will for that matter, have their money on Thomas Fewtrell to win. Of course, our money and that of our Jacobite friends in government and associates in the Hellfire will be on *you*, Mr Buck. I will advise the King as to the outcome of the bout in Fewtrell's favour, and between Flint's highly potent *manny* and O'Donahue's treachery we shall all make a small mountain of gold guineas and at the same time ruin the reputations of two of the most talented pugilists in the world. Reputations that will take years to recover and during those years Mr Buck, you ... " he turned to Flint, " ... with the help of Flint's witchcraft brew will be the undefeated boxing champion of Britain." He left the words hanging in the room's dusty summer air for a second before finishing his sentence. "What say you, Mr Buck?" Joe Buck's normal expression of a spoilt child was replaced by a broad grin which now spread across his face and holding his glass of port high he toasted,

"Here's to Mandrake and the end of Thomas Fewtrell's beginning!" Dashwood, Flint and the weasel raised their glasses. The three conspirators shared a secret smile at the American's naivety and little did Joe Buck realise he was about to become a perfect scapegoat for the Jacobite coup about to take place. Buck thought himself just a simple pugilist who had crossed the ocean to box England's best, and he *was* to all intensive purposes just that. The Jacobite plan to assassinate King George III of England would need a fall-man if things went awry, Joe Buck would be such a man. A self-confessed American Republican that fitted the role perfectly, unwittingly playing his part in the coup and only finding out how culpable he was when it was too late and the King was dead. The American had eaten a horse, and now he was about to become one, a *Trojan* horse.

The Red Snake

CHAPTER 17

S ykesy stood in the shadows watching the carriages clatter down the street towards their destination of *the Old Cheshire Cheese Inn,* the venue for the most anticipated match of pugilism in years. A sudden summer shower had caught all by surprise with its ferocity and the horses pulling the elegant carriages skittered and slipped amid a racket of horse-brass and bridles on the shiny cobbles.

The old coaching inn had been chosen as the venue for Joe Buck's debut British fight. Word spread like wildfire to anyone in the know that the large room in the pub with its concertina rear doors leading onto a huge, open roofless yard was to be a venue for the battle between America's finest fighter and Britain's newest hope, one *Thomas Fewtrell.* The excitement about the fight had spread far and wide from the lowest street-dwellers of the capital to the most superior courtiers who gathered in gaudy-coloured gaggles nattering in the halls and corridors throughout the courts of the grandest palaces of London. The rumour that King George was going to be attending the fight had created levels of anticipation throughout the city that London hadn't seen since Bonny Prince Charlie had threatened to take the capital at the head of his tartan army of Highlanders, over forty years before.

Sykey stood under the shelter of the inn's large porched entrance to protect himself from the unpredictable rain and waited for his friend's carriage to come into view. Secretly he was glad of the summer downfall as it enabled him to hide beneath the wide brim of his hat and the turned up leather collar on his black duster coat. His clandestine presence amongst the shadows reminded him of his life with Thomas as highwaymen only six months previously. He eyed the passing coaches suspiciously looking for any familiar faces inside their velvet-lined interiors lest he should be recognised by one of his former card-game victims who might want to deliver a dose of payback on the swindler Captain. London was not a safe place for a man like Captain Henry Sykes to find himself on the wrong side of the toffs. He held the limp, damp collar up around his cheeks, peering over the top of the dark leather. Thomas was late, no doubt due to the rain.

"He should've been here by now!" He thought to himself, perhaps Mendoza had kicked off about the fight again and at this very moment, the two boxers were still on the other side of town arguing like an old married couple about whether Thomas should fight the American at all. God knows Mendoza had made his opinion clear over the few days since O'Donahue had persuaded Thomas to take the fight, even offering the ex-highwayman some prize money in advance if he didn't fight. However, Henry had heard rumours amongst his old London contacts about the Irish boxer's real intentions and exactly who O'Donahue was serving, and it wasn't Thomas Fewtrell. Sykesy was so concerned about his old friend that he'd broken his self-induced exile from the capital to warn Thomas about the treachery at hand. When Henry presented himself at Mendoza's gym earlier that week to warn the pugilists about O'Donahue's true intentions, he found the treacherous Irishman sitting, smiling at the side of the training ring watching Thomas and Daniel arguing as they trained. Sykesy felt unable to speak candidly in front of the Irishman for fear of warning him and his masters that he was onto their scheme. The row between Mendoza and his student had nearly come to blows over what Mendoza felt was Thomas's disloyalty to the Mendoza school of Pugilism as his gym was now called. Mendoza made no secret what he thought about the Hellfire sponsored event saying, "Those Aristocrats want to pervert the sport for their own agenda just for money and not the art."

"Of course they bleeding did." Sykesy thought. "The Toffs want to control everything for a profit. That's how the world works ain't it?" However, the bad atmosphere in the Fewtrell / Mendoza camp surrounding that evening's fight only helped to fuel a forest fire of rumour and speculation as to Thomas Fewtrell's fighting prowess, creating of an even bigger draw than had initially been expected. Thus the Cheshire Cheese Inn was already full to capacity, and the town watchmen had been called upon to quell the growing crowd who tussled for space on the street outside the inn, all vying for a glimpse inside the building's wide-open windows. Inside only the high and mighty were allowed a ringside seat, whilst those not so high and mighty watched from wherever they could get a view.

To call the fighting area a ring at all was stretching the imagination. For the circle created inside the room was nothing more than a set of wooden hurdles interlinked together by small wrought iron pegs and slots, each one holding the weight of the next, until the circle was completed, thus making a very sturdy circular structure to separate the rowdy spectators from the fighters inside. Leaving each man free to battle away to their heart's content.

Unfortunately for both Thomas and Sykesy, Thomas's coach had arrived at the rear trademan's entrance to the Inn. Trundling its way along the dark alleyways that crisscrossed London and acted as the delivery routes and short cuts for tradesmen and the like, thus avoiding the growing mob around the venue, which by now had swollen to nearly a thousand eager fight fans.

Thomas stepped from the coach behind the Inn and peered through a gap in the huge gates separating the alleyway from the Inns rear court yard. In the relative stillness of the dark alleyway, he watched the chaotic scene of three or four hundred, drunken dandy's, Fops and various members of the British gentry; drinking and smoking their long white clay pipes, in a cloud of tobacco smoke, which hung over the whole scene like some sort of malevolent spirit. An atmosphere of aggression filled the space, which made Thomas's heart flutter. He stood dumbfounded for a few seconds before O'Donahue, who had accompanied him on his journey across town, grew impatient and kicked the small hatchway in the gate, bent and stepped through. Thomas stared at the hatchway for a second, frozen with anticipation. Mendoza's words played in his mind.

"You're better than this Thomas, you should be fighting for the art of boxing, not just the money. Are you nothing but a whore? Dancing to the aristocracy's whim?"

Maybe he was right, it wasn't too late to pull out. The Irishman's big, red head stuck back out of the hatchway.

"For feck's sake Thomas, are ye gonna stand in this piss-stinking alleyway all night? Get your arse in here!" Thomas noticed the man's voice had a touch of aggression in it. The friendly 'we're in this together' tone had all but vanished from O'Donahue's thick brogue.

"Jesus man come on, people are waiting!" Without thinking too much about it, Thomas followed the Irishman's order and bent beneath the hatch's small frame and stepped across the threshold to the yard. The waiting crowd, almost as one, turned to watch his entrance, a hush falling over the place as he straightened up inside the gate. He stood to his full height of six feet three inches, his bandaged knuckles held out in front of his bare chest, a pair of black, leather breeches to the knee wrapped twice around the waist with a bright-red, silk scarf tied in a bow at his side. In a time when most people carried little or no excess weight on their bodies, his muscle-ripped abdomen, wide shoulders and thick-set arms made quite an impression on the waiting crowd, of whom many had never seen a man like him except possibly in an old painting of a Greek god. The silence soon turned to one of positive murmurings around the packed yard, as the inquisitive stares became a sea of smiling approval.

Memories of the Rookery flooded Thomas's mind, accompanied by an overwhelming feeling of deja vu, as he pictured the Bear's entrance into the Rookery on that frosty night six months ago. The Bear had no doubt he would kill anyone placed in front of him if indeed he was thinking anything at all, but how wrong he'd been. However, now it was *Thomas* the crowd stared at with awe as he entered, The only difference was that Thomas didn't feel the confidence the Bear had felt on that night. Thomas was filled with self-doubt and a growing feeling of guilt towards the man who had taken him in and trained him so hard over the last six months. He only hoped things ended better for him than they had for the Bear.

The crowd began to part as O'Donahue pushed his way through the packed audience. Thomas was surprised at how many people knew the Irishman, patting his back and shaking his huge hands, broad smiles on their excited faces as he passed through the crowd. Thomas received the same welcome which helped to relax the nervousness that had begun to flutter in his stomach like a thousand horseflies. On reaching the wooden hurdles, Thomas knew what was expected of him and in one jump, placing his hands on the hurdle top, he hopped over the fence landing inside the ring to a rousing cheer from almost everyone inside the yard. The second Thomas's feet hit the straw-covered floor inside the hurdles he felt the oppressive, intimidating atmosphere of the ring. The difference between inside and out was almost palpable. Unlike the ring at the Rookery which on reflection had been little more than a place of archaic torture for the amusement of a psychopathic gangster, this ring was set up purely for the sport of pugilism. Although it looked pretty much the same, it was somehow more professional, a place of work for gladiators, a place of pain, punishment and perseverance. Thomas had trained hard for this moment, but nothing prepared him for the feeling of vulnerability, not the sort of emotion that would help him get out of this wooden circle in one piece. Thomas looked around at the baying crowd, and even though he could hear O'Donahue talking to him,

"Drink some ale, Thomas, bolster your strength!" But even in the midst of the throng, he felt totally alone, especially as Mendoza, the man who had been by his side at every training bout for the last six months wasn't going to be there to act as his second. A sensory overload washed over Thomas as he stood in the ring automatically slamming his bandaged fists together. His autonomous actions gave him something to concentrate on. However, somewhere in the back of his mind in a place buried deep in his psyche he started to ask himself a question, a question that all fighters must ask themselves at the outset of any battle.

"What the *fuck* am I doing here?" The noise of the crowd faded into the distance, and the boxer found himself in an almost silent world inside his own mind. A world where normality had been replaced by blood lust and depravity, a place where Thomas stood at the epicentre of that depravity, ready and willing to destroy another human being with his bare hands purely for money and the entertainment of the paying public.

"Drink Thomas!" O'Donahue pressed him from behind, but Thomas's mind had moved on to his opponent, or, more's to the point, the lack of his opponent. Where was the American? Due to the crowd, Thomas had arrived late, but the American *still* wasn't anywhere to be seen. Thomas's heart jumped as he thought about the possibility of a no show.

"That would be the best outcome for all involved," he thought, Thomas mulled the idea over in his mind. Mendoza would come around if there wasn't a fight due to there being no opponent, he was sure of it, and the prize money would go to Thomas regardless. "Yes, yes, this was the best outcome. The American has lost his nerve."

"Thomas!" The Irishman's thick brogue made him turn around, and he could see the concern on O'Donahue's face. "Take a bloody drink of ale man." The big man pushed a jug of brown ale towards him. Thomas took the pewter tankard from him and smiled.

"Looks like the American has chickened out, James!" He shouted over the din of the audience's rowdy banter. He lifted the pewter jug. "Cheers James, here's to success!" As he drank, he looked through the glass bottom of the tankard. He could see the Irishman staring at him with a strange look on his face. The ale wasn't a good one. Thomas noticed a bitterness underneath the normal, sugary, yeasty flavour. The glass-bottomed tankard allowed Thomas to see O'Donahue raise his hand and touch the bottom of the glass with his index finger.

"Come on Thomas!" O'Donahue shouted over the din. "Get it down ya man, drain the jug, it'll fill ya with . . . " But through the glass Thomas saw another hand raised towards the tankard accompanied by a familiar voice, interrupting the Irishman's command.

"Don't drink that piss Thomas, have a shot of whisky instead."

Thomas dropped the tankard after gulping only one mouthful of O'Donahue's ale.

"Sykesy!" Thomas shouted happily over the noisy crowd. O'Donahue glared at the other man, shocked by his interruption. "Sykesy what are you doing here? I thought you were still in Birmingham with Bridget . . . ?" Henry glanced around him, tipping the peak of his tricorn hat a little further over his eyebrows.

"Shhh Thomas, I'm a wanted man around here, remember!" He half whispered. Turning to O'Donahue, he pushed the tankard away from Thomas replacing it with a small, metal hip flask, forcing it into Thomas's hand. "Irish whisky Thomas, a proper fighting drink, ain't that right James?" The Irishman didn't answer, only stood there dumfounded, not knowing what to say. Sykesy smiled at the big man, letting him know that he was onto his scheme. Turning back to Thomas he gestured. "Go on Thomas, have a good swig me old mate, it'll get you in the mood to beat seven shades out of that American. After all, you'll want to put on a good show for Eleanor. I just saw her carriage pulling up outside the tavern so you'll want to make a good impression me old mate!" Thomas took a slug of the strong whisky.

"Jesus!" He said grimacing. "I think I'd rather stick to the ale, that stuff's rough as rats. Eleanor's here?" He enquired, Sykesy nodded.

"Yeah, I tried to talk to her outside, but she was ushered in by her servant, I can't see her now but she's here somewhere." Thomas handed the flask back to his friend and turned to see if he could see Eleanor in the crowd. O'Donahue saw his chance and pressed the tankard back towards Thomas again. Sykesy went to grab it from the Irishman's hand, but O'Donahue saw his move and slammed his big hand into the smaller man's chest and gave a little push. Sykesy took an involuntary step backwards and tripping over his heels he stumbled backwards where he was swallowed up by the merry crowd.

"Come Thomas, be God we haven't got time for this shite!"The Irishman's voice had an urgency to it that made no sense to Thomas. Turning away from the crowd Thomas took the cup from the

Irishman. "Drink your ale boy, Joe Buck will be here soon enough."
Thomas, suddenly felt unsure about the Irishman, unable to explain
his sudden discomfort in his friend he just nodded and took the
tankard anyway.

"Yeah, I gotta wash that bleeding whisky taste out of my mouth!"
He said screwing his face up into another exaggerated grimace.
"Where did Sykesy go?"

"Never mind that gobshite." O'Donahue said sternly, "Keep
your mind on the fight Thomas!" Taking the pewter cup he took a
long gulp of the muddy-brown liquid inside. Suddenly the tankard
was knocked from his hand.

"Don't drink the ale Thomas!"

"What, why?" Thomas said surprised as Sykesy stepped back
towards the ringside after extricating himself from the group he'd
been pushed into.

"Just don't drink it, not if you want to win this fight anyway!"
O'Donahue grabbed Sykesy by the collar of his waistcoat.

"Stay out of this you little shite. What difference does it make
to you what he drinks?" Sykesy stood to his full height, which was
still a head smaller than the Irishman.

"You know why it makes a difference mate? He's my friend
which is more than can be said for *you*!" The smaller man prod-
ded his finger into the Irishman's chest as he snarled into his face.
O'Donahue brought his fist back behind him and grabbed Sykes's
collar again. Much to Thomas's surprise, Sykesy threw a punch at
the big man, however the blow had no power to it and although
it hit the Irishman full in the jaw, the punch didn't register on
O'Donahue, except to make him even angrier than he already was.
The realisation that his couldn't fight the big man and unable to
protect himself, Henry just shut his eyes and waited for the blow.
The Irishman was about to drive his clenched fist into Sykes's face
when they were interrupted by a woman's voice.

"*Gentlemen!*" All three men turned to see a young lady in a
pale-green, silk gown and cloak. Her white-wigged hair standing
in a bundle upon her head. Her beautiful powdered face, well, that
what could be seen of it beneath the jewelled venetian mask which

covered almost all of the left hand side of her face glowed in the semi-darkness of the tavern, as if she were not of this world but from some other spiritual place. The sight of her took Thomas's breath away.

"*Eleanor!*" He gasped. The lady bowed slightly.

"Thomas!" Her eyes wandered over his body taking in his perfect physique. Thomas stared at her, dumbfounded by her beauty which was somehow made all the more appealing by the addition of the ivory-coloured mask. "Have I come at a bad moment gentlemen?" She addressed O'Donahue, who at the sight of the woman had dropped Sykesy back to his feet and taken a step away from his would-be victim.

"Me lady!" The Irishman bowed clumsily. Eleanor returned his bow with a delicate smile. Sykesy, on the other hand giving a short burst of manic laughter, partly due to the sight of the girl but mainly because he had just escaped a pummelling from the Irishman.

"Me lady!" He took his hat from his head and bowing he swept it in a long arc in front of him. Eleanor leant forward and pulled him back up.

"Stand up Henry, I'm not the bloody queen!" She said laughing, turning towards Thomas she said, "If you would excuse us, gentlemen, I need to talk with Mr Fewtrell." She smiled again, but neither men moved. "In private if you please gentlemen." On her words, both Sykesy and the Irishman bowed and began to back away into the crowd. Sykesy glanced at the big man, who was staring at him menacingly and Henry knew that the altercation wasn't over by a long shot. The Irishman wanted blood, Sykes's blood. Henry saw his opportunity to escape a good beating and vanished into the throng, gone within the blink of an eye. O'Donahue, on seeing the ex- highwayman's flight gave pursuit by pushing his way into the mass following his tricorn hat as it darted this way and that through the crowd.

"Eleanor, Sykesy said you were here, but why?" The woman stepped in closer to the hurdle and gestured with her finger that he should do the same. Thomas came nearer to the girl, and she brought her face next to Thomas's and whispered,

"I came to watch you fight Thomas." Thomas closed his eyes. The smell of the girl washed over him. The same smell he'd enjoyed six months before. An intoxicating honey-like sweetness floated around Eleanor, heavy with sexual promise, too delicate and fleeting to grasp, which in itself had the effect of making the scent even more addictive than it already was.

The presence of the woman made the aggression Thomas had been storing up for months in the build up for a fight, simply fall away. His mind swam in a multi-coloured daydream of lust, and he began to sway on his feet. She was speaking to him but her words were too far away for him to hear. His mind suddenly felt detached from the moment somehow as it created small animations of tiny dancing skeletons and devils which jerked and sprang to a music, deep within his soul.

"*Thomas!*" He opened his eyes, Eleanor was shouting at him, but he wondered why her voice came from so far away. She reached for him and grabbed his bare arm. "*Thomas!*" She shouted over the din of the room. Suddenly, as if he had stepped through an impenetrable invisible portal, he was there again, next to her, back in the chaos of the tavern, where his body had been all along. The noise of the crowd was suddenly deafeningly loud, bringing him back to the moment with a shock that showed on his face. "Thomas, I'm talking to you . . . " Thomas blinked, as if doing so would clear his mind from the growing foggy confusion that threatened to overwhelm him again.

"Eleanor . . . I feel . . . !" He was talking but the sound he was making made no sense. Eleanor couldn't understand the words, if that's what they were, as they fell from his mouth. He bent forward and coughed up a stream of the brown ale. A rowdy cheer went up from the watching gamblers around the ring at the sight of the fighter being sick.

"Thomas, what's *wrong* with you?"

Thomas's eyes rolled into the back of his head as the mandrake's psychoactive ingredient, hidden within O'Donahue's ale began to do its work. Eleanor became impatient, snapping. "Are you drunk?" Sykes's warning about O'Donahue's drink ran through Thomas's mind. He suddenly understood what his friend was trying to warn him about.

"Eleanor . . . the ale!" His head swam into a shadowy place again as his eyes rolled once more and he thought he might fall over. Reaching out he grabbed the woman's shoulder. He opened his eyes again and found Eleanor holding the tankard of poisoned ale.

"You're bloody drunk, aren't you?" Thomas shook his head.

"No, the ale, Sykesy tried to warn . . . !" Eleanor turned the tankard upside down, spilling its contents on the straw at Thomas's feet.

"I think you've had enough don't you? Pathetic!" The realisation that the fight was fixed finally dawned on the young boxer bringing with it a short moment of clarity. The depth of treachery shown by O'Donahue hit Thomas hard, not so much towards himself, he hardly knew the man at all but towards his friend Daniel Mendoza. The Irishman's unexplained deceit would destroy Mendoza's reputation as well as his own and at that point Thomas knew that the whole fight had been a set up from the start.

"The fight's rigged Eleanor!" He blurted. "They've poisoned me!" The girl just stood dumbfounded, trying to understand his statement.

"Poisoned?" She questioned.

"Something in the ale . . . Sykesy tried to warn me, but . . . O'Do-nahue, it was something in the ale!" Thomas, bent again and threw up to another roar of laughter from around the room.

"We must call the fight off Thomas, we must . . . !"

"*My lords, ladies and gentlemen!*" A voice bellowed from the far end of the room and everyone by surprise. Thomas joined almost everyone else in the room and spun towards the sound and where a well-dressed gentleman with a long scar down his left cheek stood a few feet above the heads of the crowd on a wooden trunk.

"Quiet, please gentlemen quiet . . . let's have a wee bit of order in the house!" He shouted in his thick brogue over the racket of three hundred excited voices. Shushing began around him, well-dressed dandies and fops passed the instruction for quiet along to the people next to them and the message quickly spread through the crowd bringing the tavern to an expectant hush. Thomas turned back to Eleanor.

"That's the same man that was at the Rookery on the night of your father's death!" Eleanor stared at the scarred man on the box as he began to announce the arrival of the American into the tavern. "I *have* to fight him Eleanor." The woman turned back towards the boxer, she stepped closer bringing her hand up to his cheek, then realising she was being watched by the men surrounding scarred man on the box, quickly checked herself, removed her fingers from Thomas's face saying.

"You can't fight Thomas, you can barely stand, we must call off the fight, as you said, this fight was fixed from the start, we must tell the organisers that James O'Donahue has poisoned the ale!" Thomas was struggling to stay focussed on what she was saying.

"No, Eleanor, you don't understand. The people that killed your father are the same people that have organised tonight's fight, *the Hellfire club*, I don't know why, but O'Donahue must be working for them . . . I heard through Daniel that he had debts but I would never have thought he'd stoop so low to pay them off. None of that matters now, I have no choice but to fight the American!"

Eleanor stared at him for a second as the full meaning of his words sank in. Thomas saw her face redden as rage swept over her.

"They mean to destroy you Thomas. You're the favourite to win tonight's bout, almost everyone has bet on you, as have I. They mean to throw the fight in favour of their man!" Thomas nodded. He swayed unsteadily as he fought the effects of the drug, thankful he hadn't drained the whole tankard as O'Donahue had encouraged him to do. Yet, even with only the small amount of mandrake in his system, the comical cartoons and pleasant, multi-coloured Aztec style patterns, that had initially danced around his field of vision as the drug kicked in were quickly being replaced by more horrific hallucinations by the second as the hallucinogen worked through his blood stream. This created ever bigger three-dimensional demons from the depths of his worst nightmares which floated from the shadows of the tavern's yard like hellish devils eating away at Thomas's self-confidence.

"I have no choice Eleanor, I . . . I have to fight him!" The man on the trunk began to talk again as the room fell silent.

"Ladies and gentlemen!" The scarred man bowed towards Eleanor, who returned his bow with a glare that was made all the more menacing because of her Venetian mask. Flint ignored her and continued. "Please welcome his Lordship and sponsor of tonight's pugilist bout. I give you Lord . . . Dashwood!" A loud round of applause and cheers greeted the elderly gentleman who entered the room well dressed in a red velvet coat and ostrich feather-trimmed tricorn hat of the same colour. Dashwood nodded towards Flint who continued to introduce the party. "And all the way from the new world of America, please give a grand London welcome to America's best boxer . . . Mr. Joseph Buck!" The room exploded into some cheering and applause with a fairly loud amount of booing too, which had the affect of adding to the chaotic cacophony emanating from every corner of the building. The arrival of the American meant the fight was on!

****

The first punch came from within a mist of twisted psychedelic visions that swirled upon the thick tobacco smoke hanging in the air around the ring. After Eleanor's furious exchange with Lord Dashwood at the ringside followed quickly by her even more furious exit from the venue, Thomas was now totally alone on his side of the hurdled fighting pit. He had momentarily lapsed into a hallucinogenic stupor, having no choice but to give himself over completely to the drug's powerful effects. Unable to make any sense of Flint's introductory speech to the fighters and the following rapturous applause, he had just stood in his corner, dribbling from the corner of his mouth. He was losing his battle against being drawn into the nightmarish tide of confusion that threatened to wash him away completely. *Wham!* The punch caught him totally off guard and should have floored him. However, instead of knocking Thomas out with his first punch, as was his intention, Joe Buck shocked the British boxer out of his stupor and back to reality. *Wham . . . bam,* Buck struck again and again, once to the ribs followed by a tremendous blow to Thomas's jaw. The British boxer stumbled to his knees but caught himself on the hurdle. Smelling an early victory, the American moved in for the kill. The room fell silent as he stepped in close to the crouched man. Bringing his fist back, Joe Buck drove his hand down into Thomas's unprotected jaw in what looked like a killer blow.

"Och this fight is over before it started!" Flint whispered mockingly to his master.

"That's why we bet on the American's victory in the first round." The old man glanced around the room at the others watching the fight. "The less time I have to spend with these scum the better Flint!" The manservant gestured with his head towards a group of men dressed in a ridiculous array of brightly coloured gypsy styled garb, surrounded by a group of six poorly disguised men who were obviously soldiers.

"The King my Lord?" Dashwood nodded and rolled his eyes.

"*Incognito* Flint!" Both men laughed sarcastically and turned back to the fight, not wishing to miss their man's first round knockout.

Joe Buck looked down on Thomas with no pity in his heart at all. The crouching man seemed lost in world of his own with no focus in his dilated eyes and even by the standards of a barnyard scrapper like Buck, this seemed like a despicably easy kill. Nevertheless, here he was, all the way from America and this was his first fight, so he must make a good impression on the hushed crowd by destroying their best within one round and so, with not so heavy a heart, Joe Buck threw his best punch at Thomas Fewtrell's jaw as the British boxer cowered from the devils that had begun to dance around the fighting pit. However, as the fist flew towards him, something in Thomas's mind told him to simply move his head to one side. Whether it was his pugilist training with Mendoza or the natural, lighting-fast reactions from his childhood beatings, it was hard to tell because things happened so quickly. Buck threw down and Thomas moved the target, leaving Joe Buck's bare fist free to fly past Thomas's jaw and into the sharp, metal latch that held the hurdles together. The bare skin smashed into the rusty latch with so much force that it drove the latch deep into the American's knuckle, lodging itself between the bones of the two knuckles on either side. Joe Buck squealed a high-pitched, pig-like scream of pain, as the nerve endings in his hand sent their agonising messages to his brain, filling it with white light agony. Thomas rolled along the straw-covered floor into the middle of the ring. The audience cheered at the sight of the boxer freeing himself from his trapped position. Buck pulled himself together at the sound of the cheering. Ignoring the pain from his right hand, he braced his foot on the hurdle and pulled his injured arm backwards towards himself, forcing the bone in his knuckles aside and freeing the metal latch. A spurt of dark blood shot into the smoky air, splashing over the watching gamblers, packed tightly against the fighting pit hurdle next to him. The sight of the blood-splattered faces brought gleeful smiles from the soaked men and another more macabre cheer from the bloodthirsty crowd. Buck turned towards the centre of the ring, a look of disbelief on his face. Thomas was still crouched on his haunches but this time, instead of being a cowering wreck, he was primed in a low stance; legs wide, knees bent, his arms spread and his hands open. Joe Buck had never seen anything like this man, who at this moment, looked more like a cat ready to pounce upon its prey. A deep dizziness came over Joe Buck as a new level of anger filled him at the thought that this fight wasn't already over. He glanced at Flint, who just stared on in disbelief that Thomas hadn't succumbed fully to the mandrake. The American turned back to the fighter opposite him who hadn't moved a muscle so still was he that it seemed to all he had become a statue. Buck crossed the ring, fists held out in front of him in a traditional boxer's stance. As he inched forward, blinking away a sudden burst of sweat, he looked through the defence of his bloody fists into the other man's large, dark eyes with their black dilated irises. For a split second Buck felt as if he were trapped in the fighting pit with a wild animal. Thomas's mouth hung open, a white saliva foam had formed at the side of his twisted mouth, a side effect from the hallucinogen and the sight of Thomas's grimace sent a shiver of cold sweat prickling up Buck's spine. However, Thomas was also battling an animal, only Thomas's' animal, wasn't of this world. He was trapped in a horrific, three-dimensional hallucination that could in Thomas's mind lead only to one thing, his death at the hands of the many armed and many headed monster closing in on him. There was no doubt in Thomas's befuddled brain as he stubbornly gave himself over to the powerful drug, that he was losing his fragile finger-tipped grip on reality. He was fighting for his life.

Buck came in cautiously, inching closer, wary of the animal in front of him, but the other boxer didn't move, not even to blink his blank eyes. The American came close enough to jab and landed a shocking, short, left-hand punch to the end of the other man's jaw, then another, softening him up for a real blow with his right hand. Thomas didn't seem to register the jabs. Instead he just stood unmoved by the tentative punches. The American seemed to gather confidence from the other man's immobility and drew his bleeding right hand back for what was to be a much more powerful throw than the first two jabs. Thomas remained in his trance, that was until Joe Buck's fist was about to smash into his cheek bone and as the American's fist closed in, with only an inch or so to go before making contact, Thomas burst into life. He threw his head down to his left, forcing Joe Buck's punch to sail over his head, harmlessly swinging into mid air and unbalancing him as he over reached his target. This time Thomas was ready, swinging his head back, he brought his clenched right fist up in line with his shoulder and drove the power of his punch all the way from his back foot, through his torso, shoulder and down into his right fist until it landed perfectly on the other man's jaw. *Bam,* the American stumbled backwards senselessly, until he crashed into the hurdle ring behind him. The crowd exploded into a cheer that rattled the glass oil lamps in their metal baskets around the yard. The men around Joe Buck began to push the unfortunate boxer back towards Thomas in the centre of the ring, baying at the British boxer that he should follow up his devastating blow with another. However, Thomas had bigger, more other-worldly problems. The red, silk scarf tied around his waist had become trapped in the top of his fighting breeches, the bow had been pulled and the knot was slowly tightening with every movement. A simple tug of the knot would have released the scarf, yet to Thomas, in his world of psychedelic shadows and dread-inducing devilish spirits, the red scarf he wore to signify the colour of St. George in contrast with the American's blue scarf, had now changed from a symbol of patronage to a long red silken snake which coiled itself around his torso with every minute move, threatening to squeeze him so tightly that it would cut him in two. The long tassels at the scarf's end had in Thomas's hallucinogenic state become three inch long fangs that dripped with crimson blood, as the snake's head swung this way and that around the boxer's right knee. Thomas stood perfectly still, lest he get bitten by the reptile. He watched as Joe Buck slowly gathered himself together after Thomas's devastating blow to his jaw. The look of befuddled panic on the American's face spoke volumes and if Thomas had been himself, Buck would never have made it off the hurdle. However, the frozen British boxer could only stand and watch as the American came back to his senses and pulled himself together again.

Joe Buck stared towards Flint and Lord Dashwood's position on the risen platform where they stood. Both men's faces were ashen with concern that their man was about to throw in the towel after only *one* of Fewtrell's punches hitting its mark.

"If this fight were lost ... " Dashwood mulled over the huge wager he'd placed with the King and a cold sweat broke across his brow, " ... then *I* am lost, and the Hellfire too!" An idea that was too horrific to contemplate.

"What the fuck are ye waiting for man? Get back in there and kill the bastard!" Flint yelled above the din. Dashwood came closer beside his manservant.

"I thought you said the mandrake would bring him down, but look, Flint, the fucker still stands!" Flint glared at the two boxers.

"I donny know what's going on, the manny's always worked before. It must be that Irish bastard, he's fucked it up your lordship, I'll have to deal with him later!" Dashwood grabbed Flint's arm.

"Later ... fuck later, there won't be a fucking later if we lose this fight, the American must win or I'm ... we're lost Flint, *we* are lost. I bet big on this with His Majesty and you can be sure that bloated bastard will call in every penny of my debts. Fewtrell must go down, make it happen man!" Flint turned to him, he saw the desperation on the old man's face and felt compelled to do something extreme in order to save the day. Pushing his way through the crowd he came up behind Buck who was still recovering on the ringside wall.

"Stop fucking around Buck and hammer the bastard!" He half-whispered into the boxer's ear. Joe Buck turned at the sound of the familiar voice.

"You said he'd be useless, you said he wouldn't be able to fight . . . !" Flint grabbed the man's hair and pulled it towards him,

"Fuck what I said, you're acting like a wee lass, get in there and fight him, you're America's best are ye not? Cos I have ne seen anything at all. Ye had better show us what you got Joe, otherwise you, me and Lord Dashwood are gonna have a falling out mate, and that'll only mean one thing for you son!"

"Oh yeah, and what's that then?" Buck snarled.

"Put it this way wee lad . . . " Flint said through gritted teeth, " . . . ye won't have to worry about being seasick on the way home to your wee mother cos you'll already be fucking dead!" The two men stared into each other's eyes with a hatred that threatened to set the whole inn alight.

"Fuck you, Flint. Fuck you and all you God damned British bastards, I'll show you what I got alright!" The adrenalin of hatred forced the American from his resting place on the hurdle and back into the centre of the ring where Thomas stood like a frozen sentinel. The crowd's cheering and booing at the American's recovery became deafening as Buck slowly inched his way back towards his opponent. The knowledge that this British boxer could deliver such powerful punches made the American cautious. Slowly, creeping step by tiny step towards the frozen man, he came close enough to start his left-handed jabs again, aimed first at Thomas' face then the ribs. *Wham*, *wham!* The American could see the other man was feeling his punches but seemed unable to do anything about it. Instead, he seemed obsessed with the red scarf hanging at his knee. *Wham,* another cruel blow to the jaw then Buck moved in with his right. Thomas could feel the snake snapping his jaws around his face and ribs, nipping him but not yet sinking his teeth into his flesh to deliver its venom. In Thomas's mind, the

American didn't even register, only the red snake with it's bleeding fangs mattered and then *bam*! The snake bit him, a fast hard strike on the jaw. The bite was deep to the bone, almost knocking him off his feet. Thomas's knees buckled, and he stumbled backwards but caught himself before he fell. Then the snake's head was there again, coming at him out of the psychedelic fog, lighting fast and deadly. He instinctively ducked beneath its gaping jaws and let the strike pass over his head. The crowd roared their approval as Thomas dodged the blow and the cheering filled the space with its deafening volume. Thomas registered the sound of the crowd, the din washing away the fog that had enveloped him in his own private, multicoloured nightmare and for a few seconds, he could see the American and the screaming faces of the gamblers and whores in the chaos around him. The snake was gone, and suddenly his mind followed the path back to the real world. All of this happened within a blink of an eye, a millisecond to the watchers but felt like a lifetime to Thomas, for whom time had slowed to a standstill. *Bam*! The American was on him again, only this time instead of adding to his hallucinogenic confusion, Joe Buck's punch shook the stupor from Thomas's mind completely, bringing him back to the moment with a clarity of mind and a single purpose; to survive this onslaught. *Wham,* another blow then another and it looked to all that Thomas was drunk and must fall under such a punishing and unprotected attack. Thomas could see things clearly now. However, the mandrake hadn't finished with him yet, instead of creating another dimension within the boxer's mind, this new wave of horror had the effect of weakening him to the point of paralysis. Thomas tried to raise his thick, muscle-set arms but found the power he held within his muscles had instead turned to lead. *Wham, wham,* Buck saw his chance, as the man opposite seemed to have lost another level of consciousness. The American's confidence had grown over the last ten minutes, he'd landed blow after blow without the British boxer even raising his hand against him. He was throwing his best punches and landing them perfectly, yet the British man refused to fall or perhaps he was too *stupid* to fall. *Bam, bam*, one, two, another to the head, to the ribs, to the stomach, the pounding went on. Then he saw it. Joe Buck spotted what he was looking for, no one else in the room could see it, but to Buck, it was plain for all to see. A tiny sway, a minute stagger, possibly even only a shiver yet to Buck it was momentous. The British boxer's movement meant only one thing, Joe Buck had seen it many times before in the bouts back in America. The tiny, involuntary movement that signalled the end of the fight. *Bam*, *bam*, he drove on, desperate to bring the fight to a successful conclusion before the bell rang indicating the end of the first fifteen minute round. Time to dig deep, put this British dog down once and for all. Buck stepped inside the other man's defence and drew his right arm back to deliver the coup-de-grace. Thomas could barely hold his eyelids open as he watched the blow coming and as the American's fist closed in on his face, Thomas watched the scene as his drug-induced brain slowed the American's actions down to a snail's crawl. Somewhere in the fog he felt something, it was the feeling he'd felt six months before when fighting the Bear. Hardly anything at first, just a millisecond as nerve endings danced within his body, then something more, a tingling in his hand. Beginning in his fingertips, the electric current spread into his wrist, then his arm, all the while growing in strength and intensity until, to Thomas, it felt as if his whole fist would burst into flames and he had no choice but to let it fly. As Joe Buck's fist landed a badly aimed glancing blow to his nose, Thomas brought his own fist up under the American's chin and drove his knuckles deep into the jaw bone of his opponent, slamming his fist into the American for all he was worth. Yet as he did, the Mandrake showed its final hand; flooding Thomas's brain with an overwhelming unconsciousness that the boxer had no choice but to let himself be washed away on a tidal wave of blackness that enveloped him completely.

The Pariah

CHAPTER 18

Bridget wasn't happy to see him, not this way, all bruised, torn up and crazed. It had been two weeks since the fight, and yet, Thomas had only just stopped ranting and raving his nonsensical gibberish. To all who saw him, he was suffering the effects of the fight with the American. '*Punch drunk*' was how the old men around the Birmingham Bull Ring explained it. Little did they know the ongoing effects of the Mandrake took weeks to leave one's system and it was only now, after two weeks of drifting in and out of consciousness that the boxer's body was beginning to react to the spoon-fed medicine.

He felt he was finally emerging into the world afresh, breaking the surface of deep cold water escaping the blackness of a drowning death, suddenly presented with a new chance at life and this, almost religious experience overwhelmed him.

Thomas opened his tear-filled, crusty eyes as a beam of light shone across his face, the sunbeam streamed in through the casement window in his old room at the Market Tavern. He drew in a deep breath as if he'd been starved of air for days and as he drew in the dusty air, it revived him, flooded his mind with clarity, washing away the confusing nightmares created by the mandrake. Physically, he was exhausted, he could feel it as soon as he became conscious. Exhausted and hungry, no hungry wasn't the right word, ravenous, that's what the pain in his stomach was, ravenous for ale, bread and meat. He swung his legs over the edge of the bed. The movement was painful and took all his effort. Something shuffled near the fireside, and it was then that he realised there was someone else in the room with him. However, Thomas couldn't see who it was, mainly due to the sleepy gunk that filled his eyes making his vision blurred.

"Thomas, you're awake!" Thomas recognised Bridget's concerned voice. She crossed the room and sat on the edge of his bed, taking a cloth from the small bedside table, she dipped it in a bowl of water and wiped Thomas's eyes. He flinched at the water but instantly felt the effect on his vision which cleared, leaving him able to see around him.

"Was it all a dream?" Bridget smiled her friendly, reassuring smile but Thomas could see a bemused look on her face.

"Dream, what do you mean?"

"London, Mendoza . . . the American, did I dream it all? It was so real." Bridget sighed her reply,

"I wish it *had* been a dream, Thomas!" The boxer turned to her.

"So it *was* real?" The girl nodded. "Then why am I here and not in London?" Even though she had nursed him since his arrival in Birmingham, two weeks ago, Bridget seemed shocked that he didn't have a clue where he'd been or what had happened since the fight.

"They brought you back here."

"Who?" Bridget stood and walked to the end of the long bed. She leaned over the footboard, her hands on the large wooden globes on its corners.

"I don't know Thomas, they were posh, that's for sure, well-dressed with weird accents, all *lar-de-dar*. You arrived in a fine, black carriage pulled by *six* horses!"

Thomas tried to remember, closing his eyes, digging deep into his thoughts but there was nothing, only the build up to the fight, his argument with Mendoza and . . .

"Sykesy . . . where's Sykesy, he was there, he'll know what happened to me."

Bridget scrunched her face up in puzzlement.

"What happened to you, what do you mean Thomas?" She

looked at his blank expression and realised how silly her question was.

"You really don't remember a thing do you?" Thomas shook his head.

"Only flashes of memory Bridget, a fight, I was in a fight, it was something to do with a snake, I think it bit me?" The girl laughed.

"A snake?" She saw the growing look of horror on Thomas's face and stopped herself laughing. "I'm sorry, there was no snake Thomas but there was a fight, a bloody big fight too, the King was there, it might be just gossip, but that's who everyone said brought you back here!" She said the words in a wondrous way as if describing the almighty himself, instead of the bloated, alcoholic monarch. "King George himself!" She checked herself. "Well, they never said he was actually King George, but they were bloody posh people!" Thomas cut her short.

"The fight, tell me what you know about the fight!" Bridget's face fell from its excited expression.

"Oh . . . well you lost it Thomas, although, according to the King's men you did knock the American bloke out cold with your final punch. Apparently you hit the floor first and so you lost the fight." The girl's words seemed to release a flood of memories for Thomas.

"Poisoned, that's it, I remember now. Sykesy warned me, I was poisoned. O'Donahue was there, he did it, he was working for the Hellfire Club, they were the ones who put the whole fight together." Thomas's memories came fast now, he spoke aloud, as much to remind himself as to explain to the girl. "Eleanor was there too. She tried to stop the fight but I was poisoned by the Irishman, that's all I remember." Bridget shook her head trying to hide her excitement at hearing Eleanor's name.

"Well, none of that matters now Thomas, your fighting days are over!" Thomas stood up on hearing the girl's words but wished he hadn't.

"*Over*, what do you mean?" Bridget looked at him as he swayed slightly in front of her, trying to regain his natural balance.

"The gentleman in charge of the toffs who brought you here

said you're fighting career was over, that . . . !" She hesitated, Thomas pressed her,

" . . . that what? Well, girl, spit it out!" The girl's face suddenly looked sad.

"He said you were a laughing stock, no one would take you seriously anymore. He said so many people had lost money on their wagers when they bet on you to win, that he and his friends had felt the need to get you out of London lest the mob lynched your unconscious body!" Thomas stared at her for a few seconds. Mendoza's warning about the fight rang in his head. Bridget's smile returned.

"It ain't all that bad Thomas, I had a word with your old bosses down the market, and they said you can have your old job back shifting meat, they said you can start when you're better." She seemed pleased with herself. Thomas smiled back at the girl, and he looked her over as they stood in silence of the room. He could hear the world outside coming to life in the summer morning sunlight which was streaming through the tiny roof window and illuminating her dark beauty. Even though Thomas knew about her lost innocence, the girl's naivety about success and failure made her all the more appealing to him. Thomas's stomach rumbled loudly, breaking the silence. Bridget chuckled. "*And* you got your old room back, just like it was six months ago, it could've been *worse* couldn't it?" Thomas looked around himself at the dirty, little room and trying to disguise the devastating news that he'd lost the fight and was now considered a pariah in the world of pugilism. He smiled sadly, remembering the painstakingly hard work he had put in with Mendoza and the dreams he'd allowed himself back then, as he had worked towards becoming Britain's best pugilist and for the life of him he couldn't see how it could be much *worse*.

Back in the Bull Ring

CHAPTER 19

J ames O'Donahue's body wasn't discovered until nearly three weeks after the fight at the Cheshire Cheese Tavern. It was obvious to anyone willing to look at the bloated, gas-filled corpse that it had been lying in the summer heat. It had been left beneath the hull of a row boat, next to the River Thames for weeks. It was also obvious how the unfortunate Irishman had died. The long, thin, red gash across his throat and deep stab wound was testament to the quick slash and stab of an unusually long and razor-sharp knife which had opened the ex-boxer's windpipe. He had been left to bleed out to the sound of his own gurgling blood-filled breath. The murderer had then dragged his body and stowed him under the old hull until the smell had become so putrid that even the feral dogs and cats avoided the rotting stench emanating from the wreck of the boat. Only the rats were brave enough to enjoy the feast and feast they did. On the day of his discovery any distinguishing facial features O'Donahue had once had had vanished, leaving only a pulp of gnawed meat, two holes where his nose and mouth had once been and a crop of bright red hair to testify that it was once a man at all.

The news of the Irishman's death reached Birmingham one month after the discovery of the body when Captain Henry Sykes had finally resurfaced at the Bull Ring market in Birmingham in search of Thomas. He found his old friend in the centre of the human beehive that was the market, muscle-bound and shirtless with a whole pig's carcass slung across his shoulder ready to haul the dead beast across town to the affluent area of Hockley. In the heat of the mid-summer sun the very thought of such hard work sent a shiver of horror up the Captain's spine. After an initially awkward reunion, the pair fell back into their usual, confrontational friendship.

"For God's sake Thomas, throw the bloody thing over my horse and we'll walk there together, we'll stop at an inn and have a drink, I've much to tell you about what happened in London after the fight." Thomas laughed.

"You've much to tell me?" Thomas looked at his friend incredulously. "Maybe I *don't* want to hear what happened after the fight Henry, did that thought ever cross your mind!" Sykesy shook his head.

"What's all this about Thomas? Hauling meat for God's sake, you're a better man that! What about your boxing?"

"Boxing, fuck boxing, look where that got me, six months of torture under Mendoza's whip, only to be beaten in my first fight." Sykesy stopped walking, pulling on his horse's bridle so that it turned and blocked Thomas's path. Thomas was surprised by his friend's action and stopped in his tracks, his chest pressing against the horse's flank, sweating heavily from the exertion of carrying the heavy pig's carcass which lay its dead weight across his shoulders. A look of impatience grew on his face, one which Henry was pleased to see, anything was better than the subdued expression that Thomas had been hiding behind since Sykesy's arrival.

"Move it, Henry!" Sykesy crossed to the other side of the horse until both men faced each other. Even though Sykesy had only been talking with his friend for a short time, he could see something had changed about Thomas. His spark had gone out, Henry could see it, plain as day. The confidence his friend once oozed had all but disappeared, and now he seemed a shell of his former self.

"What's happened to you, Thomas? You don't seem your ... "

"Move the horse Henry, I have to get this pig to where it's going before the heat gets to it!"

"I think the heat's already got to *you* Thomas, I mean, what are you doing carrying bleeding pigs for anyway? Let's go back on the road Thomas, just the two of us, we had a laugh, and made a few guinea to boot, what say you, my old friend?"

"*Robbers*!" Thomas said with a sarcastic snigger. "There was only one way that was going to end Henry, and it wasn't a good one, at the end of a bloody, long rope. No, I'm sticking to the simple things from now on. I've tried to be a flash blade, but it ain't me. Anyway, everyone thinks I'm a laughing stock, the King of England said it himself!" Henry stared at his friend with a growing confusion.

"The King of England, what the fuck are you talking about mate? You've had a knock down that's all. The ale was poisoned, you were meant to fall straight away, but you didn't, did ya? You battled on, and in the end, you knocked that American wanker out cold. The *poison* got to you mate not Joe Buck. O'Donahue fucked it up, and I presume that's why he's dead." Thomas's eyebrows furrowed.

"Did you kill him?" Sykesy became animated at his friend's question.

"I wish it had of been me mate, truth is, I think I know who did it, but it's fair to say he was mixed up with the Hellfire Club and those rich bastards get to do anything or *anyone* they want. That's why I think he's dead Thomas, cos he fucked up Lord Dashwood's little bet with the King. That's what the word is in London anyway, although, some people are saying that O'Donahue was talking about some sort of conspiracy against the King." Thomas couldn't comprehend the Irishman being involved in such a conspiracy.

"Conspiracy against the King?" Sykesy nodded.

"Look, that's all I was told, anyway I don't think they needed a proper reason, mate. Lord Dashwood's bet went wrong thanks to you, and it was all a little too close for comfort for the old bastard. So that Scottish nutter of a manservant of his did for him with a knife." Thomas humped the pig onto his other shoulder.

"So how do you know so much?" Sykesy sniggered.

"Because I was following him." Sykesy said, half-whispering, "I was gonna do him in myself, for what he'd done to you Thomas, but that Scots fucker got to him first." Henry drew his finger across his throat. "From ear to ear, it weren't pretty, but it did the job." Henry saw a flicker of regret in his friend's eyes and added. "But if it's any consolation, it was quick, very quick, I wouldn't fancy running into that fellow Flint on a dark night I can tell ya!" Thomas hadn't been himself since the fight, everyone had said so, and now his best friend was telling him the same. Thomas felt somehow brittle, fragile, his emotions were too near the surface and he felt as if he would break down at any moment. The experience and visions of the Mandrake still haunted him somewhere deep in his psyche. Sykesy stood on the other side of the horse refusing to move, his handsome, boyish grin helping to break his melancholy. "Look!" Henry continued. "You should be boxing or robbing with me mate, not this!" He pointed at the pig.

"You're a boxer, not a butcher and fuck Joe Buck and Lord Dashwood and fuck the King of England too for that matter, the only way you're gonna get your revenge on those bastards is to hit em where it hurts!"

"Oh yeah and where's that then?" Henry sighed.

"Dashwood's rich ain't he?" Thomas nodded.

"Yeah, that's no secret?"

"Well, the best way to hurt the rich is by taking all their money away!" Sykesy laughed as he talked. "Hit em in the pocket, there's nothing hurts a toff more than taking his bleeding money away. I'm taking from experience, I've ripped off more than I care to mention and anyway you're wrong, no one who knows you thinks you're a laughing stock, far from it, there's plenty of men around who would be willing to lay a wager on you in a boxing match. Perhaps not in London yet but up here in Birmingham in the sticks we could make a good few shillings pitting you against the local hard men. *Come* on Thomas, what say you? It'd be better than hauling that smelly bastard around for the rest of your life!" He pointed at the pig. A sudden buzz of bluebottle flies attracted by the smell of the meat began to gather around the dead pig on Thomas's shoulder, they buzzed and danced in a small cloud in the air around the pig's open stomach. Thomas brushed them away before turning back to stare at Henry as he mulled over his friend's words. Sykes's enthusiasm and his positivity were infectious, and the talk of revenge had lit a spark somewhere in the young man's mind, planting a seed of retribution. He threw the dead animal over his friend's horse's saddle smiling.

"Come on, *Captain* Sykes, let's get this fellow where he's going!" He said, patting the pig's backside. "Then you can treat me to some ale. You've given me an idea."

Even as he said the words, his mind ran over the image of Eleanor's masked face on the night of the fight and how she had tried to help him. He ran over the bargain they'd made on the night of her father's death and wondered how he would ever be able to fulfil his promise of revenge to her. Sykesy nodded, smiling his broad moustachioed grin, happy he'd finally got through to his old friend.

"Thank God for that, if the *pig* don't go off in this heat I think *I* bleeding will unless I get some ale in me. Besides, I'd say we've got plans to lay!"

****

Things moved quickly over the next few months. After a few ales on that hot summer day. The two friends came up with a plan to revive their fortunes by prize-fighting around Birmingham and the surrounding areas. There was only one problem with their plan. Thomas's level of fitness had deteriorated to the point that he could barely exert himself for more than ten minutes without collapsing into a sweating heap. The Mandrake's active ingredient had been hallucinogenic which was bad enough for an unsuspecting mind, but the poison was also toxic to the liver, kidneys and heart. The after effects of the poisoning could stay in the system for months, even years and would eventually cripple him whenever he pushed his body and mind beyond their normal limits. A pugilist of Thomas's talent needed a fitness level far higher than a normal human, and in a time when most people didn't understand or even conceive of physical or mental health, Thomas found himself grasping in the dark when it came to training. Thomas and Sykes's poverty put a real training space like Mendoza's gym totally out of the question and so Thomas looked around him and decided instead to use what he did have access to, the Bull Ring Meat Market. Why did he need expensive punch bags and weights when he was surrounded by alternatives to train with? A long, steep and daunting road lay ahead of him which he knew one day, he would have to force his body *and* his mind to climb. Every day he would battle with the voice in his head telling him that they were right, that he was a laughing stock, he should just crawl back into the hole he'd crawled out of twelve months before. He knew the high and mighty in London would have simply laughed at him if they could have seen the pugilist in the first light of morning, sprinting through the market place, a pig's carcass slung over his shoulders, carrying the equivalent of a man's weight across his back as he trained to the point where he would collapse in to coughing fits, trying his best to draw breath into his damaged body. Every day a new pain threshold stood before him. Every day a new wall to hit and yet, in the freedom of his anonymity, with firstly only Sykesy and Bridget's encouragement, he worked himself though the summer heat and into the first frosts of autumn; slowly building his body and mind, until he became a familiar figure around the town accepted by the local market traders, whores and watchmen.

"*Go on Thomas!*" Encouraging calls from all, even the odd pat on his back as he sprinted through the squalid rat-infested streets of the Bull Ring until the high town of Birmingham, which at first quietly ridiculed the athlete, now came to respect him, as he worked his way towards the first prize fight of his new career.

Sykesy watched his friend's confidence return over the next few months as he put into practice everything he'd learned under Mendoza's tutelage and more. During this training period though money, or the desperate lack of it was always a worry, so instead of punch bags and weights, Thomas used the hanging cow and pig carcasses that hung around the cold warehouses surrounding the marketplace. Every day at dawn, Thomas could be found softening up the ribs and flanks of the dead animals, slamming his massively powerful punches into the meat with ever more deadly precision. After these manic bursts of energy, often held in freezing conditions, Thomas would spend the rest of the day helping to load the cumbersome dead weight of the animals onto the various barrows to be either delivered or sold off around the suburbs of the town; often unhitching the pony or mule from its bridle and dragging the heavy barrows himself. The extreme exercise began to pay off, building the man to a size, flexibility and speed that even Mendoza couldn't have achieved in his gym in London.

Incredibly even with his self-induced exile from the capital, Sykesy always seemed to have fresh gossip from London. Where and how he got this gossip was never clear to Thomas but the news that Mendoza had battled a giant of a man in early December and amazed all by beating the fellow twice his size gave Thomas something to think about. So in the first snowflakes of that year, he changed his training routine away from strength and power, to one of precision, technique and speed. The boxer spent hours running through scenarios in his mind sitting next to the fire at the Market tavern. Thomas lost himself in the fantasy boxing bouts in his head as he tried to prepare himself for all eventualities. Even the Mandrake poisoning influenced his future plans. Henry and Bridget were to be his seconds in his corner and were instructed that only water, ale or wine from one of Thomas's sealed flagons could be used, none of which would be allowed to leave their sight before or during the fight, lest one of his opponents should try the same trick again.

As Thomas's training went on the first snowflakes of winter began to fall across the town, hiding the grime of Birmingham beneath its pristine whiteness. The morning frosts slowly became harder as freezing cold mists settled on the town for weeks on end. They hung in the fridged air stinging Thomas's lungs as he drew breath during his twilight training sessions and over the weeks, a plan slowly came together. Just the seed of an idea at first, planted by the comment Sykesy had made many months before back in the summer to 'hit em where it hurts'. As Sykesy, Thomas and Bridget huddled around each other at any one of the tables in the always busy Market Tavern, Mrs Bakewell's ale and gin at hand to free their imaginations; the tiny seed slowly grew into a blossoming tree of fortune, its branches hanging heavy with the fruit of treachery, revenge, glory and gold.

Sleight of Hand

CHAPTER 20

The card game had gone on far longer than had been expected and had fairly taken over the evening completely. The weak rays of the winter morning sunlight had begun to peek between the gaps in the heavy curtains of the mansion as the final hands were being played in this most momentous of games. The fifty or so aristocrats who were still awake and sober enough to stand stood swaying around the small green-felt gaming table watching with baited breath as the beautiful girl in the Venetian mask held her cards close to her white-skinned breast watching King George III throw down his hand. The King smiled at the woman enthralled, as was every other man by Eleanor's elegant mystique and hidden beauty as she faced the King in this card game. The monarch seemed more interested in the woman's porcelain-like features than the game at hand and even though, or maybe because of her low-born status, the puffy-faced royal couldn't help notice how she held herself with so much poise, dignity and self-belief. One could have sworn she was from the bluest of blue bloodlines. The talk amongst the players as they had dealt and shuffled the cards had been about a variety of subjects but mainly about hunting and gaming. Eleanor, who had learned about the gentlemanly sports from her late father could hold her own in any given conversation. Well-bred men and women watched her every move like so many circling hawks waiting for a mistake in etiquette to pounce on her with their talon-like tongues. Eleanor gave the slightest of glances at the King's cards before revealing her own. Her white mask camouflaged the minuscule emotions she allowed herself at her winning hand.

"Remarkable my dear!" The King said, flabbergasted by the woman's skill at the game. "Truly remarkable!" He said craning his neck to men standing at his shoulder, all of whom began to fawn sycophantically. "Eleanor my dear, you have been blessed by the almighty with your skill at the cards. I am an expert myself . . . " the King announced to all in the room, " . . . and I have played against some of the best in England, yet your skill and coolness unnerve even me, truly remarkable, my dear!" The fawning men began nodding, some, including the very people that were only minutes before jealously spreading gossip about Black Foot's daughter, were now bowing their heads towards her in approval.

"Your highness is too kind!" Eleanor purred.

"Nonsense my girl, I say it as I see it. A God-given talent if ever I saw one, it must be supernatural in order to outwit your King."

"My father taught me, your highness!"

"Then I say salute to your father for teaching you well, me girl." The King raised his glass and downed a glass of port in one gulp. Then holding the glass high, a servant stepped amongst the onlookers and poured another. "Another game my dear?" Eleanor knew the King's words were not a question and a collective, almost silent sigh spread throughout the room as the watching party goers realised this would mean another couple of hours of standing around.

"If your highness wishes to lose more gold?" She chuckled softly. The King laughed, turning to the men around him.

"Ha!" The monarch patted his pocket. "You've already wiped me out me dear, but you must allow me to try and win back the crown's coffers for I do believe you would bankrupt the country if you had the chance!" Eleanor laughed politely.

She reached into the middle of the table and began to shuffle the cards. Her quickness of hand amazed all who stood close enough to see the blur of cards as she flicked them this way and that through her delicate fingers, a testament to her upbringing amongst the card sharks of Birmingham. The King watched the girl's expertise and sighed.

"As you see gentlemen, I have been lulled into a trap by Eleanor's beauty. I am going to lose as much on this hand as I did on that damned, boxing buffoon *Thomas Fewtrell*." Eleanor stopped shuffling the cards and for the first time, that night or for that matter since anyone could remember the mysterious beauty showed a glimmer of emotion. It only lasted a fraction of a second and if you blinked, you would have missed the tiny twist of the lip and dart of the eye. However, the King who had lived his whole life at the head of an English court, full of ambitious relatives, lords and barons looking out for such minute, tell-tale unconscious reactions, spotted it immediately. "Ah, I see you lost money on that bout too me dear?" Eleanor, knowing she had given herself away broke into a broad smile trying unsuccessfully, to disguise her true emotions. The King continued. "Yes, I did too, a small fortune to be honest but the buffoon was drunk . . . !" Eleanor stopped playing with the cards, she lay them on the table and stared at the King directly.

"*Drugged* not drunk your highness!" The King returned her look with a quizzical one of his own. A silence fell over the soft murmurings as the aristocrats around the room, craned their necks to hear what was being said.

"Drugged?" Eleanor nodded.

"Yes, your Highness!" The King opened his mouth to talk but said nothing. "His drink was spiked with some sort of poison your Majesty!" The King shook himself out of his stupor.

"Poison, what sort of, who did this . . . do you have proof?" The King's questions merged into one sentence. Eleanor nodded before turning to look around herself. Her eyes ran over the faces of the men and women around the room who had now all but abandoned any pretence of politeness and moved as one towards the gaming table, openly trying to eavesdrop on the monarch and the young woman in the mask.

"Leave us . . . !" This time the King's words were sharp and to the point, no false flattery in the tone, just an order which he expected to be obeyed immediately. The crowd didn't move, unsure if they had heard correctly. King George stood, "*Out now!*" He barked the words leaving no space for misinterpretation. The aristocrats, understood well enough now and moved as one towards to the tall doors and out into the dining room. The King sat back into his chair heavily. Three men came in close to the elderly monarch surrounding his chair as if protecting him from some unseen assassin. Eleanor watched them suspiciously. "Drugged you say?" Eleanor nodded.

"Yes, your Highness, drugged." She turned to watch the last of the party-goers leave the room before continuing. "He was poisoned on the night. His drink laced with some sort of drug, a potion to make him lose the fight. Luckily he didn't drink the whole jug of ale which is why he stood his ground as long as he did."

"You have proof of this?" Eleanor shook her head, glancing at the men around the King. "It's alright me dear, these men are here to protect me, you can trust them with your life."

"Are any of them members of the Hellfire Club your Highness?" The King leant forward in his chair, clasping his hands on the card table in front of him.

"The Hellfire, what has this got to do with that lot of conspirators?" Eleanor took her drink from the table, she took a sip, hoping the glass would hide any signs of her nervousness.

"They set the fight up in the first place, they had the most to gain out of Thomas losing the bout."

"Thomas . . . you mean Fewtrell, you know the man?" Eleanor nodded.

"Yes, my Lord and I can assure you, the bout was not a fair one, if it had of been, the results would have been very different. Thomas is an outstanding boxer, your highness and a good man."

"But, but . . . who . . . and why?" The King blustered, Eleanor knew she may never have this chance to talk with the monarch again and didn't have time to play with words and so said decisively.

"Lord Dashwood, your Highness, he was the man behind the bout." The King nodded.

"Dashwood, yes I know, he was the man that set the whole

thing up but to swindle the King . . . ?" Eleanor pressed home her suspicions.

"Lord Dashwood had lost a small fortune in gold on a fight at my father's . . . " she searched for the right word to describe the Rookery, " . . . gaming house. He sent an Irishman to fight a local man called the Bear but the fight didn't happen and *Thomas Fewtrell* ended up fighting the Bear instead." Eleanor chose her words carefully lest she give away the fact that it was in fact her father that had stolen Dashwood's golden guineas, the hoard that lay beneath the floorboards of her mansion in Bearwood back in Birmingham. "Lord Dashwood's gold was stolen in the build up to the fight and that is why he set up *this* fight to regain his money, by cheating you!" The King turned to his bodyguard. He couldn't help but break into a smile.

"By God but she's sharp!"

"There is something else your majesty, there is talk amongst the aristocrats of an uprising against you my Lord!"

"Bah, nonsense . . . if I listened to every whisper of revolt, I would never leave my chambers, and the country would fall in upon itself. Forget the talk of revolution my dear and tell me how do I exact my revenge on . . . "

" . . . *we*, your highness, how do *we* get revenge on Lord Dashwood? After all, it was he and his manservant that instigated my father's death."

"Your father's death?" Eleanor nodded, allowing herself a moment of reflection on her doting father. The King's mood changed. "Ah I see what's happening here, you expect *me* to avenge your father's death?" Eleanor's shock at the question was plain to see.

"Oh no, your highness, far from it, my father brought me up to deal with problems like Lord Dashwood myself. I will take great pleasure in Lord Dashwood and the downfall of his Hellfire club." The King picked his drink up again, examining the girl, partially impressed, yet with a growing concern for Eleanor's ambitions.

"I do not doubt your ability to deliver cold-hearted revenge for your father's demise. After all you have moved like a ghost through the courtiers and gentry of London, something that takes some people, who are born of a higher station than yourself a life time to achieve and yet, here you are at the King's table with your mysterious mask, hidden beauty and sharp tongue having achieved this climb in only a few short months. Nevertheless, my girl, you should take care when it comes to people like Lord Dashwood and his ilk. His bloodline have been dancing their way through the corridors of power for eight hundred years, backstabbing their way to power since the days of King William of Normandy. The Dashwoods were some of the first Norman settlers, the likes of him would have no problem with the likes of you. So although you will have my help and permission if it is sought to avenge your father, be warned that when you corner a man like Dashwood he will come at you with everything he has and *when* he does because he *will*, all of your wit, beauty *and* my protection will count for nothing. You must ask yourself, Eleanor, is it worth it? And I must ask myself for all of my royal protection which I shall bestow on you, *what* in God's name will you bestow on me? I am after all a man as well as a King." A short silence fell over the room as Eleanor mulled the King's words over, only the morning birdsong from outside the tall windows could be heard as the new day began. Eleanor realised the game she was now involved in was far more complex than any card game she had ever played, the stakes were immeasurable, and the King had just raised his stakes from one of gold to one of flesh.

"For your eyes *only* your Majesty!" The King at first seemed surprised, but quickly realised her meaning.

"Out!" The tallest of the King's bodyguards stepped forward to protest leaving the King's side. The elderly monarch's eye twitched with irritation as he stared at Eleanor.

"*OUT*..you damn . . . f . . . fuckers, *out*!" He stuttered, the twitches in his eye growing more acute. The tall bodyguard turned to the others and gestured with his head that they should leave. Eleanor waited for them to close the tall doors behind them as they stepped into the long corridor. Then with the thinnest of smiles, she lifted her hands and untied the silken bow at the back of her head, the knot released the white mask from her face and as the jewel-encrusted Venetian mask fell. The wide-eyed King and the small black boy who stood sentinel still holding the silver tray with the King's port upon it gasped in astonishment.

Come one, come all.

CHAPTER 21

Thomas stepped into the cobbled square made from the trestles and barrows from the trader's stands around the Bull Ring market. Most of the Saturday throng had returned to their warm houses around the city to escape the freezing cold after a day's bartering for food and fabric. However, the two hundred or so market traders and people in the know who lived in the area stood around gossiping about the outcome of the upcoming fight, buzzing like so many summer wasps around a jam tart. Only it wasn't summer, it was the shortest day of the year, the middle of winter as the waiting people could testify whilst they braved the stiff winter wind that blew around the square; gusting in and out of the nooks and crannies of the marketplace, searching for the slightest sign of bare skin that poked from beneath the tears in the rabble's filthy clothing. The crowd stood impatiently stomping their feet and rubbing their woollen-mittened hands together around the small fire-pits that had been hastily erected for the occasion. The embers glowed pointlessly in the friged wind, sending small showers of sparks here and there but little heat and yet for Thomas, who braved the icy wind with only his brown leather breeches and his bottle-green highwayman's cloak for warmth it seemed far colder than it did to the ragamuffins around their fires. His teeth chattered away unconsciously as he bounced around the square, throwing punches at some imaginary rival as he desperately tried to warm his muscles and stay loose, each breath hanging for a second in the frosty air like a ghostly vapour, before vanishing, driven away on another freezing gust.

Syksey stood in Thomas's corner wrapped in his long black cloak, his black tricorn pulled almost over his eyes looking more like some sort of supernatural, black raven than any resemblance of a man as he hid himself from the cold. The wind was bracing, to say the least, and as if to add insult to injury, mother nature had now played her trump card as the first flutters of snowflakes fell over the Bull Ring marketplace. As the smoke and smog from a thousand chimneys around the town cluttered the air with black coal smoke, the snowflakes collected the grime as they fell, turning their pristine, white crystals into small, black snowdrops resembling tiny devil's wings fluttering to earth in a snowfall of gloom.

The crowd stopped gossiping as the trundle of carriage's wheels upon cobbles bounced around the market square. Four, five . . . seven, eight . . . ten carriages, Sykesy counted out loud impressed by the number of people who had travelled the fifteen miles or so from the small market town of Dudley. The onlookers watched as the men climbed from their carriages and stood in tightly packed groups on one side of the square. The Brummies formed another group on the opposite side of the boxing ring. Sykesy unwrapped his cloak and stepped forward to greet the group. A tall man wearing a thick, knitted woollen cap greeted him with a toothless smile. The Brummies watched as the two men talked to each other in a firm but friendly way. Finally, a handshake sealed the deal, and the Dudley men brought their fighter out from the rearmost carriage and crossed to the square to face Thomas.

"The *Tipton Slasher!*" the toothless man announced. Thomas nodded to him and to his surprise the Slasher crossed the ring and held his hand out, Thomas took it and the two shook a long, firm handshake.

"Yam could-ve picked a fucking cowlder day ah-pal!" The Slasher's accent was a thick brogue that Thomas had heard around Birmingham before, a friendly accent from the outskirts north of the town where the inhabitants were nicknamed yam-yams by the people of Birmingham.

"Yeah, I'm bloody frozen!" The Slasher snorted a long vapour of air from his nose as he laughed his reply.

"Well, don't worry ah-kid, yam ain't gonna feel fuck all in a minute cos yam gonna be spark out cold ah-pal!" Then turning he crossed to the other corner of the ring and much to Thomas's' surprise began to snarl like an animal slamming his fists together and against his chest. The friendly smile replaced by a vicious grimace that left Thomas with no illusions as to what the Slasher's intentions were.

Sykesy was too busy collecting the bets from the scrabbling crowd who had gathered around him to lay their bets, to notice the Tipton man's theatricals but Bridget, who had brought Thomas some cider that she had warmed over the fire in the Market Tavern couldn't help but notice the man's roaring.

"What's wrong with him?" she asked and Thomas who had just watched the transformation of the man from human to animal looked at her, perplexed,

"I dunno, one minute he was just chatting, the next he'd turned into that!" The Slasher's face was screwed into a tight ball of red-faced anger as he screamed at Thomas from the other side of the square.

"He looks a bit emotional Thomas, is he all right?" The Slasher on hearing the woman's words became even more excited.

"I ain't too sure?" Thomas replied. "But I can tell you one thing Bridget, he's not cut out for this line of work, look at him, he's an emotional wreck!" The Slasher roared even louder.

"I gunna fucking kill *yow* . . . I'm gonna hit yow so hard, it's gonna hurt yow family!"

Bridget laughed.

"Maybe, he fancies you, Thomas?"

"Yeah or maybe he's trying to scare me!" Bridget giggled loudly.

"Nah . . . I know what it is, he must be in season, that's why he's all wound up." Thomas burst into laughter. The Slasher turned to the toothless man and snarled.

"Fucking hurry up will yow, get the bets over and done with!" He pointed at Thomas. "Cos him's gonna get a bloody good hiding!" Thomas laughed.

"Jesus Slasher, you've really got to work on your pre-fight wind-ups."

"Ladies and Gentlemen!" Sykesy screamed from the footboards of one of the carriages, hat in hand, full almost to the brim with coins. "All bets have now been laid . . . no more bets." Turning to the two pugilists, he shouted. "Gentlemen, please, we will have a fair fight, no biting, kicking or gouging. We will have twelve rounds of fifteen minutes or until the last man stands!" Turning back to address the crowd, who had all become silent, listening to his words. "We will have no interference of any kind from outside of the ring, anyone that helps either of the boxers will forfeit the fight to the other boxer . . . so *please* everyone, act like gentlemen and no fucking around!" The crowd broke into a round of applause. Bridget crossed to Sykesy and took the hat full of coins. "This lady will hold all bets until a champion stands alone in the ring. Gentlemen if you please, shake hands and let's begin!" Thomas and the Slasher crossed to the middle of the ring and touched each other's knuckles delicately.

"*Fight!*" Sykesy screamed. The Slasher instantly came at Thomas with a huge wide haymaker driven from his massive shoulders accompanied by a blood-curdling snarl.

"*Aghhhhh!*" Thomas casually ducked under the man's clumsy swing and brought his own fist up as the man over reached himself, bringing his cold bare knuckles straight into the Slasher's chin, *bam!*

****

Mrs Bakewell fussed over the Slasher as he regained consciousness on the flagstones next to the roaring fire in the Market Tavern.

"You bloody brute!" She said angrily to Thomas. "You've broken his nose!"

"Mrs Bakewell . . . it was a boxing match . . . !" The woman was busy wiping the large amount of caked blood away from the man's nostrils.

"So you've gone from *wanking* in your room to punching people in the market. You must be very proud of yourself Thomas Fewtrell!"

"No, no, it wasn't like that Mrs Bakewell . . . it was a boxing . . . !" The woman had lost interest in him and had begun doting on the Slasher. Thomas shrugged and walked back to Sykesy and Bridget who were in a deep conversation with the toothless man.

"Yeah, I'm happy with that." The toothless man shook Sykesy's hand.

"Good!" he rapped the bar counter with his knuckles. "Get all of these nice folk a round of drinks on Thomas Fewtrell's tab!" The barman nodded and began gathering the pewter tankards from the bar-top as the Tipton and Dudley men gathered around.

Sykesy gestured to Thomas and Bridget that they should retire to one of the bar's snugs for some privacy. Thomas followed his friends and sat opposite the two.

"Well, there it is Thomas!" Sykesy spilt the hat's contents onto the table. The coins jingled on the hard black oak. "There's a pretty penny there me old mate, a bloody good day's work I'd say." Bridget began to count the coins.

"And all from one punch Thomas!" Sykesy smiled.

"That bloke!" He pointed at the toothless man. "He told me that the Tipton Slasher has never been beat and you did it with one punch mate, one fucking punch!" Thomas nodded, watching the girl as she counted the coins.

"One fucking punch." He said under his breath.

****

As the days grew longer and warmer, so the fighters came and went. Hard men from all over the Midlands came to test their metal against Thomas Fewtrell yet not one could better him. Tough guys and hard hitters came, and not one came near to winning a bout. Cheats were beaten, boasters were bettered and the year rolled on from one fight to another and, more importantly, the money kept piling in. Success gave the trio the confidence to move things to another level. Thomas stepped up his training schedule as the fights became more regular from once a month to two or even three fights a week, all of them bringing in more money than any of them knew what to do with. Fine clothes, horses and finery brought the trio a reputation that they were on the up and there was nothing a Brummie liked more than seeing a fellow Brummie do well in the world. The town fell behind him until the word around the high town of Birmingham was that Thomas Fewtrell was unstoppable. The word spread far and wide, initially from the market men and barrow boys who had witnessed the first few fights then on to the meat carriers, butchers, farmers and so on until it finally reached London. The small world of London's pugilism scene couldn't help but take notice of the rumours from up north about the up and coming boxer from Birmingham's marketplace. However as soon as the name Thomas Fewtrell was mentioned the London crowd refused to take the rumours seriously remembering the debacle at the Cheshire Cheese Tavern many months before. Which was why it took several months before an offer from a well-established pugilist from the Camden area for a fight in the capital came his way. Joe Buck, Lord Dashwood and Flint attended the bout, more out of curiosity than out of love for the sport of boxing. Their reasons for attending soon became irrelevant when they watched Thomas who bore no resemblance to the gibbering, poisoned wreck who had faced Joe Buck twelve months previously demolish his opponent in record time. The seasoned boxer who was well known around the London scene that challenged Fewtrell to a bout was pummelled to unconsciousness by Thomas within three minutes of the start of the first round. The Birmingham man didn't even seem to break a sweat and appeared somehow cheated by his opponent's lack of skill. The uproar from the crowd was instant and chaotic as scuffles and arguments broke out around the room. Some of the audience began pointing towards the American Joe Buck shouting that a rematch between the Buck and Fewtrell should take place. Flint was forced to usher Buck and Dashwood out of the venue before things got completely out of hand and turned ugly. Thomas watched them leave from his elevated position within the ring above the crowd. The shouts turned to booing as the trio snaked their way through the packed mob and when Joe Buck peeked over his shoulder towards the ring he saw Thomas Fewtrell staring directly at him, a deadly serious look on his face.

"*Hey Yankee!*" Thomas shouted, "Hey Buck, you Yankee bastard!" The room slowly fell silent at the boxer's voice, all eyes turned to Thomas and then to the fleeing American.

"I'll be here when you're brave enough Buck only this time there won't be a red snake to help you!" The crowd turned back to Thomas, puzzled looks falling over their faces as they tried to decipher to what the boxer was referring. Sykesy crossed to Thomas in the centre of the ring and stepped over the unconscious brute that Thomas had knocked out, still lying in the middle of the square.

"Red snake?" Thomas continued to stare at the American.

"It's a *private* thing Henry." Sykesy watched his friend for a second or two before climbing onto one of the barrels surrounding the fighting space.

"Gentlemen, I give you, England's *finest* boxer, *Mr. Thomas Fewtrell the gentleman jaw breaker!*" The mob burst into a cacophony of cheering and applause deafening the men in the ring. Thomas watched Flint lead the old lord and the American through the crowd to the rear doors of the venue, he followed them until they finally vanished into the darkness of the street.

"*Thomas!*" a voice was shouting from somewhere in the mob. "*Thomas!*" The voice was instantly recognisable with its latin tinge mixed with a cockney twang. Thomas spun on hearing his name being called and his eyes searched the mob for his friend, finally finding him trying to push his way towards the ring.

"Daniel Mendoza!" The boxer crossed to his old tutor and grabbed his hand, hauling him into the ring. "Daniel my old friend, it's so good to see you!" Mendoza let himself be pulled up into the ring where both men embraced each other like brothers.

"My God Thomas, what have you been doing to yourself? I've never seen such boxing!" Thomas blushed.

"I remembered what you taught me Daniel and I've been busy inventing my own style of boxing too." Mendoza glanced at the still unconscious man on the floor of the square.

"Well, I'd say it's working for you." Turning back to his friend he enquired. "Tell me where are you staying?" Thomas shrugged.

He nodded towards Sykesy.

"Henry, where are we staying tonight?" Sykesy laughed.

"Well, I ain't sure where you're staying mate, but I'm staying at the best whorehouse in London after tonight's takings. I might treat myself to a couple of tasty little . . . !"

"Honeypots, yeah we know!" Thomas laughed.

"Good that's settled, you will stay with me Thomas, you can have your old room, nothing's changed since you were last there. We have much to catch up on and teach each other before your next fight which I'm sure won't be long!" Thomas nodded, trying to hide any his feelings about missing the mischief Sykesy was bound to get up to.

"Thank you, Daniel, that's very kind of you, I'd love to!"

The Wager

CHAPTER 22

ord Dashwood's second meeting with the King was far less
cordial and had little in common with the first. Yes, the King
was drunk again but in this stage of King George III's life,
a day rarely passed without him downing at least one decanter of
port or Spanish Madeira, so this was nothing unusual. The thing
that stood out to Dashwood as rather odd on his second meeting
with the monarch wasn't the King at all; it was the elegantly dressed
woman with the jewelled, Venetian mask that sat silently at the
desk in the corner of the room, where the blue-liveried page had
sat on his previous visit, twelve months before.

"Sssss . . . *sit*!" The King stuttered. Dashwood obliged, taking the
seat delicately beside the fire. He could see remnants of splintered
furniture on the marble hearth next to the roaring fire and the old
Lord wondered what other priceless pieces the King had reduced
to firewood since their last meeting. "The American!" The King
barked. Dashwood nodded.

"Yes, your highness?" Dashwood waited for the monarch to
answer but the King seemed lost in his thoughts as he stared into
the fire. Dashwood glanced at the girl in the mask and finally recognised her as the one he'd seen at Joe Buck's fight with Fewtrell.
He nodded towards the girl, but she remained unmoved, watching
him with distrustful, blue eyes from behind her mysterious mask.
The woman's stare unnerved the old Lord.

"The *American,* Dashwood!" The King repeated.

"Yes, my Lord, the American, what of him?" The King turned to face Dashwood, his face puffed and red. "He'll fight Thomas Fewtrell again!"

"My Lord?" Dashwood said, his brows furrowed in puzzlement as to why the King was paying so much attention to the subject.

"I am not used to repeating myself Dashwood however, I am aware of your age and will take that into account for making me do so." Dashwood shook his head.

"My Lord?" He said again. The King's already-flushed face grew almost purple with rising rage.

"I am not a *Lord*, I am a fucking *King,* Dashwood!" He almost spat the words at the old man. He glared at Dashwood for nearly a full minute until his anger began to subside as quickly as it had risen. "The American will fight Thomas Fewtrell."

"But my lo, sorry, your Highness, Joseph Buck has already beaten Fewtrell, twelve months ago, it was a ... "

" ... it was a fucking farce man, a fucking liberty that *you* created to steal my gold!"

"Your Highness, I must protest ... !" He pointed his long thin finger, glaring at the King with a hatred he found almost impossible to hide. King George returned his look just as hatefully before leaping from his ornate chair like a man of twenty. The jump took Dashwood by surprise.

"How fucking dare you? You, y ... you, *insolent* bastard! Lower your fucking eyes when you address me, d..d ... dog!" Lord Dashwood blinked with shock, before doing as the monarch instructed lowering his head subserviently.

"I apologise, your Highness."

"So you should Dashwood. We all have our place in this world given to us by God himself, and your place is licking the shit from my fucking shoes. Do you understand Dashwood?" The King stood over him, his groin almost in the old man's face.

"Yes, your Majesty !"

"Good God man but you've pushed your luck with me today!" Dashwood stared at the thick rug beneath the King's feet.

"I'm sorry your highness, please forgive me!" The King stared at the man's thick grey mop of hair for a few seconds. He reached behind his head and scratched the bald patch beneath his silken, pill box cap. His mind wandered for a second to his youth back to when he had a full head of hair and he hated the old man in front of him even more for still having his.

"You're sorry Dashwood?"

"Yes, your Highness!"

"Good, then put the fucking fight on. I want my bloody gold back. You and that fucking American rebel made me look a fool but if he wins again then fair enough. I will even show good sporting spirit by shaking his rebel hand after the fight . . . " The King bent down bringing himself face to face with the old man " . . . and I'll be watching out for any of your back-handed shenanigans Dashwood, don't you fucking forget it!"

Lord Dashwood gripped the arms of the ornate armchair as he tried to control his anger lest it burst from his veins and throttle the royal in front of him.

"Of course my lord!" The King stood abruptly and began searching around the pockets of his long dress jacket, finally pulling an old piece of paper and throwing it in Dashwood's face. The old man picked the paper from his lap where it had landed and stared at it. By the state of the parchment, King George had obviously held on to it for many months and examined it over and over again. He didn't need to look it over for he already knew what it said. It was a satirical cartoon of the King who appeared puffed up and bloated with a ridiculously small chin standing beside the boxing ring where Joe Buck had beaten Thomas Fewtrell. The satire in the pamphlets made fun of the King's drunkenness, his fragile grasp of reality and mocked how even at a simple boxing match King George could not keep control of the wild Americans. Dashwood knew the words, after all, it was he who had written it. He had organised the circulation of the pamphlets throughout London, and they and others like them had reduced the King and his offspring to a laughing stock amongst the aristocracy although he wasn't about to confess this to the man standing in front of him.

"And *now . . .*" the King continued, " . . . I want to redress the situation immediately, so the fight will be a private affair!"

"Private, your highness?"

"Yes, yes, yes, private. Do you think I'm going to be humiliated in front of half of London again?"

"Humiliated? No, my Lord!"

"Humiliated man, no, no, not again Dashwood!"

"Where do you suggest we hold the fight this time, your majesty?"

The King looked at the old man as if he were a child.

"At your fucking Hellfire club Dashwood, wherever that is."

"The Hellfire?" The King became even more impatient.

"There you go again, making me repeat myself again. I f..f.. fucking hate repeating myself man, yes the *Hellfire club.* We will see the rematch there!" Dashwood's eyes betrayed his surprise, but as the idea sank in he became more excited.

"Yes, my King!" The King sat heavily back into his chair.

"Of course fucking yes, however for security reasons I will need the names of *all* of your members, and I will be inviting a select list of my trusted friends, associates and of course my bodyguard!"

"But my King . . ." the old man said in a sickly sycophantic tone, " . . . the members of the Hellfire will wish to remain anonymous, after all, it is a secret society which is why we all cover our eyes with masks." The Monarch mulled over the Lord's words for a few seconds.

"Nothing should be kept secret from the King, Dashwood." He said with a lighter tone. "However, I will allow your members' anonymity to remain, and so we shall all wear the eye masks to protect our identity, but I still need the names of your members!" Dashwood grimaced.

"Thank you, your majesty!" The King's smile dropped.

"Every name Dashwood, every name." An uncomfortable silence fell between the two men before the King grew bored and decided to conclude their meeting. "So it's agreed, I will inform you of the date of the rematch, and you shall inform me of the venue, and I want that list of names Dashwood!" The old man nodded. "Good, now get the fuck out of my palace!" Dashwood didn't need to be told twice. He rose from his chair and backed away towards the door where he'd come in. When he got halfway across the room, he turned and strode towards the page boy next to the large double doors. The boy reached for the handle, and as he did, Dashwood turned towards the lady in the mask. She was still watching him as he crossed the room, only this time, he thought he saw a thin smile spread across her lips. The smile sent a shiver of rage through the old man and in the seconds it took to cross to the door Lord Dashwood swore that he would see this masked beauty dragged to the Hellfire club and would laugh with Flint and the other members whilst Eleanor Blackfoot was defiled and eaten by Lord Harrington's giant dogs.

The Fight

CHAPTER 23

"*It's on!*" Bridget threw a pamphlet onto the table of the Market Tavern. Sykesy grabbed at it like a greedy school boy, his eyes wide with excitement. He scanned the page, his eyes darting along its black, scrawling print. Bridget stood over him and at that moment was joined by Mrs Bakewell, the landlady. The pair watched the ex-highwayman reading the parchment that advertised the boxing bout between the *American rebel rouser*, Joseph Buck, as he was now known and one Thomas Fewtrell, *the Gentleman jaw breaker,* as *he* was now known. Mrs Bakewell laughed,

"You can't read, can you Henry?" Sykesy peered over the top of the parchment.

"What? Of course, I can read!" he said angrily, Bridget laughed,

"No, you can't Henry, it's nothing to be ashamed of, lots of people can't read."

"I *can* bleeding read!" He said pointing at the words on the parchment. Mrs Bakewell turned to Bridget.

"Nah, he ain't got a bloody clue what's on that parchment, why don't you let Bridget read it for ya?" Bridget sighed.

"Look, Henry, we know you can't read!" Sykesy held the parchment up in front of his face, blocking the women out of sight.

"Oh yeah and how do you know that then?" Mrs Bakewell snapped.

"Because you're holding the bleeding parchment upside down,

you twat!" Sykesy flinched at the woman's words and hid further behind the paper, slowly rotating it in his hands. He mumbled something about women always knowing best before Bridget snatched the parchment and read aloud.

Two masters in the noble art of Pugilism,
JOSEPH BUCK
The American Rebel Rouser
&
THOMAS FEWTRELL
The Gentleman Jaw breaker
Brought together for the intention of boxing his opponent into submission or unconsciousness or which so ever comes first. For the period of twenty rounds, each of which shall be no less than fifteen minutes in length.
At the ruins of Rye church on the feast day of St Patrick 17th of March 1784
On invitation of the Hellfire Club
The event shall be attended by the King of England, Ireland and Wales as well as his highness's family, associates and other members of the high born and fashionable.
All members of the London Hellfire Club are required to attend.

Bridget handed the paper back to Sykesy, raising her eyes as she did. She turned to the landlady.

"It was brought this morning by a soldier horseman, very handsome he was, posh too, all official!" Mrs Bakewell said, letting her mind wander off into one of her romantic daydreams. Bridget smiled at the elderly woman's expression.

"I'd say Thomas would want to know about this!" Henry said, taking the paper sheepishly.

"Yeah, it would've been nice of them to ask us first!" Mrs Bakewell returned to her bar duties, sneering over her shoulder.

"Bloody toffs, they think they can do anything they want them lot." At that moment the creaking floorboards on the staircase announced Thomas's entrance to the room. Sykesy snatched the parchment back from Bridget and shook it above his head.

"It's on Thomas . . . the fight with the Yankee is on!"

"*When?*" Thomas said slumping into the bench on the other side of the snug's table. Henry held the paper up in front of his face and pretended to read the pamphlet. Thomas gave Bridget a bemused glance, the girl rolled her eyes at Sykes's pretence.

"17th March, Thomas, St. Patrick's day, I don't suppose you got a bit of Irish in ya to bring us a bit of Irish good luck!" Thomas laughed.

"No, Henry, sorry!" Sykesy turned his attention to the girl who was still hovering over the table drinking her breakfast ale.

"Well, Bridget O'Hara has, and she'll bring us all the Irish luck we'll need!" Henry raised his tankard and clinked it with Bridget's. The pair laughed like mischievous children, Thomas stared at them sternly.

"You can wear all the bleeding shamrocks you want Sykesy. We're gonna need a lot more than Irish luck to pull this one off boys and girls; and if this thing is going to go to plan, the timing's gonna have to be perfect cos if it ain't, we're gonna all end up doing the Tyburn dance and as you may or may not know, I fucking hate dancing. Now, Henry, you need to get word to our contact in London, find out where we stand with the wager situation and how many toffs we can expect and while you're doing that get me a fucking big horse!" Sykesy and the others seemed puzzled by his request.

"A big horse?" Sykesy repeated. Thomas shook his head.

"No, I didn't say a big horse did I? I said *fucking* big horse!" Bridget butted in.

"But some horses are bigger than others, how's he meant to know exactly how big you want this horse to be?" Thomas sighed.

"I don't bloody know, do I?" He said exasperated.

"Horses come in all sizes don't they Bridget!" The girl nodded, laughing. Thomas rolled his eyes.

"You ain't listening are ya? I didn't say a small horse or a medium horse or a big horse!" The other two stared blankly at him, he continued. He said the words very slowly "I said a *fucking ... big ... horse* ... Use your imagination!"

"What do we need a fucking ... big ... horse *for*?" Sykesy asked.

"Never mind what it's for, if we want this to go off without a hitch get me a me the horse, the biggest one you can find and he can't be too slow neither." Sykesy laughed sarcastically.

"Oh, ok boss no problem, any particular colour?" Thomas ignored his sarcasm and continued explaining his plans.

"I'll get in touch with Edward back in Shropshire, none of this will work without him, I just hope he's up for it!"

****

The ride to Easthope seemed longer to Thomas than it had on that day, years before, when he had made the trek from the hamlet to Birmingham with Edward. They had been so innocent back then. Thomas and his look-a-like younger brother thought they would take the town by storm but Birmingham had just swallowed them up and spat them out on to the filthy cobbles of the Bull Ring. If it hadn't been for boxing and God, the pair might have ended up drunk, destitute or hanging from a tree somewhere along the old Bristol Road. The latter was still a very strong possibility if Edward wouldn't play along, which, if he was still as fervent a Quaker as he had been whilst in Birmingham, Thomas was sure he'd refuse. However, Thomas *had* to ask him if he'd help their cause in this up and coming boxing match. Edward's role was pivotal to their plans.

After a long day's ride heading west from Birmingham through the market town of Bridgnorth, Bridget and Thomas finally arrived at the hamlet of Easthope. Thomas stopped his horse at the brow of the hill that he and Edward had climbed all that time ago, the memories of his tough childhood came back to him in a flood of images that swirled together creating a kaleidoscope of emotions that brought a lump to his throat. He swallowed the melancholy and pressed on. After a short visit to his family's small holding for information and a brief reunion with the two siblings who had remained behind to work their father's farm Thomas went to find his brother at St. Peter's church where he had found work as a minister for the local area. Thomas felt happy that his brother still had his passion for the teachings of Christ but at the back of his mind he also knew that this passion was the one thing that might stop him helping Bridget, Sykesy and himself achieving their goal.

Thomas was also learned of some darker news about his father, Samuel Fewtrell and his untimely death, at the hands of one of the Lutwhiche brothers. The old man had been attacked during a petty row at the local Star Inn frequented by the Lutwhiche brothers and had been sucker punched so hard from behind that it had sent him into a coma he'd never awoken from.

The Lutwhiche clan had plagued the Fewtrell family as well as many others in the area for generations, and on hearing the news of his father's death, he swore that this plague would have to be cured and he knew exactly how to do it. Bridget tried her best to calm Thomas by reminding him why they were there but to no avail. Finally, after a heated row between the pair, Thomas reluctantly agreed that he would talk to Edward *before* settling his score with the Lutwhiches.

On finding Edward, Thomas was shocked at how depressed his younger brother seemed. The Ministry had more to do with care taking for the church than anything to do with serving God he said, and Edward wanted to serve God.

"I want to travel to the new world and build my own congregation, start afresh in the virgin forests of America." Thomas nodded, seeing a way that his scheme could benefit both of them.

"You'll need plenty of cash for that Edward, building churches and travel to the Americas doesn't come cheap!" Edward sighed.

"I am trapped here, penniless and bullied!"

"Bullied?" Edward was reluctant to expand further, but Thomas pressed him, until reluctantly Edward explained that since the death of their father, the Lutwhiche brothers were running roughshod over everything and everyone around. Thomas's head swam with rage at the thought of his father's death.

"Ok, Edward, I can see a way we can help each other here." He said, finally calming himself down enough to put his plans to his brother. Edward sat patiently and listened, shaking his head occasionally, or drawing in a full breath every now and then, but he still listened without too much fuss or judgement. Thomas explained that only *he* could do the job he was asking him to do. No one else in the world was capable, and if Edward wanted to travel to the New World and set up his own church, then this was the way to do it. Yes, it involved an element of risk, quite a large element as it happened and it involved boxing, trickery and theft. Much to Thomas and Bridget's surprise, Edward agreed without too much of a fuss, his only stipulation was that no one would die. Neither Thomas nor Bridget could promise him that. Edward's face went pale but he held his hand out anyway, and the twin like brothers shook firmly and sealed the deal. "Now for the other business!" Thomas rose from the pew inside the old church and held his hands out in front of him. He clasped his fingers together and stretched them backwards, the loud crunching sound from his knuckles bounced around the stone walls of the old building. "I'll see you in two weeks in Birmingham Edward, we'll go over the details then!" Without looking back, he strode out of the church, "Come on Bridget, this is gonna be fun!"

"No, Thomas . . . " Edward shouted, surprising them all," . . . this is too important a thing to risk messing things up with those Lutwhiche boys. We can deal with them later. Keep your anger at the back of your mind until this is over, God will smite them down Thomas!"

"He's right Thomas, we have too much to lose!" Thomas stood in the old church doorway mulling over his brother's words and realising that both Bridget and Edward were right, he reluctantly agreed.

"I don't know if God will smite them down or not Edward. I'm not on talking terms with the almighty like you are, but I tell you this brother, when all this is over and done with, the Lutwhiches will rue the day they ever crossed with the Fewtrells!"

The Long Knife

CHAPTER 24

J oseph Buck listened at the large door for a mention of his name through the thick wood panelling, he struggled to hear anything over the barking of dogs and the rattle of servants' trays emanating from the kitchen level below as the house went about its business. The mutterings of Lord Dashwood and Flint simply could not be heard through the doors, and the odd word he could hear was too quiet to make any sense to him. If he could have heard the conversation inside, he would have turned around and found the first ship back to Massachusetts never to return. He stepped nearer the wood panelling and placed his ear against the door. The paranoia that plagued him, since falling into the hands of his jailers over the last twelve months was becoming chronic, to say the least. Something was in the air. The boxing matches were all well and good, and if truth be told, Joseph Buck's boxing ability had gone from strength to strength since arriving in England. The American could now hold his own against anyone that faced him, with or *without* the use of Flint's Mandrake potion. But lately, the Lord and Flint would not let him out of their sight, they held secret meetings which Buck was not allowed to attend, and he was sure that these meetings were about him, or at least their plans for him. And he was certain these plans did not have his best interests at heart, he was certain of that, yet the proof alluded him, and so he found himself with his ear pressed to another door, listening for a hint, a word or a clue as to what treachery was a-foot.

"Look, Flint, it's a simple plan!" Flint stood with his back to the old Lord staring from the long window out onto the greyness of the day outside. His gaze wandered lazily across the over grown gardens to the rear of Lord Dashwood's mansion. The Lord didn't mind his manservant showing his back to him, the lack of respect was tolerated as long as they were in private. Flint sighed deeply, he wasn't sure he agreed with what his master was saying.

"My Lord, Thomas Fewtrell will be on the lookout for anything unusual on the build up to this fight." Dashwood muttered under his breath.

"You did it once Flint, give him another Mandrake drink!" Flint's eyes followed a small movement by one of the trees in the garden, a red squirrel scampered across a branch before vanishing into the foliage.

"Ai my Lord, I'll do my best, but let's not go off track here, the main thing is we achieve our end goal!" The Lord nodded.

"Yes, of course, but that can't happen until we nip Thomas Fewtrell in the bud can it. If Fewtrell beats Buck and knocks him unconscious, then how are we going to blame the American for the assassination . . . explain that to me Flint . . . If you can!" Flint sighed again.

"Yes, my Lord, I see your point, sir, but with the greatest of respect." Flint said impatiently. "I'm telling you the same trick we used on Fewtrell won't work twice. We need another plan, something that will fill your coffers with the royal gold as well as killing the King!"

"Shhh, man . . . !" Dashwood hissed. "Never mention the King in this house again Flint . . . good God man there are ears everywhere. Who knows how many spies the bastard has in my household amongst my servants, one whisper of this little conspiracy and we'll both be hung, drawn and quartered!" Flint nodded sheepishly.

"Yes, my Lord, I'm sorry but my point stays the same, our wee trick simply will not work again." Dashwood held his head in his hands.

"Well, we must think of something. The King will want to shake hands with the winner after the fight, we have to make sure that it's the American who shakes that hand, then, whilst the crowd is packed tightly around him, and the American is with the King, you will deliver the killing strike!" Flint flinched at the words. He spun from his place by the window to face the old man.

"The killing strike!" He repeated, leaving the words hanging in the air, almost too scared to think about the meaning. "And how exactly is that to be delivered my Lord, I doubt whether we'll be able to smuggle a mighty claymore into his Majesty's company although I'd very much like to see the bastard's head come off his shoulders with a swing of a good basket hilt broadsword!" Dashwood laughed.

"My Scottish friend there are more ways than one to skin a cat, and however passionate I am about your Highlander habits, this job must be done with a finesse that would be hard to find in a swing from your mighty claymore!" Dashwood pointed towards the desk in the corner of the large room. "I have a weapon made just for the job. It's in the desk, fetch it out Flint, there's a good fellow!" Without thinking, Flint immediately crossed the room to the desk. "Middle drawer!" The Scot pulled the drawer of the low desk open and saw nothing. "Search along the rear of the draw, it's wrapped in a suede cloth." Flint bent and reached inside the narrow drawer, his thick forearm finding it difficult to reach the back of the shelf. Rolling the thick buttoned cuff on the sleeve of his jacket up, he plunged his hand forcefully into the dark confines of the drawer. He swept his hand this way and that blindly until his thick-set fingers found the bundle of suede in the rearmost recesses of the drawer. Flint froze. On seeing his manservant's expression, Dashwood spoke again. "I've had it for many years Flint, since the days of the Jacobite rising, when weapons were . . . less gentlemanly than they are in these modern times, maybe you'll recognise it?" Flint withdrew his hand holding the bundle. He examined it for a second before laying it on the desk and untying the red silk ribbon that bound the shammy leather in a long roll. As he opened the wrap, Dashwood watched his servant's eyes open, a look of aston-ishment and awe seemed to illuminate the Scot's face.

"*My God*!" Flint recognised the weapon immediately as the one given to his father by Prince Charles Stuart forty years before.

Holding the knife up to the light, he let his eyes wander over the weapon with its fourteen inches long, incredibly thin, razor sharp blade which disappeared into its engraved ivory handle. On the handle was carved an oak leaf and acorns and along the blade a tiny depiction of the Greek goddess Medusa, both symbols synonymous with the old Jacobite cause. The sight of them instantly took Flint back to his youth, filling his mind with memories of his father, the murder of the officer on the ship and his first meeting with his Lord and master. The Scot's eyes filled with tears. He coughed, trying to hide his emotions.

"My Lord . . . it's . . . it's beautiful . . . but, h . . . how!" Dashwood smiled, pleased he'd kept the weapon secret until such a time as this.

"That knife is yours Flint, given to your father by the Prince himself. I took it from the captain of the brigatine, and have kept it for you all these years and although I could have sold it many times over, for ridiculous amounts to any of the Jacobites hidden in our London circles, I knew that one day you would use it as it was intended to be used, to bring the Stuart King back across the sea to his rightful place on the throne of England. Although initially, the public will think that the American delivered the coup-de-grace on that lunatic of a King we suffer with, in time it will be *your* name that will forever go down in history as the man who brought an end to King George III and the house of Hanover!" A creak from the doorway forced the two men to stop talking, they sat for a few seconds in silence, listening for another tell-tale sign that they were being spied on from the doorway. Flint's eyes searched the small gap beneath the door where he could see the shadow of a man's feet on the other side. He turned and nodded to Dashwood. The old man smiled.

"One more thing Flint!" He whispered. "I want the masked harlot . . . Eleanor Blackfoot!" Flint raised his eyebrows, puzzled by the mention of the girl. The old man continued. "She's a complication we don't need, she has something to do with Fewtrell!" Flint's bemused look turned from one of puzzlement to one of hope.

"Och, that's it, your lordship!"

"Shh . . . !" Dashwood pointed at the door, Flint shrugged.

"Sorry my Lord!" He whispered. "The girl with the mask, maybe she's our way to win the fight!" The old man nodded, contemplating his servant's words, his bleak white face breaking into an evil smile as he imagined the treason he could muster amongst the Jacobites within the Hellfire Club.

Joe Buck could sense that his presence had been noticed behind the door by the drop in volume of the voices from the two men within. He slowly stepped back from the doorway. Careful not to trigger any creaking or squeaks from the old floorboards beneath his feet, he stepped backwards, his heart pounding in his broad chest, all the time staring at the doorway, expecting Flint or Dashwood to fling the doors apart and discover his prying at any moment. When he'd covered a large enough space so as not to be noticed, he allowed himself to breathe normally, his breath came out in a long relieving sigh, his heart slowly relaxing again, but as he spun on his heel to walk away, he came face to face with the weasel-faced minder.

"So this is how Americans repay their host's hospitality, is it? By spying on them at every opportunity?" Buck just stared at the minder, his mouth open, mid breath. He didn't know how to reply. If he remonstrated with the man, it would draw Dashwood and Flint from the room beyond.

"I . . . I!" He muttered uselessly.

"Shh!" The weasel whispered before holding his index finger up to Buck's mouth. "We need to have a little chat, Mr Buck!" He whispered. Joe Buck pushed his hand away.

"I don't have anything to say to you, sir!" Buck said, trying to hide his embarrassment at being caught.

"Shh!" The weasel repeated. "I have something to say to you Mr Buck, and unless you want those pair to come out here and catch you red-handed, I suggest you listen to me very carefully." The American shook his head, confused about the weasel's intentions. "Come on, we can't talk here if they catch you listening they'll have your guts for garters. Follow me, I need you to tell me how much of their conversation you heard!" He turned and began to walk away. Joe Buck just stood there watching the little man walk away down the corridor. A shuffle of chairs indicated that the two men inside Lord Dashwood's study had finished their meeting and were about to leave the room. The weasel turned at the other end of the corridor and was alarmed to see the American hadn't moved and mouthed the words, "*Come on*!"

The door behind the altar

CHAPTER 25

The villagers of Rye knew it was time to lay low when the local coffin-maker was approached by a well-heeled dandy from London who enquired about the construction of a large, risen platform and handrail within the ruins of the old church on the banks of the River Dew Gill. They knew that the aristocrats and lorded Gentry would once again descend upon their sleepy corner of England in the pursuit of debauchery and everyone from the innkeeper to the village idiot knew they had best keep a very low profile until the toffs had finished their villainy and returned to their townhouses, mansions and country piles or wherever it was these gaudy-coloured people came from. The village folk had seen it all before, lords, dandies, fops, mollies and of course their wretched workhouse victims dragged to the old chapel ruins for whatever perversion the rich fancied indulging themselves in on that particular night. They were unmistakable, arriving in gold and black guilt-framed coaches behind teams of beautiful, thoroughbred horses, who, by the look of their shiny coats were better fed and treated than anyone within the village. The wealth of these people astounded the villagers who in contrast, spent their lives, like so many others in England, struggling to survive day to day, putting scraps of food together on a their filthy tables in one of the wattle and daub houses that lined the dirt-packed road through Rye.

The boxing ring within the ruins was a small one, far smaller than those seen in London. Lord Dashwood made this decision so that the fighters would have no choice but to box each other senseless rather than making space between themselves to avoid their opponent's blows. A 12 x 12 foot platform stood in the centre of the ruins beneath a huge hole in the slate-tiled roof forty feet above, which, much to the coffin-maker's annoyance was letting the drizzle fall upon his new creation. The church's rotten pews were dragged out of the way and now lined the walls instead of facing the altar as they had done for many years when the church had been used for more Christian practices. A seating area had also been constructed where the altar had once been for use by the King, his royal entourage and bodyguard. It was risen so that the King could witness the action in the ring without having to stand or crane his chubby neck.

The Hellfire Club members and any of the King's other guests would be allowed to stand, sit or wander wherever they fancied within the ruins. All would be searched for weapons of any kind, including Lord Dashwood and his crew of servants, minders and sycophantic homosexuals and only the King's bodyguard permitted their long pikes, swords and pistols within the walls of the building and the King's presence. Dashwood and his cronies would watch the fight from the musician's balcony at the other end of the church which sat above the main entrance of the ruins. This suited both King George and Lord Dashwood equally as their mutual hatred for one another had grown substantially in the weeks building up to the fight, both flying into uncontrollable rages at the slightest mention of the other's name. In fact, the atmosphere had become so strained between the two that go-betweens had to be used in order to agree conditions on the wagers laid on the outcome of the fight. Both men agreed after lengthy negotiations that they would place their bets on the night of the fight, in front of the watching audience so that neither man could back out of his promise to the other. Wagers were to be met either in silver or gold and if that couldn't be matched, then the property deeds would have to be forfeited to satisfy any debts. The negotiations were non-stop, lengthy and frustratingly boring and almost filled the three-week build-up to the fight.

The boxers, on the other hand, found the time flew by in a blur of sparring and training. Joe Buck seemed to have developed into a different man compared with the fellow that had arrived from the new world twelve months before. His boxing prowess had matured as he'd settled into his role as London champion. Initially, it must be said, with the help of a few 'mannys'. After a short while, however, the potions were no longer needed as the American's fitness and boxing technique matured to the point that he was winning the bouts fair and square and with surprising speed and power. This was to be his last fight in England, and he'd insisted on that being written into the contract between the King and Dashwood, even threatening to pull out of the fight altogether if it wasn't. Lord Dashwood happily agreed to the clause knowing that if everything went to plan this would *definitely* be Joseph Buck's final fight.

Thomas Fewtrell on the other hand, agreed to the fight on one stipulation, that he had a private area within the ruin, a space that only he and his seconds were allowed to use. No one was to be permitted entrance to this area, except of course the King and his bodyguard. Thomas said he needed the space to prepare himself for the bout and would not fight unless this stipulation was adhered to. A small antechamber to the rear of the altar was offered as a changing room. Thomas inspected it and agreed it was perfect for his needs. It had two doors, one to the main hall and another door on the opposite wall leading out of the antechamber and into the overgrown graveyard at the rear of the church.

****

Bridget, Mendoza and Thomas sat within the small, dark room listening to the hubbub of the arriving guests. The sound of a violin being tuned rose softly above the murmuring of people, its strings cutting through the muffled voices and clatter of heels on the stone floor. The lone instrument was accompanied by another stringed instrument, only this time much lower in tone which provided bass to the cheerful tune the violin had now started to play. The music bounced around the moss-covered wall of the old church creating reverberation making the music seem as if it were coming from far away.

Thomas sat wringing the knuckles on his left hand nervously as Daniel wrapped a thin layer of bandages around his right fist. Bridget was busy with three flagons of sugary ale she had brought with her from Birmingham, their cork-stoppers jammed into place, a thick layer of wax protecting the seals around their tops which would indicate if the contents had been tampered with. No one spoke. Each knew what was at stake here and each knew the consequences should things not work out as planned.

"Have you made sure the door works?" Thomas said, pointing to the rear door that led out to the graveyard.

"Yes, Thomas, I've cleared away all the brambles, so it opens without any obstruction!" Bridget said impatiently as she fussed over the flagons.

"Just make sure that it opens without any fuss, because ... "

" ... yes, I know ... I've done it!" She snapped.

"Ok, you two, calm down, try and think about this as if it's just another fight, don't let your nerves get the better of you." Mendoza said sternly, trying to quell the rising tension. He slapped Thomas's bandaged hands. "There, try them out, make sure the wrap isn't too tight." Thomas stood shaking his hands at the wrists. He raised his arms and began to shadow box in the small space. Daniel and Bridget stood back and watched his fists snap at the air, amazed by the man's speed and strength. They watched him silently until the sound of the music in the main hall stopped, announcing the arrival of the King. The trio turned to each other, Daniel smiled. "Showtime my friends!" Thomas and Bridget glanced at each other, noticing the worried expression on each other's face. Mendoza crossed his head. "Holy Mary Mother of God will you pair lighten up? By the way Thomas, I just want to say thank you for choosing me as your second. I thought you would have chosen Sykesy or your brother Edward. Why aren't they here by the way?" Bridget laughed nervously and went to answer but was cut short by Thomas.

"Don't worry Daniel, they'll be here. Anyway ... " he said changing the subject, " ... let's stop nattering and get out there and meet the King!"

Thomas stepped through the small door and into the main hall and found himself behind the King's high-backed, ornate throne which had been brought from his palace and set up on the centre of the old altar. The others followed him and all three stood gazing with amazement at what can only be described as the fairytale scene in front of them. The cold stone building that had stood like a grim reminder of past tragedy was now lit up by what must have been over a thousand candles hanging from wrought-iron chandeliers and candelabras. Bright, flaming torches lined the walls in metal baskets, their light illuminating the brightly-coloured tapestries which had been hung around the room, giving the impression that one stood in a richly furnished, fantasy castle instead of the damp ruin it had been earlier that day. Thomas's bare feet felt the rich carpet beneath him on the altar and he noticed that the old flagstone floor which ran throughout the church had now been covered with a hundred or so thick, red Persian rugs. They were trampled on by the feet of two hundred people in loudly-coloured garb, styles and fashions of the day, all of them in fantastically exotic Venetian styled masks. Grey-wigged men mingled and flirted anonymously with elegantly dressed ladies, some of whom wore their wigs almost three feet high above their white-powdered, masked faces. All indulged in the wine, ale and spirits served by one of the many dark blue and yellow liveried servants who circled the room with their trays of drinks or canapés like so many summer starlings.

The trio stood behind the throne in awe, gazing like excited children at the splendour and opulence of the scene. The realisation dawning on them that the boxing match was only *one* of the reason for London's most powerful and fashionable to be there that night. The sight of so many rich people made Thomas's heart flutter with excitement and self-doubt as he watched the scene. Abruptly, the gossiping crowd hushed and turned as one to face the main entrance at the far end of the room. Another page entered the building and announced that the King had arrived. Those sat on the old pews stood and the room fell silent. The trio watched as the shadow of an ornately dressed, chubby man stepped into view holding the hand of a small black serving boy for balance. Judging by the man's gait, Thomas thought, he looked drunk. Eight bodyguards rushed forward along the aisle of the church and cleared the way for the King, pushing the crowd back rudely as the monarch came further into the church.

"*Make way for the King*!" The head of the King's bodyguard shouted. As the monarch walked so the crowd bowed as if the sun's shadow fell across a field of wilting flowers until he arrived at the foot of the altar. As the King stepped up the first of the stone steps he over balanced and the servant boy at his arm, unable to take his weight also began to topple over. Thomas sprang from behind the throne and took the King's arm saving him from his stumble. Thomas's action caught all by surprise, not least the King and his alarmed bodyguard, who leapt to the monarch's defence, bringing their long, pole-axes to the boxer's throat. The King stared up into Thomas's face, his pink, puffy eyes glistened in the yellow candlelight as recognition spread across his rosy, pockmarked face.

"Ha . . . by God it's you . . . the drunken pugilist from the Cheshire Cheese!" Thomas tried to hide his reaction to the King's remark behind a smile and helped him right himself. The guards' ceremonial pole-axes still at his neck. The King waved them away. "For God's sake, stand down you dogs, can't you see the man's trying to help me climb these infernal steps!" The bodyguards stepped back as one resuming their positions around the foot of the altar, their backs to the King, facing the crowd, the pole-axes pointing to the ceiling and broadswords at their sides.

Thomas helped the King to his seat just as Mendoza and Bridget stepped from behind bowing subserviently. The bloated monarch stared at them with a smile recognising the now familiar face of Daniel Mendoza. "Ah . . . the Portuguese pugilist!" Mendoza bowed lower.

"My King!" The monarch laughed loudly.

"I have watched your fights many times Mendoza, and you've made me a small fortune over the last twelve months. Let's hope you can do it again with this man here!" Mendoza bowed again.

"Yes, your majesty!" Thomas saw his friend's reaction and lowered his own head. "I hope you can keep him sober tonight

Mendoza, I've bet my bloody crown on the bastard!" The King burst into laughter, followed almost instantly by a crowd of family and friends who had begun to join him on the platform, gathering tightly around him as if to display their position to those around them.

"Yes, your majesty!" Mendoza fawned. "He is sober now and will remain so until he wins the fight. After that, I cannot vouch for him, my King!"

"Ha!" The King slapped the arm of the throne. "That's the spirit, man!" He broke away from Thomas's grip waving him towards the boxing platform which sat beneath two, wrought-iron chandeliers each casting a soft, yellow glow over the fighting ring. "Go on Fewtrell, show us what you're made of!" Thomas bowed again and began to back away down the steps to the altar. He glanced at Mendoza, gesturing that he should follow. Bridget, Mendoza and Thomas left the King's company and walked towards the platform. The crowd surged toward him as Thomas crossed the room slapping his back and shoulders with encouragement until the trio were swallowed by the throng of aristocrats and members of the Hellfire club. The crowd were packed together tightly in the small hall making it hard to push through the mob towards the boxing ring. Thomas searched the faces of the masked crowd as he passed. Turning to Bridget, he shouted into her ear over the din of the party.

"Where's Eleanor?" Bridget shrugged and shouted back above the rising din,

"It's hard to tell if she's here at all with all these masks. I can't tell who's who."

They reached the handrail of the ring, and Thomas pulled a small milking stool from beneath the platform, stepped on it and climbed into the ring. Mendoza followed, and Bridget began to push the crowd back aggressively making space for her to put the three small glass flagons of ale down beside the platform's edge. A huge cheer spread throughout the ruins as Thomas took his corner of the ring. He ignored the mob and began bounce on the spot throwing punches into the air as he did. Mendoza searched the room for the American but couldn't see anyone from the opposing side at all, only the excited up-turned faces of around two hundred or so bizarrely dressed and masked gentlefolk with a craving for blood.

"*My lords, ladies and gentlemen!*" A booming voice brought the music and chatter to a sudden stop, "Wagers may now be laid!" Thomas and Daniel turned to see to whom the voice belonged and both were surprised when they saw it was small, fat page in his late twenties booming out the King's commands. As soon as his words were spoken, a team of four men in black gowns and wigs, looking more like courtroom judges than touts, took up their positions along the bottom of the altar steps in front of the King. A flurry of betting began in earnest as the whole crowd seemed to raise their arms at once, their bodies pressed tightly as they tried to lay their wagers. A cacophony of music, laughter and shouting began. All the while the white noise of gold and silver coins jingling in leather pouches rang in the background drowning out the flutter of a hundred or so hands waving white-parchment credit notes, all trying to gain the attention of the stern, white-wigged bookies. Thomas turned from the chaos towards Bridget leaning over the handrail to whisper to her as best he could over the racket.

"By God but there's some money here tonight!" She returned his words with a look of awe. She had never seen so much wealth under one roof not even at Blackfoot's Rookery.

"London's banks must be empty Thomas, these rich fools have brought all their wealth with them!" Thomas smiled.

"Let's hope so Bridget . . . let's hope so!" After what seemed like an eternity, the betting panic began to abate and as it did so the fat page's voice rang out above the crowd once again.

"My lords, ladies and gentlemen, now the main wager of this evening's sport is to be placed as instructed by his majesty the King . . . " The page left the words hanging for a second, the audience picked up on the pause and taking it as a cue, began to cheer.

"God save the King!" a voice called out.

"Good King George!" Another sang, satisfied with the positive comments the fat page began talking again,

" . . . and our most gracious host here tonight at the infamous Hellfire Club, his lordship . . . Lord Dashwood!" Once again the page stopped talking for a few seconds to await a response. A drunken club member lost in the crowd began to clap his hand and stopped again when no one else joined him. The room fell into silence. Again, the page seemed happy with the correct response from the crowd and so began to talk once more. "My Lord Dashwood!" He shouted in a low but clear voice, pointing up towards the musician's balcony above the entrance to the church. All heads turned towards the risen structure which sat amongst shadows of the roof's structure. Thomas, Bridget and Mendoza also turned to look. The balcony remained still and dark. The candelabra that hung just in front and underneath the platform created shadows that danced along the front of the thick wooden handrail. Everything behind the handrail lay in blackness. "My Lord Dashwood!" The King twitched impatiently in his throne. Still, silence from the balcony. The page turned to the King and raised his eyebrows as if to ask the monarch what he should do next. The King waved his index finger towards the musician's platform. The page called again.

"My Lord . . . !" A tall, thin man dressed in a long, crimson dress coat emerged from the shadows like a ghost. He took up his position overlooking the crowd and great hall. He stopped just on the edge of the candelabra light with his hands resting on the bannister rail at the front of the balcony. The flickering candlelight played with the man's sharp facial features, the white plaster mask he wore almost indiscernible from his grey waxy skin, giving the watching crowd the impression that the man were some sort of other-worldly malevolent spirit who had crossed the great divide between life and death to partake in that night's macabre sport.

"I am here!" He said in a low, gravelly monotone as if just by answering he was committing treason against the King that he obviously hated at the other end of the room. "State your business page!" The page turned to the King once more. The monarch shifted uncomfortably before nodding that the deal should be struck. The fat page clapped his hands loudly.

"Bring them in!" Almost instantly a group of six soldiers pushed their way into the room. In their midst were two men struggling to carry a small, metal strong-box. Two soldiers pulled an old table from one of the cloisters and placed it at the foot of the altar steps. The men carrying the strong box heaved it onto the table, which looked as if it may collapse under the weight, its legs creaking and top bending under the strain. Thomas and Bridget glanced at each other, eyes wide with excitement and uncertainty. The captain of the guard stepped forward and drew a key from a small pouch in his belt and proceeded to unlock the box. The King stood as he did so, and many in the crowd began to bow.

"Raise your eyes my friends!" The King ordered. "It is for your eyes I have brought my gold here tonight so do not bow your heads, witness my wager with Lord Dashwood!" He climbed clumsily down the stone steps towards the strong box, the young black boy at his arm. When he reached the old table, he leant forward and flipped the lid to the box back. A bright but soft yellow glow emanated from inside the box as the gold within reflected in the guttering candlelight. The spectacle sent shivers down the spines of those nearest the gold and a sigh of almost orgasmic awe spread throughout the hall. A shuffle from the balcony made Thomas turn back towards Lord Dashwood's position as he did, a man in his late fifties stepped forward into the light in order to see the gold's glow. He was standing closely behind a tall, young woman in another Venetian mask. Only unlike all the other masks, Thomas recognised it as the elegant one worn by Eleanor. She seemed to be standing at an uncomfortable angle, her arm raised at the elbow to her side and Thomas could just make out a man behind her gripping her arm tightly just above the elbow. Thomas's head surged with rage.

"Looks like we weren't the only ones looking for Eleanor." He said under his breath. The old man was talking but Thomas heard not one of his words. He wanted to leap over the handrail and battle his way onto that balcony and tear the head from the man holding Eleanor. At that moment he felt a tug on the claret fighter's sash which was tied around his waist, aggressive enough to get his attention. Turning, he saw man with shoulder-length, greasy black hair, strips of grey running its length and a long scar down the side of his face. He beckoned Thomas down towards him. Thomas bent until he came face to face with Flint. The Scot looked at the boxer's expression. He saw the hatred and barely controlled rage that battled within the man's eyes and he savoured it for a second, enjoying its power and his control over it. Thomas recognised him as one of Lord Dashwood's men from the fight at the Cheshire Cheese Tavern. "What do *you* want?" Thomas spat.

"Ye go *down* in round two!" Thomas's anger subsided, replaced with puzzlement.

"Round two?" he repeated.

"Ai, round two!" Thomas snarled at the Scot.

"And if I don't?" Flint gestured towards the balcony.

"If ye don't . . . " Flint said smirking, " . . . then old Lord Harrington up there will feed that wee lassie to his fucking dogs, that's if he can withstand the temptation to just cut her tits off right in front of you, right now. *Ai,* he's an unpredictable bastard that fellow. Anyways, do you understand me big man, round two?" Thomas reached to grab the man's face but as quickly as Thomas's well-trained reflexes were, Flint brought the long knife up under his chin quicker. The action was hidden to all but Thomas by Flint's body. Thomas stopped instantly as he felt the sharp prick of pain in his throat. "That's it big man!" Flint said, enjoying the moment of control over such a powerful man as Thomas Fewtrell. "Now you've got the message, ai, round two or the girl's gonna be dog food!" With that Flint vanished into the throng. Thomas spun around to Bridget and Mendoza, but neither had seen a thing. Everyone, including his friends, were watching the King and Lord Dashwood rowing furiously over the heads of the watching audience. Eventually, Dashwood agreed that his bet would be on Joseph Buck to win in round two as he talked his own strong box appeared from its hiding place in the shadows of the balcony, carried by two of Lords Dashwood and Harrington's minders. They placed them on the rickety table at the King's feet. The crowd's reaction to the sight of another strong box of gold and silver coins was equally as enthusiastic. The King upped the stakes betting one of the royal hunting lodges in the forest of Dean against a moated palace belonging to Lord Dashwood on the coast, near Hastings.

"Stone and silver!" Thomas muttered under his breath. After a conversation between the man in charge of the grey-wigged touts and the page, it was announced that the betting had gone in favour of the American. Joe Buck was the favourite to win, on hearing this the King's face flushed with anger and impatience.

"Right, Dashwood, let's see this rebel, is he here?" Once again all eyes turned to the balcony. Dashwood, Harrington and Eleanor were joined in the pool of light on the platform by the bare-chested boxer from the new world. To Mendoza and Thomas's surprise Buck had filled out substantially since their bout at the Cheshire Cheese. His arms, chest and shoulders had become a mass of rippling muscle, his short, thick neck was surrounded by his shoulder muscles so that it seemed to disappear into the base of his head giving the impression that he had no neck at all. He wasn't the same man Thomas had fought twelve months ago. *This* man seemed to have more in common with a beast than a human. The candlelight shimmered on Joe Buck's greased chest as he strained the muscles in his torso to reveal his abdominals to the crowd. Thomas's heart sank, his shoulders physically slumping. Mendoza noticing his reaction spoke,

"What you're giving up just because he's got a few muscles . . . ?" Thomas shrugged.

"I'd pictured something else . . . I'd pictured . . . !" Mendoza slapped his back.

"You should fight with your fists my friend not your eyes. He may look powerful, and I'm sure he is but speed beats power and accuracy beats speed. You can take him, Thomas . . . !" Thomas raised his eyebrows, unsure of Daniel's words. Mendoza continued. "I have fought men twice his size and won. Why? Because I remained disciplined and took away their power using movement and boxing technique." A roar rose from the crowd. Both men turned to the balcony once more to see Joe Buck throwing lighting fast punches into the air showing off to the waiting crowd. Mendoza laughed. "Having said that, he does look pretty quick Thomas."

"Yeah, I've heard it all before Daniel!" Thomas said earnestly, "Tell me what do you really think, have I got a chance?" Mendoza sighed and made the sign of the cross.

"I think you'll be fine ..." He said, Thomas smiled, "...but I have just said a prayer to God and he thinks you're fucked!" An uncomfortable silence fell between them before both men burst into morbid laughter. Thomas glanced up towards Lord Harrington's position who still held the girl only now he was supping on a large glass of port or wine, and by the look of Eleanor's body, his grip had relaxed somewhat.

Thomas knelt down and dragged Mendoza with him. He beckoned Bridget over, and the three huddled in his corner of the ring. To all that were watching it looked as if they were praying together, but inside the huddle, Thomas was instructing Bridget what to do once the fight had reached round two.

****

"For fuck's sake Edward, it's just a bleeding horse!" Sykesy held the reins of the huge dray horse as Edward tried to mount the beast.

"This ain't no horse it's a bloody monster. Where did you find it?" Sykesy rolled his eyes at the preacher's awkwardness as he tried to mount.

"I got it from behind a brewery in London. Look ..." he said pointing to one of the thick ropes Sykesy had tied to the pommel of the large saddle, "...just grab one of the ropes and haul yourself up!" Edward stopped trying to throw his leg over the animal's back and looked at Sykesy.

"You mean you stole it Henry!" Sykesy became impatient.

"Look your holiness!" He said sarcastically. "Your brother said we needed a fucking big horse so that's what I got him, a fucking big horse. Edward you're not meant to be giving it bleeding holy communion so stop getting your cassock in a twirl and get on the bleeding thing, we're gonna be late!" He spoke to Edward as if he were a child. Edward didn't move.

"Late for what exactly?" Sykesy's impatience turned to one of embarrassment.

"Well ..." he replied stumbling over his words, "...I ain't too sure but whatever it is, it's important enough to warrant me nicking a fucking big horse ... so come on, chop chop, this ain't one of your

Sunday services!" Edward clumsily complied, painfully straddling the horse's huge flanks with his legs. Sykesy led the horse from the old, dilapidated barn hidden amongst the brush and pointed down the tree-lined highway. Edward followed his gesture which pointed at nothing in particular. Orange dusk illuminated the rising river mist that would soon engulf the highway, its brightness dimmed by the over-hanging trees which created shadows along the dirt-packed road. In the last rays of sunlight, two or three miles distant, Edward could just make out the spire of an old, ruined church poking out above this rising mist, its tiled spike and wrought iron crucifix still bathed in the sunset's glow.

"Just follow this road, it'll take you straight to that church." Edward noticed Sykesy's voice now had a more serious tone. "Thomas said you should wait until after dark, and *don't* let anyone see you arrive! There's an overgrown path on the right of the highway that will lead you from the road to the back of the church, take it. Leave the horse tied and enter through the rear door of the church, the pathway's been cleared so it will be easy to find in the dark, they'll be waiting for you!"

Edward became alarmed.

"What, you're not coming?" Sykesy laughed.

"Don't fret preacher, Thomas said I should wait here. Don't ask me why but when you see him, tell him I'm at the appointed place and I've got everything he told me to bring!" With that Sykesy slapped the horse's rump with his gloved hand. The horse barely noticed and turned its huge head to look at the cloaked man beside him.

"Come on Edward, give me a bit of help, kick him on or something, he's a big brute but too bleeding docile if you ask me!" Edward looked down at Henry who seemed far below him from his high perch on the nag's back.

"Docile's good Sykesy, I like docile." Gripping the reins tightly, he kicked the beast's flank with his heels muttering prayers beneath his breath. The horse began to clip clop slowly forward onto the darkening highway towards the village of Rye.

The fight began cautiously with both men unwilling to give the other a chance to open up any gaps in the other's defence to deliver a blow that would bring an early end to the bout. Jabs and blocks were the order of the first few minutes of round one as both boxers searched the other for any weaknesses in technique. The crowd, on the other hand, wanted blood, plenty of it and sooner rather than later. The dance in the boxing ring had become tedious and so, even though the fight was in its first minutes, the cat calls had already started. Thomas didn't hear any of them. He was busy watching Buck step around him. He saw that although the American had become a well-disciplined boxer, using his top half to position himself defensively as well as offensively, his footwork was clumsy and slow. There was something else too, something Thomas hadn't seen in any of the fifty or so fights he'd had since last battling the American, Joe Buck had a look in his eye that betrayed what he felt in his heart. A look that Thomas could have sworn was a look of fear, a distraction to something outside the ring. Thomas knew he would have to exploit that fear, just as Joe Buck would exploit his own distraction of Eleanor at the hands of Lord Harrington on the balcony. He glanced up at the shadowy figures watching him from above and saw Eleanor, her pale beauty almost glowing in the darkness, the fear in her eyes beneath the mask. He let his eye rest on her features a millisecond more that he knew he should have something he knew the American would take full advantage of. Bam! The punch was hard to his jaw shaking him to his very foundations. His moment of pleasurable distraction shattered into a thousand fireworks exploding painfully in his head. Buck quickly followed his left with another punch intended to floor Fewtrell, but Thomas's reactions were too fast. Turning his head to the side, the right hook glanced off of his chin and spun into the air behind his ear. Even so, the throw was a good one, forcing Thomas to step backwards, much to the approval of the watching aristocrats who began to scream for the American to close in for the kill. However Joe Buck had learned his lesson from his first fight with Fewtrell, and he stepped forward slowly, one foot at a time, arms raised in front of his face, eyes glaring with menace. What he lacked in movement with his feet he more than made up for with heaviness of body which he planted like a tree roots into the canvas, sail sheet beneath his feet, daring Thomas to try and topple him. Buck knew that he had all the time he needed and the knockout punch the audience were waiting for wouldn't be happening anytime soon, at least not whilst Fewtrell was still so fresh. He'd have to wear him down over the next fifteen minutes. Jab, jab, left, left, trying to open up Fewtrell's defence. But Buck's initial punch had the opposite effect than what he intended, and instead of shaking Thomas's belief in himself, Fewtrell now became totally focused on the fight. No more distractions, all of that was out of his hands for the time being. He needed to survive, now he must concentrate on the man in front of him, not the new world amateur he'd knocked out many months before, this American was now a real fighter, and the brute was there for one reason, and one reason only, his destruction.

"Use your feet, Thomas . . . move man!" Mendoza screamed from the corner of the ring. His voice hoarse, struggling to rise above the racket of the crowd. Thomas heard his words, and as Buck came in for another jab, Thomas shifted his head to the side, and the jab went wide. Quick as a flash, Thomas brought his own fist up at the over balanced American aiming a reactive blow at the man's jaw. Joe Buck saw the punch coming and tried to turn his head, but his reactions were too slow, and Thomas's fist landed well, clipping the end of Buck's chin. Although the punch was delivered well, Joe Buck didn't register it coming on, just as determined to destroy his opponent. Jab, jab, Buck tried to open the defence, stepping foot by foot forward, slowly pressing Fewtrell, searching for a way in. Thomas bobbed his head this way and that dodging the jabs, hiding behind his forearms, peering through the gap, watching the American's every movement.

****

Flint watched the scene from his place next to Lord Dashwood on the balcony. Whilst everyone else was watching the two boxers sound each other out in the ring, the Scot never took his eyes off the King. The sight of the puffy-faced monarch laughing and joking at the far end of the church made his head swim with rage. He fingered the long blade hidden within his jacket inside pocket, imagining the deadly weapon sliding into the King's bloated body as he whispered the last words the monarch would ever hear, unmistakable treasonous words, telling him that it was the blade of Charles James Stuart, the rightful King that had put an end to his life and the Hanover reign.

"Come my little scarred trollop, let me see those big blue eyes of yours!" Harrington twisted Eleanor's arm as he tried to remove her Venetian mask, she seemed frozen with fear as he moved in closer to her, "The thought of one of my prize dogs humping away on you is giving me a bloody good horn!" He whispered as he reached for her mask. Her lack of reaction was a ruse and as Harrington raised his finger to push the mask from her face, she snapped and bringing her teeth tightly around his grubby index finger she bit down as hard as she could. Her teeth biting through the flesh down to the bone. Harrington yelped with the pain of the woman's bite. He tried to pull his finger from her mouth but Eleanor bit even harder letting her teeth grind into the finger bone. Flint and Dashwood turned towards the sound. Harrington's eyes were wide with panic and excruciating pain and now he seemed to be frozen, unable to free his finger and due to the position of his other arm, unable to force the girl's mouth open with his free hand. Lord Dashwood burst into laughter. Flint on seeing his master's reaction joined him laughing. Harrington continued to yelp in a high-pitched female tone. "Help me Flint!" He screamed. But the two men didn't move. "Please Dashwood!" Harrington pleaded. "Get the bitch off me!" Dashwood nudged his servant's shoulder, nodding towards his friend. Flint smiled and crossed to Harrington. He stared at the girl for a second, realising that this was the first time he'd actually seen the girl show any signs of emotion since he'd kidnapped her twenty-four hours before. Eleanor's self-control impressed Flint. For he could see a hatred in her eyes that he himself had carried for so long. He brought his thick set arm up in a flash and struck the girl with a hard, open-handed blow to the face. The strike knocked the mask from her face and it hung to the side, caught by the ribbons which held it in place. Flint's knuckles had burst her bottom lip and her own blood flowed with that of Harrington's finger, covering her lips and chin. Harrington pulled his hand towards him and held it up to the yellow candlelight examining the incision made by the girl's teeth. His eyes reflected the flickering light, horrified by his injury, the flesh from the top of his index finger was missing, leaving only a red bloody bone protruding from the grizzly stump.

"*Bitch*!" He brought the hand up and punched Eleanor as hard as he could. He wished he hadn't as the blow opened up his wound even more and the bone still attached to the finger came off at the first knuckle. Harrington screamed once more. Eleanor recoiled from the blow, nearly losing her feet but soon regained her composure and stood silently watching Harrington's painful dance. Harrington saw her look of defiance and raised his other hand to strike again, but Flint who impressed by the girl's resilience stopped him. Harrington turned to Flint. "Let me go you bastard!" Flint smiled.

"No, my Lord, she's not to be harmed until the end of round two!" Harrington glared at him, then at Dashwood who was smiling, eyebrows raised. On seeing Dashwood, Harrington spun to Eleanor who to his surprise was smiling. "I'll fucking have the last laugh, bitch!" Eleanor opened her mouth slightly as if to speak. Harrington stopped to hear what she had to say. However the words never came. Instead she spat Harrington's bloody finger into his face. Flint burst out laughing and turning to his master he said,

"My lord, I like this wee lass. I'd lay bets on her eating Harrington's dogs!" Dashwood's smile dropped from his face.

"Keep your fucking mind on the game at hand Flint, this trollop means nothing. You are about to make history. Don't fuck it up because of this little tart!"

****

Thomas ducked beneath a long haymaker thrown by Buck as he ducked under the arm, he brought his own fist up to pound the ribs beneath Joe Buck's armpit. The searching and toying moments of the fight were truly over. Now each man closed on the other, punching flesh with sickeningly powerful blows. Thomas's eyes stung with sweat which hung from his blonde fringe in large beads. Strangely, the sweat seemed to concern him more than the actual pain he felt from the punches landed around his face and ribs. He could see the American's technique clearly now, a close cautious attack that was how Joe Buck was playing it. He could see his weak points, but the American wasn't giving him a chance to take advantage of them. Each time he closed in Buck retreated before Thomas could counter attack.

The mob were growing impatient by the caution shown by the boxers, and their lack of ferocity and hissing began to be heard around the room. At that moment Thomas saw a chance and took it, *bam,* finally landing a classic punch to Joe Buck's jawbone that clearly shook the man to the core. He stumbled backwards. Thomas came in for the kill, but Buck kept stepping backwards buying time to recover. Thomas's footwork came into play, and he crossed the ring at surprising speed catching the American totally by surprise. Thomas jabbed with his left then brought his right up to deliver what should have been a devastating blow, Joe Buck clumsily stepped to his right, leaving Thomas's fist to sail into nothing but air. The American had tricked him. Thomas was too late in seeing the deception as Joe Buck recovered from his apparent stupor and slammed his fist into his opponent's face without mercy. Thomas's head spun to his left as the other man's knuckles found bone. *Boom!* Thomas's ears rang from the power of the blow. Stars danced around his eyes. Subconsciously he knew that there would be another punch following almost instantaneously and without registering the movement in his brain, Thomas dropped his head low just in time to feel the backdraft of Joe Buck's fist flying over his head. He brought his own fist up into Buck's ribs again and the punch caught him just right and Thomas could hear the American's rib crack beneath his knuckles. Joe Buck let out a deep breath as the air was forced from him. Thomas brought his left arm over the top of Buck's shoulder, trying to trap the man, he pulled his arm back again ready to slam the same rib with his fist, however, Buck simply slipped from his grip, stepping away from him and as Thomas turned he found Joe Buck's fists waiting for him. The American could wait no longer and he threw any caution he had to the wind and began pummelling away with abandon at the man in front of him. Buck's attack was relentless, catching Thomas off-guard as he spun from his own previous attack. The punches flew freely between both men now, a new level of aggressive energy rising from both boxers as the minutes of round one were counted down. *Bam, bam, bam,* the incredible blows landing on the face of the other began to take their toll. Joe Buck's nose was broken and his blood flowed freely into the blood of his lower lip which was also cut deeply, the claret liquid dripping down his chest and onto the white canvas sheeting at his feet where it lay in puddles smudged by the boxers' feet. Thomas's face wasn't much better, his right eyebrow had ballooned into a huge red bubble above the eye where the blood was trapped beneath the skin. There were other bruises too, mainly around the ribs and internal bleeding around the torso left dark blue patches on both pugilist's bodies as they threw everything into the battle. The bloodletting in the ring was a sickeningly, macabre sight and the audience, who only ten minutes before had been baying for blood, now stood almost silent as both men continued to pound away at each other relentlessly. The hush spread throughout the hall until it was silent and only the sound of tired, heavy breathing from the pugilists and the sickening sound of blood-covered knuckles slamming into raw flesh and bone could be heard. Finally the sound of a bell brought both exhausted men to a halt. Each man stood watching the other until from Joe Buck's corner, the weasel sprang into the ring and placed his arms on the boxer's shoulder.

"Come on Joe this way, you must rest!" He led the boxer away. Thomas blinked away the sweat and turned to see Mendoza patting a small milking stool whilst holding Thomas's sugary ale.

"Come Thomas, sit, take some ale, we have to see to that eye before it closes completely!" Thomas nodded and crossed to his corner of the ring where he slumped onto the stool. Mendoza was talking to him, but words were lost in the chatter as the crowd began to shake themselves out of their silence to talk about the boxing bout. Thomas stared at the American. Daniel understanding his expression continued, "He's nearly spent said Daniel, you can finish him in this round!" Bridget, who was standing next to the handrail listening to Mendoza's words handed Daniel one of the flagons. Thomas took the glass container and examined the wax seal around its stopper.

"Daniel's right Thomas, Joe Buck wore himself out on that last flurry of punches!" Thomas screwed the lid from the flagon breaking its wax seal, and after taking a short swig he turned to Bridget saying sarcastically,

"He's not the only one who's worn himself out!" Bridget held her hand under the flagon and pushed the bottom upwards so that Thomas would drink more of the liquid. The ale had an almost instant effect, and as his body absorbed its sugary contents, it revived his mind and body. He dropped the flagon from his mouth and indicated that the other two should come close. He knew there was no chance of being overheard because of the rising din of the crowd, but he didn't know if any of the bystanders were working with Lord Dashwood.

"Bridget . . . " he said, a new tone to his voice, the dusky girl stepped close, poking her head under the handrail, " . . . Bridget, you must do something for me!" The girl nodded agreeing without enquiring what exactly she was to do. Thomas continued, this time addressing Mendoza. "The fight's rigged!" a cloud passed over Mendoza's face.

"Rigged . . . how so?" Now Thomas turned once more to Bridget.

"Are you still searching the crowd for Eleanor?" Bridget nodded.

"Yes, she said she would be here to meet us but . . . !" Thomas placed his finger on her lips.

"She's here alright, you probably can't see her from where you're standing but I can." Bridget began to search the room full of masked faces again.

"Where is she . . . ?" She asked, a mixture of concern and confusion in her voice. Thomas gestured with his head.

"Don't all go looking at once or you'll give the game away. She's up on the musician's balcony with Lord Dashwood's men!" Bridget peered over Thomas's shoulder, but she couldn't see anything in the shadowy recess.

"I can't see her."

"Trust me she's there." Now he addressed them both, "One of Dashwood's men just warned me that if I don't go down in the next round, they're going to kill her!" Bridget became alarmed, almost breaking into a panic.

"What!" Her eyes began to fill. Thomas was curious about her reaction but pressed on with the plan he'd come up with whilst battling Buck.

"You gotta go up there, Bridget!" He pleaded. "She's being held by someone called Lord Harrington, he's a total nutter apparently, so I've been told by Dashwood's ma . . . !" He didn't finish his sentence, Flint was suddenly beside Bridget, pushing her out of the way as if she were one of the many serving wenches working that night. His dark eyes glared with hatred in the candlelight as he stared at Thomas and Mendoza in the ring.

"Don't forget big man, ye go down in round two!" He spat the words in his guttural brogue. Thomas's nostrils flared with rage, the Scot saw this and laughed. "You had best save your anger for Joe Buck big man because if ye don't go down when my Lordship wants ye to . . . " He pulled the long-bladed, jacobite dagger from a hidden pocket inside his jacket and held it in his fingertips, displaying its vicious blade to the boxer. The trio ran their eyes along the blade's razor sharp edge. Flint saw their horror at the sight of the weapon and began to twirl it in the air. "I'm gonna slide this wee pig stick into ya lady's spine until she's little more than a bag of blood and bone . . . then we'll see how attractive she is!" Flint's sudden appearance with his weapon and threats had caught the three by surprise, and Thomas was clearly shocked. Bridget, on seeing her friend's reaction to the Scot's appearance bowed her head and reached subserviently for the flagon in Thomas's hand and took it saying,

"Thank you, sir!" She turned to Flint, eyes lowered, "Would you care for a drink kind sir?" Flint looked the girl up and down, an expression of total disdain crossed his face as if he'd come across something unpleasant on one of his silver-buckled shoes. Bridget smiled innocently. Flint turned back to Thomas. "This round . . . you go down." He twirled the knife one more time before replacing it back into his secret jacket pocket. As he turned to leave, Bridget gathered the flagon of ale in one arm and tried to push passed the Scot, however, the space between the ring and the bystanders was small, and she clumsily fell into Flint, dropping the half empty flagon from her arm as she did. The Scot quickly grabbed at the glass jar before it hit the floor and shattered, but he was too slow. The flagon smashed, and Bridget jumped to avoid the smashing glass, falling into Flint's arms, almost toppling the man. Flint caught himself.

"*Clumsy bitch*!" He screamed into Bridget's face. He pushed her chest, forcing the girl away from him. "Get off me *nigger*!" Bridget stepped backwards, bowing her head, she curtsied.

"Sorry master." She muttered. Flint glared at her then at the men in the ring, before storming off into the packed crowd.

"What an arsehole!" Mendoza said, trying to follow the sight of the man's figure as he vanished into the crowd. Thomas shook his head. His mind swimming with desperation.

"Now you see what I was talking about. He's going to kill Eleanor with that dirk unless we do something." Bridget gave him a mischievous smile.

"You worry about the fight Thomas. I'll worry about Eleanor." Addressing Mendoza, she said sternly. "Don't let him go down in this round Daniel whatever happens make sure he keeps fighting!" She passed the remaining two flagons onto the ringside before disappearing into the throng in the same direction Flint had taken a minute before. The bell rang loudly, Thomas looked at Mendoza and both men turned to face Joe Buck. The American was already on his feet, the weasel at his shoulder whispering something into his ear and if Buck's expression was anything to go by the whispered conversation was an important one. Mendoza broke another seal on the glass jar nearest him and instructed Thomas to drink. Thomas obliged him, taking a long swig of the light brown ale from the flagon.

"Come now Thomas, back to work, let's put some of those new techniques we've been working on to use!" Feeling fully revived and now with a mental possession of the American's weaknesses, Thomas turned away from Joe Buck and gave Mendoza a cheeky wink.

"To hell or the hangman!" he said morbidly.

****

Edward timidly rode the horse along the silent dirt-packed road aware that at any moment, the huge horse's clip clopping might bring unwanted attention from the picket of King's horse guards, who were stationed two hundred yards ahead of him in the growing darkness and mist. As he got closer to the old ruin, he could clearly make out the figures of the men scattered amongst the many carriages parked along the highway. The guards and coach drivers chatted to each other as they smoked their long clay pipes. A long branch was balanced upon two barrels forming a barricade and blocking the road. He pulled on the horse's reigns, trying to stop the animal trotting and bring him to a slower walk but the beast was so big that Edward's remonstrations went unnoticed and horse carried on at its own pace. Suddenly an opening appeared on his right in the thick bush that ran along the side of the road. A gap that was just big enough for his horse to get through if he lay across its back and tucked his head in behind the beast's neck.

"This must be the place?" Edward thought to himself pulling hard on the reigns. This time the beast did obey and turned abruptly into the dark gap in the trees. Edward sank into the saddle and the tree's leafy branches scraped across his cloaked back as rode into the shadows of the trees blindly. He was still lying across the horse's back, and had covered around thirty or forty yards when suddenly the horse's bridle was pulled up, bringing the beast to a standstill. Edward sat up and was surprised to see he was in a hidden clearing amongst the trees. A brutal-faced man was holding his bridal. All around the clearing were the grey silhouettes of some twenty or thirty rough-looking men peering from the gaps between the trees. At first he assumed they were another attachment of the King's horse guards or foot soldiers but if they were, they were the roughest, scruffiest soldiers he'd ever seen.

"Who goes there?" The man whispered, Edward was thrown by the question. He opened his mouth to speak but in truth was lost for words. The first man was joined by another who Edward thought as tough-looking as the first fellow.

"Is he one of ours or theirs?" the second man enquired from the first who still gripped the bridle tightly.

"That's what I'm trying to find out sir!"

Sir, Edward thought to himself so they must be soldiers but the man's remark, *ours or theirs* made no sense to him. Edward's mind ran over the situation. The men on the highway were King George's men of that there was no doubt. Yet these men who on closer inspection were clearly all armed to the teeth with braces of pistols, swords and various knives looked to the preacher more like members of the ruffian, robber gangs that had begun to work the towns and cities around England. All wore raggedy uniforms and large-brimmed, frayed hats with ridiculously large colourful cockades but their uniforms were jumbled together and in no particular order or military company. Perhaps they were deserters he thought Edward, however, by the look of the men who had stepped from the misty shadows amongst the trees to see the newcomer these men were unmistakably battle-hardened and as tough as they came. "Mercenaries!" He thought to himself. The man shook the bridle.

"Well . . . " he said sternly, " . . . are you with *them* or *us*?" The man who acted as captain for the group looked Edward over suspiciously taking in the long, dark-green cloak with its black, velvet collar and his large, battered tricorn hat and bottle-green cockade.

"He don't look like one of them!" The bridle holder said to the captain. On realising who was in charge of the situation, Edward leant down from the massive animal and spoke to the captain. He gestured with his head to the highway and the King's picket of guards and whispered.

"I am certainly not with them, brother!"

"Then who are you? You're not one of my men and you're not with the King?" The man holding the bridle blurted.

"So you're with Lord Dashwood ... maybe he's one of Flint's men, sir?" The captain glared at the man, angry that he had given so much information away but to Edward, the man's words were like music to his ears. Without hesitation, Edward sat back up in his saddle aggressively,

"Yes, I am Lord Dashwood's man. Flint is waiting for me to play my part in tonight's mischief and you sir are delaying me ...!" The captain was taken aback for a second, Edward had seen men like this before when amongst the Quakers in the taverns of Birmingham. They wore their honour on their sleeves, and any affront to it would almost always end in bloodshed. Edward had to give the man a way out, a way to keep his honour in front of his own men. "I understand your position captain and to be sure, I wasn't told by Flint that you and your men would be here." Edward's mind formulated a story as he was talking, hoping that the captain wouldn't notice his shaking hands. "For you have formed and camouflaged your men so well that I, a trained military man myself could not have discovered you unless I rode upon you, which of course I did!" He said laughing, "Well done sir ... Well done. You are obviously a man of high degree." He fawned. The compliment worked. The captain smiled in the dusky twilight, a bright smile for one so violent looking as he.

"Thank you, Mr. ...?" He left the question hanging in the misty air.

"Do forgive me ... " Edward stifled his growing panic trying to sound as comfortable as he could in the situation, " ... but Flint said we must neither give nor ask each other's names!" The captain nodded, feeling foolish for asking the man in the first place.

"Yes, sir, quite correct ... ehh ... it was a trick question, sir." The men around him began to nod and smile, happy with the quick thinking of their leader. Edward knew it was a bluff but said nothing.

"Forgive me captain but by the look of your ... " he scanned the group and decided a little bit more flattery wouldn't do any harm,

" ... tough company of men, you look as if you're expecting or about to start a fight!" He realised his question sounded suspicious so disguised it by adding. "And by the look of this lively bunch of rascals, it's going to be a hell of a scrap. I tell you, brave captain I wouldn't want to be on the receiving end of one of your merry lads' swords, they look terrifying!" Edward laughed and much to his relief so did many of the men around him. Even the captain smiled before remembering his duty.

"*Shh dogs* ..." he spat, " ... or we will be discovered." He waved his hand, and the watching men vanished into the darkening mist leaving only himself, Edward and the bridle-holder to talk in the clearing. "We have orders to attack at Lord Dashwood's command, who and why is none of my business. I am paid gold for the use of my sword, and that's as far as it goes with any of us. I presume Flint wants you on the inside tonight?" Edward nodded without saying anything more lest he give himself away. "Good!" The captain continued. "Then God speed sir, you go about your business as I shall be about mine but ..." he looked into Edward's face, " ... when the killing starts and the bloodlust begins you had best keep your head low because my men will give no quarter to friend nor foe, you had best remember it!" Edward shivered just what had Thomas and Sykesy got him into.

"I will captain, I will!"

With that, the captain slapped the horse's rump, and Edward trotted into the gloom of the trees towards the rear of the old church and the sound of a baying crowd.

****

Back inside the old ruin, neither boxer had tried to communicate with the other except with their fists of which the conversation had been non-stop. Now that round two was well under way Joe Buck had begun to taunt Thomas with spiteful jibes trying to get under his skin. But Thomas knew these tricks having seen and heard them all before in the bouts leading up to this fight. One of the benefits of prizefighting in the Midlands was this *catcalling* was common practice amongst the brawlers of that area. He knew it was the first sign of weakness in a boxer and the confidence that Joe Buck initially had was dissipating by the second. Jabs and punches were swapped between the men with a power and ferocity that few had ever witnessed in a boxing match before. But the American's punches to all with a trained eye had become clumsy, mistimed, inaccurate.

"You punch like a penny whore Fewtrell!" Buck snarled into Thomas's ear as the two became entangled in each other's arms. As the two were in close, Buck tried to head butt Thomas but he saw his intentions and threw his own head at the American catching Buck on the nose with his forehead. As Buck stumbled under the blow, Thomas unravelled himself from Buck's arms and threw a punch which caught the American just under the eye. The sound of bone on bone crashing together made a sickeningly dull thud as Joe Buck's cheekbone collapsed under the power of the right hook. The bone cracked and sank into his face making Buck's facial features appear freakish beneath the smear of blood which now covered the whole left side of his face. Thomas retorted as the other boxer stumbled to his knees.

"I don't know what type of penny whores you've been shagging Joseph Buck but if they can punch like that perhaps you should've sent one of them to the fight instead of coming yourself!" Thomas stood over the man who was now a blood-soaked, swollen-faced wreck kneeling unsteadily on one knee looking up at his attacker, arms raised in defence. Thomas could see the American still had fight left in him and he knew that a lucky punch was always possible but in truth both men knew the fight was already decided. The last five minutes of round two were just for show, a chance for Joe Buck to reclaim some level of dignity by withstanding the better pugilist and for Thomas Fewtrell to show the crowd, the King, Lord Dashwood and of course Joe Buck himself, how devastatingly destructive he could actually be. The weasel screamed at Buck to rouse himself but Joe Buck couldn't seem to get off his knees. His eyes swam in confusion as he tried to regain his feet. Thomas dropped his guard and crossed to the boxer, he held out his hand, in gesture of gentlemanliness to the American who looked at it for a second, before accepting the offer of help. He took Thomas's open hand and began slowly to climb to his feet. At seeing the good sportsmanship of the Englishman the watching audience exploded into applause and cheering. Even King George roused himself from his throne as Thomas pulled the man off the canvas and patted his shoulder with his free hand but as Joe Buck raised himself with his left hand, he brought his right hand around in a sweeping haymaker to land on Thomas's jaw. The underhanded blow caught everyone, least of all Thomas, by surprise. The punch knocked his head sideways with such force that he stumbled back into the handrail of his own corner of the ring. Buck didn't waste any time as the crowd began booing his un-sportsmanly behaviour. He stepped in for the kill whilst Thomas was still trapped in his punch drunk stupor.

Bam, bam, boom, the blows came quick and fast, one after the other to Thomas's face and body. He took the punches as best he could trying all the time to hide behind his forearms. Mendoza looked up at his man and wondered how long Thomas could take the punishment and to all, it looked as if Thomas would soon succumb to the attack. Yet as Mendoza watched he could see the strength of the attack was wavering. The slightest of movements and mistiming by the American, unnoticed by all except for his trained pugilist's eye told him that the attack was a last ditched effort to break Thomas. Mendoza called out to his man as he looked up at the battle from the corner of the ring.

"Stay with it Thomas, he's losing his energy!" To Mendoza's surprise Thomas turned his face towards him. Sheltered from the American's blows Thomas gave Mendoza the same cheeky wink he had when he'd stepped into the ring.

"I've got this!" He mouthed as Joe Buck threw his exhausted arms about him, slowly the power in those punches dissipated, absorbed by the weight and bulk of Thomas Fewtrell's muscles until they were little more than a pathetic set of clumsily aimed slaps that one might find in any bar room brawl. The crowd exploded into cheering again as Thomas, who had curled the top half of his body into a tight ball to protect himself from the unexpected attack, burst into life from the corner of the ring. Joe Buck was now the one to be caught by surprise. As Thomas threw his all into the attack on the American, who's earlier unsporting behaviour now acted as the motivation for his own destruction. There was no time for probing defences by jabbing and searching, this was an all-out, no mercy attack on the American. Blow after blow pummelled into the red raw skin of Buck's face until after nearly two minutes of non-stop killer punches the American's face resembled a pulp of flayed raw meat found on any butcher's chopping block. Then with an almighty effort, Thomas saw his chance and delivered a punch that had never been witnessed before, a punch he had invented himself. It came from the lower quarter of his body. A swing that he had learnt from his days as a farmer's son as if he were swinging a sickle or machete. The fist came in lightning fast, low at first using the shoulder as a pivot, the action similar to that of cutting barley in the fields back home in Shropshire as the fist rose bringing it high from beneath coming in from under the chin to catch the poor wretch directly under his jaw. *Boom!* Thomas's fist lifted the sixteen stone American twelve inches off the canvas. The moment froze in a split second of silence as the man's body seemed to hang in the air for a millisecond too long before plummeting to the canvas on his back with a loud thud. Instantly the audience went wild, screaming, cheering and clapping their approval at the spectacle inside the ring. Of course, not everyone in the room was so elated. Thomas stared at the prostrate man in the centre of the square. He was out cold, eyes rolling this way and that, his body quivering as the nerve-endings within his brain sent electrical pulses here and there throughout his body. Thomas heaved a sigh of relief before looking up at the balcony searching for Eleanor. He could see Lord Dashwood's stern, angry face staring back at him with disbelief, as he witnessed the scene inside the ring and behind him, Thomas could see Lord Harrington and Eleanor, her bright, blue, fearful eyes shining from beneath the mask. The fight inside the ring was over, but now the fight outside was about to begin.

Stone and silver

CHAPTER 26

The manservant at the top of the rickety stairwell leading up to the musician's balcony hadn't been watching the fight. The whole affair was none of his business. Lord Harrington had brought him along as he always did to these *Hellfire* meetings to serve whatever food and drinks he was asked for. A task he was not happy with or accustomed to, being the gentleman's housemaster, it was his job to order the other servants around, not to serve drinks *himself*. So when the dusky serving maid appeared at the top of the stairwell with a tray of the King's canapés and a sexy smile, he was more than happy to let the dark-skinned strumpet serve the morsels of food to his master's fifteen or so guests without too much fuss.

"Besides!" He thought to himself. "Better the little negro tart trip herself up in the darkness of the balcony than I!"

Lord Dashwood glared with alarm and astonishment from his perch at the banister rail. His hawk-like eyes scanned the spontaneous celebrations below him as the fight came to its dramatic end. The American, the rebel hero and deliverer of his fortune, now lay in a semi-conscious daze as Dashwood's weasel-faced associate busily attended to him as he lay unmoving in the centre on the blood-splattered canvas floor of the ring. The old man turned to the Scottish manservant standing next to his right shoulder. He was also staring down at the unexpected turn of events with a growing feeling of dread growing in his stomach.

"You said Fewtrell would go down Flint!" The Scot continued to stare at the crowd below, avoiding his master's glowering look.

"But I told him my Lord, I said ... " The old man pointed at Thomas.

"Well, it doesn't look like he was fucking listening does it? And now, because of your incompetence we have lost our chance!" Flint shook his head.

"No, my Lord, the King will die!" Dashwood turned to face Flint.

"Oh really!" He said spitefully. "And how are we going to make that happen? We can hardly blame the American if he is out fucking cold!"

"I shall do it, my Lord!" Dashwood laughed,

"Well, that was the plan all along Flint, you would deliver the killing thrust, but how, may I ask you are you going to get Mr. Buck to take the blame for it when,when, well just look at the oaf!" The Lord gestured to the fallen man in the ring. Flint glanced down at the American again, his mind running through various scenarios of how things might play out. He saw Thomas in the ring scowling up at them both, a look of defiance in his bruised eyes. Flint turned to his master and said with a quiver of emotion in his voice.

"I shall do it my Lord and if I'm caught and our wee plan goes awry, I shall take sole responsibility for it!" If Dashwood was surprised by the manservant's word, he didn't show it, instead without turning to look at the Scot he said coldly.

"If our plan goes awry we shall both hang!"

"No, my Lord, I have fifty good men hidden in the trees behind the church to make sure none of those Hanoverian bastards ever steps foot on the streets of London again. All they wait for is my signal!" Lord Dashwood frowned.

"Which is?"

"When I shout the King is dead, they shall attack the King's guard and anyone else that gets in their way!"

"Good!" Dashwood said impatiently. "Well, what are you waiting for? Get on with it!" Flint stood for a second, watching his master's expressionless face. The memories of his life ran through his mind. "A life's servitude to the old man was all he'd known for the past forty years and now, at the point of no return!" He thought to himself. The old Lord wouldn't even return his look or say farewell. Flint bowed slightly and backed away into the shadows of the balcony.

****

Bridget wandered the tightly packed balcony until she spotted Eleanor and Lord Harrington. She placed the silver tray of food in her left hand and reached inside the corset of her dress for the long dagger she had pick-pocketed from the Scotsman when she had feigned a stumble against him at the ringside. She concealed the long knife beneath the tray and stepped in close behind the well-dressed gentleman holding the girl. Only when she was in the shadow of the man's back did she reveal the knife. Bringing it up with lightening speed to the man's throat, its razor sharp spike prodding painfully into the lord's skin.

"Release the girl!" Bridget ordered with a whisper. The old man was taken totally by surprise. Bridget pressed the dagger harder. The man already smarting over his missing finger winced with pain. "Release her . . . do it now!" Harrington brought his open hand up as he let go of Eleanor's arm. Instantly the girl spun to face him. She reached for her fallen mask and put it back in place. She reached up to her hair and pulled a six inch long hairpin from her white wig. Harrington's eyes widened with horror as without hesitation she turned the hairpin upon him, driving it into his adam's apple. The thin, steel needle slid directly into his throat and the man blinked in astonishment at her action. He tried to talk but only a pathetic gurgle emanated from his open mouth. He searched the girl's eyes for some mercy but found none. Her bright, innocent eyes were now cold blue disks of hatred that sparkled from the confines of her mask. Eleanor was not finished with him yet, she grabbed at Bridget's hand, snatching the long dagger from her. Expertly spinning the blade in her own hand she brought the tip of the razor sharp knife up to the man's throat, just the way her late father had trained her to do many years before. Harrington raised his hands for protection but now Bridget, seeing what Eleanor had in mind grabbed his arms and pulled them down to his sides, gripping them tightly. Panicking, he desperately tried to shake the dark girl off but he had no chance as the two women worked together in the darkness of the balcony. Eleanor raised her left hand taking a handful of the man's hair as she did so. She pushed her right hand, containing the long-bladed dagger in a smooth thrust that sent the weapon's deadly point upwards into the Lord's neck, through the roof of his mouth and finally into his brain. Both women held onto him tightly as he quivered his final death throes. Eleanor examined his expression and smiled as it slowly changed before her eyes. Where once the man's eyes were cruel spiteful, they were now pools of horror and regret in the pain of his awful death. Bridget, on the other hand, watched Eleanor's beautiful features from behind the man's shoulder with a growing admiration of the girl's strength. She also watched the unsuspecting crowd around them, who it must be said, were all far too interested in the commotion in the hall below to notice the murder of one of their fellow Hellfire members right next to them. The man began to shudder and shake as the knife found the base of his spinal cord. He let out a whimper of pain which Bridget stifled by holding her hand over his mouth. Then Eleanor gave a twist of her wrist, driving the blade deeper into Lord Harrington's brain. He became limp, letting out a long sigh and the stout legs which held him suddenly went limp and the girls let him fall into the shadowy corner of the balcony, the dagger's handle still protruding from his throat. Shoving his arms and legs into the corner so he wouldn't be discovered until the daylight illuminated the church, Eleanor turned to Bridget and hugged her.

"You came for me!" She whispered. Bridget smiled and kissed the girl's cheek.

"Of course I came for you . . . " her words were said matter of factually, she continued, " . . . we need to get out of here because things are about to get very lively." The two girls crept along the wall at the rear of the balcony until they came to the staircase. The manservant who had allowed Bridget to enter was still watching the entrance to the balcony and he eyed the girl's approach with some suspicion.

"Lord Harrington's had an attack!" Eleanor said feigning alarm.

"My lady?" The manservant replied, puzzled.

"Your lordship has collapsed!" Eleanor continued. The servant became pale in the candlelight on the stairwell.

"Collapsed you say?" Bridget stepped into the doorway to the stairwell and grabbed the man's coat sleeve.

"Yes, he's over there . . . he seems to have something stuck in his throat!" The man stared blankly from one girl to the other before sprinting into the throng on the balcony, muttering comments of horror under his breath. Bridget smiled.

"This way my lady!" Eleanor laughed a cruel laugh that Bridget had never heard before.

"Something stuck in his throat!"

****

Thomas turned from the balcony towards the King's throne. The monarch was on his feet smiling and clapping his hands in Thomas's direction. The boxer bowed. The monarch gestured that Thomas should come to him. Thomas nodded and bowed again before turning to his Portuguese friends. Mendoza was in the ring now, patting Thomas's shoulders.

"Well done, Thomas, you really upset the apple cart tonight my friend!" He said excitedly. Thomas shook his head. Mendoza laughed. "Most of the wagers were in the American's favour, and now as you see, the losers are becoming very sore." Thomas turned to see that the crowd had begun to argue amongst themselves, small scuffles and rows were breaking out around the room as the gamblers argued over their various debts and wagers. The King's guard noticed the change in atmosphere. The captain ordering his men to stand at arms to protect both the King and his newly acquired gold. "This could get very ugly Thomas!" Mendoza continued, Thomas turned to his friend with a new look of concern spreading across his face.

"You have no idea just how ugly this is going to get Daniel!" He glanced at the gold-laden table in front of the King, its two strong boxes guarded by the four, well-armed men at arms. The monarch was looking around himself at the growing chaos, alarm apparent on his face. Thomas turned to stare back to the balcony. He could see Lord Dashwood still at his perch, glaring towards King George's position. However, Flint had disappeared from his side and there was a commotion beginning behind them, where Eleanor and Lord Harrington had been standing. He could see with some alarm, that Lord Harrington and Eleanor were no longer there and he wondered if Harrington had carried out his threat to kill the girl. His suppressed his urge to climb the steps to the balcony and confront the Hellfire members. Recognising that the atmosphere in the hall now had the same tinder box undercurrent that he had witnessed many months before in Birmingham's Rookery he knew that things could take a major turn for the worse at any moment.

"Find the girls Daniel!" He said urgently. "Then meet me in the antechamber!" Daniel seemed confused. Thomas scowled. "I don't have time to explain right now just do as I . . . " At that moment a gunshot from outside the church brought the rowdy proceedings to a halt. Everyone fell silent, listening for another shot. They weren't disappointed. A volley of several musket shots broke the silence and the crowd on hearing this became even more animated and looked to the King as if for some explanation. Thomas slapped Mendoza's shoulder. "Go, Daniel, *go* find the girls. I'll be waiting in the antechamber behind the altar." Daniel nodded and dropped from the fighting stage. Thomas watched him for a second as he worked his way through the packed excited audience that was quickly transforming into a violent mob. He turned to Joe Buck, who was now, with the help of the weasel-faced minder on his knees in the middle of the canvas. He crossed to his fallen opponent. "Here!" He held his hand out to the boxer. "Let me help you, Mr Buck!" Joe Buck and the weasel were taken by surprise. The American sat back on his haunches and stared up at Thomas. "Come on man, you put up a hell of a fight, but it's over now, I'm sure the King will want to meet us both. Besides, I've got a feeling that pretty soon, this isn't somewhere you're gonna want to be!"

"Thank you!" Buck held his hand out to Thomas, and the latter pulled the heavy weight onto his feet. The weasel helped Joe by placing his head under the boxer's shoulder, and the three made their way out of the ring, pushing their way through the throng towards the King's throne. Flint, who had descended the stairs from the musician's balcony and was working his way to the King, saw Buck rise from the canvas and couldn't believe his luck. The American would take the blame for the assassination, after all, he thought to himself. He looked up towards his master, who was leaning over the bannister rail staring with hatred towards the monarch and hadn't noticed Joe Buck leaving the ring. Flint turned once more to the job at hand. He knew he had to time things just right if his plans were going to work. The gunshots from outside told him that the group of mercenaries he'd hired had either been discovered by the King's guard or had grown impatient with awaiting his signal and just taken it upon themselves to attack the soldiers protecting the highway for the King, his family and associates who had accompanied him. If he could get his chance to deliver the fatal wound, then he and his soldiers of fortune would systematically kill all of the King's entourage, thus leaving the crown of England to be placed back on the rightful God-appointed head of Charles Edward Stuart. Flint said the name over in his mind as he crossed the room to the King's throne. Just the thought of it made his head swim with rage as he pictured his father's face and his miserable death at the hands of a bloodthirsty Hanoverian redcoat in the cold, wet heather of Culloden moor all those years ago. He followed the two boxers and the weasel-faced minder as they forced their way through the room. Without either Joe Buck or Thomas knowing that he was behind them Flint tapped the weasel on the shoulder and nodded, the weasel seemed surprised to see him, but returned his nod and the four made their way to the altar. As the group reached the foot of the stone alter the Captain of the King's bodyguard shouted his command.

"Halt!" Instantly the pickets standing to attention at the bottom step of the stone altar crossed their pikes, blocking the way to the King.

"Nonsense captain!" The King shouted, leaving his throne. "Let them through, let them through!" He ordered. A cloud passed over the young captain's face.

"But your highness!" The captain said, alarm in his voice. "The gunshots outside, maybe somethings a-foot . . . a plot your majesty?" The King crossed the space with the help of the small black boy and took a step down towards the captain. The King came in close to the young soldier and half-whispered.

"If I worried myself about every bloody gun shot your drunken bodyguard let off, I would constantly be in hiding . . . besides, if something is a-foot, then it's your job to deal with it, not mine, and if you ever question me again I'll make sure you spend the rest of your heroic military career emptying the shit from my chamber pots . . . understand *captain*?" He spat the words into the young man's face. The captain lowered his head in an unquestioningly subservient bow.

"Yes, your highness!"

"Yes, yes, of course, fucking yes, now fuck off and let my guests through you oaf!" The King's face developed a purple hue as he shouted his command. The Captain sheepishly ordered his men to stand at ease. An order they followed instantly by snapping to attention, their pikes at their shoulders swords at their sides. Thomas and Joe Buck watched the scene with bemusement as the King ushered the boxers into his company with some excitement. The weasel followed closely behind them and Flint bringing up the rear of the group. As Thomas climbed the steps, he saw Mendoza skirting around the foot of the steps and enter the antechamber at the rear of the altar. To his relief, he saw Bridget and Eleanor following closely behind. He wondered how Eleanor had escaped Harrington's clutches but knew he'd have to wait until later to hear the explanation as the King was about to address him.

"Good God man but that was a great bout was it not?" Thomas bowed.

"Your highness is too kind!" Thomas fawned. The King turned to his royal companions and smiling shouted.

"You see, you inebriated bunch of parasites, here is a real man, the best pugilist in England!" The group began to clap their hands politely. The King turned his attention to Joe Buck. "Ahh, and as for you, our American cousin . . . or should I say American rebel, now you see what we British are capable of when we set our minds to it." He slapped Buck's bare shoulder. "But do not fear man, we are a generous nation, and your efforts will be rewarded handsomely!" He pointed to the two strong boxes on the table. "Your loss is my gain Mr Buck for I do believe that your sponsor Lord Dashwood has wagered everything he has on the outcome of this fight and now, his fortune belongs to me!" He slapped the man's shoulder again and turning to Thomas he continued. "Reward, revenge . . . and a bloody good night's sport all in one sitting . . . and all thanks to you Fewtrell, all thanks to you!" His smile dropped for a second as he scanned the boxers' concerned faces. "There will be rewards for you both gentlemen and the royal household thanks you for your effort." Buck and Thomas both bowed again.

"Thank you, your majesty!" The boxers said simultaneously. The King smiled.

"You see!" He said to the sycophantic aristocrats at his shoulder. "The American rebel rouser is struck down with obedience in the face of his King, all thoughts of rebellion vanish in the face of the royalty!" Joe Buck bristled at the man's words. Thomas glanced at the American and was just about to tell the American to calm himself when the King spoke again. "Tell me Fewtrell, was that the famous Mendoza in your corner tonight?" Thomas nodded.

"Yes, my King!" The monarch looked confused. He glanced at the weasel and Flint.

"Well, where is he?" Thomas followed the King's gaze and for the first time saw that Flint had followed him onto the altar. His alarm was noticeable, but the King chose to ignore it. Thomas was about to warn the King that the Scot was one of Dashwood's men but as he opened his mouth to talk the King interrupted him, "Come on man, the great Mendoza, where is he?" Thomas pointed to the antechamber and bowed slightly.

"He is waiting for me in my changing room, your majesty!" The King turned to see what Thomas was pointing at. He saw the small door to the antechamber for the first time.

"Mendoza is in there?" Thomas nodded. "Well, go get him, man, the King wishes to meet him!" Thomas bowed slightly lower and backed down the steps. The King watched him for a second before turning back to his guests and began talking about the boxing bouts he'd witnessed where Daniel Mendoza had triumphed over men twice his size as if it were some sort of magical trick rather than a calculated boxing technique. The aristocrats listened intently, feigning interest in the King's favourite new sport. On reaching the bottom step, Thomas turned and followed the step around the foot of the altar and into the antechamber. As he stepped into the candlelit room, he saw Daniel, Eleanor and Bridget talking earnestly to a tall, cloaked figure. Thomas recognised the bottle-green cloak as his own and smiling, he crossed the room.

"Brother ... you came!" He said grabbing his lookalike and hugging him closely. Edward grunted as the air was forced out of him by his brother's strength.

"All right all right, calm down, I'm here, get off me, you're soaking wet with sweat?" Thomas laughed and turned to Mendoza.

"You're about to meet the King, Daniel!" Mendoza scowled.

"I am?" Thomas nodded as he slouched onto a small pew next to the wall.

"Yes, he's asked for you, so get out there and lick his royal arse!" He said laughing.

"Aren't you coming with me?" Mendoza said earnestly.

"Just tell him I'm dressing myself and I will join him shortly!" Mendoza's brow furrowed but he agreed and turned and left the chamber. As soon as the door shut behind him Thomas sprang to his feet. He crossed to Eleanor and hugged her. She kissed his cheek and smiled. Thomas released her. She looked up at him, her eyes sparkling blue pools beneath the mask. She raised her hands and undid the bow at the rear of her head. The mask fell from her face.

"Thank God I won't have to wear this anymore!" She said softly revealing the perfect unscarred face beneath.

Bridget's heart jumped at the sight of the girl's beauty, but instantly became concerned.

"How many people saw you without the mask. Could you be recognised?" Eleanor gave her a reassuring smile.

"Don't worry Bridget, only the King saw my face without it, I cannot be recognised by anyone apart from him, and he is hardly going to tell anyone it was I who pointed the finger at Lord Dashwood!" Thomas placed his hand on the girl's shoulder.

"Your identity must remain secret Eleanor. Although you've brought down Dashwood, any one of his Hellfire club members could take revenge on you at any moment that's why we had to keep your identity hidden. This way you can walk the streets of England without having to look over your shoulder for the rest of your life. Anyway . . . " He continued, " . . . thank God you're safe. How did you escape Lord Harrington?" Eleanor pointed her elegant finger towards Bridget and crossed to her where she hugged Eleanor lovingly. Thomas smiled at the girls, then addressing all of them he said. "Ok, this is the moment we've been waiting for, you all know what to do, so don't fuck it up or they'll have our heads!"

Thomas and Edward began to exchange clothes. Edward shed the green cloak, brown leather britches, waistcoat and shirt swapping them with Thomas's fighting britches and tied a red scarf around his waist just as Thomas had in the fight. Bridget busied herself by wiping away the congealed blood around Thomas's nose and mouth and cleaning him up after his fight. She soaked a cloth in the bucket of cold water she had left there earlier and gently dabbed it around Thomas's bruised left eye to bring the swelling down. Edward, on the other hand, was receiving attention from Eleanor, who was applying dark soot around his left eye, creating what, at a quick glance would look like a bruise, and then she smeared dark red rouge to the ends of his nostrils and bottom lip. Now the look-a-like brothers had swapped their identities completely. The only difference was Edward's body, or lack of it, for even though he looked similar in face, his body lacked the bulk of his older sibling. However, Thomas had seen this miscalculation and prepared for it. Giving his younger brother a linen shirt to wear which, by design, was far too small for him, for in its sleeves, were sown thick linen padding around the shoulders and tops of the arms. The padding gave the impression that the wearer was indeed a man of substantial build and even though it wasn't a perfect copy of Thomas's physique, it would in the packed crowd and dim candlelight of the hall be enough of a resemblance to pass as the real thing. Finally, Thomas handed Eleanor back her mask, telling her she must wear it one more time, at least until she was far enough away from the hall, so as never to be recognised. She protested, but Thomas was insistent, saying that it was just a precaution. Bridget agreed, adding that Eleanor's beauty is not something one forgets in a hurry. Thomas placed his hands into his cloak's pocket, and to his surprise, he found the small leather eye-mask which had been moulded whilst wet into the shape of his features. He studied it for a second, remembering the royal mail coach heist that had kicked off this bizarre chain of events all those months ago. Placing the mask back in his pocket he pulled his broad-brimmed tricorn upon his head, before breaking into a broad, tooth-filled grin that helped to hide the growing uneasiness he felt in the pit of his stomach. Suddenly Mendoza was back in the room.

"The King is asking for you, T . . . " Daniel stopped talking abruptly. He looked at Edward next to the door he'd just entered through, then he took a second take at Thomas by the far door. He stood opened-mouthed at the sight of the two Thomas's. Mendoza's face darted between the two men, unable to find an explanation.

"Ha Daniel!" Thomas said in a friendly tone. "Do not let our little trick concern you. There are more important matters afoot right now." Daniel just stood there, unable to make sense of the situation, Thomas continued. "I want you to escort the girls to the village. It's very important no one sees you. Eleanor has a carriage there that will take you all back to London." Edward placed his hand on Mendoza's shoulder.

"Avoid the clearing in the forest at all cost. Go through the brush if you must, but whatever you do avoid the men in the trees for they are real killers!" Edward's words met a silence from all, especially Daniel Mendoza.

"Come now go all of you, get clear and let us all play our parts!" Eleanor grabbed Daniel's hand and followed Bridget through the small door to the rear graveyard out into the blackness of the night. As they left the antechamber, Thomas searched the faces of his friends for any signs of nerves and saw by their pallor that they too were feeling the mounting pressure of the moment. As Daniel stepped out of the room, Thomas stopped in the doorway and turned to his brother.

"Right!" He said quietly to Edward. "I'll see you in back in Birmingham!" Edward laughed, placing his hand on the antechamber's door-handle on the opposite wall.

"Birmingham town or the Tyburn Tree!" He said as he stepped through the door, into the noisy hall beyond.

****

The scuffles between the King's guests and the Hellfire club members had grown considerably since Thomas and Edward had switched places. Instead of the excitement of the earlier boxing bout, the atmosphere was now purely one of aggression. There was now a stand off between the Hellfire club who had lost their wagers on the American and who had now armed themselves with whatever lay at hand and the King's guests who had gathered at the far end of the church as near to the altar and the King's guards as possible for protection from their would-be attackers. The King on the other hand stood in a relative oasis of calmness upon the stone platform. He was talking as lightheartedly as he could to the group surrounding the American boxer but however much he tried to put a calm face on the proceedings, the sporadic and increasing gunfire from outside made him start and stutter with every rapport of the muskets.

"W ... we must ssss ... set an example to the others ... one must never show fear in the face of adversity!" Flint had positioned himself to the rear and side of the King as he talked to Joe Buck about the New world. The American, head still bowed, answered the monarch's questions with nods and short sentences, leaving King George to do most of the talking. The weasel stood to the side of Buck, his hands in the pockets of his long riding coat. Edward, who to all present now appeared as *Thomas* stepped from the rear of the altar and joined the group. The King smiled graciously and instantly turned his attention from the American, who he'd been trying to extract words from as if ringing blood from a stone, to Thomas, who to all there, looked as if he'd just retired and cleaned himself up, in order to appear to the King of England in a condition befitting such an occasion.

"A . . . a . . . ah Fewtrell, you are with us again!" Edward bowed.

"I am your highness, thank you for your patience." The King laughed.

"Ha! . . . patience, that all..w..we royals have . . . is . . . is bloody patience. We wait around from one hour to the next to be attended on or assassinated by those around us!" The words made the Scotsman bristle as if his intentions had been discovered. He slowly raised his right hand to the chest pocket of the long, dress coat, his fingers began to search for the Jacobite dagger he thought concealed there. The weasel watched him intently, waiting for his moment and the blade to be drawn but instead of seeing Flint's hand whip the dagger free, the weasel saw the man's eyes fill with confusion as his fingers searched fruitlessly for the knife. As the search went on, so Flint's subtlety of movement grew less and less until he became so animated that he drew attention to himself from the rest of the group of royals, aristocrats, boxers and bodyguards. They all watched his growingly-erratic behaviour with some interest and alarm. Edward and Joe Buck watched on as the Scottish manservant became more desperate by the second. He looked up to his master on the balcony at the far end of the room, still stood at the handrail watching the events on the altar with his dark, predatorily eyes. Finally, Flint, on realising that the knife was gone and unaware that Bridget O'Hara had pick-pocketed the weapon and that it was, at that very moment protruding from Lord Harrington's throat, turned his attention to one of the King's bodyguards who stood watching the growing chaos within the ring of steel created by the soldiers. He flashed the weasel and Buck a quick glance with his desperate hate-filled eyes before lunging to the soldier's side and drawing the long, basket hilt broadsword from its sheath. Before the guard could react, the Scot had drawn the sword and spun on his feet and raising the razor-sharp blade over his head, he swung it with all his might towards the King's head. If the thrust had landed it would have surely have taken the monarch's head clean off at the shoulder. The King didn't flinch, he just watched the crazed Scotsman's lunge without, it seemed to all who witnessed the scene with horror, any concern at all. As the huge blade swooped down towards the King's neck, another blade met it. This blade from one of the pikes was being held steadfast by the captain of the guard. The broadsword smashed with a loud clang into the steel spike at the pike's end. Its drive and power dissipated along the pike's seven foot shaft. Flint looked at the captain and drew the basket hilt back again, in order to make another attempt at the King's life. However, as his arm drew back, Flint heard the unmistakable click of a pistol's hammer at his ear and the cold metal of a muzzle at his temple.

"James Flint, I arrest you in the name of King George for treason against the crown. Drop the sword or I'll turn your Scottish skull into a bowl of raw haggis!" Flint froze for a millisecond, before turning to the voice. His eyes betrayed the shock of seeing the weasel-faced man holding two pistols in hand, one of which was resting its long barrel at his temple. Flint scowled.

"Ye wee bastard turncoat, how could ye betray Lord Dashwood?" The weasel smiled and began to speak but was stopped by the King.

"Ah, surprise at your fellow conspirator's betrayal to your Jacobite cause?" Flint's eyes darted this way and that, as he searched for a way to strike the blow before the weasel could pull his trigger. The King continued, "Well, Jacobite, let me introduce you to Sir James Marshall!" He pointed at the weasel-faced man, who had now brought both barrels up to Flint's face. The monarch continued. "He is our royal household bodyguard and my personal spy." The King saw the shock on the Scotsman's face and took delight in explaining the trap the Jacobite had stepped into. "Did you really think that I could not have foreseen such a clumsy scheme such as yours and Dashwood's?" He turned to see the Lord Dashwood watching from the far end of the hall an opened-mouthed look of horror on his face. The old lord turned to leave but was stopped by another company of King's guard who had ascended the stairs and were beginning to arrest everyone on the balcony. The King turned back to Flint, who was now being held tightly by two of the pike men, the broadsword taken from his hand by a burly guardsman. "You see, the King has eyes and ears in every plot in the Kingdom. *Yours* was brought to my attention by Mr Buck who on seeing our great country and on being pressed into service by you and your master, decided to break free of your oppression and come to me to tell all and there within is the lesson for you to learn, Jacobite. Our American cousins are not to be taken lightly, especially when one is trying to take away their freedom!" Joe Buck gave the King a quick glance of disbelief, wondering if the monarch could even recognise the irony in of his words. "To the Tower of London captain!" The King said, gesturing with his index finger to nowhere in particular. "I can see this is going to be a busy summer in our courts *and* executioners . . . take them away and arrest their fellow conspirators!" The captain ordered his men to take the Scot away. Flint searched for his master, but Lord Dashwood had already been led into the shadows, and now he was grabbed roughly by the arms and marched towards the front of the church by two bodyguards. Suddenly the gunfire was coming from inside the building as the King's guard who had been guarding the highway outside, were now being driven back by the overwhelming fire power of the mercenaries attempting to force their way inside the ruin. A detachment of guard were backing into the building covering each other's backs but were falling one by one to the well-aimed shots of the expert fire of the brigands. The young captain ran to his men's side to find out what was happening. After a hasty conversation with the sergeant at arms in which he ordered a barricade of church pews to be piled upon one another to block the main doorway, he quickly returned to the King's side with his report.

"Your highness, I think it would be prudent to leave now. My guards can only hold these men for so long." The King's brow furrowed,

"Yes, captain but who are these men, what is this about?" The weasel spoke up.

"My King, I think it is safe to assume that they are part of Lord Dashwood's conspiracy!" The King pondered his words for a second.

"Then I think we had better wait until the road outside the church is clear of these brigands before the royal party leaves." The captain, irritated that the monarch didn't seem to have a grasp of the seriousness of the situation opened his mouth to protest, but on seeing the scowl upon the King's puffy face, decided against it, and simply bowed instead.

"I'm sorry to say my Lord, that the brigand's control the highway outside!"

"These rascals control the King's highway!" The monarch said incredulously. "Good God man, what type of soldier are you sir? Go about your business man and kill the bastards!" The captain froze for a second beneath the King's glare. "Well, what are you waiting for?" Edward stepped forward.

"My King . . . if I may suggest?" The King turned to Edward.

"Fewtrell . . . yes . . . y . . . yes of course man, go ahead talk!" The King said trying to hide the quiver of nerves in his voice, Edward bowed.

"Your highness, there is a room behind you with a door to the rear of the church. If your highness wishes to leave without anyone seeing you do so, then there could be no better way than through that door." The King looked the man over distrustfully. Edward continued. "From the back of the church there is a concealed path, it leads to safety my King, one could skirt around the fight and reappear along the highway and no one would be any the wiser. Perhaps some of the King's guard could bring your carriage there to meet you after the fight is over?" The captain stepped into the circle.

"My lord . . . I must protest, your highness will not be safe without his bodyguard!" The King laughed.

"Bodyguard you say, how could I not be safe guarded by two of England's greatest boxers?"

"But my King . . . !"

"*Enough!*" The King snapped at the captain. "It is settled, we leave incognito via your door, Fewtrell!" Turning to the young captain, he ordered. "We will take shelter in one of the houses in the village beyond the river until the skirmish is over, you captain will meet us there." The captain seemed uncomfortable.

"What about the gold your majesty?" The King raised his eyebrows, having forgotten the two strong boxes, he turned to the young man to answer. But just as he did, the young captain's head exploded into a cloud of red mist and gore as a lead musket ball fired from inside the foyer of the church found its mark and killed the unfortunate soldier instantly. The aristocrats around the King froze in horror at the sight of the man's body slumping lifelessly to the cold flagstones. The King stood opened mouthed and wide-eyed. His face speckled with blood and brain from the fallen man. Flabbergasted at the turn of events, he seemed suddenly incapable of moving. A crash of musket fire broke the moment, and all on the altar turned to the barricaded doorway at the front of the church. As they did, the room seemed to explode with a gunshot volley from the King's dwindling bodyguard. On hearing this and taking it as their cue, the Hellfire club violently attacked the King's guests, and a riot spread like a wildfire through the ruin. The aristocrats protected themselves and returned the attack as best they could with whatever items of furniture and masonry lay around them. Suddenly a lone figure sprang over the barricade, sword in one hand, a pistol in the other and a large Spanish style cavalier style hat with it long, brightly-coloured feather brocade announcing that he was a hired gun. He leapt into the fray, firing at the soldier in front of him, hitting the man dead centre of the chest. The man's back exploded leaving a hole the size of a fist which you could clearly see the guttering candlelight through. The guard fell to his knees and collapsed into a crumpled hump, dead before he'd hit the floor. The attacker was followed by more men, all leaping over the barricade with blood-curdling screams, waving their swords around their heads to cower the soldiers inside. Flint on seeing the men broke free from his guard, dropping him with a head butt to the nose. The stunned soldier dropped his pike and stumbled backwards. Flint grabbed the man's basket-hilt sword and drew the three foot of steel from its leather scabbard. He brought the sword around him in an expert swing and caught the bodyguard on the collarbone.

The weight of the heavy blade drove itself twelve inches into the man's body, slicing the top half of the victim in two from the neck to the solar plexus. The guard stood motionless for a second, his eyes a mixture of pain and puzzlement until finally, he fell almost in slow motion. Flint turned to the King's position sword in hand and devilment in his eyes. King George saw him advance towards him, both men locked in a moment of death. Flint raised his arm and gave a terrifying but unintelligible highland battlecry as he charged to the altar towards the King. Just as he stepped onto the first step, his broadsword flying over his head, the weasel-faced spy stepped in front of the King, his pistols in hand. He pulled the trigger to the flintlock in his right hand but instead of the deafening rapport as the gun let go its missile as would be expected, there was a dull whoosh as the powder in the pan ignited but didn't follow though to the rest of the barrel. The gun had misfired. On seeing this, Sir James Marshall, King's watchman and spy brought the other pistol up to fire but it was too late. The highlander had cleared the steps and thrust the basket hilt claymore with such ferocity that the blade pierced the spy's throat and slid all the way up to the hilt of the blade. The man behind Sir James was pierced too, straight through the heart killing him instantly, which is more than can be said for the poor weasel who even though impaled, stubbornly clung to life. The weasel determined to be professional to the end attempted to bring the other pistol to bare on the Jacobite, but Flint saw his hand rise and grabbed it by the wrist. The other pistol fired, this time successfully but the lead bullet just ricocheted into the floor spinning off into the crowd uselessly. Flint and Sir James glared at each other, face to face. Flint's brutal, scarred features dominating the dying spy. Finally Flint withdrew the sword from the dying man. He did it agonisingly slowly trying to extract as much pain from the weapon as he could, all the while whispering his Scottish curses into the weasel's ear. The sword came free and the spy fell to the ground. Flint stood panting with pleasure, his wild eyes glaring in the dim light, staring down on the dying man's blood-soaked body beneath him.

"Now my wee turncoat, ye shall see the death of your Hanoverian

King and know this, Prince Charlie will come across the sea and take his rightful place on the throne of England, Scotland, Ireland and ..." *Bam!* Flint never finished his sentence. The American who had watched the proceedings without a word all night now brought his right fist into action and laid the Scotsman out with a perfect right hook, breaking the man's jaw, knocking him out cold.

"Goddamn, that bastard likes to talk!" Buck said irritably looking down on the man. Edward bent to Sir James who had already started to pass out with the loss of blood. The man's eyes had developed a peaceful look about them as he saw what had happened to Flint. He tried to speak but found it difficult due to the amount of blood that curdled in his mouth.

"Don't try to talk. I will administer the last rights." Edward said under his breath. Sir James smiled staring into Edward's kind face.

"Save ... the ... K ... K ... King!" His smile turned into a grimace as he gave the order with his final breath. Edward looked up to King George who stood gazing at the dead man, incapable of comprehending the turn of events. In the space of only a few minutes a badly organised plot had turned into a very real coup. Edward rose from the spy.

"My Lord, it's time to leave!" He pointed towards the door of the antechamber. "This way!" He pushed his way through the group until he stood at the rear door. "My King!" He shouted. The words seemed to wake the monarch from his horrified stupor and he instantly began pushing his family and friends aside in order to reach the door. As he got to Edward he stopped.

"My gold!" He mumbled. Edward placed his hand on the King's shoulder. The King looked at Edward with some confusion.

"My Lord, the gold is lost!" He pointed towards the thirty or so brigands who having killed all the bodyguards had now taken over the room completely. Lord Dashwood at their centre organising the rebellion. These mercenaries were not interested in any plots for the crown they were there purely for the gold. It seemed to Edward and the King who had also turned to watch the events that they had no respect for Lord Dashwood's commands. "Let's concentrate on saving your life, sire!" Edward ushered the King through the rear door into the antechamber and out into the black night beyond. They were followed by the American and various family and friends who had the chance to follow before being spotted by one of the mercenaries who gave chase but missed his chance to capture the King and boxers who fled into the shelter of the dark tree line. As the group escaped through the trees, they could hear those still held in the church being systematically butchered, their pleas for mercy turning to screams of pain and terror as the hellish noise of human suffering emanated from within the church and into the night sky as the brigand thieves massacred the helpless aristocrats and Hellfire members. They were determined not to leave one person alive to witnesses their crimes. The run through the trees to the village took thirty minutes and all the way the King could hear his subjects' screams rise into the moonless sky in what seemed like a never-ending slaughter behind him.

To Hell or the hangman!

CHAPTER 27

The rider sat motionless in the blackness of the tree line, he listened intently to the night for any telltale signs of movement on the highway. A soft rustle of leaves was the only distraction as every now, and then a gentle breeze disturbed the uppermost branches of the tree that he sat beneath, awaiting his prey on this darkest of nights. The god-awful noise emanating from the burning ruin had stopped over an hour before. The horrific hellish cacophony of men and women's pain and anguish finally ceasing, giving over to the relative silence of the forest and the distant sound of crackling firewood. The smell of roasted flesh that carried on the breeze reminded him of the Rookery fire where so many had perished. Thomas tried to shake these recollections from his head and instead turned his attention to his partner in crime, who was waiting in the shadows across the clearing, and he knew, however bloody this night's work would be, Henry Sykes would be by his side, sabre and dagger in hand to cover his back.

In the distance, Thomas could see the soft, flickering orange glow from the burning roof of the ruin. He didn't allow his eye to dwell on the flames though, as he knew it would ruin his night vision and he would need all five senses working perfectly for what lay ahead. He assumed that the fight inside the church had been far more violent than any of the partygoers had realised it would be. From the number of gunshots he'd heard, things had got well and truly out of hand, and he hoped his brother Edward had got away with his disguised subterfuge and managed to escape the slaughter. Thomas ached all over. His face throbbed relentlessly where Joe Buck's punches had found their mark, and his bruised ribs made his flanks stiff and sore. Sitting astride the huge dray horse didn't help matters, but he knew it wouldn't be long until his prey came into view, so he constantly shifted his weight in the saddle to stop himself getting cramp in his thighs.

A mist had risen from the river near the village now, slowly climbing its banks, spreading across the flood plain until it had reached the trees where it had initially halted. But much to the highwayman's relief it had softly consumed the tree line until now it made the night blacker than it already had been along the forest highway. For if their plan was to work the night had to be as dark as death. Even so, the fire's distant glow cast shadows amongst the trees creating more light than they wanted and Thomas hoped it wouldn't ruin their moment by illuminating their presence. As he waited, Thomas felt that familiar tingling in his knuckles. Just nerves, he told himself, and he found comfort in the fact that Sykesy had scouted the area several times on the build-up to the fight and he would know every crook, cranny and path along the deserted, dirt highway. Henry's knowledge of their escape route would be the difference between life or death. Thomas felt reassured that he could just about make out his friend in the darkness, his brass pistol butts glimmering in the distant fire's glow, the rest of him a shadow amongst shadows, a ghostly portent of the robbery to come.

Suddenly the unmistakable sound of horses' hooves on packed dirt broke the silence. Thomas instantly became alert as did Henry across the way. Two horses could clearly be heard approaching their position. Their bridles made no noise as the mercenaries came closer. These men knew their game and had wound cloth taken from their victims' clothes to wrap around anything that might jingle in the silence of the forest. Thomas wished he'd taken the same precautions

"Two scouts!" Thomas said under his breath. "Let them pass on!" He prayed to himself as both riders came closer and as they drew nearer, he could see the two silhouettes of the men, black against the flickering orange mist, both were armed to the teeth with long swords and a brace of pistols across their chests. Their unmistakable, large-brimmed hats with their feather cockades giving away the fact that they were hired guns who would kill on command for reward. Thomas held his breath, his heart pounded in his bruised chest as he prayed that his dray wouldn't shuffle and snort or that Sykesy wouldn't get an attack of nerves and fall on the two as they passed on their way as they rode point for the main group that was bound to be following behind. The seconds passed like hours as the horsemen clip-clopped along the road, until finally, they were two shadows in the distance. Then a muffled sound came along the road leading to the church. A much louder noise, as the sound of heavy horses, lots of them and the squeak and trundle of a laden wagon. However much these men had tried to quieten their passage by tying up their bridles with cloth, they could not, however, conceal the sound of their horses riding together, which although still quiet was a cacophony of snorting and thuds in the silence of the forest. Thomas lowered his head to hide behind the brim of his tricorn hat lest his eyes reflect the fire's glow and warn some outrider in the main group. He glimpsed the main body of men from his hideout in the brush as they began to pass between him and Henry. They rode in silence, each of them running over their part in the slaughter inside the church. One or two of them trying to forget the bloodletting yet more of them savouring the power of the battle's bloodlust. Thomas listened as the caravan carried along its way. The soft shuffle of hooves on the packed dirt of the road, almost noiseless except for one sound, barely audible at first but there nonetheless. A high-pitched sound, muffled, yet to Thomas and Henry, clear as a crow's craw in the dawn, the unmistakable jingle of gold coins jostling together from somewhere within the carriage. Thomas's heart fluttered in his chest. It pounded so hard he was sure that the riders would hear it beating but the boxer knew how to control such feelings and began to breathe steadily just as he did when in the ring. He felt a tang of guilt as he watched the procession. This guilt like his heart had to be brought under control.

These mercenaries, he reasoned to himself, had just murdered men, women, lords and ladies and as far as he knew, his own brother and even the King may lie dead inside the old ruin. Guilt had no place here, he was about to scourge the Earth of these brigands who knew nothing of the worth of a man's life, and he was going to get rich doing it.

The black shadow of the carriage trundled along in front of him, just a silhouette against the light cast by the fire which gave the thick mist an orange hue. Every time its wheel hit the slightest of indents in the potholed road, the gold within jingled an intoxicating invitation to the highwaymen.

The majority of the riders were in front of the wagon, two rode abreast, and two brought up the rear guard. These unfortunates would have to be the first to die. Their clip-clopping passed Thomas's position, and as it did, Thomas saw Henry on the other side of the highway bring his horse out of the shadows. Thomas followed his example, pistol in hand. Sykesy, on the other hand, was brandishing his three-foot long sabre with its curved blade and in the other hand was a dagger almost as long and equally vicious. Thomas had only ever seen these weapons drawn in one of Henry's drunken displays around the Birmingham Rag market, now he would see just how deadly these instruments of war could be.

Both highwaymen brought their horses silently in line with the rearmost riders and walked along behind them for a short distance, slowly advancing until both were almost alongside the mercenaries. The men in the wagon train perceived the newcomers at the exactly the same moment. They turned, initially with surprise and a friendly smile, believing that the dark riders who had appeared from nowhere were from their own party but as the realisation that the tricorn hat-wearing men were not, both brigands went for their saddle-holstered pistols. For Thomas it was an easy option, he just drew his fist back and punched the man on the bridge of his nose, which cracked audibly as it burst in an explosion of blood, knocking him unconscious instantly, leaving the mercenary to droop forward onto the pommel of his horse's saddle. Sykesy, on the other hand, had the fastest of the two, this man reactions were lightning fast, drawing his weapon in the blink of an eye. Henry Sykes had seen his intentions and reacted just as quickly by bringing his long sabre over his head flaying it down with perfect precision, its razor-sharp blade chopping the man's hand off at the wrist, pistol and all. The brigand's eyes opened wide with horror, his mouth dropped ready to scream in pain and to warn to his fellow bandits. But the mercenary could find no breath in which to produce his final warning; for Henry's long dagger was already lodged in the man's Adam's apple and was held there solidly until the man's terrified eyes rolled into his head and he fell from the saddle onto the black highway with a dull thump. Thomas was shocked by his friend's lightning-fast reactions. He'd always thought of Sykesy as a comical character not to be taken too seriously. He'd even made fun of the long sabre his friend always carried with him, but in the instant it took to slay the brigand and in the time it took for the man to fall dead from his saddle to the floor, Thomas's opinion of his friend had changed forever. Now he saw just how deadly Henry's skill with the blade was.

"You get the gold, I'll deal with these bastards!" Sykesy whispered. Thomas nodded obediently, still in shock by how fast things had escalated. But there was no time for reflection, events had begun to take on a life of their own. One of the outriders had heard the thud of his fellow mercenary's dead body hitting the dirt and Thomas's victim's horse had panicked and cantered off into the brush, carrying its unconscious rider with it. The outrider on the right-hand side of the carriage turned to see what had happened and in the split second it took to turn, Henry was upon him, his silver sword flashing the fire's reflection on its long faultless blade. Sykes's actions were too fast to see, but the result of the attack was plain; another man fell dead to the ground. Thomas trotted to the left side of the coach and unceremoniously punched the unsuspecting guard in the jaw. The heavyweight sucker punch had the desired effect, and the man fell silently from his horse. Sykesy guided his horse back around the rear of the trundling carriage and came alongside his friend.

"Ok, Thomas . . . " he whispered, " . . . you play your part, and

I'll play mine. If all goes well we'll meet at the pre-arranged place!"
Thomas nodded. Henry returned the nod and gave his friend a
mischievous grin before pulling his black neckerchief over his face
and spurring his horse he yelled "*To hell or the hangman*!" Thomas
watched as his black-cloaked silhouette vanished into the orange
mist, his sabre's blade flashing in the darkness as he galloped at full
pelt between the two lines of mercenaries ahead of him, delivering
deadly thrusts left and right at the surprised brigands. The guard
instinctively pulled on the reins of the wagon which unbeknown
to him was exactly what Thomas had hoped for. Thomas dropped
from the huge, dray horse and still holding the beast's reins, opened
the carriage door. The interior of the coach was lit by a single candle
on its metal stand on the carriage's wall. The light inside the coach
which had been completely invisible from outside shocked him, and
he froze as he tried to take in the situation. For instead of an empty
carriage, he found Lord Dashwood and his Scottish manservant
Flint, who had also been caught by surprise at the highwayman's
sudden appearance. They were sitting facing each other, their feet
resting on the two strong boxes containing the jingling gold between
them. The three men stared at each other for what seemed like a
full minute but in fact only a heartbeat. Surprisingly, the old man
was the first to move, drawing a pistol from a leather pocket in
the rear of the carriage's wall. As he did so, Thomas grabbed at the
old man's ankle and yanked it as hard as he could. As he did the
Lord's pistol fired its shot which smashed uselessly into the front
of the coach's walls, splintering the wood. The lead shot traveled
straight through the timber and came to rest in the spine of the
coach driver who flopped forward paralysed. The Lord slid from
his leather seat and on to the two boxes on the floor with a painful
yelp. In the blink of an eye Flint was upon Thomas with a shower of
blows with his left hand and the Scottish dirk, which he'd retrieved
from Lord Harrington's throat, in his right. The blade tore through
the air towards Thomas's face but the boxer's reactions were too
fast and he withdrew his jaw. However, the blade's tip caught the
neckerchief disguising Thomas and ripped the silken fabric from
his face, leaving the old man and his servant in no doubt about

the highwayman's identity. Both stared at Thomas for a second, recognition sinking in.

"It's you . . . Fewtrell . . . the pugilist!" Lord Dashwood's mouth opened wide as he tried to make sense of the situation. Flint, on the other hand, had already done so and his swift reaction nearly caught Thomas off-guard with another thrust of the eighteen inch long dirk. Thomas instinctively grabbed at the knife's blade which luckily for Thomas was not a sharp one, the Scottish dirk being used mainly as a thrusting weapon instead of a cutting one. He held the blade in his huge, left hand. The Scot tried to free the weapon by pulling and twisting the blade, but Thomas held it in a vice-like grip as the blade dug into his skin. Thomas took the pain and bringing his right hand up grabbed Lord Dashwood's empty pistol by its barrel and swung it into the Scotsman's face with as much force as he could muster. The brass butt smashed into the man's mouth shattering his blackened front teeth and sending him backwards in a bloody shower of teeth and red spittle where for the second time that night he lay unconscious. Dashwood looked at the highwayman, and whimpering held his thin arm across his face awaiting the blow that he was sure would render him as unconscious as his manservant but it never came. Thomas reached in and lifted the frail old man from the strongboxes and placed him on the seat.

"I don't hit old men . . ." Thomas said sternly, " . . . but if you move one muscle, I'll make an exception for you, understand Dashwood?" The old man nodded, his eyes darting this way and that distrustfully as he searched for an escape route. "I'm only here for the gold, King George will deal with you." With that Thomas hauled both boxes from the floor of the carriage. They were indeed as heavy as he'd predicted and he was glad he'd insisted that Henry had found the big dray to carry them. Pulling both boxes onto the floor outside the carriage, he slammed the coach door and found himself in the blackness of the night once more. He lifted the first strong box onto the saddle of the dray and tied it there with the thick ropes that hung from its side. The weight of the box pulled the saddle to one side, but Thomas heaved the other from the floor and crossed to the left hand side of the dray, where he repeated the operation until the saddle sat central on the horse's back once more. Using one of the coach's wheel spokes as a hurdle, he climbed into the saddle. The big horse didn't even seem to register the extra weight, and Thomas kicked the beast on and pulled on the reins, bringing the horse into the brush at the side of the highway. He could hear a battle ahead of him as he found his way along the bridlepath running parallel to the highway where he kicked the dray into a trot. As he drew along the road, he could hear the deafening rapport of gunshot, and he hoped Henry was able to deal with the brigands. Thomas drew his own brace of pistols as he came upon the battle on the highway. He could just make out his friend, a shadow amongst a whirlwind of orange mist and gun-smoke. The mercenaries were scattered in confusion and darkness along the highway. Henry used the road to his advantage cramming the assailants against the thick brush of the tree line as if he were a Spartan battling Xerxes' Persians at the gates of Thermopylae. His sabre swinging this way and that, his left arm holding the dagger, making movements in the opposite direction protecting his rear. Thomas watched from the safety and shadow of the bridlepath. His overwhelming reaction was to go the aid of his friend, but Sykesy had been adamant that he should leave and go about his business and by the look of things Thomas thought to himself, business was good.

One after another the horsemen fell upon the lone defender. Pistol shots whizzed past Henry's head as they were either misfired of badly aimed in the mist. Anyone that came within reach of the deadly sabre swing was a deadman. Left and right his attackers came at full pelt though the fire's glow, swords levelled to impale the highwayman. To Thomas it was as if Sykesy had a sixth sense as he parried their attacks from left and right with lightning-fast dagger and sword, instantly setting up another parry for the next attack with almost animalistic instinct. His black cloak flew about him as if he were some devilish spirit of death as the men came to die on his blades. His heels controlled his horse with expert precision, turning this way and that to meet his attackers who over the first few minutes of the battle had begun to pile up dead or wounded at his horse's hooves. The leader of the mercenaries cantered around at the front of the line of men, ordering his men to attack and kill the highwayman, but the narrowness of the road hampered their formation, only allowing two a breast to charge Sykes's position and as they came, so they fell. Thomas sat atop the huge dray watching with a macabre fascination and in the dim light, amidst the fury and violence of the melee he thought he saw his friend smiling, enjoying the bloodlust of battle, a wrath in a dance of death within the orange mist. Slowly the battle abated. Henry sat awaiting the next attack, but from Thomas's position he could just about make out the group of ten or fifteen remaining brigands bringing some form of order to their ranks, thirty or forty yards along the road. Their leader was ordering his men from their horses and to prime their pistols and muskets. They did so and began to form a line of five men abreast, slowly walking towards Henry, picking their way through the darkness, guns in hand. As they came within view of the highwayman's shadow, they levelled their guns at him. Thomas watched on, he knew he should warn his friend but he and Henry had discussed this exact situation whilst planning and both had agreed that the gold would be their main priority. However, Thomas couldn't help himself. He stood in his stirrups and opened his mouth to warn Henry of the oncoming musket volley that would surely kill him but before he could the guns fired their deafening rapport. Sykesy gambolled backwards over the rump of his horse, blades in hand. To Thomas who was much nearer to his friend than the gunmen, it looked as if Henry had moved before the shots were fired but he couldn't be sure. The gunmen, who were partially blinded by the gun smoke, believed that the highwayman had definitely been blown from the saddle and must surely be dead. Thomas desperately scanned the area for his friend, but the mist shrouding the scene made it impossible to see what had become of Henry. A rousing cheer rose from the mercenaries, and it was with a very heavy heart and a growing panic that Thomas left the scene.

Two lovers

CHAPTER 28

The old Star Inn had stood on this Shropshire site since the days of the Anglo-Saxons. Its thatched roof had turned green with neglect and a small, smoking chimney poked up from the thatch, sending a thin line of wood smoke skywards in the evening breeze. The wattle and daub plastered stonework on the exterior of the building was coated with Belladonna ivy with its large white flowers, complimenting the beautiful tree-lined backdrop in the shallow valley where the Old Star Inn stood. A small brook of fresh spring water ran along one side of the Inn. The trickling sound of water creating a peacefulness within the valley. It was as if this was a place that had never been, and never would be, discovered by the outside world. Behind was a small holding of land which provided enough space to grow food and have sheep, goats and chickens without it becoming too serious or hard work, yet still providing enough to live one's life with plentiful food, water, ale and cider. There was a cider press with its huge pressing stone and behind that an orchard of ten or fifteen acres with what must have been a thousand, healthy-looking apple trees.

Thomas, Bridget, Eleanor and Edward stopped at the brow of the hill and looked down at the scene of peacefulness and contentment for a whole minute. The sound of their horses clip-clopping seemed too loud for such a paradise as this, and yet, Thomas knew that he must ride down there and create merry hell with the four

burly Lutwhiche brothers; who, at that very moment, stood outside the inn by the horse rail, laughing and joking as they drunk
from their cider flagons. The brothers' attention now turned from
their cider and their boasts of sexual prowess with local girls to the
riders on the hill. As they came closer, they became mesmerised
by Bridget O'Hara. In truth, none of the brothers had ever seen
a woman like her before, her mocha skin puzzled them and they
couldn't take their eyes from her as she stared back at them. They
had heard tell of black people but had never actually encountered
any, and as Thomas, Bridget and the others rode slowly into the
quiet valley, the insults began in earnest.

"It's a nigger!" shouted one of the brothers excitedly.

"Nah, that ain't no nigger, she's too light!" Came the reply in a
country bumpkin brogue. "Niggers is black as old oak, that there is
a jiggerboo!" retorted another, bursting into laughter. Bridget didn't
rise to the abuse, she had heard much worse in the slave markets in
Bristol, and in the whore houses, she had worked in than anything
these ignorant country bumpkins could come up with. There was
nothing these idiots could say that would upset her. Thomas, on
the other hand, *was* upset not so much by the catcalls more by the
fact one of these bastards had murdered his father.

The fight that followed was unfair from the start. The Lutwhiche bullies didn't really stand a chance against the professional
pugilist even if there was four of them. Swift and brutal is the best
way to describe what followed and in a world of brutality this was
particularly brutal. Head-butts, punches and kicks were liberally
dealt out by both sides but only Thomas's punches were finding
their mark. One of the Lutwhiche brothers got lucky with a right
hook to Thomas's chin, but the instant his knuckles made contact
with the boxer's granite jaw he wished he hadn't, the blow breaking
his wrist as well as his fingers. Eventually, Thomas stood alone
having knocked all four of the brothers unconscious. They lay
about him like so many scruffy bloody-faced rag dolls, their dirty
breeches filled with their own excrement and their teeth and noses
sticking out at weird angles. After his hard work, which took all of
three minutes the unconscious men began to stir into agonising

consciousness, their moans and groans ruining the tranquillity of the vale. Bridget instructed one of the customers from inside the pub who knew the brothers to help them back to their farm and to instruct them, when they regained the use of their broken jaws, never to utter the name Fewtrell again or return to the valley as it now belonged to Thomas Fewtrell.

Thomas already bored with the Lutwhiche brother's company had already disappeared inside the inn. He returned with two tankards of ale for himself and his friends and a bill of sale for the Star Inn and all the land around it, lock stock and barrel. Within the hour the happy landlord hurriedly went on his way with a heavy purse and a huge grin, and so, Thomas, Edward and the girls took possession of the building in a deal which took less than an hour from start to finish.

Edward seemed eager to be on his way and raised the subject of sharing out the proceeds of the heist but Thomas couldn't bring himself to do so until he had found out the fate of his friend Henry Sykes. So until news arrived, the four settled in for the duration, busying themselves tidying up the inn as best they could and bringing the surrounding farm and orchards into some sort of order. It was in the second week after the heist, whilst the men were chopping wood in the orchard for the inn's fire that Thomas saw a lone figure riding towards them across the land behind the house. The man was slumped over his saddle and was obviously in need of some assistance. Thomas's heart skipped as he recognised the captain.

"Henry . . . *Henry!*" Thomas leapt across the cut logs and ran towards his friend through the overgrown field. Sykesy raised his head slightly before falling from the horse into the wet grass.

****

The Star Inn was the perfect place to lie low as word of the attempted coup on his majesty's crown and the brutal retribution that followed in its aftermath spread like wildfire throughout the country. The search for the robber brigands who had survived Sykes's attack, swept the East end docks of the capital and all but one or two of the killers were rounded up within a week of the bloody heist. Lord Dashwood refused to accept his fate arguing that it was not *his* men who had ultimately taken the King's gold but *Thomas Fewtrell*, the King's favourite pugilist, who had stolen the treasure from the King's coach and Dashwood had *seen* him with his own eyes. The Lord's testimony only seemed to make matters worse for him. "How can a man be in two places at once?" The King questioned, assuring the investigation that Thomas Fewtrell had not only been in his presence for the whole evening and so couldn't have done the robbery and was ultimately responsible for his escape from the massacre in the old church. The King recounted to the court how Thomas Fewtrell had led his small party of escapees though the forest to the village of Rye, where the monarch had been given shelter and protection by the loyal villagers. Dashwood was at a loss for a reasonable explanation.

"There must have been two Thomas Fewtrells." The old man stuttered from behind the bar of the dock.

After the judges had stopped laughing at the old man's preposterous explanation they found Dashwood guilty of the terrible massacre carried out by the brigands and the theft of the King's gold. He was sentenced to the most terrible punishment England had to offer and so, as he stood on the platform of execution, less than one week after his attempted coup. Lord Dashwood, founder of the Hellfire club was hung until barely alive, then taken down, his limbs spread across a wooden style where the executioner drew his long blade slowly across the man's stomach, releasing the old man's stinking bowels. After the Lord had been shown his own innards, his limbs were hacked off until only Lord Dashwood's torso and head were left intact. It was during this moment of overwhelming pain, when it reaches its highest threshold, and saturates the brain that Dashwood reflected upon his manservant's fate. The Scot had been sold as a slave into hard labour to be worked to death in the sugarcane fields of the Caribbean. The old man wondered whether it would have been better for all if he had just let the boy hang as a child after the battle of Culloden Moor, all those years before.

****

Even though Sykesy had been attended to by a surgeon at some point before his arrival at the farm, his wounds refused to heal and had started to fester. He drifted fitfully in and out of consciousness for several days as Eleanor and Bridget tried their best to nurse him back to health. But the going was slow, and the ever-present threat of gangrene taking hold never left their minds. After much soul searching, Thomas and Edward decided they needed to remove the lead shot lodged in Henry's rib. This in itself was not too serious an operation, but the rib in question was so near Henry's heart that neither brother relished the idea of opening the highwayman's chest and chance killing him. However, day by day, the wound grew darker, and all knew that the green blood would kill him unless the bullet and the trapped piece of shirt causing the gangrene were removed. And so they carried Henry into the old bar room and laid the semi-conscious highwayman upon a long, oak table and placed candles around him.

Thomas leant over his friend, a set of horseshoe pliers in hand to remove the bullet. Henry's dagger sat in the burning coals ready to cauterise the wound after the operation. Henry opened his eyes and stared at Thomas who patted his shoulder, trying to calm the highwayman's nerves. Sykesy could see the concerned faces around him.

"I watched your battle with the brigands Henry!" Thomas said, as much to calm his own nerves as to take his friends mind away from the pain of his wound. Sykesy tried to smile. Thomas continued. "I have never seen a better swordsman than you, my friend!"

"Was I good Thomas?" Henry whispered. Thomas laughed softly.

"*Good?*" Thomas said incredulously. "You were death on horseback Henry and you were right all along, you would have made an excellent soldier!" Henry smiled at Thomas's words, but the effort of talking was becoming too much for him. Each breath bringing a deeper level of pain. Thomas tried to calm his friend, but he could see Henry wanted to talk and so brought his ear close to Henry's mouth.

"We did it, Thomas," Sykesy whispered. "We pulled off the biggest robbery of our lives, we'll die rich men." Thomas brushed his hand across his face, trying unsuccessfully to hide the tear that had begun to well in his eyes.

"Yeah, rich *old* men!" He said reassuringly, Edward and the women tried to listen to the conversation, but the words were so softly spoken between the friends that it was impossible to hear what was being said.

"So what will you do Thomas?" Sykesy said, a smile breaking his parched lips. Thomas looked at him, a puzzled look on his face.

"What will I do?" He repeated the question.

"Yes, with all your money?" Thomas sighed.

"I don't know." He shrugged. "I'll probably get married." Thomas glanced at Eleanor and Bridget as he said the words, Sykesy followed his look with a bemused expression. "To be honest Henry," Thomas whispered, "I'm at odds to which of the girls I shall wed, after all, I'm in love with the pair of them."

"What ... but ... ?" Henry tried to talk but broke into an attack of coughing. Thomas continued patting his friend's shoulder as the coughing attack abated. He continued to explain. "I love Bridget for different reasons than Eleanor. Bridget is streetwise, worldly and tough yet still beautiful and exotic, whereas Eleanor is refined, elegant and so beautiful but I wonder if I could give her the lifestyle she's used to. I do know one thing though Henry, whoever I choose, it'll break the other's, heart." Henry stared up at Thomas with a growing look of disbelief on his face. He burst into laughter which instantly brought on another coughing fit. "Calm, Henry calm, save your strength, you can help me choose my bride when you're well." Henry's coughing fit grew worse.

"My God Thomas but you're naive!" He said spluttering the words. Thomas stared at him blankly. Henry tried to talk, controlling his breathing as he did. "I don't think you'll be marrying either of them ... These girls are for each other Thomas. I thought you knew ... " Thomas smiled, unable to make sense of his friend's words. Henry watched Thomas's face for a second and on realising he wasn't getting through to the man he pressed his point. "Let

me put it this way, some girls enjoy a honeypot rather than a . . ."
Another bout of coughing cut the sentence short, Thomas shook
his head.

"What are you trying to say, Henry?" Sykesy breathed deeply. The
pain of his spluttering was clear to see, but he continued trying to talk.

"You've been barking up the wrong tree all this time, Thomas,"
Henry said loudly. "Eleanor and Bridget are . . . !" The coughing was
back, only this time it tinged with uncontrollable laughter. Thomas
turned to the others who stood at the far end of the dark wood table,
watching with embarrassed expressions.

"We need to operate right away, the poor man's becoming more
delirious by the second!" The laughing fit became too much for Henry
who fell back onto his pillow semi-conscious. Bridget, Eleanor and
Edward looked at each other awkwardly before Edward broke the
moment's silence by taking a glass of gin and passing it to Thomas who
tipped the liquid into his friend's mouth. Even in this state, Henry
managed to drain the whole glass, spluttering its contents down,
knowing that this would be the only pain relief he would receive.

"To Hell or the hangman!" He muttered softly under his breath.

"To Hell or the hangman!" Thomas replied with a lump in his
throat, before Sykesy closed his eyes with a peaceful smile, falling
once more under the spell of his fever. Edward nodded.

"It's time Thomas!" Thomas searched the eyes of the others, who
stood around the table, their ashen faces white in the dim candlelight. Thomas's face whitest of all knowing that Henry's life was in
his hands. The operation took an agonising hour as Henry lay in a
gin-induced stupor. His once handsome smile was now a disfigured
grimace as he swung between life and death. The dim light and heat
of the fire seemed to make the small room even more claustropho-
bic than it already was as Thomas and Edward tried to remove the
offending bullet. Finally, the sound of the lead shot plonking loudly
into a pewter cup signalled the end of the procedure and Henry was
carried into the small master bedroom to regain his strength. Only
time would tell if they had stopped the green blood creeping along
the highwayman's veins.

A place beneath the apple tree.

CHAPTER 29

Henry Sykes was buried on a bright late spring morning. Thomas chose a peaceful spot beneath a large apple tree to the rear of the Star Inn in the sleepy vale in Shropshire. His bones and sabre still lie there to this day, two of the brightest of King George's gold coins placed upon his eyes, still wrapped in the linen sheet buried deep in the good soil that can be found in abundance in that part of old England. Edward said prayers to his God asking for Henry's forgiveness. Should the good lord have had any doubts about taking the highwayman into his bosom, Edward assured Thomas that *he* would take responsibility for Sykes's soul even if God would not. Thomas teased young brother explaining that Henry Sykes would never have asked for forgiveness from anyone, least of all God for if the Lord made the mistake of forgiving Henry his sins on earth and allowed highwayman into paradise, he would probably take advantage of the situation to rob the place.

The King's golden hoard was divided between the four remaining friends, with Sykes's share being put to one side. Thomas insisted that it be split in two, and sent anonymously to both Daniel Mendoza and Joe Buck under the guise of a fictitious but generous patron. Throughout this adventure, Mendoza had remained honest to Thomas and to the art of pugilism. Joe Buck would return to America, as promised, far richer than he had arrived, even if his mother would curse the loss of his good looks at the hands of

Thomas Fewtrell. He would travel the eastern seaboard of America, telling tales of his fights and the generosity he'd received from King George III for his remaining years.

To Thomas the stolen loot had lost its sparkle now Henry was no longer there to share it and he had no idea what he'd do now that he was a wealthy man. His plans to marry either Eleanor or Bridget were pulled from beneath his feet like the proverbial rug when he accidentally discovered the girls embraced in each other's arms in a moment of sexual passion. Suddenly Henry's words made sense. His initial shock at discovering the lesbians soon dissipated though. The girls explained that they had been in love with one another since the days of the Rookery. Eleanor told him that they intended to return to Birmingham and take up residence in her father's old house on the outskirts of the town once the heat had died down. Here, thanks to her father's stash of treasure and the gold coin from the heist, they would live out their lives in privacy and the comfort of each other's company for the rest of their days. Thomas's initial disappointment was soon replaced with happiness for the women.

Edward announced that he wanted to take advantage of the summer's good weather and travel to the New world as a missionary. And so it was that the day came when the friends split their share equally and went on their separate ways, leaving Thomas waving from the doorway of the Star Inn as his comrades climbed the incline of the peaceful vale, never to return.

The years rolled on, and when Thomas grew bored, he came out of retirement to box a few rounds here and there, always drawing a huge crowd whenever he did. Until one day he was beaten by a young fellow and outsider fighting under the name Gentleman John Jackson, and that was it, his boxing days were over. In his retirement, Thomas even found the time to write a book with the grand title of *Boxing reviewed, the science of manual defence* and to his amazement, it sold in great numbers and still does to this day. When he became lonely, he visited his friend Daniel Mendoza in London, and the two talked pugilism into the early hours over a glass of port and a roaring fire. When a more sombre mood took him he would take a flagon of his homemade cider and sit beneath the apple tree at the rear of the inn, rest his back on an ornate headstone intricately carved with the words *Captain Henry Sykes* and he talk to his old friend about their adventures on the road when they had been young men. In time he married a local Shropshire girl and settled into the life of a landlord and gentleman farmer, and for the remaining years of his life he was as content as any man that had enjoyed a great adventure in his youth. When in old age his time came, Thomas Fewtrell was carried in a procession of hundreds to be entombed alongside his ancestors in the Fewtrell family burial site which still to this day sits on the land of the great, Tudor manor house that once belonged to the Fewtrell family.

And so, just as the earth travels through its celestial orbit around the sun, so our own adventure comes full circle to its conclusion.

The End

Daniel Mendoza

AUTHOR'S NOTE

Thomas Fewtrell, the original notorious

After the unexpected success of my first book *The Accidental Gangster* and during my on-going research into Birmingham's most infamous family the Fewtrells for the bestselling book series, I had a brief but inspirational conversation with the award-winning *Birmingham Evening Mail* journalist Mike Lockley. We discussed gangster folklore and the legends that had built up around the Fewtrells' now legendary battle with the London underworld. Mike made a prediction that the book series, probably the most controversial books to be written about Birmingham would go on to be very popular. I don't think either of us realised at the time how close to the truth his prediction would prove to be. It was during this conversation that Mike mentioned that this generation of the Fewtrell family were not the first notorious fighters to come out of Birmingham and also that the *Accidental Gangster* wasn't the first bestselling book to be written by a member of the Fewtrell family. *Boxing Reviewed-The Science of Manual Defence* had been written years before by legendary pugilist and ancestor of the Fewtrell family Thomas Fewtrell in 1790.

Our conversation ignited an interest in me to find out more about this famous ancestor. So with help of my wife Abi Fewtrell it was with some difficulty that we began to descend the Fewtrell family tree in search of the original notorious, Thomas Fewtrell. Thanks to the relative rarity of the family name, we managed to trace the Fewtrell family tree all the way back to the 1500s, to the days of King Henry the VIII. Back in those times the family were rich land owners in the village of Easthope in the county of Shropshire, even legitimately having their own coat of arms as well as 1000 acres of land. A large black and white tudor manor house and a family crypt were all part of the family riches right up until the 1700s, when for some unknown reason, the family pile was lost. Although the manor house, land and family crypt are still there to this day, they are now owned by an English Lord. Yet if one visits the crypt as Abi and I did, one can still see the strange inscriptions carved into the stone surface of the burial site. Thomas Fewtrell's name can still be clearly read, if a little faded by over a hundred or so winter storms.

The further I dug into Thomas Fewtrell's life and times the more I uncovered about the man himself and the world he lived in.

Pugilism of the 1700s was in comparison with today's boxing, a brutal, corrupt and, at times, deadly affair. Thomas must have been a tough man indeed to stand against the best of his day and not only win his bouts but become champion to King George III, friend and sparring partner with the undisputed pugilist champion of the day, *the Great Mendoza* and hold the key to his home town of Birmingham. Although his name is now largely forgotten, Thomas Fewtrell was as famous in his day as the *Notorious Conor McGregor* is in ours.

After years of prizefighting, gambling and his ever-increasing drinking binges, Thomas's defeat at the hands of *Gentleman John Jackson* sent him into retirement a very wealthy man. He returned to his birthplace of Shropshire to become an innkeeper, boxing trainer and author of his bestselling pugilist instruction book mentioned above.

Nine generations have past since Thomas Fewtrell swung his fists in the boxing ring and entertained people in his public house. It therefore seems almost surreal to me that 170 years later, in 1960, that history repeated itself with the rise of Thomas Fewtrell's direct descendants, Eddie Fewtrell and his seven brothers, most of them boxers too, who went onto entertain Birmingham city with their clubs and pubs for over 50 years.

As with all my books, I have used real people and wound my plot around them tightly, mixing fact with fiction in order to create a world for the reader to inhabit the past. The sights, sounds and smells of the filthy streets and aristocratic palaces of 18th century England and the political intrigues of the day, all lie within these pages and to my knowledge are all historically correct.

Thank you.
D J KEOGH

Printed in Poland
by Amazon Fulfillment
Poland Sp. z o.o., Wrocław

R00190